BOOK EIGHTEEN IN THE RAIDING FORCES SERIES

MILITARY DECEPTION

PHIL WARD

A RAIDING FORCES SERIES NOVEL

This book is a work of fiction. Names, characters, businesses, organizations, places, events and incidents are either a product of the author's imagination or are used fictitiously. Any resemblance to actual persons, living or dead, events or locales is entirely coincidental.

Published by Military Publishers, LLC
Distributed by Military Publishers, LLC Austin, Texas

www.philwardauthor.com

ISBN: 979-8-9920645-2-0

Cover design by Stewart A. Williams

For ordering information or special discounts for bulk purchases, contact
Military Publishers LLC
3616 Far West Blvd., Suite 117, Box 215 Austin, TX 78731

~~

The Raiding Forces Series continues all the way to VE Day.

Be the first to get updates and know about upcoming releases. To be on our notification list, scan the QR below and sign up!

phil@philward.com

GETTING THE MOST FROM THE RAIDING FORCES SERIES

The Raiding Forces WWII Series is written like a continuous WWII special operations campaign. It unfolds raid by raid. Missions are high intensity, rapid tempo of short duration, characterized by surprise, speed and violence of action. Characters rotate based on tasking and operational necessity while command relationships and strategic objectives remain fixed – win the war. Raiding Forces, the unit, is constantly being reconfigured to meet the demands of different theaters and mission profiles as the conflict develops.

These books are designed to be read in sequence, with tempo, reach and lethality escalating as the war progresses. Jump in and hang on. It's a wild ride.

Phil

Phil Ward
RLTW

PS: I recommend researching even the minor characters. Many are real people with amazing tales of their own. You may be surprised at some of the famous names that show up in the story from time to time.

DEDICATION

Military Deception is Dedicated to

Lieutenant Colonel Glynn R. Donaho, Army Ranger Republic of Vietnam 1968-69

"So, what did you do in the war?"

Here's what then-Lieutenant Donaho did during his year's tour. Fought in the Tet Offensive, pursued the NVA into the mountains, helped relieve the siege of Khe Sahn, reopened Route 9, invaded the A Shau Valley, operated in villages, mountains, hills, sands, rice paddies, jungles, in heat, monsoons and typhoons, captured four 37mm M1939 AA, captured 37 new in the cosmoline Russian Makarov pistols, recovered (rescued) a company command party that had been ambushed – all WIA, recovered a downed Huey UH1 helicopter, blew up one of the largest munition and demolition supply caches of the war, captured a cache of Chinese military radios, served as the Camp Evans Reaction Force, provided security for mine sweep operations on both Highway 1 and Route 9, never lost a fight, never left a soldier behind… enough said.

Rangers Lead the Way.

RANDAL'S RULES FOR RAIDING

RULE 1: The first rule is there ain't no rules.

RULE 2: Keep it short and simple.

RULE 3: It never hurts to cheat.

RULE 4: Right man, right job.

RULE 5: Plan missions backward (know how to get home).

RULE 6: It's good to have a Plan B.

RULE 7: ~~Expect the unexpected~~. *INACTIVE*

RANKS, DECORATIONS AND NICKNAMES

RANK PROTOCOL:
The first time a person is named in a chapter or after a chapter break their full rank and name is given. Addressing military personnel by their rank is a mark of respect. At all levels rank is earned and those who have it - from a corporal to a four star general are proud of it.

DECORATIONS:
In the British military officers are authorized to put the initials of their decorations after their name. In the Raiding Forces Series the protocol is the first time an officer is introduced in a book the initials of his decorations are listed following his name. After that for the rest of the book they are not.

In the U.S. military officers do not have the same privilege.

NICKNAMES:
In the British military nicknames are endemic. Radio operators are called Sparks, red heads are called Ginger, tall people are called Lofty but sometimes short people are called that too etc.

In the U.S. military there are a lot of nicknames but nothing like the British.

MILITARY DECEPTION
ONGOING OPERATIONS

OPERATION BODYGUARD A comprehensive deception campaign covering the D-Day invasion – a bodyguard of lies, code named "BODYGUARD"

OPERATION CARPETBAGGER Operation to provide aerial supply of weapons and other matériel to resistance fighters in France, Italy and the Low Countries by the U.S. Army Air Forces

OPERATION FORTITUDE, A deception plan to convince the Germans that the D-Day landing would occur in Pas-de-Calais instead of Normandy.

OPERATION FORTITUDE SOUTH – A subset of FORTITUDE is aimed at presenting Pas-de-Calais as the target for the invasion.

OPERATION JEDBURG – The arming, equipping and advising of the French Marquis SOE supported, by individual operators from OSS, SO and OG, will be dropping teams into France flanking and forward of – up to thirty miles behind the invasion beaches. The idea is to raise a guerrilla army that, commencing of the night of D-1, will knock down phone lines, blow bridges, cut railway tracks, ambush road networks etc.

OPERATION LONG NECK *(previously OPERATION LEAF EATER)*
Diamond interdiction program / Eliminate diamond smugglers
Command and Control team – code name **CARD GAME**, consisting of Col. Randal, Major the Lady Jane Seaborn, Captain "Geronimo" Joe McKoy, Captain Billy Jack Jaxx, Waldo Treywick, Captain Pamala Plum-Martin, Mandy Paige, Beverly Blackwell, Captain Roy Kidd, Captain Preston Butterfield, MSgt. Mack Beckwith, King

OPERATION OVERLORD – The eventual invasion of enemy-occupied France being marshalled in Great Britain

OPERATION TOMCAT Conduct a parachute raid on an enemy signals station/lighthouse complex, capture or kill the enemy personnel in the target area, collect any equipment or documents of intelligence value, and withdraw by sea.

1

DECEPTION IS THE BASIS OF ALL WARFARE

COLONEL JOHN RANDAL WAS NOT SUPPOSED TO BE HERE . . . somewhere in France lying beside a couple of strands of droopy barbed wire in the middle of the night in his Class A uniform hoping a German patrol did not appear out of the dark. He was fully cognizant of the fact that in Raiding Forces "hope was not a course of action," being the one who coined the saying, or at least stolen it fair and square from the person who did.

The reason for the "somewhere" was because dense fog had confused the skipper of the Motor Torpedo Boat (MTB) from the 15 Motor Torpedo Squadron who had delivered the ten-man patrol from Seaborn House across the narrowest twenty-one-mile section of the English Channel to enemy-occupied France. The young Royal Navy Volunteer Reserve officer (RNVR) who sported a DSC on his blouse – the British Navy equivalent of the U.S. Silver Star – was what was euphemistically described in military terms as being "disoriented."

Col. Randal was pretty sure they were dead lost. What he did not know was it was perfectly fine with the gentlemen who had ordered the mission – the ones now back home safe in their beds, if Col. Randal and his men were.

Provided, that is, as long as the Raiding Forces' team landed in the Pas-de-Calais region of enemy-occupied France – a generously sized target 2,576 square miles in area. Certain individuals in the shadowy seven-member organization called the London Controlling Section (LCS) only required a quick in-and-out recce of short duration the Germans would know had taken place. Or as one wit on the LCS described the concept of the recently launched deception campaign using small-scale reconnaissance missions to a fellow Section officer over cocktails in the St. James Club, "The Raiding Forces' operations are designed to be clandestine in the retrograde."

Whatever that meant.

Lieutenant Colonel John Henry Bevan, MC, Major the Lady Jane Seaborn's godfather, was the Controlling Officer, aka the Chief of Deception, of the LCS. Col. Randal knew that. He did not know exactly what LCS did. And he had no idea his future godfather-in-law was behind tonight's mission. And Lt. Col. Bevan was unaware Col. Randal was out tonight. He was supposed to be at the five-star Bradford Hotel with his goddaughter.

It has been said, "If you want to make God smile, make a plan."

Also unknown to Col. Randal was that Lt. Col. Bevan and his merry mischief makers in the TOP SECRET/MOST SECRET "Need to Know Eyes Only" London Controlling Section had recently begun to plan using Raiding Forces (E) – Europe – to carry out certain aspects of OPERATION FORTITUDE SOUTH – one of the Deception phases of OPERATION BODYGUARD. Both highly classified operations were designed to cover the location of the upcoming invasion of France. [(i)]

The idea, at least as far as Raiding Forces was concerned, was to carry out a series of small-scale intelligence-gathering operations/raids on the French coast opposite Seaborn House with the intent of making the Germans believe the Allies were initiating extensive forward reconnaissance incidental to invading Calais. The LCS was in the deception business. Its mission was to fool Hitler. The real invasion, when it came, was going to take place in Normandy.

Raiding Forces was tasked with performing what amounted to live-fire smoke-and-mirror type minidramas up and down the French coast across the Dover Straits from Seaborn House. Only neither they nor the Germans on the far shore understood it that way. Both sides were under the impression the incursions were for real. They shot at each other given the chance.

So what was Col. Randal doing on a reconnaissance mission somewhere in the Pas-de-Calais region? That was going to take some explaining when Lady Jane found out. He was supposed to be on a two-week leave in London – a holiday.

WHEN THE RAIDING FORCES' PARTY HAD ARRIVED AT THE Bradford Hotel from Castelrozzo earlier that day, Lady Jane corralled Captain Billy Jack Jaxx and immediately departed in one of the hotel's limousines. She took him to her family's – and HRH King George VI's – tailor, Mr. Chatterley at Pembrook's Military Tailors. She had arranged for new U.S. Army Class A uniforms for Jack Cool with a stop at Blood's Bootmakers for a brown leather pistol belt and a dress holster for his 1911 Colt .38 Super.

Captain Pamala Plum-Martin, DSO, OBE, DFC, RM, Mandy Paige and Beverly Blackwell had taken off in another limousine to go on a shopping safari. The rest of the party was free to explore London on their own. Or to hang around the hotel, which was an interesting place to be in wartime London.

Captain Penelope "Legs" Honeycutt-Parker, OBE, GM, RM, was planning to catch the train to the tiny village outside of Seaborn House to visit her husband, Lieutenant Colonel Lionel Honeycutt-Parker, who was commanding Raiding Forces (E), usually referred to simply as "Seaborn House." Since King had never been to Seaborn House, on impulse Col. Randal decided the two of them would accompany her. The idea was for the Merc to have an opportunity to familiarize himself with ongoing operations.

This plan was flawed from inception. The only train back to London would not arrive until 0700 hrs the next morning. Lady Jane was not likely to be enthusiastic about being stood up on her first night back in England.

The Bradford provided a limo from its seemingly inexhaustible fleet to drive the three to Victoria Station. The train station was jam-packed with soldiers, sailors and airmen. The train was standing room only. Until, that is, it headed out of the city toward the Restricted Zone, a heavily fortified ten-mile buffer along the coastline, off limits to civilians and nonessential military personnel.

Nonessential, meaning anyone not permanently assigned to some military establishment inside the Zone or having a special pass with a date/time stamp to visit for Official Business. A great many civilians living in the area had been forcibly relocated. The Military Commander Home Forces desired to limit prying eyes from observing developments during the buildup for the D-Day invasion. The greater good trumped individual rights. Security was the number one concern and would remain so for the remainder of the war.

Every "enemy alien" living in England, meaning foreign nationals from countries at war with the United Kingdom, was forcibly interned even if married to a British citizen. There was great fear across the country about an enemy Fifth Column. Tribunals were set up to evaluate each alien's case, and individuals were classified as Category A, B or C. Category A people were interned for the duration as a potential national security threat. Those in Category B were allowed to remain free but subject to restrictions on travel and certain activities. Category C, which included many genuine refugees from Nazi persecution, was exempt from both internment and restrictions.

Everyone, including the Germans, knew the Allies intended to invade the continent of Europe. The question was when and where. Most people on both sides believed the invasion armada would take the shortest route, meaning Dover to Calais – twenty-one miles. When? To the knowledgeable military observer that could be calculated. Once the buildup phase was complete, moon and tide data would dictate which days each month would be favorable to launch the assault. Army, Navy and Air Forces all had differing requirements, dramatically reducing the number of days acceptable to all three. If the Germans could predict the month, it would be easy to determine the approximate date of the invasion within a day or two.

The Allies were preparing for the largest amphibious/airborne operation in history. Planning for D-Day had been ongoing for some time but finalizing the details were still in the preliminary phase. The Allied Commander had yet to be appointed, though the odds-on favorite was General George C. Marshall, Chief of Staff of the United States Army. A line of departure (LD) time of 1 May 44 had been tentatively picked for the invasion – a little over five months from now. Almost no one knew that.

It was the most closely guarded secret of the twentieth century.

Prime Minister Winston Churchill was on record as stating, “In time of war truth is so precious she must always be attended by a bodyguard of lies.”

Lieutenant General “Geronimo” Joe McKoy was known to say, “There’s been many a’ slip betwixt the cup and the lip.”

Both were right.

The future of the free world depended on victory when the Allied Forces went ashore. As important as it was, D-Day was going to be a near-run thing. There was no way to stack the deck in the Allies’ favor – never good in any military endeavor. An attacker going against an entrenched enemy needs at least three-to-one odds in their favor. More, a lot more, was better.

The German defenders, ensconced behind their fortifications along the Atlantic Wall overlooking potential landing sites, would outnumber the Allied troops in the initial assault. The landing was going to be weakness going against strength. Never a good thing.

In addition, German reinforcements to include armor were strategically prepositioned to the rear behind the Atlantic Wall. They could be rushed to counterattack the invasion beaches once the first wave came ashore. If there was one maneuver the German Army was known for, it was the counterattack. When the initial wave of the Allies went in on D-Day they would be at their most vulnerable. They would have to fight their way ashore, get off the beaches, crack the Atlantic Wall and go inland knowing a counterattack was coming – guaranteed.

Nowhere would the Allies have a three-to-one numerical advantage.

Field Marshal Erwin Rommel’s newly formed Army Group B was a formidable formation consisting of the 2nd, 21st and 116th Panzer Divisions, the 352nd Infantry Division plus the 716th, 243rd, and 709th Static Coastal Defense Divisions. The legendary Desert Fox also had the crack 91st Airlanding Division w/6th Parachute Regiment attached. It was a highly mobile, specially trained division designed to rush to Allied drop zones/landing zones to annihilate Allied parachute and glider airheads – which are at their most vulnerable when they first touch down.

Army Group B Headquarters had recently been transferred from Northern Italy to France. FM Rommel was now in command of the

Normandy sector of the Atlantic Wall – the exact stretch of French coastline where the Allies were preparing to come ashore on D-Day. His orders were to defeat the invasion at the water's edge. It was well accepted that the Desert Fox knew an invasion was coming, being in the dark only about when and where.

On the Allied side, those in the know understood that as important as it was, the landing would be a roll of the dice. That was bad enough, but increasing the stress level for the planners was the knowledge that D-Day was a one-off. If the attack failed there would be no do-overs. The Allied coalition would be forced to negotiate terms short of the "Unconditional Surrender" President Franklin D. Roosevelt laid down as the only acceptable end to the war.

The trio from Raiding Forces (ME) on the train en route to Seaborn House were not cleared for nor had any knowledge of what was taking place in the halls of power at the strategic, intelligence, deception or any other level of D-Day planning/preparation/organization. Legs Parker was going to spend the next two weeks with her husband. Col. Randal and King were on a sightseeing day trip.

A command car picked them up from the station. When the three arrived at Seaborn House, an Operations Order for an upcoming cross-channel reconnaissance mission was in progress. Col. Randal and King sat in. A young officer Col. Randal had never met before, Captain Sinclair Lovelace, MC, was conducting the briefing of a team consisting of ten operators, most of whom were new to him as well. The majority of the Life Guards and the Blues polo players who had composed the initial draft of volunteers when Raiding Forces was first formed had made their way out to serve in Force N's guerrilla mule cavalry or at Oasis X running desert gun jeep patrols prior to the move to Castelrozzo. These troops being briefed were men badged in after he left.

Capt. Lovelace was doing it by the book, which is how an Operations Order should be issued. Though very little of what Raiding Forces did was by the book, Warning and Operations Orders were a key aspect of mission success – the one component a commander could control. The operators composing the team for the night's mission were tightly focused on everything the captain was saying. This level of professionalism would not be taking place had not Lt. Col. Honeycutt-Parker been an exacting taskmaster. It was clear he demanded a high standard of soldiering from his officers and men.

Col. Randal was well pleased.

Following the briefing Capt. Lovelace led the team outside and conducted a short rehearsal. The mission called for the patrol to land ashore in France with the idea being to conduct an onsite reconnaissance of an enemy Range Finding/Direction Finding (RF/DF) Station. There were two models in the German inventory – Freya Apparatus and Wuerzburg Apparatus. It was not known which type would be found on the objective. That was one of the intentions of the night's mission. Identify make and model.

The RF/DF Stations along the French coast were proving to be a problem for Allied shipping in the Channel, especially for the Royal Navy's small units like the 15th Motor Gun Boat Flotilla (Special Duties) that operated in and around the Dover Straits. And for those nonflagged vessels – boats operated by the intelligence services were not allowed to fly the White Ensign – used to insert/extract MI-6 or SOE agents on covert assignments.

The primary purpose of the night's mission, as briefed by Capt. Lovelace, was to "gather actionable intelligence for a raid to destroy the site by Combined Operations to be conducted at a later date."

This was, in fact, not true. No raid was planned. Nor would one be.

There was an absence of information on how many enemy personnel were expected to be found on the RF/DF Station though the number was thought to be less than a dozen. While this was a sneak-and-peek, in the event the opportunity presented itself Capt. Lovelace was authorized to snatch a German prisoner to bring back for interrogation if doing so did not compromise the mission.

Since the exercise aimed to gather intelligence on an enemy position about which little was known, there was not enough information available regarding the target to conduct a detailed rehearsal of the actions on the objective. However, with the Raiding Forces' long established principle of "Fail to Plan – You Plan to Fail," in mind, Capt. Lovelace simulated the team landing ashore, establishing an Initial Rally Point (IRP) / Extraction Rally Point (ERP) – when infiltrating it was the IRP, when exfiltrating it became the ERP – advancing to the RF/DF location, setting up security at an Objective Rally Point (ORP), carrying out a reconnaissance of the target and the withdrawal to the ERP. Then the row back to the Motor Torpedo Boat.

The drill was simple play acting but also a vital precursor to mission success. This was how professionals did it. Col. Randal liked what he was seeing – attention to detail.

Capt. Lovelace loaded his team aboard a Bedford truck to drive them to the dock to link up with the MTB. Col. Randal and King decided to hitch a ride with the troops to observe their departure. The idea was to see them off then return to Seaborn House. They rode in the cab with Capt. Lovelace.

Col. Randal said, "So, how did you wind up in Raiding Forces, Captain?"

Capt. Lovelace said, "Rather not say. You shall think I am a flaming idiot, sir."

"Try me."

Capt. Lovelace said, "In 1811 sir, the Duke of Gordon raised the Gordon Highland Regiment. His beautiful wife stood in the town square in Aberdeen with a golden Guinea in her lips and welcomed each new recruit with a kiss.

"At the start of the war in 1939 within an hour of hearing the story, believing it to still be the tradition, I reported to the nearest recruiting station and attempted to sign up for the Gordons. In no uncertain terms I was informed Scottish regiments did *not* accept Englishmen. However I refused to take no for an answer, sir.

"After a long day of haggling, needing men – the Gordon's recruiting sergeant finally agreed to enlist me. He also added a year to my age – I was only seventeen, which meant I was too young to serve overseas with the regiment in the event it deployed. And he changed my religion to Presbyterian. Next day when the new recruits were paraded by our Instructor Sergeant he demanded to know what motivated an Englishman to join a Scottish regiment. He laughed when I explained. However, it came to be known that five of the other recruits had also joined expecting to be kissed by a beautiful duchess, sir."

Col. Randal said, "Works for me."

Capt. Lovelace said, "After a minimal period of training, not atypical in those early dark days of the war, the Gordons deployed to France as part of the British Expeditionary Force. Following a disastrous campaign what was left of my battalion straggled out through the evacuation beaches at Dunkirk. sir.

"Not long after we returned home Combined Operations put out a call for volunteers. I signed up for No. 11 Commando (Scottish). We began a series of pinprick raids against the enemy-occupied British Isles – more like slapstick comedy than actual military operations, sir."

Col. Randal did not feel the need to interrupt the captain's story to mention he had been on the first raid against the Channel Islands during which No. 11 Commando played a part. Comedy was a pretty good description. The Commandos invaded the wrong island. But then no one on that particular operation had covered themselves in glory.

Capt. Lovelace said, "After a bit of hit and miss raiding I was selected to attend Officer Cadet Training School. Not for any potential as a leader of men I might have exhibited, but most likely because the Scots had quite enough of having an Englishman serving in their ranks. Upon graduation from OCTS the Army packed me off straightaway to the new Commando Basic Training Center at Achnacarry.

"While on the course I was pulled aside by one of the instructors who had a word with me about a hush-hush formation that conducted highly classified small-scale operations. He offered to recommend me. Following a stop at the Central Landing School for parachute training, here I am, sir. By the time I arrived you had already departed for an undisclosed location."

Col. Randal said, "You ever get that kiss?"

"Negative, but I was allowed to visit the Regiment's museum to see an oil painting of the duchess and touch the hat she wore on that glorious day in 1811, sir."

Col. Randal said, "Not much of a consolation prize."

When the truck reached the dock the troops unloaded and immediately boarded the Motor Torpedo Boat. The team moved with the ease of men who had done this before. They were well-trained.

At the last minute, again acting on impulse, Col. Randal and King decided to board as well. The new plan was to accompany Capt. Lovelace to the point of his team disembarking. The intent was to remain on the MTB while the operators went ashore and carried out the recce. The boat should arrive back at Seaborn House in time to make the train to London.

It seemed reasonable.

Then the fog set in. A classic pea souper. Most skippers would have aborted the mission then and there. Not Lieutenant Cavin Prescott-Davies,

DSC, RNVR. The highly coveted Distinguished Service Cross ribbon on his blouse was the only purely Royal Navy award on the British honors list. Equivalent to the U.S. Silver Star, it could only be awarded for valor. Lt. Prescott-Davies stood on navigating by dead reckoning. Fortunately, tonight the Channel was calm for a change. However, there was a risk of collision with Royal Navy or Kriegsmarine traffic due to the limited visibility.

Col. Randal and King rode on the open-air bridge with Lt. Prescott-Davies listening to him describe the vicious battles conducted nightly in the Channel between Coastal Forces 15th Motor Gunboat Flotilla and their opposite number – the heavier armed German E-Boats of the Kriegsmarine 6th and 9th Flotillas. The MGBs and E-Boats, known derisively in Royal Navy circles as the "dust of the sea," were fighting their own private navy war virtually unknown to anyone except the sailors involved.

Most of the British officers and crew in the 15th MGB Flotilla were "Hostilities Only" Reservists – primarily yachtsmen. They went out night after night On His Majesty's Service to do the King's business.

It was quite a tale.

After a little over an hour the First Officer, who served as the MTB's navigator, came up on deck to announce the coast was three miles ahead. Since the fog was so thick it was barely possible to see the bow, they took his word for it. Lt. Prescott-Davies ordered speed reduced to "Dead Slow Ahead." The main engines were shut down and the silent auxiliary motor was activated for the final run in to the shore. The intent was to prevent the RF/DF Station on the site Capt. Lovelace was intending to reconnoiter from picking them up on its sound locator.

The German sound detection device resembled two pairs of giant musical horns mounted on stands called "sound tubas." In fact, they looked more like the long fanfare trumpets seen in Robin Hood movies. While they were a primitive detection system invented prior to radar, the devices still had their use for identifying small surface craft with a low radar signature.

An Able Body (AB) seaman went forward and started taking soundings with a weighted plumb line. Great care had to be taken not to run aground on the approach to their point of debarkation. The French coast was not a place you could always sail over to and go ashore. Parts of the French coast were treacherous. A slight miscalculation and the MGB risked being holed on submerged rocks. In that case, the Raiding Forces' party might find itself stranded on the enemy shore with the sun coming up – which was officially, in typical British understatement, "not good."

After what seemed like forever, Lt. Prescott-Davies rang for the engine room to come to Full Stop. An anchor was put over the side. Capt. Lovelace had his team come up from below and assemble on the deck. There was the muffled rattle of equipment as the men shook out their gear in preparation for going ashore. Stealth was paramount from this point on. Every item had been taped to eliminate metal-on-metal contact. The submachine guns' (SMG) barrels were wrapped in oilskins. There was not a lot of noise.

Adrenaline was surging at the anticipation of what was to come. Everyone was hyped up. Ready to land. The men were all armed with .45 M-1928 Thompson submachine guns obtained through Lend-Lease, though some may have been provided by the National Rifle Association which had solicited its members to donate their personally owned SMGs. Raiding Forces (E) refused to carry the British Army issue 9mm Sten guns. The operators were of the belief any weapon that cost the equivalent of $10 U.S. to manufacture had to be a "piece of junk." Stens looked like something bolted together in a junior high school shop class but in fact, performed reasonably well when compared to the American .45 1928 Thompson or German 9mm Maschinenpistole 40 (MP-40). Still, none of the men was carrying a Sten tonight.

The Thompsons cost over $200 each and looked like what they were – the weapon of choice of Chicago gangsters. And that contributed to giving the men a sort of deadly gunfighter feel. Which is not a bad thing when going into harm's way.

Col. Randal was under the impression a shipment of 9mm Beretta M-1938s had been sent to Seaborn House from the massive stores captured when the Italian Army surrendered in Egypt. He made a mental note to check on that. Also, he needed to get a status report on the U.S. M3 "Grease Guns" with the 9mm conversion kits Brigadier General Donovan promised. They had not arrived on Castelrozzo yet. The compact Grease Guns would come in handy for Raiding Forces (E)'s cross-channel raiding.

The troops could put .30 M1s to use as well. They were wildly popular with the British operators working out of RFHQ. He would have a supply shipped in from Castelrozzo.

There was nothing wrong with the Thompson SMGs other than they were heavy, slightly awkward and it was not possible to carry as much .45 ammunition as 9mm. Little details like the ammo are important for small-scale raiders who have no means of resupply and have to fight with what they carry. What weapon an individual operator chose to use was not all that important. Ammunition compatibility was. In a tight situation the team members needed to be able to share ammo. It could mean all the difference.

Two Goatley dories were put over the side, each with a pair of Life Boat Service Men (LBSM) from the National Lifeboat Service Institution (NLSI) as boat handlers. They were from the group of original personnel Lady Jane had brought with her the first night she arrived at Seaborn House to solve then-Major Randal's seemingly insurmountable small boat problem – in what now seemed like a long time ago.

The troops climbed into the boats.

Col. Randal looked at King. Then they scrambled down with them.

King said, "This is a really bad idea, Chief."

"Roger that."

Capt. Lovelace said, "I am in serious trouble if you get killed on my watch, Colonel. Do you have any weapon besides your service automatic, sir?"

In fact, he did. His suppressed .22 High Standard Military Model D was in a shoulder holster under his blouse – the Pembrook's tailored uniform jacket had been cut fuller on the left side to accommodate it. And the "self-aiming" .380 Remington Model 51 Beverly Blackwell had given him was in a Mexican slide holster around back under it.

King was armed with his 9mm Lahti from the Winter War and a custom Fairbairn Fighting Knife he never went anywhere without – the blade had been shortened from seven to four and a half inches. The stiletto was strapped to his left forearm under his suit jacket.

Col. Randal said, "I do, but we're only along to observe, Captain."

Capt. Lovelace, who was in full-on patrol leader, movement to contact, high intensity, in charge of everything in sight around him mode – exactly the way he should be – said, "Have you adhered to any aspect of your plan from the moment we departed Seaborn House, sir?"

"That would be a negative."

"Now would be a good time to start, Colonel. You stay right in my bloody hip pocket, sir. If you two are not at the ERP when we withdraw you shall be left behind. No sending out a search party or waiting for you to show up."

Col. Randal said, "Understood."

The LBSM navigated the Goatley through great outcrops of rocks and foaming water. The approach was silent but what no one noticed in the dark was that a strong current had carried them off course. Not that it mattered. The MTB had delivered Capt. Lovelace's team to a point nowhere near the RF/DF Station they had come to reconnoiter.

Eventually the dories landed on a tiny shelving beach. It was clearly not where they had intended to come ashore. Which meant there was not going to be any reconnaissance of the assigned RF/DF target.

Capt. Lovelace did not hesitate. He was not one to be easily discouraged by minor setbacks like being lost in enemy territory. His orders were to conduct a recce, so he pulled his team together in a tight perimeter at the IRP/ERP and issued a new set of orders.

"We are on Planet Earth somewhere on the European continent. At least I choose to believe that to be the case. Disregard your previous instructions concerning recceing a RF/DF Station. We shall go up this bluff and see what we can find on top."

In training exercises, in order to enhance the learning experience it is acceptable to call an "administrative halt" to explain certain aspects of what was about to take place next. However, it is not considered best practice when on an actual operation. Col. Randal thought it a good move.

"Point element move out."

Col. Randal noted the troops appeared unruffled by the turn of events. As per the plan, the LBSM stayed behind at the IRP/ERP to secure the Goatleys. He and King fell in behind Capt. Lovelace on the climb up the steep slope that was not quite what would be described as a cliff. Nevertheless, it took effort to scramble up the thirty or so feet to the top.

It was dark but the men had spent countless hours on night exercises. In fact, most of their training and none of their actual cross-channel operations escorting or extracting "Joes" for MI-6 or SOE had ever been conducted during daylight hours. The team moved with the ease of a well-oiled machine. Once on top of the escarpment they traveled at a good pace over rough ground and through ploughed fields. Then the two-man point element halted.

Capt. Lovelace moved forward alone to confer. He was back quickly. "They spotted the shadow of what is believed to be a small house directly ahead in the distance."

He gave three raps on the wooden stock of his M1928 .45 Thompson SMG. Up ahead the point moved out again. The rest of the patrol closed up. They came to a barbed wire fence. It was not much of an obstacle. The droopy wire was easy to cut. But the process required a few extra minutes because Capt. Lovelace ordered the strands be pulled back to make a wide, easy-to-find opening in the event they had to come back this way on the double with Nazi stormtroopers in hot pursuit.

Col. Randal observed and approved.

The patrol moved another twenty-five yards or so before running into a second obstacle consisting of accordion-like coils of concertina wire that resembled a jumbo-sized spring. This was a much more challenging obstruction – three and a half feet high by fifteen feet wide. The wire was heavy-duty military grade with razor-sharp barbs. It was proving difficult for the small cutters each of the men carried on their web gear.

The silhouette of a German sentry sitting in a chair could be seen on the far side of the obstacle next to what appeared to be a guard hut – the "house" the point men had spotted. Guard huts had not been part of the limited intelligence supplied prior to the mission. If the structure was truly a guard hut, it provided additional confirmation the patrol had come ashore in the wrong location.

In truth, Capt. Lovelace's team had arrived at German Defense Post No. 9. It was one of a series of interconnecting squad-sized defensive positions manned by troops drawn from Static Beach Defense Divisions strung along the length of the French coastline. Defense Posts were the initial point of contact the Allies were going to run into when they stormed the Atlantic Wall.

Col. Randal was interested in its layout.

Efforts to cut through the wire silently were proving to be a challenge for the element attempting to do the breaching. Not one to be deterred, Capt. Lovelace dispatched four additional people to take their place with instructions to make the cuts more quietly. How they were supposed to accomplish that was problematic. He then reinforced the original point element with two more operators with orders to scout along the wire barrier to determine if there was a gap that could be exploited.

Time was now running short for when the patrol would have to begin withdrawing to the ERP in order to avoid being caught in the Channel after daybreak. Up to now Capt. Lovelace's people had not achieved much other than the most basic reconnaissance – having found France.

The scouts returned after a few minutes to report there was a larger building not far away that appeared to be an aircraft hangar – but no gap in the wire. Nothing like that had been part of the intelligence brief. Any lingering doubts they were in the wrong location were now completely dispelled.

Eventually the attempts at breaching the wire drew the attention of the lone German sentry, who may have been dozing at his post. The guard realized something was going on – but what? He disappeared into the hut and returned with two men.

The patrol froze and watched transfixed as the Germans advanced toward where they were attempting to cut their way through the wire. This development, while seeming to take place in slow motion, was happening fast. There was no time to evaluate the turn of events and react.

When the three Nazis were directly opposite their position Col. Randal shot two of them center of mass with his suppressed .22 High Standard Military Model D three times each.

WHIIIIIICH, WHIIIIIICH, WHIIIIIICH –

WHIIIIIICH, WHIIIIIICH, WHIIIIIICH.

King, having managed to wiggle under the wire, performed a perfectly executed "Rear Takedown and Stranglehold" on the third German, causing the man to black out. The Merc stopped short of killing him – barely. A prisoner snatch had been authorized.

Then King dragged the German back under the razor-sharp concertina wire making him "do the chicken" the whole way by applying pressure to the choke hold when he appeared to regain his senses. The idea was for his prisoner to be too busy having uncontrollable spasms to attempt to resist. Now the patrol had a prisoner who was of intelligence value. They could go home moderately successful.

Capt. Lovelace said, "By Jove you reacted fast, sir!"

The patrol made their way back to the Extraction Rally Point dragging their prisoner the entire distance. He was protesting but not making a lot of noise because of the gag in his mouth. When they reached the top of the escarpment above the ERP Capt. Lovelace's men rolled the bound captive down the bluff.

The Seaborn House operators hated Nazis. They considered every German to be one whether they were a member of the National Socialist German Workers Party or not. Their hatred was fueled in no small part by Hitler's Commando Order of 1942 stipulating all captured Commandos be immediately executed. The men felt like they were doing their prisoner a favor by not killing him.

As the team was preparing to board the Goatleys for the return to the MTB, Col. Randal handed Capt. Lovelace his green beret. It was adorned with the Raiding Forces' flash stitched over what the British called three "stars." In fact they were squared off diamonds – his captain's rank.

Col. Randal said, "You dropped this."

"Negative, sir," Capt. Lovelace said. "I was ordered to leave it behind. The idea I suppose is to let the Nazis know who came calling. Colonel Honeycutt-Parker did not explain his reasoning."

Col. Randal said, "In that case, pitch it on one of the rocks above the waterline. They'll get the message."

Leaving a calling card behind had not been mentioned in the Operations Order. Col. Randal wondered why. It seemed to negate the concept of a clandestine operation. The dead German soldiers could have been attributed to the French Resistance.

When the team returned to Seaborn House, Major the Lady Jane Seaborn was there in the Tactical Operations Center (TOC). She had been driven down from London in one of the Bradford Hotel's limousines to collect her errant boyfriend. Except for Lt. Col. Honeycutt-Parker, none of the Seaborn House people present had ever met her. They were somewhat awestruck. Lady Jane's reputation had preceded her.

The duty personnel present in the TOC were in lockstep agreement: she lived up to advanced billing in the drop-dead gorgeous department.

Lady Jane was less than thrilled to be spending her first night back in England tracking down Col. Randal. Nevertheless, she had a difficult time keeping a straight face when he and King appeared covered in mud from the time spent climbing the bluff and low crawling around outside German

Defense Post No. 9. Walking out uniforms and tailored business suits are not designed for field work.

Lady Jane was even less pleased to learn Col. Randal was away on a mission to France. That was not part of the plan. They were supposed to have a two week furlough in London. However, it was noted she perked up when he came in looking like he had been sleeping under a bridge.

Lady Jane said, “Enjoying your leave?”

Col. Randal said, “One thing led to another then spiraled out of control.”

Lady Jane said, “I can see that.”

She opened her purse to show a pair of handcuffs borrowed from hotel security. “Am I going to need these?”

Col. Randal said, “Maybe later.”

Lady Jane laughed. “You are having your meeting with Uncle Johnny at White’s this afternoon at 1400 hours. I need to take you back to the hotel first. We cannot have you calling on my godfather at London’s most posh gentlemen’s club looking like a transient.”

Col. Randal said, “Give me a few minutes to confer with Colonel Honeycutt-Parker and Captain Lovelace then we’re out of here.”

Lady Jane said, “Now would be a good time to exercise brevity.”

Col. Randal said, “Wilco, you have my word.”

He pulled Lt. Col. Honeycutt-Parker and Capt. Lovelace aside. “I can’t stay for the debrief. I’ll give you my assessment of last night’s operation right now. Captain Lovelace exhibited outstanding leadership throughout. The troops were highly disciplined, performed well, responded to a change in mission seamlessly when things did not go as planned and maintained excellent patrol integrity at all times. I was well-satisfied with the preparation for and conduct of the operation from start to finish.

“However, certain equipment deficiencies were observed.”

Lt. Col. Honeycutt-Parker said, “Oh?”

Col. Randal said, “One, we experienced difficulty attempting to breach the wire surrounding a potential target with the small wire cutters the men carried. In future, a pair of heavy-duty cable cutters needs to be TO&E for every mission.

“Two, experiment using something to prop up concertina wire in order to infiltrate under it. As you recall Colonel, we did that with forked sticks in Abyssinia operating against the Italian road watch outposts. Make whatever works best organic to every team as well.

"Three, you need suppressed weapons. Mine was the only one along tonight. I'll supply the quiet sidearms. You arrange for training in their use – Captain Jaxx will come down to conduct it. Make the pistols part of every operation going forward."

Lt. Col. Honeycutt-Parker had served in Raiding Forces from before the time it acquired the name and been one of the senior officers in Force N during the Abyssinian campaign. He was fully cognizant Col. Randal was a hard grader when it came to tactics and leadership. The commander of Raiding Forces (E) was much relieved to hear such a lavish report.

It was typical of the colonel that he was identifying weakness that could be addressed to improve performance – taking care of his troops.

"Very good, sir." He did not mention this was the first cross-channel mission in well over a year where Raiding Forces landed and went inland. He had been expecting to hear his operators were a little rusty.

Capt. Lovelace said, "A pleasure having you accompany us last night, sir."

Col. Randal said, "Yeah, I bet it was, Captain."

"Sir!"

Col. Randal turned to Lt. Col. Honeycutt-Parker. "Lady Jane and I'll expect you and Penelope at the Bradford as soon as you feel you can break away here, Colonel. Jane has accommodations reserved. You and I need to discuss plans for Raiding Forces going forward."

Lt. Col. Honeycutt-Parker said, "Looking forward to it, sir."

Col. Randal said, "Captain Lovelace report to me at the hotel as soon as Colonel Honeycutt-Parker releases you. There are people I want to introduce you to."

As Col. Randal, Lady Jane and King were being driven off the estate in the limousine, she said, "Being back at Seaborn House evokes memories. We had our first date here. Dinner alone by candlelight. I was infatuated but desperately not wanting you to know."

Col. Randal said, "I remember thinking you were a pretty little brunette with a big smile – great meal."

Lady Jane laughed, "We never got around to eating it."

ENDNOTES – CHAPTER 1

(1) Almost no one possessed the "Need to Know" of the existence of the two operations, much less what constituted their mission statement.

2

BETTING ON RAINDROPS

MAJOR THE LADY JANE SEABORN WAS FLUTTERING AROUND the suite at the Bradford Hotel. Normally the epitome of composure, today she was rattled. Colonel John Randal had never seen her like this before. Amused, he was watching her closely but trying to conceal it. His butler when in England – formerly her husband's butler – Sergeant Major Maurice Chauncy, had delivered a fresh Pembrook's-made U.S. Army Class A uniform to their suite complete with decorations and a highly polished pair of his brown Corcoran jump boots. You could see your reflection in the spit-shined toes. The idea was to give him his best opportunity to make a good impression on her godfather, Lieutenant Colonel John Henry Bevan, MC, Chief of the LCS. They were meeting at White's – that is Col. Randal and Lt. Col. Bevan were. Women were not allowed inside the Club – not even in the lobby.

Lady Jane laid out his blouse and was double- then triple-checking to make sure everything was letter-perfect. It was. The sergeant major had already done that having checked the spacing with a tape measure. Even though Lady Jane tried to downplay today's meeting as nothing more than an opportunity for her godfather to get to know him better, the event having a harmonious outcome was obviously important to her. She helped Col.

Randal into the beautifully tailored blouse she had ordered six months earlier in anticipation of an eventual trip to London. Mr. Chatterley at Pembrook's Military Tailors had all his measurements on file. She anxiously smoothed down the shoulders – which did not need any smoothing.

Lady Jane said, "You look ravishing."

Col. Randal said, "That sounds good."

The new uniforms – Lady Jane had ordered three sets – had been picked up the day before when she took Captain Billy Jack Jaxx to Pembrook's. In Jack Cool's case, she had secretly shipped Mr. Chatterley one of his old Class As to use as a pattern.

Lady Jane also brought Col. Randal a duty holster from Blood's Bootmakers for his second 1911 Colt .38 Super. It was a replacement for the one for the 9mm Browning P-35's holster she commandeered from him after being shot in Cairo. How Lady Jane managed the holster was a mystery. Fathers in the Six Hundred registered their newborn sons with Blood's at birth to be on the list for leather goods. Even so the waiting period was up to two years.

Col. Randal noticed an attractive rectangular infantry-blue metal device he had never seen before pinned above the rows of ribbons denoting his decorations – a Combat Infantry Badge. The CIB was a recently authorized service award for U.S. officers – in the rank of Colonel and below, and U.S. enlisted men engaged in ground combat operations. The award was so new there were no regulations out yet as to where it was to be worn on the uniform. In Airborne units some paratroopers pinned their CIBs under their Jump Wings while others in different outfits wore theirs above them.

Lady Jane had placed his CIB above the wings. As an artist, her choice of where the award should be placed, was arrived at after a fair amount of experimentation. The location was finally chosen because she "liked the composition." That worked for Col. Randal although he was never comfortable wearing Class As with full decorations. He favored adhering to Raiding Forces' Rule No. 2: "Keep It Short and Simple" – parachute wings and that was it.

Nevertheless, Lady Jane was calling the shots for his command performance and he let her. She wanted him to wear the "whole bit." The idea being to make a good impression. Lt. Col. Bevan was a military snob who did not trust anyone not in uniform. He placed a premium on those who had been decorated for valor. She was not worried about that aspect of the meeting – just everything else.

Typically Col. Randal teased Lady Jane nonstop when they were together – but not too hard. It was their way of entertaining each other and they never tired of it. However, he had to be careful. She was fully capable of holding her own with lightning quick riposte. No teasing today. She was too keyed up.

To her credit while doing everything possible to ensure he would make his best appearance – "the stitching on one's buttonholes is enormously important" – she did not engage in telling him what to do, not do, say or not say. Lady Jane's only desire was for everything to go smoothly.

He respected that.

She need not have worried. Col. Randal was planning to take the sitdown at White's with all due seriousness out of respect for her. By mutual understanding he and Lady Jane had an unspoken, never-to-be-violated rule – neither of them ever intentionally embarrassed the other.

They were very careful about that.

Lt. Col. Bevan was a central figure in her life, and she wanted Col. Randal to have a relationship with him. All he needed to know. Besides Brigadier General William "Wild Bill" Donovan had ordered him to "insinuate himself into the London Controlling Section" – whatever that meant. Today was a chance to kill two birds with one stone. The part about insinuating himself being classified – meaning not known to Lady Jane.

Col. Randal suspected Lt. Col. Bevan had an ulterior motive for inviting him to White's today. He did not have a clue what that might be. But he was pretty sure it had nothing to do with the stitching on his buttonholes.

One of the Bradford's long black limousines with a silver "B" monogram painted on the door drove Col. Randal to the club. Founded in 1693, White's was the oldest private member club in the world, and the most exclusive in London, with annual dues rumored to be in the range of $350,000 per year. Aristocrats do have need of a place to relax in a convivial atmosphere surrounded by their peers.

The chauffeur came around and opened the door for Col. Randal who at this point, if not apprehensive, was at least clicked on. He had flown over

2,000 miles for this meeting – some of it through enemy-contested air space. Why?

The driver said, "I shall be standing by here when you conclude your visit with Colonel Bevan, sir."

Col. Randal said, "Let's hope you have a short wait, Rollins."

Lady Jane had briefed him not to offer a tip. According to her, the chauffeur would be offended. The British upper class and those who served them really were different. Col. Randal could not see how a gratuity for a service rendered might be taken as an insult – but his was not to reason why. He did not buck the system.

Many of the guests at the Bradford Hotel never actually touched cash. They signed for everything. Most likely the members of White's were equally indisposed to handling cash, though apparently they had no qualms about gambling it.

Rollins said, "All the best, sir."

Apparently there was no keeping secrets from the staff at the Bradford, though how Rollins could know he might need luck was worth noting. He might want to tap into the hotel's back door intelligence network in the future. Never hurt to know what the people around him were thinking.

Nearly four years had passed since the last time he had been to White's to meet with then-colonel, and now-Major General Sir Stewart Menzies aka "C," the head of MI-6. A lot of official business from all branches of the government was conducted on the club's premises. Inside, exactly the way he remembered, the place reeked of elegance, wealth, and power.

As if it were only yesterday the hall porter said, "Welcome back, Colonel Randal. Nice to see you again, sir. If you shall come this way, Colonel Bevan has already arrived."

Col. Randal said, "Good to see you too Groom – anyone betting on raindrops these days?"

"Not that I am aware of, sir."

As he was escorting him to the small drawing room on the first floor where Lt. Col. Bevan was waiting, Groom said, "I read Flight Lieutenant Wheatley's book about you and Colonel Stone, sir. Quite an amazing exploit the two of you parachuting onto that remote island and capturing the Italian admiral such as you did."

Col. Randal said, "Wheatley was an Army captain when he interviewed us in Cairo."

Groom said, "I believe that was only a temporary rank until he could be gazetted by the Royal Air Force, sir – flight lieutenant is the same grade. Since then a subsequent promotion to Squadron Leader has come through."

Col. Randal said, "The only thing amazing about *Jump on Bela* was that hack Wheatley managed to spell our names right."

Groom said, "Colonel Stone voiced the exact sentiment, sir."

"You've seen Terry?"

"He is here now, sir. Visiting the Duke."

Lt. Col. Bevan stood up to shake hands when Col. Randal entered the room. He seemed genuinely pleased to see him. "Jane has kept me apprised of your activities since we last met, Colonel. The array of gongs on your tunic tells me she did not exaggerate – failed to mention those, actually. Quite the war record, well done."

Lt. Col. Bevan was a great believer an officer should be smartly turned out. It was said he wore the "best polished shoes in the British Army." Thanks to Lady Jane and Mr. Chatterley at Pembrook's Military Tailors, Col. Randal passed the command presence test. He was off to a good start.

It took a lot to impress Lt. Col. Bevan. A graduate of Eton and member of Pop, he was married to Lady Barbara Bingham whose ancestor, Lord Lucan, had commanded the cavalry division during the charge of the Light Brigade – into the Valley of Death. His brother-in-law, Field Marshal Sir Harold Alexander was currently in the process of stepping in to assume General Dwight D. Eisenhower's position as Commander Mediterranean Theatre of Operations – although that piece of information had not been released to the general public. Several times a week he dined with Field Marshal Sir Alan Brooke, the Chief of the Imperial General Staff at the exclusive Army & Navy Club, to discuss deception planning for D-Day.

And while only a lieutenant colonel, as Controlling Officer LCS he wielded enormous powers almost without precedence in modern history though almost no one knew why – or whom he reported to – it was Prime Minister Winston Churchill.

Had the Prime Minister not been the PM he would have been a member of LCS. The two met weekly, often more, at Checkers to drink brandy, smoke cigars and dream up schoolboy tricks to play on the Germans designed to convince them of what they already believed . . . that the invasion would come ashore at Pas-de-Calais – the shortest straight-line distance across the English Channel to enemy-occupied France.[1]

That was not where Allied Forces were going to land.

Through his contacts with Prime Minister Churchill, Lt. Col. Bevan was able to command the attention of President Roosevelt. As controller of LCS he could direct any government agency in London to do his bidding and – working through the Joint Security Control – any in Washington. Senior officers who attempted to obstruct the doings of LCS suddenly found themselves quietly posted to the China, Burma, India (CBI) Theatre of Operations where they would no longer be in a position to interfere. Lt. Col. Bevan's contemporaries, many far senior in rank, regarded him in much the same way as they would a public executioner . . . with caution, respect and a healthy dose of fear. [2]

While they were meeting at White's today, it was not Lt. Col. Bevan's personal favorite choice of clubs. That would be Brooks where he was also a member – his "LCS annex." He could be found there almost daily. Lieutenant Colonel Sir Terry "Zorro" Stone, KBE, DSO, MC, once described Brooks to Col. Randal as "the most political club that will ever exist in London." It too was not without its history of colorful wagers. In 1785, two years after the first recorded flight of a hot air balloon, a bet was registered in the club's book on which of its members would be the first to "fornicate with a woman 1,000 yards in the sky."

So why was today's meeting being held at White's instead of Brooks? Because as soon as his business with Lady Jane's significant other – a turn of a phrase he found extraordinarily distasteful in this particular case – was concluded, Lt. Col. Bevan would move to another room to confer with two other high-level players in the world of British secret intelligence. The outcome of those talks would shape the direction LCS would take in carrying out a great many of its cover and deception schemes for the remainder of the all-important run-up to D-Day.

The meeting with Col. Randal was a job interview.

Col. Randal and Lt. Col. Bevan sat and had a polite conversation for nearly an hour. However, the talk did not seem to go anywhere in particular. Virtually no personal questions – which was odd considering the stated purpose of the meeting was for them to get to know each other better.

The Controller of Deception inquired about Force N guerrilla operations in Abyssinia, desert patrolling out of Oasis X and seemed particularly interested in Raiding Forces' small-scale raiding in the Aegean. It was a polite conversation.

Not said was, "Welcome to the family."

When Col. Randal returned to the limousine Lady Jane was waiting inside. "How was your visit?"

Col. Randal said, "I have no idea."

AS SOON AS COLONEL JOHN RANDAL LEFT THE BUILDING Groom escorted James "Baldie" Taylor, looking as sleek as a seal in one of the late Big Five criminals' beautifully tailored navy blue Egyptian silk suits, to the small drawing room. He had been waiting in private to confer with Lieutenant Colonel John Henry Bevan. The two had never met. However, Jim came highly recommended. The Chief of LCS had been briefed on the MI-6 agent's wartime role in intelligence and was aware he held the local rank of major general in the Middle East and other places but not in England.

As had been the case in Col. Randal's meeting, today was to be a job interview. That was the purpose of Jim traveling to London. He had been summoned – just like Col. Randal.

Lt. Col. Bevan went straight to the main point. "Let me see if I understand correctly, Mr. Taylor. You serve as MI-6's liaison to Raiding Forces. You are also SOE's liaison to Raiding Forces. You are Raiding Force's liaison to OSS and vice versa for General Donovan. Now Brigadier Clarke of A-Force has proposed you as my LCS liaison to Raiding Forces and MI-5 as well?"

Jim said, "More or less. In addition I also assist in coordinating certain activities with Brigadier Raymond J. Maunsell's SIME and Brigadier Dudley Clarke's A-Force for Colonel Randal. Prior to the war my primary responsibility was to assess the ground warfare capabilities of foreign powers to include non-state actors."

Lt. Col. Bevan said, “Quite possibly the most byzantine job description ever. Do all those agencies know the nature of your relationship with the other organizations?”

“Not entirely,” Jim said, “though it is not a complete secret. I report to MI-6. I liaise with the rest – a fine distinction. SOE may have the mistaken impression that I report to them. As for Colonel Randal, he does not care what I do in my spare time.”

“A complicated life you live, Mr. Taylor, though it puts you in a unique position to represent the London Controlling Section at a critical juncture of the war.”

“Not any more complicated than dealing with my three ex-wives,” Jim said.

“Has Dudley Clarke briefed you on the scope of LCS?”

Jim said, “He informed me you would do so in the event you found me suitable – though he did not say suitable for what. I am aware of much of what A-Force is involved with in the Middle East and elsewhere. That said, Dudley has his finger in a lot of pies I may not be privy to.”

Lt. Col. Bevan said, “I understand you accompany Raiding Forces on operations on occasion. Unusual for such a senior intelligence officer with a portfolio as diverse as yours. Once you are fully read in on the LCS mission brief, those adventures shall no longer be possible – nonnegotiable.”

“I understand, Colonel.”

“Start out by telling me what you know about Randal and my goddaughter.”

Jim said, “As I am sure you are aware, early in the war Lady Seaborn was a talent spotter for MI-6. She put them on to Colonel Randal when he was attempting to stand up a pinprick Commando unit for small-scale raids on the French coast. Ever since that time Raiding Forces has been conducting operations for Broadway. On occasion with full knowledge SIS initiated the mission and at other times not.”

Lt. Col. Bevan said, “That seems a bit odd.”

“The Colonel does not have an agenda or ask unnecessary questions. Given a mission he salutes and carries on. Though he will take liberty to modify the assignment when he deems it has been designed, as he calls it, ‘by some armchair commando.’”

Lt. Col. Bevan said, “Happen often?”

“More than not.”

“And how does Jane’s connection to MI-6 play into all that?”

Jim said, “Over the years, Lady Seaborn has distanced herself from MI-6. My impression is the split loyalty did not suit her. She is all Raiding Forces, all the time, one hundred percent.”

Lt. Col. Bevan said, “I offered Jane the opportunity to serve on the LCS in order to have a woman’s perspective. Turned me down. Did not want to leave Castelrozzo – likely she meant Randal, not the island.”

“Lady Seaborn and the colonel are unusually close. Particularly since she was shot,” Jim said. “People enjoy being in their company. I have never known of any serious disagreements between the two of them. Never enjoyed that type of relationship with any of my wives.”

Lt. Col. Bevan said, “If I take you on as my liaison officer I shall expect you to keep me briefed on the strengths and weaknesses of Raiding Forces’ key officers. I need to be apprised of their performance level at all times, particularly if it should ever change for any reason. LCS shall be dependent on them for extremely high-value tasks that in the big picture are considerably more vital than they might seem.

“Start with a sketch of Colonel Randal.”

Jim said, “Before the war he operated against Huk bandits in the Philippine jungles for two years on detached assignment to a flying squad of the Constabulary from the U.S. 26th Cavalry Regiment. After leaving the U.S. Army under a cloud . . .”

Lt. Col. Bevan interrupted. “What sort of cloud?”

“He was accused of cutting off the head of a bandit named Smiling Jack and sending it to General MacArthur’s intelligence officer,” Jim said. “The officer had openly questioned whether Randal was exaggerating his team’s success rate in combating the guerrillas. Claimed Randal simply went into the jungle, killed the first Filipino he came to and said he was a Huk.

“Eisenhower, then a lieutenant colonel on MacArthur’s staff, was not the addressee. Unfortunately, his secretary opened the box by mistake. She ended up in hospital.

“May still be hard feelings over the incident.”

“Good for Randal – stood his ground, took up for his troops,” Lt. Col. Bevan said.

Jim said, "He came to the UK in late 1939. Enlisted in The Rangers Regiment – one of the three Territorial feeder regiments of the King's Royal Rifle Corps. Served in the British Expeditionary Force for a brief period at Calais for which he was awarded the Military Cross. After an epic escape, bringing out his surviving troops against all odds, Randal joined the Commandos where he organized a small-scale raiding unit for cross-Channel raids. Later he raised a mobile guerrilla army called Force N behind the lines in Abyssinia. From there he moved to the desert and conducted around-the-clock hit-and-run gun jeep patrols against Rommel's lines of communications from a remote base named Oasis X in the Great Sand Sea. He is currently engaged in carrying out a series of airborne and amphibious raids against targets in the Aegean."

Lt. Col. Bevan said, "Personal traits?"

"The Colonel is a charismatic leader. Easy to like. Difficult to know. He is a daring small-unit tactician specializing in unconventional warfare – with an eye for the main chance. Very good with light highly mobile forces. He possesses a cool brain, does not get rattled and is decisive when crafting plans, giving orders or under fire. Gives off the impression of having a plan to kill everyone he meets."

Lt. Col. Bevan said, "What would you say are his main strengths as a commander?"

"Colonel Randal is a master at improvising what he does not have in the way of materiel support and/or equipment, which until recently has been virtually not forthcoming except for obsolete castoffs.

"He is unparalleled at unit building – taking disparate organizations and/or individuals and instilling in them the Raiding Forces' culture. What he calls 'putting a round peg in a round hole.' He has a set of rules for his men. Number one being: 'The first rule is there ain't no rules.'

"You could not ask for a truer friend or make a more formidable enemy," Jim said.

"Weaknesses?"

"The Colonel goes his own way and takes far too many chances – always leads from the front. Lady Seaborn gives him a hard time about it. As do a number of others, myself included," Jim said. "We would rather he dial back his high-risk leadership style and become more of a commander. General Donovan concurs as does Brigadier Clarke."

Lt. Col. Bevan said, "What is it you are not telling me?"

Jim said, "We are not having this conversation?"

"Goes without saying. From this point forward, Mr. Taylor, we are not having any conversation – ever, full stop."

"I have information to the effect that Lady Seaborn's husband was taken prisoner by the Japanese after his ship was torpedoed en route to the CBI," Jim said. "Commander Seaborn was imprisoned in a slave labor POW camp where he was caught red-handed stealing food from the other inmates – a capital offense in their eyes. A mock trial was held by the prisoners.

"He was found guilty and sentenced to be boreholed."

Lt. Col. Bevan said, "What pray tell is that?"

"Commander Seaborn was held over an open latrine by his ankles, lowered head first and drowned in the excrement."

"Does Jane know?"

Jim said, "Acting on Colonel Randal's advice I chose not to inform Lady Seaborn. We concurred there was nothing to be gained by upsetting her at this time. Possibly at some later date or after the war – Admiral Ransom says maybe never."

"A wise and prudent decision," Lt. Col. Bevan said. "One I wholeheartedly endorse. Speaks well of you and demonstrates sound judgment on both your parts when there was no right answer."

"Col. Randal is very protective of Lady Seaborn."

"Excellent report. Exactly the detail I shall expect on a timely basis," Lt. Col. Bevan said. "LCS's ability to be confident in working with Raiding Forces going forward shall be dependent on my having a comprehensive understanding about everything taking place inside the unit while their knowledge of what we do, not so much – as in not at all."

Jim said, "I shall consider providing background color as an integral part of my job description."

Lt. Col. Bevan said, "I want a copy of those rules you mentioned."

"They shall be on your desk this afternoon."

"Last question . . . if I take you on will you be able to control Randal?"

"I cannot make that guarantee," Jim said.

Based on his interview with the colonel and from everything Lady Jane had told him, Lt. Col. Bevan believed the response to be forthright, accurate and true. Which was exactly what he wanted from a liaison officer – straight answers.

"Consider yourself hired, Mr. Taylor. Do not inform Colonel Randal quite yet. We need to flesh out the details of how this relationship is going to work prior to – but bear in mind at all times LCS is the executive agency. You report to me now no matter what anyone else might have to say going forward."

Maj. Gen. Menzies said, "You report to Colonel Bevan. He will pass on any information MI-6 might be interested in to me. That is not the case for any other of the agencies you liaise with.

"I understand, sir."

What Jim did not know was why LCS needed a liaison to Raiding Forces.

MAJOR GENERAL SIR STEWART MENZIES, DSO, MC, AKA "C," was waiting in the billiard room where he conducted MOST SECRET/TOP SECRET MI-6 business on a daily basis with Lieutenant Colonel John Henry Bevan and James "Baldie" Taylor.

The chief of the British Secret Intelligence Service (SIS), Maj. Gen. Menzies had been born into enormous wealth and power, as were all the other members of White's. It was said he "had no great intellect but exceptionally good social connections." His parents were members of the Prince of Wales set. He did not discourage the rumor he was the illegitimate son of King Edward VII – his mother having been a lady in waiting to the queen. The money on his father's side came from whiskey and gin distilling while his mother's family owned the Wilson Steamship Company of Hull. C's actual father, not the King, listed himself on Sir Stewart's birth certificate as a "Gentleman of Private Means." About all that was known about him publicly was he spent a great deal of time riding and fox hunting. And had a passion for the smartest London clubs.

Maj. Gen. Menzies grew up among the small group of privileged, wealthy and immensely influential families who ruled half the globe. He entered Eton as an Oppidan – the son of "noble and powerful persons, a special friend of said college," which meant not having to take the entrance exam. And more importantly he became the President of Pop, the oldest and most powerful of all British schoolboy societies. Membership marked its fellows for high public office in later life – Pop ran the British Empire. As a student athlete, Sir Stewart was considered one of the best sportsmen of his time. And he was a member of the immensely influential Beaufort Hunt, as was Major the Lady Jane Seaborn.

Though it was said by his arch-enemy, Adolf Hitler, that Maj. Gen. Menzies was the greatest spymaster in the world, he did have his detractors. The Brigadier was not Prime Minister Churchill's first choice to be the Chief of MI-6. But over time, their relationship had matured into a fine-tuned partnership.

Maj. Gen. Menzies and Lt. Col. Bevan's lives were intertwined socially, financially – the Chief of LCS was C's stockbroker – and militarily. Both had served during the last war, both decorated for their actions. Now they were in the top tier of players of the Great Game in England. In every sense of the word they were cut from the same cloth – card-carrying members in the upper, upper echelon of the "Old Boy Network."

Both had a relationship with Colonel John Randal though neither man knew him well.

Maj. Gen. Menzies said, "I take it you have decided to avail yourself of Mr. Taylor's services."

Lt. Col. Bevan said, "I have."

"Briefed him on the LCS mission statement yet?"

"Only tangentially. I shall send him off to MI-5 first for what doubtless shall be an illuminating orientation about the state of their current activities. Then later today we shall have Mr. Taylor to my office to introduce him to the staff, at which time he shall be indoctrinated into the mysteries of strategic deception as conducted by LCS on a worldwide scale.

"Following those two briefings, life as Mr. Taylor has known it shall never be the same."

Maj. Gen. Menzies said, "Excellent . . . now for the matter at hand, which is how to deal with the Office of Strategic Services moving forward – a top priority. There is no way to keep the Yanks at bay forever. Donovan shall want in on Secret Intelligence and Deception. Even though his people are rank amateurs at espionage with no existing network of contacts on the European continent and no experience with handling them if they did."

Lt. Col. Bevan said, "I see no clear path forward for preventing OSS from becoming involved, Sir Stewart."

"SIS has been able to fend off General Donovan up until now by throwing OSS a few crumbs. That shall not always work. Which is unfortunate," Maj. Gen. Menzies said.

"We simply cannot afford to allow the Yanks to be involved in SI in Europe. It is bad enough having to deal with SOE who seem to have forgotten its charter is to organize guerrilla armies in enemy-occupied countries. Not poach on our ancient commission to collect information. Secret Intelligence is a business best left to those who appreciate – shall we say – the finer points of how to play the game."

Lt. Col. Bevan said, "The last thing LCS needs is SOE or OSS muscling in on Deception."

Maj. Gen. Menzies said, "Possibly you have a thought, Mr. Taylor."

Up until now they had been talking about him as if he were not in the room. Jim, who had been adhering to the age-old intelligence operative's idiom of "listen first, talk second" said, "They do not call General Donovan 'Wild Bill' without cause. He can be what the Yanks describe as a 'bull in a China closet.' Went ashore in the first wave with the U.S. 1st Infantry Division in North Africa – waded in under fire. Contrary to every principle of security.

"It would be unrealistic to believe the general is going to stand idly by while MI-6 and LCS carry out the cover and deception program for the largest amphibious invasion since the Spanish Armada set sail without wanting a piece of the action."

This was not what Maj. Gen. Menzies and Lt. Col. Bevan wanted to hear but it was no great surprise.

"Donovan will not be denied," Jim said. "Not this time. That is why the idea of using Raiding Forces for whatever purpose you have in mind provides the perfect opportunity to deflect his attention from the main object."

Lt. Col. Bevan said, "Elaborate, please, Mr. Taylor."

Jim said, "As you know, a strategic deception campaign consists of two phases – planning and execution the same as any other military operation. You cannot develop a strategic deception program without a strategy and *that* is what you want to control.

"Let Raiding Forces be a surrogate for OSS. Col. Randal can carry out the boots on the ground aspects of the tactical cover and deception – the execution phase. At least certain parts of it.

"In that way," Jim said, "you make Donovan feel OSS is an intrinsic part of LCS's deception campaign while keeping him away from strategic planning."

Lt. Col. Bevan said, "And that would work, why?"

Jim said, "Because in Donovan's mind, Raiding Forces is a wholly owned OSS asset."

Maj. Gen. Menzies said, "Randal has proven useful in the past. There is no reason to believe that shall not continue. He and General Donovan appear to enjoy good rapport. That could be useful for MI-6 and LCS purposes."

"The two enjoy an enviable working relationship," Jim said. "As does Raiding Forces with MI-6. There is no reason that kind of cooperation should not extend to LCS."

Maj. Gen. Menzies said, "We have the same end game objective – winning the war. The only friction between our services is how we go about accomplishing it. Turf wars between MI-6, OSS, SOE and LCS – even MI-5 – are inevitable. But they need to be kept to a minimum in the national interest."

"I believe you will find General Donovan easy enough to work with," Jim said. "Provided he does not feel he is being shut out – that would be a mistake."

Lt. Col. Bevan said, "That shall be a major part of your brief, Mr. Taylor. To keep our relationships on an even keel. You are the man in the middle. A thankless task – one well worth doing, nevertheless."

Jim said, "Make no mistake . . . do not underestimate Donovan. Lie or attempt to mislead him and he shall eventually find you out. The result shall be unpleasant repercussions coming from the highest levels of the U.S. government.

"The general can be a formidable opponent."

Lt. Col. Bevan said, "What does that mean?"

"Donovan and General McKoy have known each other since the American incursion into Mexico. "Geronimo" Joe has been a friend of the Roosevelt family since he led Teddy's horse up San Juan Hill. The President went to college with Donovan and thinks of him as his old football hero. We will be dealing with three men who have known and respected each other for twenty-five years," Jim said. "They will – as the Yanks like to describe it, 'have each other's back."

Lt. Col. Bevan said, "Point taken."

Maj. Gen. Menzies said, "Utilizing Raiding Forces to participate in strategic deception for LCS, thereby satisfying OSS's desire to be included, is an elegant solution, Mr. Taylor. Do you have a suggestion on how best to go about implementing it?"

"I shall have to get back to you on that after Colonel Bevan reads me into LCS."

"We shall lean heavily on you for advice about dealing with our OSS friends," Maj. Gen. Menzies said. "And fending off those bunglers at SOE. Amateurs really have no place in SI or the extraordinarily sophisticated art of military deception."

Lt. Col. Bevan said, "Agreed."

What neither Maj. Gen. Menzies or Lt. Col. Bevan mentioned was the primary reason LCS had initially considered working with Raiding Forces was Rikke Runborg's relationship with Field Marshal Erwin Rommel. She was slated to play a starring role in MI-5's Double Cross System deception campaign as part of OPERATION FORTITUDE SOUTH. Based on an assessment from Brigadier Dudley Clarke, it was believed Rocky would only cooperate if she remained under the protection of Col. Randal.

Rikke Runborg did not trust the British intelligence services.

JAMES "BALDIE" TAYLOR WALKED OUT OF WHITE'S AND entered the Bradford Hotel's limousine left behind for him by Major the Lady Jane Seaborn when she came to the club to link up with Colonel John Randal. Lady Jane's godfather had asked her to provide the transportation. He had not told her why.

"Fifty-eight Saint James Street."

The address was just over twenty blocks straight up the street from White's. Jim knew the place. It was the brand new London Office HQ of the MI-5 Security Service (SS) – not the best of acronyms considering the Nazis used it too for their concentration camp guards, among other things. Nowadays MI-5 rarely used the abbreviation.

The Saint James Street headquarters was known as "The Box" for its postal address of PO Box 500. The old headquarters had been located in Wormwood Scrubs, a Victorian era prison in West London. Offices were former cells. The doors still had functioning locks and if one was accidentally closed the MI-5 officer working at his desk was locked inside. It was funny the first few times it happened. Luckily for the Security Service staff stationed there – some said imprisoned – the Luftwaffe bombed the place. Staff ever after referred to the move to new quarters as the "Great Jailbreak."

The motto of the Security Service was *Regnum Defende* – Defend the Realm. Its job was to catch spies. MI-5 was very good at it.

Jim had no idea what to expect. Lieutenant Colonel John Henry Bevan had simply directed him to repair to MI-5 for a briefing straight away. He needed the Security Service orientation prior to coming to the London Controlling Section at 1 Horse Guards for his indoctrination into the murky world of Military Deception. Baldie did not know it but he was about to have his most interesting day since becoming an intelligence officer.

His instructions were to meet with John C. Masterman, Oxford don, author, international sportsman – a cricketer – the chairman of "Twenty" as the super-secret Twenty Committee was sometimes called. It was also known as Double Cross, The Double Cross System or as The Club, by its members. The name Twenty was chosen because in Roman numerals it is written as XX – double cross. Code names are not supposed to be chosen like that. They should have no relationship to what they are concealing, but someone in MI-5 had a sense of humor and clearly did not mind flouting the rules.

The XX joke was likely not appreciated by the Nazi spies the Security Service ruthlessly hunted down, interrogated, turned, then made available to the Club to do their mischief.

COLONEL JOHN RANDAL WAS IN THE LOBBY OF THE BRADFORD Hotel sitting on a couch in the VIP conversation area with Beverly Blackwell. The hotel was decorated like a magical fairyland for the Christmas season. Sparkling lights behind heavy blackout curtains and a giant fern with an angel on top created a spectacular holiday atmosphere. Nighttime restrictions as laid out in Blackout Leaflet No. 2 distributed in 1939 prior to the beginning of the war were in full force and effect. The Blitz was over but the occasional German Heinkel He 111 intruder still showed up from time to time.

Major the Lady Jane Seaborn ordered a section of prime lobby real estate to be cordoned off with velvet rope for the exclusive use of her party during their stay at the hotel. It provided a panoramic view of the bulk of the ground floor to include the entrance. Two couches and several large overstuffed leather chairs allowed for several people to congregate in palatial comfort. It would also be possible to hold a private meeting in the VIP area . . . in plain sight.

A rather muscular-looking individual in a tuxedo, one of several identically dressed, hard-eyed, very aware gentlemen stationed around the lobby, was standing at a modified position of parade rest at the velvet rope's gate. The discerning eye would notice a slight bulge under his left shoulder.

Col. Randal casually inquired about his day job, aware the London Police Force were armed for the duration – which meant he would most likely be an off-duty policeman moonlighting as hotel security. He was surprised when the man said, "I work for you, sir."

"Really?"

"Vulnerable Points Wing assigned to Seaborn House. Lady Seaborn requested the extra security during your stay. My orders are not to allow anyone to disturb you or your guests, Colonel."

"Badged Raiding Forces' operator?"

"I am, sir."

"Good – if any man so much as looks crosswise at Beverly when I'm not physically present, shoot him."

"With pleasure, sir."

People-watching was the principal sport in the lobby of the hotel. Col. Randal and Beverly were watching the people watching them. The roped-off VIP section, being a new development, attracted attention. Who would rate the privilege was of no small interest to those passing by – Bradford guests took their perks seriously. A mere U.S. Army colonel and a beautiful blonde . . . possibly *she* was somebody.

A lot of VIPs were in residence at the hotel. Three exiled heads of state from European countries and one deposed king, from countries the Nazis now occupied, made their home in the Bradford. Members of the peerage were thick on the ground. It was said on any given night a quorum of the House of Lords could be found in the main bar. Cabinet Ministers, air marshals, field marshals, admirals, and general officers of all grades were coming and going on real and imagined very important business. Slinky women in full-length furs as well as those in uniform glided through.

A commotion at the entrance to the hotel drew Col. Randal and Beverly's attention. Major General Sam Houston Blackwell – friends called him "Bronc" – had arrived with his entourage. He knew how to make an entrance. Red, the stunning Clipper Girl who was now spending most of her flight time serving on his personal C-47, was with him as were his two military aides – one captain, one lieutenant, as prescribed for USAAF major generals. Bronc seemed to be enjoying his war.

Maj. Gen. Blackwell was a big, handsome rancher, former University of Texas football player and one of the richest men in the state due to the discovery of oil on his extensive South Texas spread which turned his cattle operation into a hobby overnight. Beverly described her father as an "international playboy" in pointy-toed cowboy boots . . . with a taste for fast women.

He was wearing a plank of medal ribbons that covered most of his chest topped off by a pair of Command Pilot's Wings, Jump Wings, and Glider Pilot Wings – Bronc and Beverly had qualified as glider pilots with the 82nd Airborne Division's 325th Glider Infantry Regiment at its base in Kairouan, Tunisia, to familiarize themselves with piloting the "canvas coffins" his TTC planes towed. If a Hollywood producer needed an actor to play the role of movie star general, Maj. Gen. Blackwell would be the type he was searching for.

At that moment the doors of the private elevator to the penthouse floor opened and Lady Jane and her cousin Brandy Seaborn stepped out.

Beverly said, "Uh-oh!"

For months, she had been doing everything possible to prevent her father from meeting Brandy in the belief it would not end well. In his blockbuster novel For Whom the Bell Tolls, novelist Ernest Hemingway wrote "the earth moved" when describing a similar encounter. That is not exactly what happened when Maj. Gen. Blackwell and Brandy made eye contact for the first time.

It was more like one of the Luftwaffe's 4,400-pound Satan bombs hit the building. The hotel shook – or it seemed to.

Beverly said, "I knew that was going to happen."

ENDNOTES – CHAPTER 2

(1) While simple sounding, even juvenile, when described on paper, these high jinks were in fact high-level, military-grade deceptions designed to be played out on the world stage with the intention of mystifying and misleading the Nazi regime from the top down as to the time and place of the D-Day invasion. The purpose of the exercise was to trick the Wehrmacht into stationing the bulk of their air and land forces in the Pas-de-Calais region while the rest were spread out along a 2,000-mile-long front making them weak everywhere. And even after the Allies eventually landed, they wanted the German High Command to question if the D-Day landing was the real invasion or merely a feint. A suspicion that the actual main attack would be led by Lieutenant General George S. Patton's First United States Army Group later at Calais would freeze the bulk of the German forces in place. The idea was to buy time for the Allies to get ashore in Normandy and consolidate the beachhead.

(2) London Controlling Section (LCS) conducted cerebral cover and deception operations in conjunction with MI-6. Dirty tricks were left to the knuckle draggers at SOE. For the most part OSS was to be kept on the sidelines until after the invasion.

3

THE STUD HISSELF

JAMES "BALDIE" TAYLOR WAS SITTING ALONE AT THE BAR IN the Bradford. He was contemplating what had taken place earlier that day. While the intelligence officer would have never admitted it, he was more than a little rattled by the experience. In fact, at one point previously during his briefing at MI-5, he thought his brain was going to explode. He needed time to process what he had heard.

There was no way to have foreseen what happened when he walked into 58 St. James Street – the MI-5 headquarters, aka "The Box." Upon arrival Jim was immediately subjected to a no-nonsense security check by stone-faced plain clothes MI-5 officers who exhibited a total absence of any sign of a personality. The Security Service was the senior British intelligence agency. Its mission was to catch spies. In the British Isles, everyone was a suspect until proven otherwise. Even the members of sister intelligence organizations.

The men and women who worked for MI-5 took their job seriously, though the tendency to hire beautiful debutantes as secretaries and the number of eligible bachelors among the officers gave the place somewhat of a party atmosphere.

Eventually Jim was escorted to the office of Lieutenant Colonel Thomas Argyll Robertson, Seaforth Highlanders, aka "Tar" for his initials. He was Chief of MI-5 Section B1-A – the unit responsible for playing double agents back at the Germans. Lt. Col. Robertson was a legendary counterintelligence officer only no one knew why, exactly. One reason for that was because no currently serving member of Security possessed the "Need to Know."

The story no one was cleared for . . . one night in 1936 Tar found himself in a phone booth tapping into a phone conversation emanating from 145 Piccadilly – the Duke of York's home. The call was between King Edward VIII and the Duke, his younger brother.

It was a black operation. Unsanctioned. Classified above MOST SECRET. Being carried out at the behest of the Prime Minister, off the record. With Tar was an engineer from MI-5's technical department sworn to secrecy on pain of being imprisoned in the Tower of London in solitary confinement for life or maybe wrapped in chains and dropped in the Thames if he breathed so much as a word of the night's activities. The technician was needed to do the actual phone tapping. He was not privy to the conversation being eavesdropped on.

A British constitutional crisis was at hand. Rumor was – and it turned out to be more than just a rumor – the King was planning to abdicate the throne and marry American divorcée Wallis Simpson. It was a scandalous prospect with enormous political and social implications at a time the British Empire was teetering on the brink of war.

MI-5 was called in to confirm or debunk.

Nowadays, Lt. Col. Robertson was in charge of what was sometimes described within the Security Service as the spy-vs.-spy department – Section B1-A. Known as a *bon vivant par excellence*, Tar was a recovering womanizer and longtime drinking pal of his old Sandhurst classmate Lieutenant Colonel David Niven, of General Headquarters (GHQ) Liaison Regiment, "Phantom."

That aside today Lt. Col. Robertson was all business. He produced a box of the type that might contain a ring or some other small piece of jewelry such as a pair of cuff links. Handing it to Jim he said, "You do know what this is."

Jim cracked the lid on the box. Inside was a small oval object the size of a pea encased in brown rubber to protect the thin glass vial it covered – an L-pill for lethal. Bite down, the glass ampoule encased in the rubber broke, poison cyanide was released – you are dead. As simple as 1, 2, 3.

"I do."

"Carry it on your person at all times going forward. At night keep it by your bedside. Under no circumstances are you to allow yourself to become captured. National security is at stake," Lt. Col. Robertson said. "You have likely heard that before but in this case consider it true. In a few moments you are about to be read into one of the absolute MOST SECRET/TOP SECRETS of the war – almost no one possesses the Need to Know.

"From now on, Mr. Taylor, you had best pray you do not talk in your sleep. Not that anyone would believe you if you did. Tell me after we finish your briefing if you believe I exaggerate."

Jim said, "I hear you loud and clear."

Having been a longtime MI-6 officer he was taking the melodrama with a healthy dose of skepticism. Intelligence types can be overly dramatic. They relish tradecraft and love their secrets. "Need to Know" was often nothing more than a form of conceit about who had the need and who did not. Biting down on a suicide pill . . . a little over the top considering he was slated to be nothing more than a mere liaison officer.

That, as it turned out, was wrong.

Lt. Col. Robertson said, "Effective immediately you shall be seconded to MI-5, as an honorary member – welcome to Security, old boy. We feel it is essential so when you sit in on the weekly Double Cross Committee meetings you can report back to the London Controlling Section with more authority. It is imperative you make it clear to LCS the script it develops does not deviate in substance from the outline for controlled agent traffic XX authorizes. And one other thing old boy, MI-6 is prohibited by law from operating in the United Kingdom – MI-5 can and does.

"You may occasionally get in on arresting Nazi spies."

Jim had no idea what the Double Cross Committee/Double Cross System/XX was but felt reasonably sure Major General Sir Stewart Menzies and Lieutenant Colonel John Henry Bevan were going to have differing views on the subject of who he worked for. He kept that thought to himself. Taking down a spy or two – might have possibilities.

"I understand, Colonel."

The life of a liaison officer is comparable to being a ping-pong ball. Back and forth. Dealing with people in the different units or agencies requires a certain degree of tact and diplomacy. Normally that meant between two organizations – *both* of whom wanted it made clear to the other *they did not work for them*. In this case Jim was going to have at least four to deal with – MI-6, LCS, OSS, MI-5, SOE and now possibly the Double Cross Committee – a lot of egos to juggle. He wondered how OSS Raiding Forces fit in the picture.

Lt. Col. Robertson took Jim to meet the chairman of the Twenty Committee, J. C. Masterman. The initials stood for John Cecil only no one ever called him that. A former Oxford don he was a brilliant, urbane, intelligence officer who carried himself with impeccable bearing. While holding the rank of lieutenant colonel in Military Intelligence, he never used it or wore the uniform.

Masterman was the chairman of the Twenty or Double Cross Committee, sometimes called the Double Cross System, most often written as XX – known to the members as "The Club." The committee chose the name and Roman Numeral XX because of its acronym. The two XXs made a double cross – which is what it did, double-crossed the Germans by turning their spies and playing them back against the Third Reich.=While the XX Committee worked most closely with MI-5 Security Service, it was a standalone organization made up of people from all the intelligence organizations to include the military, prewar professional and amateur, hostilities-only officers. Jim was beginning to comprehend the names of the different organizations within organizations – somewhat.

XX's job was to provide the "chicken feed" – which was true, partially true, out of date and/or of no use intelligence. Lieutenant Colonel John Henry Bevan's London Controlling Section then used this worthless "intelligence" to craft a narrative for deceptions called "traffic." Once LCS's script was written it was passed back to XX to be reviewed, then on to Lt. Col. Robertson's MI-5 Section B1-A who oversaw – under tight control – its dissemination to the Nazi "customers by having the turned former German spies send it back to their handlers in the Abwehr."

The principal means of transmitting chicken feed to the Germans was by real and "notional" double agents using wireless messages, letters written in invisible ink and other spy craft. The content was ordained by XX, composed by LCS, then reviewed and reapproved by XX before being disseminated by B1-A who transmitted the traffic to the other side.

Additional ingenious subterfuges were used to get the traffic into the Nazis' hands. Allied diplomats, both in England and abroad serving in neutral countries, would have seemingly indiscreet conversations at social events that they intended to be overheard and passed along to the Germans, pillow talk with a known Nazi agent, etc.

One such story containing chicken feed being pushed was that the Allies had an arsenal of "secret scientific weapons" of enormous power that would be deployed once the invasion began. Not true. But it gave the Germans something to think about. Far and away the largest deception being played against the Nazis on a worldwide stage was designed to cover the when and where of the D-Day invasion – OPERATION FORTITUDE SOUTH.

Clues were being planted all around the world like pieces of a puzzle. The intent was for the German intelligence apparatus to "discover" them, put the pieces together and arrive at the desired wrong conclusion. The idea was to make the Germans work for it but not too hard – which would result in a eureka moment. Their conclusion would be accurate but not true. But because they had to figure it out piece by piece the Abwehr would believe it.

The idea was to play to the opposition's vanity.

Jim knew "chicken feed" was often genuine but not damaging intelligence a double agent under MI-5 control could feed his Abwehr handlers to establish his or her bona fides. The purpose of the exercise was to convince the Germans their agent was capable of producing accurate intel by providing them true but useless information. The Nazis could verify the traffic was accurate only it never quite got there in time for the enemy to react to it.

Jim's prewar intelligence background was evaluating foreign military capabilities. As such, he was a student of war. While he was listening to Masterman, it began to dawn on him he might have been hasty in his initial ho-hum assessment of MI-5 and XX. The Chairman of the XX Committee was describing an incredibly sophisticated multifaceted grand grandmaster-level counterintelligence game being played on the world stage for high stakes – the saving of thousands, possibly tens of thousands, of Allied soldiers' lives on D-Day.

Deception might not need to be reserved for the upper-class elite who possessed qualities of honor, discretion and the spirit of gentlemanly amateurism as some in MI-6 and MI-5 believed. But the members of the LCS and XX Committee did have to be exceedingly bright. And creative. And they had to get it right.

Jim knew there was no aspect of warfare more important and more difficult to control than the element of surprise. It was perfectly clear to him if the Germans could be misled as to the when and where of the D-Day landings and kept in the wrong place then the Nazis would not be able to shift reinforcements in time to prevent the Allies from getting established ashore.

The deception needed to go further than D-Day. If the Germans could be convinced the Normandy landing was a feint, then they would not rush all their forces to the area to participate in a counterattack. The 15th Army would be tied down protecting the wrong beaches in Pas-de-Calais. Even a small delay would buy the Allies critical time to get their beachhead established.

And if they could trick the Germans into dispersing their troops to defend the entire French coastline the numerical superiority of the Wehrmacht in France, which would outnumber the Allied invaders by a staggering margin, would not be so daunting.

Masterman was at MI-5 today specifically to meet Jim and conduct the initial part of his orientation. He wasted no time in drilling down to the basic core principles of the XX Committee. The liaison officer's indoctrination was of utmost importance. Jim had to understand every detail of the deception campaign in order to facilitate keeping all the moving parts of the intelligence community involved on the same page. It was going to be no small task.

"We have a seven-point plan to deceive, mystify, and mislead the other side while at the same time gaining invaluable intelligence insight about the opposition in the process. To wit: One, control the enemy foreign espionage system or as much of it as we can get our hands on. Two, catch fresh spies as they appear – being made easy because upon arriving in England the newcomers unknowingly report to enemy agents we already have under our control. Three, to gain knowledge of the Abwehr. Four, to obtain information about the code and cipher work of the German Service. Five, to get evidence of enemy plans and intentions from the questions they ask their agents under our control to report on. Six, to influence enemy plans by the answers we send back. Seven, to deceive the enemy about our plans and intentions.

"Only late in the game did we come to fully appreciate the added value of deception the Double Cross System provided us. We can thank Colonel Robertson for recognizing the possibilities that facet of our double agent work offered. He changed the game."

Masterman delivered his lecture in classic bullet point format, fitting for a former Oxford don. Jim was not overly impressed. From the counterintelligence angle the concept of the operation he outlined was not earth-shattering. However, the deception aspect of sending carefully crafted responses to the spies' Abwehr handlers held possibilities he had never considered – unlimited possibilities. That part of the program was breaking new ground.

J.C. said, "It has been said, 'One must never hold your enemy in contempt.' Respect the other side's perseverance. And recognize eliminating a spy only spurs the opposition to replace him with another. Far better to observe an enemy agent and provide him with misinformation to unknowingly send back to Germany. Better yet, of course, is to persuade the spy to work instead for us as a double agent.

"XX Committee and B1-A are not actively involved in the major MI-5 counterintelligence mission which is the hunting down of enemy agents. Our charter is to manage the double agents we have captured and turned, which I shall explain in greater detail at a later time. Your role at MI-5 shall be to attend the weekly XX Committee meetings and serve as liaison between XX, LCS and B1-A – fascinating work; you shall not be bored."

Jim said, "That's what Tar said."

Masterman said, "Thanks to the good efforts of Colonel Robertson – whom I am quite sure was too modest to take credit – MI-5 now actively controls and runs the *entire* German espionage system in this country. More importantly we have turned it back against the Nazis."

Jim was gobsmacked. He must have heard wrong. Never in the history of state-sponsored warfare, to the best of his knowledge, had there ever been a case where anything like what Masterman described having ever occurred. Control an adversary's entire foreign spy network then play it back at them – a counterintelligence agent's fantasy.

"Are you saying . . ."

"Tar has every single German agent in England under management working for us. Except for one who committed suicide. And of course those we executed."

While this unbelievable piece of information was an earth-shaking revelation in the greater scope of wartime intelligence there was something else that became apparent to Jim he needed to consider. If a diagram were drawn composed of a large circle with MI-6, MI-5, XX, B1-A, LCS, A-Force, OSS, SOE, NID, Rocky, Rommel and Eisenhower labeled all the way around the perimeter with lines drawn from each running through the center they would intersect in the middle on one name – Randal.

Jim touched the pocket of his suit coat to make sure the pill box was still there.

BRIGADIER GENERAL WILLIAM "WILD BILL" DONOVAN walked into the lobby of the Bradford Hotel. Obtaining a room at the hotel was a virtual impossibility. It was booked up far into the future by flag officers, peers of the realm, Members of Parliament (MP), high government officials, visiting congressmen and senators from the States, A-list movie stars, exiled heads of state and the like. However, Major the Lady Jane Seaborn kept a suite on the penthouse floor permanently reserved for him. Wild Bill stayed there when he was in the city, which was more and more frequent now with the buildup to D-Day gaining traction. Men, equipment and materiel were pouring into England. There was a vibrance in the air. People knew they were living in a historic moment. The locals joked the U.S. Forces were, "Overpaid, oversexed and over here – glad to have them."

It was time to go for Hitler.

Across the room Brig. Gen. Donovan spotted Colonel John Randal in the VIP section sitting with Lady Jane and Captain Billy Jack Jaxx. His longtime friend, client and quail hunting buddy, Major General Sam Houston Blackwell, was also there off to one side talking to Brandy Seaborn. Lieutenant Colonel Sir Terry "Zorro" Stone and Red were in another pair of overstuffed chairs. The private section was designed to be rearranged so several different conversations could take place simultaneously.

It was a clever piece of tradecraft on Lady Jane's part. Those sitting behind the velvet rope could conduct classified business in full view with no one able to overhear what was being said. And it seemed innocent enough. Military and government officials visiting socially. Those same people seen coming and going from a private room would raise eyebrows.

Intelligence operatives rendezvous with their contacts in seedy bars and low-life dives, at least in paperback novels and the movies. The lobby of the five-star Bradford Hotel was a better idea. High-ranking military officers and government officials socializing was nothing out of the ordinary. The perfect cover. No one paid any undue attention – except to note the women behind the velvet rope were exceedingly attractive.

The Vulnerable Points Wing security officer stationed at the gate opened it for Brig. Gen. Donovan. As he walked in Capt. Jaxx was saying, "Mr. Chatterley asked me to tell you he wants an autographed copy of Jump on Bela..."

"A word, Colonel?"

The two moved to a pair of oversized chairs where they could talk in private.

Brig. Gen. Donovan said, "I've just come from a meeting at White's with General Menzies and Colonel Bevan. They informed me you were there earlier."

Col. Randal said, "I met with Colonel Bevan. It was a social call, sir. He's Lady Jane's godfather."

"Well, maybe so, but it's exactly what I instructed you to do," Brig. Gen. Donovan said. "Here's what is about to happen next. Raiding Forces Europe is going to be tasked with conducting strategic reconnaissance and small-scale raids on the French Coast as part of the run-up to D-Day – more on that later."

Col. Randal clicked on. "Yes, sir."

Brig. Gen. Donovan said, "Start making plans to relocate your HQ to Seaborn House in anticipation of running missions across the Dover Strait. You need to oversee this phase of Raiding Forces' operations personally. I'm working out the details of an additional job description for you in the future – probably some variation for OSS like your being Bronc's Airborne Advisor. Is that going to present a problem?"

"Colonel Honeycutt-Parker will be here later this evening or tomorrow, sir. I'll get a more detailed report on the status of Raiding Forces Europe at that time," Col. Randal said. "All I know at this point is our recruiting efforts have not been supported by Combined Operations or any of the other armed services."

"What does that mean?"

"Small-scale cross-channel raiding has been shut down for the last year and a half. Apparently Combined Operations decided it was counterproductive," Col. Randal said. "Word is they wanted to focus on larger operations but the result was pretty much all raiding came to a halt, sir."

Brig. Gen. Donovan said, "It's well-known Hitler obsesses over pinprick Commando raids. Even more so than losing ten thousand men killed in a single day on the Russian Front. Why would COHQ choose to do that?"

"No idea, sir. The Vice Admiral in Charge of Channel Operations placed a ban on cross-channel ops eighteen months ago. Refuses to authorize anything other than a single small unit craft crossing to France as needed to insert or extract agents for the intelligence services. Colonel Honeycutt-Parker said last night's recon mission was the first since that ban went into effect."

"Based on my conversation with Colonel Bevan that's about to be resolved. Small-scale raids are back on in a big way," Brig. Gen. Donovan said. "And I have nominated you to command them."

Col. Randal said, "A return to full operational tempo out of Seaborn House is going to require an infusion of personnel from Castelrozzo. When we do, Raiding Forces Middle East will be drawn down to dangerous levels, sir."

"You feel that's absolutely necessary?"

Col. Randal said, "Raiding Forces Europe was understrength from inception and there's been attrition, sir. Colonel Honeycutt-Parker hasn't been able to recruit from Achnacarry or existing Commando units because Combined Operations is raising four Special Service brigades. It won't release volunteers."

"Get me a report on your manpower situation ASAP," Brig. Gen. Donovan said. "OSS can probably scrape up a few more MUs and unassigned OG personnel. I'll find the people even though we have a worldwide commitment and are stretched to the breaking point."

Col. Randal said, "Understood sir."

"You just keep doing what you're doing, Colonel."

"Yes, sir."

Col. Randal wondered what it was he was doing that he needed to keep doing.

MANDY PAIGE ARRIVED AT 58 ST. JAMES STREET IN LONDON'S West End, the MI-5 building known as The Box, having been delivered by one of the Bradford Hotel's limousines. While the building housing the Security Service had a nickname, the Security Service itself did not have anything comparable to OSS's "The Outfit," MI-6's "The Firm" or SOE's "Ministry of Ungentlemanly Warfare/Baker Street Irregulars." It was a no-nonsense government agency with a party atmosphere. Mandy's instructions were to ask for Lieutenant Colonel Thomas Argyll Robertson. She had no idea why.

There was no doorbell so she knocked on the door and was let inside. She found two decidedly stoic individuals in dark suits who were on duty in the lobby. Armed security. The Box was clearly a place where visitors were not welcome. She wondered if they practiced frowning in front of a mirror.

Mandy said, "I have an appointment to see Colonel Robertson."

One of the security men spoke into a telephone. Within minutes a charming officer sporting the tartan trousers of his old regiment, the Seaforth Highlanders, arrived.

"You must be Mandy. Brigadier Maunsell has extraordinarily nice things to say about you. Any friend of R.J.'s is a friend of mine. Call me Tar, my initials – T-A-R. – or Tommy; everyone does."

Mandy said, "Nice to meet you, Tar."

Lt. Col. Robertson said, "I would like to start off by showing you around another of our facilities . . . a place we call Camp Zero-two-Zero. Would it be possible for us to use your limousine? I have a story to tell and you can hear it on the way."

Mandy wondered what R.J. had to do with her being summoned to MI-5. She had the sensation of being swept up in something – but what? And she was curious how Tar knew she had arrived in one of the hotel's limousines.

In the car Lt. Col. Robertson gave the chauffeur instructions to drive to Latchmere House. During the last war the place had been a rehabilitation hospital for soldiers who had been gassed. This time around the estate had been commandeered by His Majesty's Prison Service (HMPS) and turned into a maximum security holding facility. The large foreboding building was surrounded by concertina wire with armed guards patrolling the perimeter.

On the drive over, Lt. Col. Robertson told Mandy a tale she found difficult to believe. "Conventional wisdom held by most, to include those in government and the military, is the Abwehr has England saturated with an elite corps of highly trained secret agents. It is widely thought a sinister German spy is lurking behind every potted plant.

"To combat the perceived threat of a vast Nazi intelligence apparatus spying on the realm the British Ministry of Information has plastered posters everywhere that show glamorous women smoking cigarettes out of long holders above slogans like KEEP MUM, SHE'S NOT DUMB or LOOSE LIPS SINK SHIPS above a picture of a ship going down. The domestic propaganda campaign designed to constantly remind the already mistrustful general public to be vigilant and exercise restraint when talking to strangers has been underway full bore since the beginning of the war."

Mandy said, "*Perceived* threat?"

"The idea of a vast German spy network in the country is nothing more than an urban legend – a full-blown myth," Lt. Col. Robertson said.

Mandy was shocked.

Lt. Col. Robertson said, "In 1940 the Nazis overwhelmed France in six weeks. Prior to that time German intelligence had not paid much attention to our military. But when Hitler decided to invade the UK, the need for high-grade intelligence about the state of our defenses became a priority for the Abwehr. However, there was a problem. The Germans only had one agent in all England . . ."

Mandy thought, *that cannot possibly be true.*

". . . a hard-drinking Irishman who had worked on several government contracts," Lt. Col. Robertson continued. "He was in it for the profit supplying the Germans with minor bits of military information in exchange for money. When the war broke out, realizing the depth of trouble he was in as an Abwehr mercenary spy, Mr. . . . we shall call him Mr. Jones . . . immediately came forward and confessed his sins to MI-5. Instead of standing him up in front of a firing squad we kept him on as a double agent – our first of the war. Only we wrote the script for the intel he sent back to the Germans.

"The Abwehr was so impressed with what they perceived as the sudden improvement in the quality and volume of Mr. Jones' intelligence, new agents were hastily recruited and dispatched to England. They came by parachute, submarine, seaplane or intermingled with the refugees flooding into the country by boat.

"The German spies sent over were mostly incompetent, hastily trained – comically inept," Lt. Col. Robertson said. "Nearly all were instructed to report in to Mr. Jones for further instructions immediately upon arrival. That made our picking them up easy enough. Others who came over did not know British laws, customs etc. As a result of our massive campaign advising the public about the threat of an enemy Fifth Column, the spies were quickly spotted and turned in to the authorities.

"MI-5 decided not to execute them all. The Nazi secret agents not stood in front of a firing squad were showed film of the executions of those who were. The idea was to demonstrate just how serious their situation was. As you can imagine when presented with the choice of options – a blindfold and last cigarette or becoming a double agent – our success rate at turning German spies has been extraordinarily high."

Mandy said, "I can see how it would be."

Lt. Col. Robertson said, "Most of the Abwehr infiltrators underestimated the caliber of MI-5's counterintelligence capabilities. Some misjudged the risk of spying believing the Nazis would invade, enjoy a quick victory like they did in France and their services would no longer be required. Virtually none of them were enthusiastic about being secret agents."

Mandy said, "That is a surprise."

"For us as well. A few Germans landed and went straight to the nearest police station to turn themselves in, having, they claimed, only agreed to become spies as a way to defect," Lt. Col. Robertson said. "Others told us they were threatened with being thrown in a concentration camp if they chose not to volunteer. One was issued a radio that only transmitted but could not receive. Another parachuted in with little or no food and after starving for a few days while hiding in a forest, gave himself up."

"Are you saying the Abwehr's spies are like the Keystone Kops? Sounds perfectly implausible, Tar."

Lt. Col. Robertson said, "It gets crazier. A Spaniard whom we shall call Mr. Smith saw possibilities. He went to the German Embassy in Spain and convinced them he had contacts in England who would be willing to spy for the Nazis if paid for their services. The Abwehr signed him on.

"Since Mr. Smith did not actually have any contacts in the UK, he repaired to the public library, researched the British Isles, then created what we in the game call a network of 'notional' agents – meaning he made them up. All his traffic to the Abwehr was open source material."

Mandy said, "That is an incredible story."

Lt. Col. Robertson said, "I am just getting started, Mandy. Pleased with the increase in the sheer volume of Mr. Smith's production of intelligence, the Germans began providing him more and more money for information they could have found in the library. So Mr. Smith, ever the entrepreneur, created more and more notional spies. Had them scattered all over England.

"Eventually, of course, he came to the attention of MI-5. We thought Mr. Smith was what he claimed to be – an Abwehr case officer running a Nazi spy ring in England. One of our gentlemen flew to neutral Spain and arranged a meeting. Mr. Smith promptly confessed to gaming German Intelligence. Smart move on his part. He was about to be liquidated with extreme prejudice."

Mandy said, "What did you do?"

"Mr. Smith volunteered his services to become a double agent working for us," Lt. Col. Robertson said. "We agreed but to keep a closer eye on him MI-5 relocated its new master spy to England. At that point we found ourselves in possession of an entire network of make-believe spies. What to do?

"I suggested taking them all on, which we did. A whole network of notional spies we could play back against the Nazis.. How are you liking the story so far, Mandy?"

"Fascinating, but what does it have to do with me, Tar?"

Lt. Col. Robertson said, "My job description is chief of MI-5 Section B1-A. We control double agents, real *and* notional. You speak fluent German as I understand?"

"Yes."

"You are a reasonably competent telegraphist?"

"I can send and receive Morse."

"And you have a relationship with a certain Rikke Runborg?"

"Correct."

Mindful of the Rules for Raiding Rule #2: Keep it Short and Simple, Mandy was careful with her answers, unsure where this conversation was leading. She did not want to commit herself. Tar was asking questions he already knew the answers to, which was a red flag.

Lt. Col. Robertson said, "How would you like to come to work for me and be Miss Runborg's case officer? She is destined to play a key role in the cover and deception campaign for the upcoming D-Day invasion of France. And that means by association you shall too."

"I would need to think about it, Tar. Sounds fascinating. Unfortunately, my other commitments shall most likely prevent me from accepting."

"Take your time," Lt. Col. Robertson said. "We may be able to mitigate those obligations somewhat. I certainly hope so."

Mandy said, "I am open to suggestions."

Lt. Col. Robertson said, "Naturally, we did not have this conversation. But then you knew that, of course. No reason to go into the tedious details of the Official Secrets Act."

He did not bring up the XX Committee or the LCS because Mandy did not possess the Need to Know at this early point in their relationship. Nor did Lt. Col. Robertson mention Ultra decrypts also aided in locating German spies for the simple reason he was not cleared for Ultra. He had nothing more than a vague idea a program existed that provided Most Secret Source (MSS) signals intelligence MI-5 could utilize to track down enemy spies.

The technicians at Bletchley Park, having broken the German Enigma code, were able to determine when and where the German spies would be landing. And they could pinpoint their location once they attempted to transmit a message to the Abwehr. The men and women the Germans sent to spy on England did not stand a chance. They were easy prey.

All of this was highly classified MOST SECRET/TOP SECRET. Need to Know and compartmentalization was in full force and effect. Officers within an intelligence agency's various departments routinely lied to each other in conversations or omitted certain details from their reports. Nothing was what it seemed. No one was immune to being deceived. Lying was an art form. It was almost like a game. A lot of it was unnecessary.

Unknown to Mandy, she was not receiving the same briefing as Jim. There was no mention of every Nazi spy in England being under MI-5 control. She did not possess the Need to Know. And she never would.

Need to Know was an obsession and a conceit.

Mandy said, "So why are we at a prison?"

Lt. Col. Robertson said, "You are about to meet the warden, Lieutenant Colonel Robin Stephens, affectionately known as "Tin Eye" for his monocle. I thought you might like to see for yourself what happens to German agents when they fall into our hands and are in the process of debating whether or not to cooperate."

Mandy said, "Love to."

MAJOR GENERAL SAM HOUSTON BLACKWELL – FRIENDS called him "Bronc" – and Brigadier General William "Wild Bill" Donovan were sitting off to the side in the VIP section with a couple of Waldo Treywick's cigars in their teeth. They were unlit. Cigar smoking was confined to the Smoking Lounge. The two generals chose not to light up in order to stay where they were. It was more interesting in the lobby.

If anyone paid undue attention to the VIP area two or three of the hard-eyed men in tuxedos would drift over and stand just outside the velvet rope in front of whoever was being stared at to block the view. And they would stare back. People soon got the message.

Brig. Gen. Donovan said, "You fly missions, Bronc, and it would be unreasonable to believe you're going to cease and desist. So I won't be able to talk to you about a lot of what's about to be taking place in the future. Don't hold that against me and don't ask questions I can't answer."

Maj. Gen. Blackwell said, "Comprende, amigo."

Brig. Gen. Donovan said, "I'm going to need your assistance. Randal will be relocating his HQ to Seaborn House. Problem is he's responsible for at least two ongoing TOP SECRET operations run out of Castelrozzo. He is going to need to travel back and forth to supervise."

Maj. Gen. Blackwell said, "I can make that happen. I'm getting a C-54 Skymaster outfitted as my new transport aircraft – lot roomier, faster cruising speed," Maj. Gen. Blackwell said. "What say I make my old Neiman Marcus interior designer C-47 available to Raiding Forces on a permanent basis?"

"That works nicely."

"Great, in that case my personal C-47's about to be shot down any day now. That's how Randal acquired the Hudson bomber you and I turned into a bullet hole cheese shredder. Force N claimed it crashed in Abyssinia back in the day. RAF wrote the plane off the books and Raiding Forces used it happily ever after until our little joy ride. Beverly lit me up about that."

Brig. Gen. Donovan said, "I bet she did."

"Any news you *can* tell me, Bill?"

"The big-picture scenario is to set up something called Supreme Headquarters Allied Expeditionary Force – SHAEF," Brig. Gen. Donovan said. "It will plan, organize and carry out the invasion of France. Then once ashore exercise command and control of the war in Europe until VE Day."

Maj. Gen. Blackwell said, "Going to be a Brit in charge I guess. That's the scuttlebutt. Field Marshal Alan Brooke."

"No, the War Department's plan all along has always been for General George Marshall to come over and have the job," Brig. Gen. Donovan said. "We're supplying most of the men and materiel. We get the top command slot. General Eisenhower was supposed to return to Washington and take his place as Chief of Staff.

"However, the President informed me recently he can't sleep nights when Marshall is away from the country. Now the word is Ike will be announced as Supreme Allied Commander any day."

Maj. Gen. Blackwell said, "I guess I'm not supposed to know that last part, huh?"

Brig. Gen. Donovan said, "No you're not, but there has to be some benefit from being a good friend of the head of the United States' only national intelligence agency."

"Can I quote you on that?"

Ignoring him, Brig. Gen. Donovan said, "Here's my dilemma, Bronc, and it's the only reason I'm confiding this much classified information to you. The Office of Naval Intelligence is reluctant to cooperate with OSS because of our 'unconventional methods,' they say. The Army would like to see the Outfit amalgamated into its Military Intelligence Branch. We both have the same SI mission statement . . . 'collect, analyze and disseminate.'

"Eisenhower's inner circle, Army *and* Navy, will try to freeze me out. And Ike, who is still trying to figure out how in the world he went from being an obscure staff lieutenant colonel a little over three years ago to being nominated by the President for promotion to full four-star general, may be unwilling to intervene in an interservice squabble on OSS's behalf. Our soon-to-be-announced Supreme Allied Commander is still feeling his way as he goes. Might not want to burn political capital on a battle he sees as petty interservice rivalry."

Maj. Gen. Blackwell said, "Can't freeze me out. I assign 'em their personal aircraft. Where do you think Ike gets his?"

Brig. Gen. Donovan said, "I was counting on you to say something like that. I need you to be my top man on the inside of SHAEF. Keep me in the loop."

"What are friends for? I can also arrange a seat at the table for Randal as my Airborne Advisor. Bound to be a major parachute/glider component to D-Day. Between the two of us we ought to be able to generate enough of a peek behind the scenes for you to have some idea what's going on at Supreme Allied Headquarters. At least at the tactical level."

Brig. Gen. Donovan said, "Very good. I'm working out the details of another assignment for Randal. Give him two bites at the apple. Your Airborne and my Operational Groups Advisor – possibly need your assistance with it."

Maj. Gen. Blackwell said, "Two bites are better than one."

Neither of the generals were regular Army. Both were successful men in civilian life who wanted to win the war and go back to what they were doing before it started. Throw away the book. Improvise and adapt. Get it done. No problem.

Infiltrating SHAEF seemed like a perfectly reasonable idea.

COLONEL JOHN RANDAL AND MAJOR THE LADY JANE SEABORN were sitting on a couch in the VIP section of the Bradford Hotel's lobby. She had her arm on his shoulder.

Lady Jane's godfather had called her earlier in the day to suggest the three of them have a private dinner together.

Lady Jane said, "Your meeting with my godfather must have gone well."

Col. Randal said, "What makes you say that?"

"When he phoned to ask if we would have dinner with him tonight here at the hotel he inquired if I thought you would like him to propose you for membership in White's."

"Really?"

Was she kidding?

It was getting late in the day. Almost everyone who had flown in from Castelrozzo was in the Bradford's VIP section as well. King, Captain Pamala Plum-Martin and Lieutenant Ted Hamilton were the only ones who were not.

Mandy had arrived back from MI-5 needing advice. What to do? There was no one she could talk to about the position offered to her in Section B1-A. It was classified Top SECRET/MOST SECRET, Need to Know and the Tower of London had been mentioned. Only one person present, Lieutenant Colonel Tommy Argyll Robertson aka "Tar" possessed the need. She had invited him back to the hotel to meet Rocky. To be more precise, he had invited himself to be introduced to her.

Waldo Treywick and Rikke Runborg were chatting with Tar. They had no idea who he was and he was not telling. That would come later.

Major General Sam Houston Blackwell was off to one side again with Brandy Seaborn. This continuing development was the center of much speculation. Everyone was trying their best not to let on how interested they were. And failing.

Beverly Blackwell and Captain Billy Jack Jaxx were talking to Captain Sinclair Lovelace, who was in from Seaborn House as per Col. Randal's instructions. The University of Texas "Ten Most" beauty queen was keeping a not-so-discreet eye on her father.

Lieutenant General "Geronimo" Joe McKoy and Brigadier General William "Wild Bill" Donovan were engaged in a highly classified exchange with James "Baldie" Taylor though none of the three was revealing everything they knew about any of the subjects under discussion. Jim was wondering what Lt. Col. Robertson was doing there. Brig. Gen. Donovan understood the reason. Lt. Gen. McKoy had no idea who he was. No one was lying, but there was a lot of information being withheld – by all three.

Secrets were layered on top of secrets. Up until recently there had not been much of that in Raiding Forces. There was now.

Brig. Gen. Donovan said, "We are in the process of falsifying our Order of Battle prior to the invasion. The plan is to give the Germans an inflated picture of U.S. troop strength deployed, en route to England or in the pipeline. I intend to have Randal involved in the deception. The Abwehr has a dossier on him. So, it will be entirely believable to them that he is being brought in to participate in some capacity – likely small-scale raids or strategic reconnaissance."

Lt. Gen. McKoy said, "How's this phony Order of Battle deal gonna work, Bill?"

Brig. Gen. Donovan said, "We create 'notional' units on paper with corps and division patches, simulated radio traffic, photographs identifying phantom units that don't exist, the whole works. The imaginary units arriving in the UK are going to find their way into the press – intentional leakage, in order for the news to make its way to the Germans."

He did not mention MI-5 Section B1-A would be feeding the information to the Abwehr via their XX System of double agents.

"Troops wearing the notional unit patches will be seen in bars, restaurants and nightclubs across the country. It's a big deal. The plan is to create an entire ghost army and have it poised and ready to launch. Mystify, mislead, misdirect and divert – as the Great Teddy says, 'Hey, Presto!'"

Lt. Gen. McKoy said, "Good idea, Bill. That'll give the other side somethin' to cogitate on. What're we gonna do to help?"

Brig. Gen. Donovan said, "Be seen in public with senior officers from Supreme Headquarters Allied Forces Europe wearing the unit patch of one of the notional units. Basically play-acting. You're good at that so we're going to give you a notional command too, General . . . what kind of outfit would you like to have?"

"Make mine a' armored cavalry corps," Lt. Gen. McKoy said. "I always did want to be Jeb Stuart."

Jim said, "A showman like you, General – cookie-cutter definition of a high-value deception operative."

Lt. Gen. McKoy said, "Those also serve who show off."

"Consider it done, General," Brig. Gen. Donovan said. "Understand this is a much more important exercise than it sounds like at first blush. We need to create a *fake* army and position it in a place that will convince the Germans to defend territory where we're *not* going to land. That way when we do go in the opposition won't be there to greet us. The intention is to bring in General Patton to command it – he will be your notional boss."

Lt. Gen. McKoy said, "Yeah, I got it, Bill. Good plan. Don't hurt to fight smart."

"Here's my question for the two of you – keep it under your hat for the time being," Brig. Gen. Donovan said. "The U.S. Army has something called 'frocking.' It's like the British Army's local rank system. I'm considering having Randal frocked to brigadier general and giving him command of a notional airborne division – he wears the rank but doesn't get the pay.

"What do you think?"

Lt. Gen. McKoy said, "If all John's gonna do is be a play actor in some D-Day melodrama he'll be headin' straight back to Castelrozzo as fast as he can get there. Frocked or not. You can put that in the bank and spend the money."

Jim said, "I tend to agree."

Brig. Gen. Donovan said, " Not to worry. I have plans for Randal that should keep him occupied."

GENERAL DWIGHT D. EISENHOWER WAS HAVING DINNER IN the main dining room of the Bradford Hotel with several American and British officers. They were members of the staff he was assembling for SHAEF – his inner circle. Ike's attractive Mechanized Transport Corps (MTC) driver, Dvr. Kay Summersby was sitting next to him. She had been his chauffeur since 1942. The jury was out on whether the two were having an affair or not – both denied it.

Gen. Eisenhower had tried to stay at the Bradford during his stay in London. Unfortunately it could not accommodate him so he had to settle for another five-star hotel in the Mayfair district. Obtaining reservations for the dinner party tonight proved almost as difficult to score as a room.

The purpose of Gen. Eisenhower's being in the city was to finalize the announcement of his appointment as Supreme Allied Commander Europe. The turn of events was a heady development for most of those at the table. All of them – at least the U.S. officers – had been obscure majors, lieutenant colonels and colonels a little over three years prior. One had outranked him. Now they were part of the Supreme Allied Commander's staff and would be running the war in Europe.

Being in the inner circle was almost like an out-of-body experience. Not one of the officers would have believed in their wildest imagination they would find themselves actually being a part of something of this magnitude. Not for one minute.

Everyone at the table had been watching a stream of people making their way to a room off the Bradford's signature dining chamber. Gen. Eisenhower only recognized a few of the officers. Different people at his table were able to identify some of the others, Major General Sir Stewart Menzies, Lieutenant General "Geronimo" Joe McKoy with his long silver gunfighter style hair was a shock – no one knew him. Brigadier General William "Wild Bill" Donovan. Major General Lawrence Grand, formerly MI-6 then SOE's Section D for Destruction, Commander Ian Fleming, several beautiful women, less senior officers ranging from captain to colonel and trailing along at the rear, Major General Sam Houston Blackwell.

Gen. Eisenhower waved him over to the table. Just as he walked up, Colonel John Randal, Major the Lady Jane Seaborn and Lieutenant Colonel John Henry Bevan came out of a small private dining room and followed the stream of new arrivals to the room – her godfather was most impressed with the Sheba Diamond.

The maître d', waiters, waitresses, busboys, even the executive chef who came out from the kitchen, immediately ceased what they were doing, rushed over, fell in and lined up shoulder-to-shoulder to greet Lady Jane.

She walked down the line trailed by Col. Randal and Lt. Col. Bevan, speaking to each person by name.

Gen. Eisenhower said, “What is going on over there, Bronc?”

Maj. Gen. Blackwell said, “An awards ceremony for one of Raiding Forces’ officers, Captain Jaxx . . . he’s getting the DSC.”

Gen. Eisenhower said, “Who is that young colonel with the stunning woman everyone lined up for?”

“John Randal – the Stud hisself.”

“Randal?”

Colonel Thomas Jefferson Davis aka “TJ,” his adjutant general, said, “That’s the son of a bitch who chopped off Smiling Jack’s head and sent it to your secretary in a box.”

Not the only time in the last year Gen. Eisenhower had been reminded of the incident. Tonight was the first time he had ever laid eyes on Col. Randal. The two had never met, though Ike knew him by reputation.

“The Butterfly.”

4

SPYING AND LYING

BRIGADIER GENERAL WILLIAM "WILD BILL" DONOVAN pulled Major the Lady Jane Seaborn aside to inquire if the Bradford had a private room where he could conduct a discreet classified briefing for Colonel John Randal and three or four other people.

Lady Jane said, "Absolutely, there is a small space we call the Phone Room on the floor where we are all staying. Before the war our penthouse suite guests placed their international phone calls from there in complete privacy. An operator was on duty around the clock. Now we are no longer able to make those calls, so it's unused."

Brig. Gen. Donovan said, "Exactly what I need."

"Anything you require for your briefing, General?"

"A chalkboard and easel would be helpful. Oh, and one of your Vulnerable Points Wing security people outside the door in the hall. Would you have Bronc, Jim and the colonel be present?"

Lady Jane said, "When?"

"Anytime in the next ten minutes will do nicely – we need to get the ball rolling."

Lady Jane laughed. "I shall make the arrangements. If anyone asks, and I know they shall, what do I say is the purpose of the briefing?"

"OSS/Raiding Forces Reorg."

"John will love that."

Brig. Gen. Donovan said, "You are invited to sit in if you like, Lady Jane."

"I shall."

She walked away then returned a few minutes later. "Everyone is moving now. The chalkboard is in the elevator with security on the way up. I am about to go make sure the room is set up. John asked if General McKoy and Beverly could attend."

Brig. Gen. Donovan said, "Beverly?"

Lady Jane laughed. "He seldom goes anywhere without her."

Brig. Gen. Donovan said, "In that case, fine. She's OSS."

The designated people discreetly made their way by ones and twos to the private elevator. It whisked them to the penthouse floor. When they stepped off, the Vulnerable Points Wing security officer standing outside the door of the Phone Room ushered them in. Brig. Gen. Donovan and Lady Jane were there waiting.

When everyone had arrived Brig. Gen. Donovan said, "Last night Bronc and I did some horse trading with Brigadier Gubbins, Chief of Special Operations Executive. SOE recently negotiated an agreement with my Chief of London Station, Lieutenant Colonel David Bruce. The plan is to fold OSS Operational Groups and Special Operations into SOE for the run-up to D-Day and for some indefinite time beyond. The stated purpose of the amalgamation was to facilitate the conduct of paramilitary operations on the Continent prior to and immediately following the Allied invasion.

"As a result a new organization is being set up called Special Forces Headquarters – SFHQ, consisting of OSS's OG, SO and SOE. Not to leave this room . . . I was not much impressed by the arrangement. That stipulated, Colonel Bruce had little choice. It was either capitulate to SOE or be left on the sidelines. We don't have the contacts with the Maquis in France they do and not enough time left prior to D-Day to develop them.

"The Brits have made their best effort to keep OSS out of the Secret Intelligence business from day one. And now they are aggressively maneuvering to curb our ability to carry out guerrilla operations on the Continent – which is our SO charter. And if we refuse to accede to his proposal, Gubbins intends to restrict our access to the French Resistance.

The bottom line is under the SFHQ concept as far as OSS operating in the ETO – we might as well stack arms and go home.

"So, with Bronc's able assistance I restructured the agreement."

There was a low murmur from the group. They did not like what they were hearing. A turf war.

Brig. Gen. Donovan said, "Before we delve into the particulars a quick rehash of the acronyms we'll be discussing is in order: Secret Intelligence-SI, Special Operations-SO, Operational Groups-OG and Special Forces Headquarters-SFHQ."

Brig. Gen. Donovan took out a piece of chalk and wrote on the board OSS & SOE. "The Gubbins plan called for SFHQ to consist of OSS's SO, OG and SOE – all of SOE, which meant the two OSS elements would be subordinated. Under that organizational structure SOE was given control of all Special Forces operations involving the French Maquis. OSS was only to be allowed to provide personnel in the form of individual operators who were to tag along with SOE teams in France on D-Day and subsequent operations.

"That deal is now off the table."

Brig. Gen. Donovan drew a line down from OSS and SOE and labeled it SFHQ. Then he drew another line down from SFHQ and labeled it SOE/SO. "Gubbins' primary concern going forward until sometime after D-Day is OPERATION JEDBURGH – that name is classified.

"JEDBURGH is the arming, equipping and advising of the French Maquis. SOE teams, as I mentioned, supported by individual operators from OSS's SO will be dropping into France flanking and forward of up to thirty miles behind the invasion beaches. The idea is to raise a guerrilla army that, commencing on the night of D-1, will knock down phone lines, blow bridges, cut railway tracks, ambush road networks, etc.

"We are going to let Gubbins have that. And he can retain control of OSS SO until the beachhead lodgment is well-established ashore – a date to be determined."

Next Brig. Gen. Donovan sketched in a long line straight down from OSS at the top of the board. It bypassed SFHQ. He labeled it OGBE.

"Now under a new OSS reorganization Bronc and I proposed, OGs worldwide will be elevated to branch status named "Operational Group Branch." Here in England it will be styled Operational Group Branch Europe – OGBE.

"Notice OG has disappeared from SFHQ. Under this new Table of Organization OGBE will be commanded by Colonel Randal and consist of Raiding Forces and attached units. It will be a standalone organization responsible for pre-invasion raids and reconnaissance on the French Coast prior to and following D-Day.

"OGBE will also have responsibility for coordinating with the French Resistance for arms, supplies and direct action strikes along a narrow corridor running along the French coastline for the length of the country. Any SOE operation carried out up to five miles inland from the coast – what the Nazi Reich Minister of Propaganda Dr. Goebbels likes to describe as the 'Zone of Death' – has to be coordinated with Colonel Randal to include JEDBURGH."

Major General Sam Houston Blackwell said, "Gubbins went up like a volcano when Wild Bill laid that one on him – *Boom*!"

Brig. Gen. Donovan said, "'M,' as Gubbins fancies being called at SOE, for his middle name 'McVean,' threatened to take my organizational changes to Eisenhower for mediation. And in the event that failed, to kick it upstairs for the Prime Minister to intervene.

"At that point, General Blackwell informed General Gubbins in that case he would pull his Troop Transport Command special operations squadrons from SOE – currently supporting OPERATION CARPET-BAGGER, the aerial resupply of the French Underground – and give it to OGBE. Blackwell told Gubbins he could indent for an aircraft from Colonel Randal next time he needed one."

Beverly Blackwell said, "Uh-oh."

Lieutenant General "Geronimo" Joe McKoy said, "I'd a' liked to have been a fly on the wall – way to go Bronc, cowboy up."

"General Blackwell's one tough negotiator," Brig. Gen. Donovan said. "Gubbins gets virtually all of his air from the two USAAF Special Operations Squadrons – Bronc's boys."

Maj. Gen. Blackwell said, "That's when Wild Bill decided to point out to Gubbins now is not exactly the best of times to pick a public fight with OSS. Apparently there's a move underway in certain quarters to disband SOE. People in high places are trying to pull M's guerrilla warfare charter and give it to MI-6."

Lady Jane said, "What motivated that development?"

"A scandal surfaced recently regarding Gubbins' mishandling of operations in the Netherlands. One of SOE's underground resistance networks was penetrated by the Abwehr," Brig. Gen. Donovan said. "SOE agents on the ground sent numerous security check warnings the mission had been compromised. The messages were disregarded – on multiple occasions."

James "Baldie" Taylor said, "Those fools kept parachuting arms and agents onto DZs set up by the Germans. This went on for months, long after the abort security check had been sent to alert SOE the operator transmitting it was under enemy control."

Visibly angry, Lady Jane said, "That is outrageous. We do not want our Raiding Forces' lads under SOE's management. Not now – not ever."

Jim said, "There is no excuse except incompetence. The security checks were repeatedly ignored for reasons still not adequately explained. Good men and women were sent to their deaths again and again. Some claim the SOE Country Section Desk Officer for the area was playing golf when the first abort message came in and simply ignored them after that."

Brig. Gen. Donovan said, "One result of the reorganization is Colonel Randal's Operational Group Branch Europe will control *all* OG missions anywhere in Europe to include those emanating out of the Middle East, Italy and the Balkans.

"Notice the diagram, Lady Jane – OGBE has no direct line connecting it to SOE.

"What are your questions?"

Col. Randal said, "So, who is OGBE supposed to use to carry out the raids? There's less than fifty badged Raiding Forces' operators at Seaborn House, sir."

Brig. Gen. Donovan said, "I'm working on that."

After the briefing those present made a point of leaving separately so as not to draw attention to the fact they had been having a meeting – spy craft was the new Raiding Forces' obsession.

Lt. Gen. McKoy called it, "Spyin' and lyin'."

COLONEL JOHN RANDAL WAS STANDING AT THE BAR WITH Mandy, Beverly and Captain Billy Jack Jaxx. There was the usual crowd of British peers and politicians but now a lot more Americans. A group of entertainers from a USO show touring bases in Great Britain had dropped in. They were attracting attention. Especially the dancers.

Mandy was taking the opportunity to tell Col. Randal a sanitized version of her meeting at MI-5. There were details that could not be discussed. But she wanted his advice on the parts that could be.

"I have been offered a position with an intelligence service that must remain unnamed for the present."

Col. Randal said, "Really – that wouldn't have anything to do with your new friend Tar, would it?"

Mandy laughed. "I can neither confirm nor deny . . ."

"Sorry, didn't mean to step on your cloak and dagger."

"As we both know," Mandy said, "Rocky has been involved with A-Force in some capacity. Apparently that activity is about to shift to England. As I understand it my role would be to serve as her handler."

Col. Randal said, "I see."

Which meant he did not have a clue what she was talking about. All he knew was from time to time Brigadier Dudley Clarke would show up at RFHQ and disappear with Rikke Runborg for a short while without leaving the building.

Mandy said, "R.J. and possibly Dudley recommended me for the assignment. I doubt they would have if it were not important. Both of them are aware of my heavy involvement in Raiding Forces' ongoing operations."

Col. Randal said, "Roger that."

"What should I do, John?"

"If you're asking me personally I don't want you to go anywhere. You're more important to me than you realize. That said . . ."

Mandy said, "I am not leaving Raiding Forces. Way too much fun giving you a hard time when you get yourself in trouble. The response I gave was my current commitments would likely prohibit me from accepting the offer."

Col. Randal said, "Any way you could work it so you're TDY to this undisclosed organization from time to time?"

"Possibly, if you are all right with that."

"I'd say play it out. See where it goes. This might be a good thing. Talk to Lady Jane – she'll definitely have a thought."

"You have no idea how I dreaded having this conversation, John."

Col. Randal said, "Lighten up. General McKoy says there's more ways to choke a cat than by feeding it butter."

Mandy laughed. "What does that mean?"

"I have no idea."

Capt. Jaxx was hitting on one of the USO entertainers, a member of "Bob Hope's Gypsy Dancers," who was mightily impressed with his chest full of medals.

She said, "If I weren't a lesbian I would so jump your bones."

Beverly said, "Best brush-off line ever."

BRIGADIER GENERAL WILLIAM "WILD BILL" DONOVAN WAS having a conversation in the Bradford's VIP area of the hotel lobby with Colonel John Randal and Beverly Blackwell. Lieutenant General "Geronimo" Joe McKoy strolled in. Col. Randal made eye contact with him. He came over and joined the group. They rearranged four tall-backed overstuffed chairs so they were completely blocked from view for additional privacy – like being in a cocoon.

Brig. Gen. Donovan said, "For starters let me run through OSS Europe's new Table of Organization again and explain each element's duties so you are absolutely clear on how all the pieces fit together. There is some mission overlap which can be confusing.

"Special Intelligence: That's the gathering of foreign intelligence. You can forget that one. Not your concern. Colonel Bruce, the head of London Station, is focusing his energies on SI. But like I said earlier, OSS is meeting a lot of push back from the British 'old boy network' about involvement in secret intelligence gathering.

"Special Operations: The raising, arming and advising of resistance fighters behind enemy lines. The major part of SO is logistics. Air dropping weapons, running guns via sea, etc. Bronc's Special Operations Squadrons play a major role in SO – US and British.

"And last but not least the one you're concerned with, Operational Groups. On paper each OG consists of four officers and thirty operators. They are designed to carry out Commando/Ranger-type direct action missions against point-type targets. As well as performing strategic reconnaissance, raids, prisoner snatches, etc. The same types of operations you have been running in the Aegean.

"As I mentioned, there is some overlap between SO and OG. Occasionally on a short-term mission-specific basis, an Operational Group may be employed to organize and lead a band of guerrillas behind the lines.

"Now this is where it can get a little difficult to follow. SO, which is also being elevated to branch status, mirrors SOE – the entire ministry. Great Britain has three major intelligence agencies – MI-5, MI-6 and SOE – plus several additional smaller ones for a total of nine. The U.S. only has OSS with the FBI handling counterintelligence in the continental U.S. and South America.

"OSS performs the function of all of the UK's intelligence services. However, under the SFHQ reorganization, OSS SO Branch is now OPCON to SOE – meaning under British operational control. Raiding Forces now styled OGBE, will control all of the OSS Operational Groups.

"Questions?"

Having known the general all her life, Beverly felt comfortable asking, "How many OG teams are here in England, Bill?"

"None at this time."

Lt. Gen. McKoy said, "You got any on the way?"

"As I told Colonel Randal earlier, I'm working on that."

Lt. Gen. McKoy said, "So, we're supposed to kick off a whole new campaign, coverin' the entire coast a' France, Italy, the Balkans and who knows where else with what we've got in the way a' manpower at Seaborn House right now – about a reinforced platoon, and that's it?"

Brig. Gen. Donovan said, "Yes and no. For national-level political reasons I am not at liberty to go into, we need to keep an American organization as much as possible. Factor that into your planning going forward. To that end, Colonel Randal informs me there will have to be a redeployment of the 575th Ranger Task Force personnel from Castelrozzo to Seaborn House."

Col. Randal said, "We can do that, but it may take time, sir."

"Bronc has indicated a willingness to supply transport aircraft."

"In that case I'll get with him to discuss details, sir."

Brig. Gen. Donovan said, "You will need a Raiding Forces' Rear HQ here in London for coordination with SHAEF, MI-6, LCS, SOE and MI-5 considering Mandy is going to be working with them. You can set up at OSS London Station located at 20 Grosvenor Square. However, I recommend against it. For reasons I won't go into OGBE needs to be completely autonomous."

Col. Randal said, "Understood, sir."

"What I do not want, Colonel, is any OSS interservice rivalry between you and Colonel Bruce," Brig. Gen. Donovan said. "As I'm sure you noticed on the organizational chart I drew there wasn't any line connecting OGBE to the OSS London Group. Bruce is not in your chain of command. There is no reason for friction between the two of you."

Col. Randal said, "Wilco."

Brig. Gen. Donovan did not mention he had decided not to have Col. Randal frocked to brigadier general because then he would outrank the OSS Chief of London Station by two grades. No need for that headache. Since Col. Randal had never known the idea was under consideration, no harm no foul.

In the interest of harmony he intended to have Lt. Col. Bruce promoted to full colonel to not be outranked by the head of OGBE.

"Any more questions?"

Lt. Gen. McKoy said, "Not much need to ask Bill. You're givin' us a big assignment. And you ain't givin' us much to do it with."

Brig. Gen. Donovan said, "That is a fact. But like I said, I'm . . ."

Col. Randal produced a folded paper from the inside pocket of his blouse. "Here's a list of weapons we require for Seaborn House."

"I'll have them flown in. Arms and equipment I can deliver immediately," Brig. Gen. Donovan said. "Personnel, that's going to take a little longer."

Col. Randal said, "There is one other detail, sir. A message arrived from Westly Slade. He's up at Achnacarry completing Commando training. The Lieutenant requests an interservice transfer from the Navy to the Marines – can you make that happen?"

"I can but why would Slade want to make the change?"

"He believes being a Marine is a better fit for his Raiding Forces MOS – Special Warfare strike team leader."

Brig. Gen. Donovan said, "Tell Westly to consider himself a U.S. Marine. My office will handle the paperwork. Anything else – now would be the time."

"I'd like the 1st Ranger Battalion or the 509th PIB attached to Seaborn House for operations, sir – preferably both," Col. Randal said.

Brig. Gen. Donovan laughed. "Nice try, Colonel. Afraid the ability to deliver on that one is above my pay grade. If I could have my way both battalions would be yours. With your OGBE mission statement plus the other commitments Seaborn House currently has, you could definitely put them to use."

Col. Randal said, "Who do I report to for orders, General?"

"A King's Messenger will arrive periodically with sealed instructions – your next assignment," Brig. Gen. Donovan said. "The KM won't be authorized to do anything other than to personally ensure the document is placed in your hands. Not left with a duty officer."

"Understood."

Brig. Gen. Donovan said, "The orders will not originate from me but act on them as if they did. Eventually OGBE will be expected to work up to an operational tempo of one cross-channel mission per week, bare minimum. You will still continue to have the commitment to escort MI-6/SOE agents to France and there is one other classified operation you are not cleared to know the details of . . . that assignment is ongoing.

"Seaborn House is about to be a very busy place."

What he did not mention was it had been decided Col. Randal would not be advised who or where the orders originated because of his insistence on personally leading missions. Risk of capture and interrogation outweighed his Need to Know. Col. Randal was never to be aware Lieutenant Colonel John Henry Bevan was handpicking his targets.

Brig. Gen. Donovan said, "Anything else?"

Col. Randal said, "What's the process for coordinating our naval transport, sir?"

"I'm afraid the Commander-in-Chief and Flag Officer-in-Charge Dover – Admiral Pridham-Whippel – is less than enthusiastic about our plans to go raiding," Brig. Gen. Donovan said. "He's imposed a ban on small-scale cross-channel traffic.

"The Admiral is not cleared to know the 'why' of what we're trying to accomplish and may never be."

That last remark, which may have been an unintentional slip by Brig. Gen. Donovan, led Col. Randal to suspect there might be more to the cross-channel ops than he was being informed of. That thought he kept to himself. He did not know the "why" for operations other than what would be stated in the alerts. And that was not much.

Lt. Gen. McKoy said, "With a fancy tongue-twister of a title like the admiral's got I bet ole Pridham-Whippel was one unhappy sea dog when he found out he wasn't authorized to know what we're up to."

Brig. Gen. Donovan said, "The Admiral is not inclined to cooperate. The Royal Navy MGB for the raid you went on was a one-off. And the U.S. Navy doesn't have a PT boat squadron operational in England at this time we can borrow one from. You're going to have to improvise.

"I'm working on that too."

Beverly said, "Wow!"

COLONEL JOHN RANDAL WAS IN THE VIP SECTION OF THE lobby talking to Lieutenant General "Geronimo" Joe McKoy and Beverly Blackwell. Col. Randal was interested in the general's take on the conversation with Brigadier General William "Wild Bill" Donovan.

Lt. Gen. McKoy said, "We need to go into this deal with our eyes wide open, John. Nobody's tellin' the whole truth and nothin' but the truth. Everbody's lyin' or at least holdin' out about somethin'.

"We could be headed down a rabbit hole and this ain't Alice in Wonderland. If we're not careful we're liable to find ourselves as collateral damage some dark night on the far side due to the obsession that's goin' on with compartmentalization and Need to Know."

Col. Randal said, "There is that."

Beverly said, "Agreed – we're soldiers, not secret agents."

Lt. Gen. McKoy said, "You're dead right, Beverly. Our job is to go places in the dark a' night and break stuff – only thing clandestine about Raidin' Forces is when and where we show up."

Commander Ian Fleming arrived. The Naval Intelligence Division (NID) officer had been trying to get a date with Beverly from the day she arrived in Raiding Forces. No joy. It would have been easy to take the NID officer as a bungling wannabe ladies' man who was essentially an errand boy for his boss at NID, Rear Admiral John Henry Godfrey.

That would be a mistake. He did very well with women, just not Beverly.

And he was nobody's errand boy.

Unknown to Col. Randal and virtually everyone else who knew him, Cdr. Fleming was one of the best wired-in intelligence officers in all of Allied Forces. He was NID's liaison to the LCS, sat on the XX Committee and was one of only twenty people in the entire world currently cleared for Ultra. Considering the Prime Minister, the King and the President were on the list, it was an exclusive group.

It was said Cdr. Fleming was extremely creative at dreaming up exotic special operations someone else had to go carry out. That was true but not for the reason implied. Being greenlighted for Ultra prohibited him from going in harm's way – ever. He carried an L-pill. When traveling outside the country a military aide was always along who had orders to shoot him if there was ever a possibility he would fall into enemy hands. Virtually everything he did was Top Secret/Most Secret. He never talked about it.

Cdr. Fleming considered himself a friend of Raiding Forces.

Col. Randal said, "What can we do for you, Commander?"

Cdr. Fleming said, "It is not what you can do for me but what I can do for you, sir."

Keeping in mind one of Lt. Gen. McKoy's redneck philosophies – "If anything is free, take as little of it as you can get," – Col. Randal said, "Let's hear it."

"General Grand mentioned to me you are in a rather bad way for finding qualified Raiding Forces' operators," Cdr. Fleming said.

"That is correct."

It was a mystery how the former head of MI-6's Section D for Destruction, who had dispatched him on certain operations at the beginning of the war, knew anything about the current state of Raiding Forces' affairs. Major General Lawrence Grand had left clandestine duty and returned to being a Royal Engineer. Possibly he had not severed all his ties to the intelligence community. Originally, then-Col. Grand was MI-6 before Section D was transferred over to SOE. It was said of SIS once a member, always a member.

Cdr. Fleming said, "Back in the dark days when the UK was expecting to be invaded in a matter of weeks, acting on orders from then-Colonel Grand, my famous, globetrotting, true-life adventure author brother set up a super hush-hush organization at the behest of the Prime Minister.

"It was euphemistically called GHQ Auxiliary Unit. A super-secret, dirty tricks, guerrilla warfare army made up of handpicked men organized into clandestine cells – an underground army if you will. They were trained in close combat, sabotage, the use of firearms, explosives, intelligence gathering etc. The idea was to have an underground British resistance organization in place and ready to rise up against the Germans after the Nazis overran our country."

This was news to Col. Randal.

Cdr. Fleming said, "Peter selected a key man in each county to recruit the personnel, oversee a continuous training program and coordinate with Army HQ. The key man recruited the *crème de la crème* of locals. Then SOE lavished arms, explosives and equipment on them. Hidden bunkers were dug where they stored their gear and conducted their meetings. The Auxiliers (AU) are so clandestine the members in one county do not know the members in the other counties.

"The Germans never invaded. But the Auxiliary Units have remained in place to this day. A secret army watching and waiting. The bottom line is – at the end of the day the UK was left with an intelligence and sabotage network composed of picked men with no one to operate against."

Col. Randal said, "I see," which meant he did not have any idea what Cdr. Fleming was talking about.

Cdr. Fleming said, "The Auxiliers are scheduled to be disbanded. Perfect man material for you to recruit for Raiding Forces. Need to be nimble though. The SAS is being bulked up to brigade strength by Special Forces Headquarters for post-D-Day paramilitary operations in France. They shall likely be wanting the AU's for themselves, manpower shortages such as they are, what?"

Lt. Gen. McKoy said, "How many men we talkin' about, Ian?"

"In the range of 3,500 in the original intake."

Col. Randal said, “How do we go about recruitin’ ’em?”

“With a great deal of finesse,” Cdr. Fleming said. “Brigadier Gubbins is less than thrilled with the creation of Operational Group Branch Europe ...”

Col. Randal wondered how Cdr. Fleming already knew about OGBE.

“ . . . wanted the OSS OGs in SFHQ under his control. He could and likely would interfere with our efforts to poach the ranks of what he sees as his Auxiliary Units. I shall work behind the scenes to have those who want to volunteer for Raiding Forces made available without SOE being the wiser.”

Lt. Gen. McKoy looked at Col. Randal. It was clear what he was thinking – “rabbit hole.”

Col. Randal said, “You’ve met Captain Lovelace. I’ll assign him to be in charge of recruiting the AU personnel. Keep me in the loop, but the captain’s your point of contact in the event I’m not available.”

“Have him get in touch with me at NID,” Cdr. Fleming said. “Beverly, possibly you would care to be the liaison on this project? We need to move on this rather quickly.”

Beverly was tempted to trot out the line the USO dancer used on Jack Cool but managed to restrain herself. “I’ll have to clear it with Lady Jane first, Ian.”

Cdr. Fleming said, “One can only hope she is agreeable.”

Col. Randal said, “I haven’t forgotten your Red Indian project, Commander. The OSS Maritime Unit Special Warfare Operators assigned to it will be having a change of duty station to Seaborn House. I’ve had them running missions in the Aegean to gain operational experience.

“When the time comes to commence your NID missions they’ll be a veteran team.”

“Outstanding!”

Col. Randal said, “On the Auxiliary Unit personnel, we’ll take as many as we can get, Commander – thanks.”

That did not mean that every one of the Auxiliers who volunteered would end up in Raiding Forces. They would have to pass the initial interview. Then selection. Followed by Jump School and amphibious training at the Combined Operations Training Center in Inveraray. Capt. Roy “Mad Dog” Reupart, MC, would have to come set up shop at Seaborn

House. His work was going to be cut out for him supervising the Auxiliary Unit integration program.

Col. Randal said, "Beverly, send a TWX to Major Hoolihan. Tell him to hop a plane and report to me here at the Bradford ASAP if not sooner."

"On the way, John."

After Cdr. Fleming departed, Col. Randal said, "What's your thought on recruiting Auxiliary Unit personnel, General?"

Lt. Gen. McKoy said, "Layin' low, spyin' and lyin,' leadin' secret lives for the last three years – might have ourselves a culture fit problem."

Col. Randal said, "We'll see."

COLONEL JOHN RANDAL WAS IN THE VIP SECTION WITH Major the Lady Jane Seaborn. She was getting ready to depart with Mandy Paige on what she described as "girl business." He wondered what that might be. And since no one was telling the entire truth much lately he suspected there might be more to it than she was letting on.

Lady Jane said, "I am very disappointed with this trip so far, John. London is depressing. Parts of the city are bombed out. Rationing is in full swing. I planned to take the girls shopping, however, the stores have hardly any merchandise. And there are no children or pets to be seen."

Col. Randal said, "What happened to them?"

"The children were evacuated to the countryside to escape the air raids during the Blitz. The pets . . . an estimated 400,000 were put down during the first few days of the war because of food rationing. It was called the Great Cat and Dog Massacre.

"I hate Nazis."

Col. Randal said, "That's a lot of dead animals."

Lady Jane said, "Wish we had brought Happy with us. I miss him."

Col. Randal said, "I'm pretty sure he misses you too, Jane."

"I do not want him to be sad."

An impeccably dressed white-haired Royal Marine captain arrived at the entrance to the VIP section. The Vulnerable Points Wing security operator spoke to him briefly then walked over to Col. Randal.

"Sir, a King's Messenger to see you."

That was quick – his first set of orders. Col. Randal decided it was probably a test run of the procedure for the delivery of OGBE's marching orders. Brig. Gen. Donovan was a force to be reckoned with when it came to getting things done in a hurry. Raiding Forces had adopted one of the legal terms he was known to drop into conversations: "Time is of the essence."

"Let him in."

The King's Messenger Service had been in existence since 1198. It did what the name implied. Delivered messages for the King or, on rare occasions, for other high-level government officials when absolute discretion was required. King's Messengers did not normally deliver in England proper except in exceptionally rare instances of extreme importance to the war effort. In this case the message being delivered was from Lady Jane's godfather at the LCS – Col. Randal was not cleared to know where it originated.

Lady Jane said, "King's Messengers serving as the conduit for our assignments is confirmation of how vitally important whoever sent the dispatch has been deemed to be – one does not simply dial them up."

Col. Randal said, "Worth knowing."

"There is an air of mystery surrounding the Service. Little is known about them other than reliable retired officers are commissioned to hand-carry important messages around the globe in service of the King," Lady Jane said. "How many there are is generally not known, but the best estimate is around twenty men at any one time – possibly more now with the war."

The KM produced a leather credentials case containing the Service's crest with a small greyhound device dangling under it and the engraved motto, *Honi Soit Qui Mal Y Pense.*

"May I see your ID, sir?"

Col. Randal produced his military identification card. The KM studied it carefully. Once satisfied he produced a wax-sealed manila envelope from his briefcase and handed it over. The wax seal was stamped with the royal cypher representing the King's signet ring.

"Thank you, Colonel. Have a good morning, sir. I shall be on my way." Then he was gone.

Col. Randal said, "Can you translate the Latin on his badge?"

Lady Jane said, "It's Norman French. 'Shame on him who thinks evil of it'."

"What does that mean?"

"Avoid negative thoughts, think well of others. Also the motto of the Most Noble Order of the Garter, which, as you are aware, I am a Lady's Companion."

Col. Randal said, "No negativity I'm for that."

Lady Jane laughed. "Are you going to read your dispatch?"

Col. Randal produced his switchblade, touched the button and slit open the envelope. He was expecting a blank piece of paper. What he found was the briefest Operations Order he had ever received to include frag orders. It consisted of a set of six-digit grid coordinates, the words "gun installation" and "Onsite reconnaissance forthwith."

In Raiding Forces'-speak that translated to "ASAP if not sooner."

This was no drill.

BRANDY SEABORN ARRIVED IN THE VIP SECTION. "BEVERLY said you needed to see me urgently."

Colonel John Randal said, "Is the *Arrow* still at Seaborn House?"

"Drydocked in the boathouse. Why do you ask?"

"Raiding Forces has been alerted for a cross-channel mission tonight. The Royal Navy is not inclined to support our operations. You up for a boat ride?"

"Love to. I shall make a call and have the Arrow serviced. Will you be along?"

"Negative."

"Unfortunate. We should talk, handsome."

"Concerning your new boyfriend?"

"You really are a crystal ball reader like Jane says. We did not have this part of the conversation."

Col. Randal said, "Yes we did."

Mandy Paige found Captain Billy Jack Jaxx and Captain Sinclair Lovelace in the linen pantry shooting dice with the hotel's porters. "The Colonel needs to see both of you straightaway."

Capt. Jaxx said, "What's up, Mandy?"

"I believe you are about to be alerted for a mission. Do you gamble with the hotel staff often?"

Capt. Jaxx said, "Yeah, on occasion . . . Roger that, why?"

Mandy said, "Perfect! See me the very instant you can. I need your help, Jack."

"No problem."

When Capt. Jaxx and Capt. Lovelace arrived in the VIP section Col. Randal handed Capt. Jaxx the sealed envelope. "Get your gear. Your orders are in this envelope. Link up with Brandy. You'll be inserted in France from her yacht tonight out of Seaborn House."

Capt. Jaxx said, "Roger, sir."

Only he did not have any gear except for a Colt .38 Super, suppressed .22 High Standard Military Model D and his Buck Rogers-looking .380 ACP Savage 1907 pocket pistol.

Col. Randal said, "You'll have to lead a team you've never met before so take King with you. Carry out the mission then get back here as fast as you can. Developments are breaking fast around here and I need you close."

"Yes, sir!"

"Make it happen, stud."

"Can do, Colonel."

Col. Randal said, "Captain Lovelace, stand fast. I have something else for you. We're about to put your recruiting skills to the test raising a new troop for Raiding Forces."

Capt. Lovelace said, "Maybe we can have Beverly or Mandy stand outside the hotel with a golden Guinea in her lips like the Duchess, sir."

Col. Randal said, "Works for me – don't mention the idea to Lady Jane. She'd do it."

So much for a quiet two weeks' vacation in London.

CAPTAIN BILLY JACK JAXX LED A TEAM OF EIGHT SEABORN House men and King on board Brandy Seaborn's private motor yacht, the *Silver Arrow*. The boat had a history with Raiding Forces that went back to long before Capt. Jaxx and King had joined. In the early days, when the unit was called the Small-Scale Raiding Company, the *Arrow* had been the only craft available and had seen hard service until a Motor Gunboat, MGB

345, had been attached for operations. Now the *Three Four Five* was in the Aegean and Brandy's yacht was once again being called to duty.

Captain Penelope "Legs" Honeycutt-Parker was along to serve as navigator. The crew consisted of former Sea Rover Scouts who had volunteered to serve in the Raiding Forces' Navy while they were still attending school. At the time they were too young to enlist or be drafted. The ex-Scouts were all old enough at this point to serve but had been assigned back to Raiding Forces at their request after their initial period of Royal Navy training for MGB/MTB sailors on the HMS Bee at Weymouth was completed.

Times had been desperate back in those days. They might be desperate now. The flying by the seat of their pants nature of this hasty mission attested to that possibility.

Capt. Jaxx was not comfortable with the mission. He had received zero intelligence other than a set of grid coordinates of where to land ashore and the words "gun emplacement." Not much to go on when issuing his Operations Order. He had to limit it to the things he knew and could control – patrol formation on landing ashore, moving off the beach, order of march, setting up of Rally Points, actions on enemy contact, actions on the objective, the withdrawal phase, signals, test-firing weapons . . .

He did not know any of the troops on his team other than King. Fortunately they knew of him. Jack Cool's reputation had preceded him.

The operators were inexperienced at raiding. They were not, however, entirely green. The men all had a number of cross-channel missions under their belts – some in the double digits – escorting agents across the Channel or extracting them for MI-6 and SOE. That entailed going ashore first to secure the landing site and then signaling the "Joe" it was safe to land. Or doing that in reverse when pulling someone out.

Tonight was a reconnaissance mission. And that meant going inland to place eyes on. The operators knew anything might happen with Capt. Jaxx leading the patrol. The men were keyed up but trying not to show it. They were finally getting to do what they were trained for. No more loitering on the beach babysitting an agent until he disappeared on his mission then going home.

Capt. Jaxx's Operations Order was highly professional. Clicked off rapid-fire in bullet points. Test- firing weapons was informal – go/no go.

The rehearsal was a no-nonsense affair. Jack Cool clearly had done this before. The interesting part the troops quickly picked up on – he did not give many orders.

He was simply in charge without ever saying he was. The team was expected to perform with precision. Which made the men lean into the drill to demonstrate to Capt. Jaxx not only did they know their job – they were good at it.

As the operators progressed through the pre-mission evolution it began to dawn on them they were witnessing a command performance by a team leader on a level they had never seen before. Capt. Jaxx made being in charge appear effortless. His casual leadership style inspired confidence. And that motivated the men to execute each movement with exacting specificity. Each step taken in slow motion. As a consequence the rehearsal flowed as if choreographed.

Exactly the way it was supposed to.

Rehearsal concluded, Capt. Jaxx led the team to the dock where they boarded the boat for the voyage to the far shore. No melodrama. No wasted movement. Strictly business. No macho pep talk.

Capt. Jaxx said, "Let's rock."

The *Arrow* slipped its berth and on the last of the ebb tide nosed downriver toward the open sea. A storm had passed through earlier that day but now there was a feeling of calm. The weather was good and by skillful dead reckoning Capt. Honeycutt-Parker kept the yacht on a course that led straight to the drop-off point. A little over twenty-one miles distance.

As the men on the bridge watched the vague shadow of the coastline take shape the Seaborn House operators realized her navigation was spot-on. Something that was not always the case with a Royal Navy gunboat or motor torpedo boat crew navigator. These new people in from the Aegean knew what they were doing.

At 2335 hrs Brandy dropped anchor in ten fathoms, a little closer inshore than usual. They were actually running ahead of schedule. The moon, still high and very bright, showed no sign of being obscured by clouds as indicated to expect by the meteorological report. It was scheduled to set at 0105 hrs.

Two Goatley dories transported on deck were put over the side. Having done this many times during their continuous training at Seaborn House and on actual missions to land or extract Joes, this always tricky process went smoothly. Capt. Jaxx was in one dory and King the other. That way if a boat failed to reach the beach for any reason the troops on the other could continue the mission with a veteran on the team.

Capt. Jaxx had never operated across the English Channel prior to tonight. He did not know crossings were not supposed to be this easy. He was unaware one attempt to drop off an MI-6 agent escorted by Raiding Forces' operators out of Seaborn House had been forced to turn back ten times before successfully landing their Joe ashore. Wind, tides, fog, faulty engines and bad navigation frequently conspired to make a relatively short voyage seem like an impossibility. Having to turn back at least once or twice was more typical of missions than not.

The Life Boat Service Men (LBSM) paddling the Goatley dories made good time. The two boats were on the beach before the moon had set, landing at the base of a steep gradient. It was not going to present a difficult climb, however, it appeared to be over fifty feet in height. Going up was likely to be easier than coming back down. Especially if they were in a hurry or had men wounded. The terrain was not ideal for a hot extraction but then no terrain was ever ideal for an extraction under fire.

Once ashore Capt. Jaxx had the team pull in tight around him. "This is the Initial Rally Point/ Extraction Point. Security detail – drop off here with the Life Boat people."

The detail consisted of two men who would help secure the IRP/ERP with the four LBSM.

"OK boys, saddle up – let's do this."

Cliff climbing was a staple of Seaborn House training. As it was at RFHQ on Castelrozzo. This was a bluff, which meant the face was more rounded, not sheer, making it much easier to scale. The team scrambled up the bank. All the operators were armed with 1928 Model .45 Thompson submachine guns with thirty 20-round box magazines. Each man had four Mills bombs – fragmentation grenades. While heavy, the operators routinely trained with this amount of equipment – often more.

Cap. Jaxx and King were each carrying a No. 69 concussion grenade in the event an opportunity to snatch a prisoner presented itself.

While that sounded like a substantial amount of firepower, it would only last a few minutes in a sustained firefight. The idea tonight was not to get into one. The mission called for a sneak and peek of a light machine gun (LMG) position. The additional intelligence on the type of gun they would be reconnoitering had been received prior to departure. Based on the original orders it could have been anything.

Typically an LMG was crewed by two or three German soldiers.

The term "Atlantic Wall" was German propaganda designed to persuade the Allies they had an impenetrable defensive system running the length of the French coast. If you believed Dr. Goebbels there were Nazi storm troopers armed to the teeth standing shoulder-to-shoulder along the coast to repel any Allied attempt at invasion. That was not exactly true. The static coastal defense divisions euphemistically called "fortress units" were manned by a motley mix of older men, young boys, convalescents recovering from wounds or other medical issues and "volunteers" from Eastern European countries the Nazis had overrun – some were Russian. The troops in these units were commonly equipped with an ad hoc mix of nonstandard captured enemy equipment with a glaring lack of ammunition compatibility which increased logistical resupply problems at the tactical level.

These were not crack troops – a "static" designator meant the division was not capable of maneuver.

In reality, the area to be guarded was so vast even by employing substandard divisions the Germans were only able to defend certain key terrain such as potential landing beaches. The Nazis did their best to turn those locations into amphibious death traps with a layered combined arms defensive system. The defenses started off shore with underwater obstacles with Teller mines affixed, preplanned artillery in advance of and on the anticipated Forward Edge of the Battle Area (FEBA), minefields, interlocking light and heavy machine guns with fields of fire covering the landing beach and a mobile panzer reserve positioned to the rear poised and ready to strike.

Also Wonder Weapons that could turn the sea into fire – or so the Nazis claimed.

The Germans' decision about which beaches to defend in depth was made easier by knowing the Allies would have to land on those located in range of fighter cover from England. More than a single beach would be required for an amphibious landing the magnitude of D-Day. And the beaches had to be close enough together to be mutually supporting. That was a must.

So, MI-6, SOE and Commando units like Raiding Forces never went anywhere near a major beach that met those standards.

Tonight Capt. Jaxx's patrol was conducting a recon of an area that was located *between* a pair of beaches that did. A Wehrmacht Division set up in a linear defense of the Atlantic Wall was responsible for defending three to five times the normal distance a division-sized unit was expected to be able to cover – called "force to space." By necessity, the Germans made up for their lack of numbers by scattering "strong points" along the forward edge of the battle area (FEBA).

Some of the so-called strong points were not all that strong. A tripod-mounted 7.92 mm MG42 with a crew of three – gunner, loader and rifleman/spotter. The German defense plan called for the crew to be located in a small underground concrete bunker with overhead cover. At least this was the plan on paper and the way the machine gun positions were described to Capt. Jaxx at Seaborn House.

In reality not all the MG positions had been provided with the concrete bunker yet, and they were not all mutually supporting due to being so spread out. The gunner in the concrete bunkers had a restricted field of fire due to the size of the firing port. It limited his ability to traverse to not much more than 180 degrees.

What that indicated to Capt. Jaxx was these type gun positions were vulnerable to attack from either flank and to the rear. And where did the Germans sleep? Three men crammed in a tiny bunker? Was one standing guard at all times? Highly unlikely. Unsupervised low-grade conscripts were not a recipe for vigilance at zero dark thirty on a lonely beach where nothing ever happened after dark.

When the patrol neared what was termed the military crest of the bluff – just below the top, Capt. Jaxx signaled a halt. The terrain to their immediate front was a danger area. He sent two scouts forward to secure it with instructions to signal when all was clear.

When he heard three slaps on the wooden butt of a .45 M1928 Thompson submachine gun, Capt. Jaxx led the rest of the team up and over to link up with the point element. The patrol found themselves in a broken field that had not been tilled in years due to being in the Restricted Zone.

Now for the big question. Where was the gun emplacement? The brief intelligence on the target gave a six-digit grid coordinate of where to land. There was no indication of where the target was located in relation to where they came ashore. A six-digit coordinate was only accurate to within 100 square yards which is a big area at night on an enemy coast with limited time to stay ashore – it was almost as if finding the gun position was not all that imperative.

Stranger still, Capt. Jaxx had one verbal instruction from Col. Randal before he departed the hotel for Seaborn House. It did not make a lot of sense. "Leave a canvas pistol belt behind with 'U.S.' stenciled on it when you withdraw." It struck him, without being said, that leaving the pistol belt behind was of as much primary importance as the reconnaissance.

His was not to reason why.

All Capt. Jaxx knew about the small German machine gun positions along the English Channel was what he had been briefed on at Seaborn House. They were placed from 200 to 300 yards apart. While that was adequate for providing interlocking fields of fire oriented toward the Channel in daytime, at night the fighting positions were not close enough to mutually support each other in any meaningful way.

If one LMG came under ground attack after dark it was on its own. It was not likely the three-man gun positions on either flank would venture out to come to their assistance. At least of their own volition. If a senior NCO or officer were present they might.

There was one other detail and it was important. The German machine gun positions were tied in to each other by a landline network. They communicated by field phone. The commo wire linking them together was strung off a man-portable spool. It lay on top of the ground.

As soon as the operators came over the bluff they stumbled across a landline. King cut it with his Fairbairn. So now the question was "Left or right?" Capt. Jaxx had no idea but he was pretty sure there would be something of interest on the end of the wire whatever direction they went.

"Which way, Jack?"

"Pick one and move out."

The Merc went right. Before following him, Capt. Jaxx dropped off two men to secure the path down the cliff, then gave the whispered instruction to the rest of the patrol, "Rally Point."

Why would he leave a detail to guard it? With the moon having set it was now dark – pitch black. He did not want to be forced to hunt for the rally point in the event of having to pull out in a hurry with the enemy hot on their trail. That meant now the maneuver element of the patrol was down to six operators. More than adequate for reconnaissance.

Why not just detail one man? Raiding Forces had a policy of not assigning an independent task to a single individual on an operation if at all possible. Two are braver than one and a pair of men did not feel so alone. After his experience on Hydra following his escape from the *Perseus,* Capt. Jaxx was sympathetic to the concept.

Following a landline to their objective might sound overly simple but there was a good reason for doing it. Periodically the Germans would send out a commo man to inspect the wire. He would trace it by walking along the line looking for signs of damage.

And that meant no land mines.

There are a lot of factors a patrol leader must constantly be taking into consideration.

King came to a halt. "Bunker straight ahead."

Capt. Jaxx whispered, "Check it out."

The Merc was the exception to the two-man policy. He liked to operate alone. No witnesses.

The patrol waited down on one knee – every other operator facing out in the opposite direction with weapons at the ready. Capt. Jaxx was pleased with how well the Seaborn House men worked. Aware they were primarily used to escorting MI-6 and SOE agents and never traveling farther inland than the landing site, he had not been expecting the level of fieldcraft the team was exhibiting. The operators were highly trained. All they were lacking was actual boots-on-the-ground experience.

King ghosted back. He whispered, "Not really a bunker. More of a half-dugout lean-to with overhead concealment – a wooden frame canopy. The Channel side is open air."

There is a difference between overhead cover and overhead concealment. Overhead cover is a substantial structure designed to protect those inside a position from small arms fire, air bursts of artillery or shrapnel from near misses. Overhead concealment is simply camouflage. Not that it was important tonight. However, there was some intelligence value in knowing the machine gun "bunkers" as they had been described were not in all cases actually fortified fighting positions.

"We can capture the Germans easy."

Capt. Jaxx whispered, "What makes you think so?"

"All three are snoring."

Capt. Jaxx had the patrol pull in tight around him so their shoulders were touching. "We're getting ready to turn this recon mission into a prisoner snatch."

There was a stir among the operators. This was getting good. When they had learned Capt. Jaxx would be leading tonight the men assigned to the mission suspected there was a possibility the assignment might turn out to be more than pure reconnaissance. It was understood Jack Cool was not a recon man. He had a reputation of having a preference for kicking in doors and shooting everyone inside.

Capt. Jaxx whispered, "Here's what's going to happen. King will take the first two men in the file around behind the gun position and come in on the far flank. I'll take the last two and we'll move up on this side. When King claps his hands he and I will toss in concussion grenades.

"The instant they detonate both teams rush in and secure the bad guys. Sling your weapons. Everyone take out a twenty-round magazine to use as a club. If any of the Germans resist there's no need to be gentle on my part."

It was possible to physically feel the tension ratchet up – or maybe it was resolve – these men were going to take it to those Nazis.

Capt. Jaxx whispered, "Questions? No? Move out, King."

The Merc led his party into the night. Without a sound. Simply vanished – Hey Presto!

Capt. Jaxx looked at his Rolex. He gave them three minutes. When it was time he turned to the two remaining operators and whispered, "Follow me – stay frosty, boys."

The Seaborn House men had no idea what that meant but it set the tone for what was to come. The men stepped off, moving on tiptoes like ballet dancers, taking great pains to be stealthy. They were ready.

It was dark, visibility limited. The machine gun (MG) position finally swam into sight as a blurred smudge up ahead. Capt. Jaxx led his people to the near side of the structure. He crouched down next to the 4x4 support beam at the front. The two operators were stacked up close behind him physically touching with their SMG magazines in hand prepared to do the King's work this night. Like the Merc said, snoring could be heard coming from the bunker.

It was almost funny.

Capt. Jaxx produced his No. 69 Grenade aka "plastic grenade" because instead of metal it was encased in Bakelite. It would fragment like a real grenade. Getting struck by a fragment would not feel great, but concussion grenades were not designed to be fatal. When thrown a linen tape with a curved lead weight unraveled in flight, freeing a ball bearing inside the fuse, initiating the "all ways" action. The concussion grenade detonated when it struck something solid – from any angle – thus the nickname, "Any Angle Grenade". The N0.69 had an "All Ways" fuse which meant no matter what it struck the grenade was going to go off.

When throwing one great care had to be taken to hit in the vicinity of your intended target. That was important. The trick with All Ways action fuses was not to detonate yourself. Things could go wrong if the grenade struck a solid object closer than what you were aiming at. Details like that are important.

"Clap, Clap."

Capt. Jaxx reached around the corner and threw the grenade inside as hard as he could. He did not care what he hit as long as it landed within the machine gun position. *WHUUUUUMP, WHUUUUUMP.*

Capt. Jaxx said, "Go!"

He stood back and allowed the two Seaborn House operators to charge inside before following them in. Capt. Jaxx wanted to take advantage of the opportunity to have the men benefit from the training aspect of the takedown by doing it themselves. King and his two people met them behind a half-moon-shaped table. It was a crude but effective firing platform constructed out of poured concrete for the 7.92mm MG 42 machine gun mounted on it.

The three Germans were incoherent – stunned. Much to the regret of the Seaborn House operators the Nazis were in no condition to put up any resistance. After gagging the prisoners and tying their hands, a quick search was conducted. It failed to turn up anything of intelligence value. Wasting no time Capt. Jaxx gave the order to commence the withdrawal to the rally point at the edge of the cliff above the Extraction Point on the beach.

Unknown to Capt. Jaxx there had been recent reports of French Resistance activity in the area. The local German commander, a battle-hardened veteran of the Russian Front, had been assigned to the Atlantic Wall to recover from having been wounded. He had experience in anti-partisan operations.

The *Hauptmann* had taken the precaution of stationing five-man reaction teams at every other machine gun position along the coast in his company's Area of Operation (AO) with orders to respond to any sign of trouble. In the Wehrmacht, failure to conduct an immediate counterattack could and probably would result in the responsible officer or NCO facing a firing squad. Germans took their counterattacks seriously.

That meant a pair of heavily armed, highly motivated parties of enemy soldiers with evil intent were now rushing toward Capt. Jaxx's patrol from opposite directions.

King led out. The going seemed torturously slow due to the prisoners being incapable of walking. Two men per Nazi were detailed to drag them. The ground was rough, which did not make the going any easier.

After what felt like a long time the challenge rang out. "Halt! Drop dead?"

Capt. Jaxx immediately responded with the countersign, "Gorgeous!"

The Seaborn House sentry at the top of the bluff was doing it by the book, "Advance Gorgeous and be . . ."

A burst of green 9mm submachine tracers cracked past like a swarm of angry fairies. They were coming from a German patrol counterattacking from their left flank. Luckily, as is common in meeting engagements, the small arms fire was high.

The patrol hit the dirt – a reflex reaction.

Capt. Jaxx ordered, "Hold your fire."

Not sure what was taking place he did not want to give away their position. The temptation was to engage. Another swarm of angry yellow fairies cracked overhead coming from behind. A second counterattacking patrol from the opposite direction mistakenly believed *it* had been fired on. The Raiding Forces' team was caught in a blue-on-blue crossfire.

Unlike the Allies who issued standardized red tracers, the Germans used what they could get. Having overrun most of Europe, the Wehrmacht captured huge stores of different colors of tracer ammunition from the countries they defeated. They promptly appropriated it for their own use.

At night a firefight was a rainbow of colors but enjoyment of the show was an acquired taste.

The first enemy patrol instantly shifted its fire toward the source of the yellow tracers. This was what was called a "blue-on-blue," meaning two elements from the same side were firing on each other. A lively engagement developed with the rounds cracking back and forth inches overhead.

Standing a mile offshore, Brandy and Capt. Honeycutt-Parker watched the flurry of tracers, alarmed by what was taking place, helpless to do anything. A prolonged firefight was close to worst-case scenario. Brandy began edging the PT boat in closer to the beach.

At the top of the cliff, Capt. Jaxx's next decision had to be made with absolute exactitude. He was in close proximity to the enemy. If the Germans pinpointed his location and assaulted it they would be in a position to place plunging fire on his troops as they attempted to make their retrograde movement down the bluff. Then for the Nazis their next step would be the simple matter of taking out the two Goatley dories beached directly below – a simple matter.

That would be game over.

Jack Cool was in his element at times like this – almost relaxed. What to do? He decided his best bet was to let the two enemy patrols fight it out. "Never interfere with an enemy in the act of embarrassing himself." Somebody said that? Napoleon?

The idea was to slide down the cliff to the ERP, board the dories and leave the Germans to it. The trick would be to spirit his team away undetected. In their favor was once a blue-on-blue gets started it is not easy for the participants shooting at each other to stop.

"Roll those prisoners off the edge."

One after the other the Nazis were sent over. The detail on the beach in the ERP was staring up at the volley of colorful tracers crisscrossing at the top of the incline, not knowing what was taking place but reasonably sure it could not be good. There was no contingency plan for anything like this. An object came bouncing downhill picking up speed. When it splatted into the sand on the small narrow beach, the ERP security team was startled to discover a bound and gagged German soldier.

Then another came tumbling down. Followed by a third. These Nazis were not having a good night – blown up by concussion grenades, captured by British Commandos, manhandled over rough ground and rolled down a cliff after having been shot at by their own side.

Up above at the top of the incline the first Raiding Forces' operator started making his way down leaning back in a controlled sideways slide. He was moving fast, bicycling his boots to gain a purchase and maintain balance, almost but not quite out of control – they actually trained for this.

The problem was not getting down the slope. It was stopping at the bottom. The ERP security detail and LBSM quickly linked arms to form a barrier like in the children's game Red Rover to slow down the operator before he crashed into something hard at speed. Or ended up in the water. It was the best they could think of under the circumstances with a firefight raging overhead. While the human chain worked to impede the operators plunging down, there was a price to be paid in pain. Men carrying weapons and gear have hard edges.

Capt. Jaxx came down last, moving fast. The blue-on-blue firefight had not abated behind him. If there was ever a classic example of the "fog of war" this extraction would be a textbook example. Getting shot at while exfiltrating seems worse than taking fire going in.

When the people at the bottom brought him up short of crashing into the water, Capt. Jaxx said, "Let's take it home, boys."

He meant it.

THE SNOW WHITE PHONE IN MAJOR THE LADY JANE'S SUITE rang. Colonel John Randal came awake instantly. He disentangled himself from Lady Jane who was sleeping with one tawny thigh on his chest and her head curled up on his shoulder in a wild tangled mass of mahogany hair. His Rolex said 0355 hrs.

"Randal."

The hotel switchboard operator said, "Sir, you have a call from Captain Jaxx."

"Put him through."

Captain Billy Jack Jaxx came on the line. "Sorry to wake you, sir – I have a situation."

"Where are you?"

"I'm calling from Seaborn House. We brought back three prisoners. What am I supposed to do with 'em, Colonel?"

"Stand by on the line."

Col. Randal got up, slipped on a pair of running shorts and went out into the hall. He nodded to the Vulnerable Points Wing security officer seated at the desk next to the private elevator and continued on down the hall to Brigadier General William "Wild Bill" Donovan's room. The general came to the door wearing one of the Bradford Hotel's monogrammed silk robes.

Col. Randal said, "Sir, I have Captain Jaxx on the phone reporting in from Seaborn House. He's brought back three prisoners. Wants to know who to turn them over to."

Brig. Gen. Donovan said, "Outstanding, absolutely outstanding, Colonel! That's four in the last three nights. I don't believe there's been a single German brought out of France since the ban on small-scale raiding went into effect.

"What was done with the first Nazi you captured?"

Col. Randal said, "Being held in the basement at Seaborn House until you advise me what to do with him, General."

Brig. Gen. Donovan said, "Keep all four Germans there under tight control until I can make arrangements with London Station's X-2 – Dr. Pearson. He's not set up for interrogations yet. I'll order him to expedite his plans."

"Yes, sir."

"The British intelligence community is doing their dead level best to freeze OSS out of SI and SO to protect their turf," Brig. Gen. Donovan said. "But they failed to take into consideration the possibility of Raiding Forces bringing in prisoners. I'm not turning our POWs over to them."

"Understood, sir."

Brig. Gen. Donovan said, "I'm on record as saying – told the President, the only way OSS is going to get in the intelligence game is to kill the umpire and steal the ball – you're doing a hell of a good job doing that, Colonel. Keep it up."

Col. Randal had no idea how to respond – not sure who he was expected to kill.

Brig. Gen. Donovan said, “Have Captain Jaxx report to me here. I want to hear his story. Tonight was supposed to be a simple reconnaissance. Go in, gather intel, leave something stamped ‘U.S.’ behind, and come out.”

“Pays to be careful when sending Jack on a mission, sir,” Col. Randal said. “He’s been known to overachieve.”

Brig. Gen. Donovan said, “That’s what we say about you.”

5

IN THE SPIDER'S WEB

MAJOR THE LADY JANE SEABORN AND MANDY PAIGE WERE in one of the Bradford's limousines en route to MI-5 to see Lieutenant Colonel Thomas Argyll Robertson, aka Tar, the Chief of Section B1-A. Lady Jane had not bothered to call ahead to make an appointment. She was confident he would make time to see them.

Acting on Colonel John Randal's suggestion, Mandy had sought out Lady Jane to ask advice on Tar's offer to join MI-5. After listening to Mandy's story Lady Jane said, "We should drop in on Colonel Robertson and get a better read on what he has in mind."

It was not really a suggestion.

When they approached the door at 58 St. James Street there was no doorbell or knocker on the double doors. And no doorknob. This did not discourage Lady Jane. She did not knock like Mandy had the first time she was there. Having attended more MI-6 and SOE training schools than she could remember she knew the door was under observation. Most likely from a room in the building across the street. So they just stood in front of the door expectantly.

It wasn't long before the door was opened by one of the two security officers Mandy had met when she first visited. While not exactly welcoming, he did allow them inside. Since the two guards were aware Mandy had a relationship with Lt. Col. Robertson they did not demand her ID or grill her with rapid-fire questions as they had on her first visit. They started to put Lady Jane through the process but thought better of it. The men recognized her. She was reported to be the richest woman in England. The Security Service kept up with details like that.

Lt. Col. Robertson arrived within minutes. Lady Jane was known to him personally. He had met her most recently at the Bradford when Mandy took him to the hotel to be introduced to Rikke Runborg. He had also met her a few years earlier when his drinking companion from Sandhurst then-Captain (now Lt. Col.) David Niven had dated – or more accurately tried to date – her before she met Colonel John Randal. Lady Jane being present today was unexpected. MI-5 did not get a lot of drop-in visitors.

He escorted the women to his office then said, “What can I do for you two ladies?”

Lady Jane said, “I understand you have offered Mandy a position with Security. You should know she has been my personal assistant for the last two years. My understanding is R.J. recommended her.”

Lt. Col. Robertson said, “He did.”

“In that case, Tar, out of our enormous respect for the Brigadier, we would like to accommodate you,” Lady Jane said “provided there is any way possible. However, before acquiescing I require a better understanding of what it is you have in mind for Mandy.”

Lt. Col. Robertson said, “I am aware of your relationship with MI-6, Lady Seaborn. That is the one and only reason I am willing to discuss any part of Mandy’s possible involvement with Security. Be advised everything we are about to say is classified and no one outside this room possesses the Need to Know.”

Lady Jane said, “Leave out the classified material.”

Lt. Col. Robertson was not used to people coming into his office and dictating terms to him. Normally, those he met with had two choices: Do what he desired or face a firing squad. That made negotiations easy.

However, he needed Mandy for a top-level intelligence assignment of national importance that only she, Lady Jane or Col. Randal were in a position to perform. Since it was unlikely the colonel or Lady Jane would always be available on call for a task that could be time-sensitive, Lt. Col. Robertson's options were limited.

He wondered if Lady Jane knew that.

"Rikke Runborg is an MI-5 asset. Both Brigadier Maunsell of SIME and Brigadier Clarke of A-Force have knowledge of her activities. As do you, Lady Seaborn. From time to time she has been required to transmit certain information useful to us to the other side. I am quite sure you are aware of that having taken place.

"Now Rocky, as you call her, is to be relocated to the U.K. for the run-up to D-Day. Her contact with the opposition being Field Marshal Erwin Rommel is top priority. I would like for Mandy to be her case officer.

"That is all I am at liberty to say."

Lady Jane said, "What do you envision Mandy's responsibilities to include?"

"Typically we set our assets up in an apartment where they are closely monitored in a controlled environment," Lt. Col. Robertson said. "They transmit from their living quarters. Because of their high value to the war effort and the fact we do not entirely trust them, the double agents are not allowed to go out unless accompanied by their handler or other Security personnel."

Lady Jane said, "You do understand Rocky only agreed to work for MI-5 on the condition Colonel Randal and/or I would be her protectors?"

"I have heard rumors to that effect," Lt. Col. Robertson lied.

He knew perfectly well it was the case.

"Over time Rocky has become a treasured member of the Raiding Forces' family – my dog does yoga with her," Lady Jane said.

Lt. Col. Robertson – the counterintelligence mastermind who almost single-handedly built a weapon as highly classified as ULTRA that brought every single German spy in England under his control and also provided him the ability to lie to Hitler at will – was beginning to feel whipsawed by the conversation.

Lady Jane said, "Here is what we are prepared to do, Tar. Mandy remains on my staff. However, she shall agree to serve as Rocky's case officer. That should work nicely as the two are quite good friends.

"Colonel Randal and I can be counted on to continue our relationship with Rocky – as I said she views us as being her protectors. Though, understand at times the colonel and I shall be traveling out of the country.

I am quite certain she shall be quite comfortable with having Mandy look after her best interests when we are away."

Lt. Col. Robertson said, "I anticipated that might be the case."

"Mandy and Rocky shall maintain residence at the Bradford," Lady Jane said. "There is not going to be any imprisonment in an apartment. However, she shall never go out alone. Hotel security is quite adequate to ensure her safety and prevent her from leaving the building unattended. You may station your own people on the premises for an additional layer of protection if you so wish.

"We have a private phone room where you can set up your transmitter permanently. Any special antenna you might require should not pose a problem. The room is located on the penthouse floor with easy access to the roof.

"If these terms are acceptable, then you have yourself a new part-time MI-5 case officer. You shall not be disappointed in Mandy's performance. On that you can rest assured."

Lt. Col. Robertson said, "Welcome aboard, Mandy. A pleasure doing business with you, Lady Seaborn."

Lady Jane said, "Naturally I shall expect you to be Mandy's MI-5 patron."

"Always my intention."

Lady Jane said, "In that case, Tar, feel free to drop by the Bradford from time to time – you are one of us now."

That was not how this was supposed to go for MI-5's premier spy catcher – had Lady Jane just recruited him?

LIEUTENANT GENERAL "GERONIMO" JOE MCKOY, BRIGADIER General William "Wild Bill" Donovan, Colonel John Randal and Captain Billy Jack Jaxx were having breakfast in the dining room of the Bradford Hotel. Jack Cool was walking them through the night's mission from the time he issued his Operations Order until the team returned to Seaborn House with the three prisoners. Brig. Gen. Donovan wanted to know every last detail. He may have been a wealthy, high-profile New York lawyer, the WWI commander of the Fighting Sixty-Ninth regiment, a recipient of the Medal of Honor, chief of America's first and only foreign intelligence agency, and a man the President of the United States thought of as his college football hero. But at heart he was still the young National Guard captain who took a cavalry troop to the border during the Mexican Punitive Expedition against Pancho Villa.

He admired small-unit leadership – and a good war story.

Brig. Gen. Donovan said, "We need to hold the German prisoners at Seaborn House until I can get with Col. Bruce. We have our OSS X-2 Counter Espionage Branch. The problem is it's been low priority for us – never staffed.

"MI-6's Section V is dedicated to counterintelligence. They have been initiating three OSS X-2 officers into the mysteries of the game. While our people are in the process of wrapping up their training, OSS London Group is not set up to handle interrogations."

Brig. Gen. Donovan did not mention he had a concern the British instructors were obfuscating aspects of certain training in areas they did not want OSS to meddle in. The officers sent to MI-6 to be tutored by Section V were brilliant academicians who could win a bar fight. One was a Rhodes Scholar. Difficult men to outsmart by being intentionally vague about certain facets of the counterintelligence program. Wild Bill's officers had reported their suspicions to their station chief, Lieutenant Colonel David Bruce.

Col. Randal said, "Why would MI-6 have a counterintelligence section, sir?"

Brig. Gen. Donovan said, "Typical bureaucratic overlap. OSS has the same problem back in the States. The FBI is responsible for counter-intelligence in the continental U.S. But that wasn't good enough for J. Edgar Hoover. Back in 1939, before there was an OSS, he managed to get the President to issue an executive order allowing the FBI the exclusive right to conduct counterintelligence in Central and Latin America. Hoover set up what is called the Special Intelligence Service within the Bureau."

Lt. Gen. McKoy said, "SIS... where do you think J. Edgar stole that name?"

Brig. Gen. Donovan said, "Now even with the war on and Nazis thick on the ground in the region OSS is still not allowed to operate down south."

He did not feel the need to mention MI-5 was in the process of waging a bureaucratic knife fight to take over MI-6's Section V making the same argument about overlap. It was a carefully thought-out plot worthy of a battle plan crafted by Sun Tzu. Great rewards were in store for the Security Service if successful.

The plan was for MI-5 to absorb Section V which just so happened to be where MI-6 obtained its Ultra intercepts. That would gut SIS of Most Secret Source (MSS) intelligence. As a result MI-6 would no longer be treated with the respect it was accorded by the other government agencies, the military and the other intelligence services.

MI-6 would find itself positioned to be swallowed up by its competitor – MI-5. As a result, England would have a single civilian intelligence agency, not counting Special Operations Executive. But then SOE was not supposed to be in the secret intelligence gathering business in the first place – its charter was guerrilla warfare and sabotage.

Which would set up another bureaucratic death match when MI-6 came after the Baker Street Irregulars.

Capt. Jaxx said, “So, who do we turn our prisoners over to, sir? We’re bound to take more.”

Brig. Gen. Donovan said, “Beverly Blackwell is Raiding Forces’ X-2 Counter Espionage officer. When Lady Jane recruited her out of my office we listed Beverly as that to have a justification for being assigned to you. Possibly she can be involved with MI-5’s interrogation program – supervise the handling of your prisoners.”

As they were leaving, Col. Randal waited until Capt. Jaxx had departed and then said, “General, a word, sir?”

“Certainly.”

Col. Randal said, “I don’t believe Beverly’s a good fit as an interrogator or an observer of interrogations, sir.”

“Oh?”

“Going in harm’s way – that’s one thing. Fly a dangerous mission – Beverly’s as brave as a lion. Enhanced interrogation – that’s something else, sir.”

Brig. Gen. Donovan said, “In what way?”

“Beverly’s a happy spirit. I don’t want to damage that, General.” Col. Randal said. “There’s some things once you’ve seen them you can’t unsee.”

Brig. Gen. Donovan said, “Point taken. I don’t wish that for her either. We need to make sure Beverly’s not involved in interrogations. But she will make an outstanding liaison officer to represent OSS or you.”

“Thanks, sir.”

Brig. Gen. Donovan said, “No, thank *you*.”

HQ ETOUSA 20 GROSVENOR SQUARE, LONDON

GENERAL DWIGHT D. EISENHOWER, GENERAL BERNARD Montgomery, Major General Walter Bedell Smith, Admiral Sir Bertram Ramsay, Major General Ira C. Eaker, Rear Admiral Alan G. Kirk, Air Chief Marshal Sir Trafford Leigh-Mallory, Major General Sir David Petrie, Major General Sir Stewart Menzies, Brigadier General William “Wild Bill” Donovan and Air Chief Marshal Sir Arthur Tedder arrived at 20 Grosvenor Square, London, the HQ of European Theatre of Operations United States (ETOUSA). These were the senior officers who would plan and control the Allied Invasion of France once Supreme Headquarters Allied Expeditionary Force (SHAEF) was officially activated. The stated purpose of the gathering was a preliminary briefing on certain aspects of the pre-D-Day campaign that was being geared up to mislead the Germans as to the time and location of the invasion. In actuality, it was a reception for the senior top tier players in the ETO to have an opportunity to meet and greet – some for the first time.

Standing in front of the room, Gen. Eisenhower said, “The people present this afternoon have it in their power to win or lose the war. Sometime in the next six months a great Allied armada is going to set sail for an undisclosed location on the coast of France, hurl itself ashore, smash its way through Nazi Germany’s Atlantic Wall then march on Berlin – OPERATION OVERLORD.

“The fate of the free world rests on the outcome of the invasion – on us. A terrible responsibility to shoulder, to be sure. But there it is. Every effort must be made to ensure success.

“Lieutenant Colonel Robertson of MI-5, the British Security Service, is here to brief you on steps now underway to help stack the deck in our favor when D-Day arrives. Pay close attention to the details. While the plan he is about to outline will sound simple, what the colonel is going to describe is in fact a highly sophisticated, multilayered counterintelligence deception campaign being conducted worldwide that very well may decide the fate of OVERLORD – and the free world.

"This is day one of operational preparation for the most momentous military undertaking in world history. It is imperative for us to start out on the same page and stay there. I say again, pay attention to the details. They are subtle… it is easy to miss them.

"The colonel won't be taking questions."

Lieutenant Colonel Thomas Argyll Robertson, as usual in his regimental tartan trousers which had earned him the nickname "Passion Pants," stepped to the front of the room. If he was daunted by the extraordinary military assemblage he did not show it. But then coolness was to be expected of the man who had tapped his King's telephone.

"At the Tehran Conference Prime Minister Churchill made the observation, 'In time of war the truth is so precious she should always be attended by a bodyguard of lies.' To that end, the D-Day invasion is to be covered by a comprehensive deception campaign – a bodyguard of lies if you will, code named appropriately, BODYGUARD.

"The central aim is a strategic deception operation engineered to mislead the Germans into believing the invasion is coming at a location it is not and that it is not coming in the place where it is. And to ensure the enemy forces deployed to defend the false invasion site are not immediately rushed to the real one . . . the deception shall be continued *after* D-Day.

"Hiding the massive buildup of men and materiel for the invasion is simply not possible. It is a given the Germans will spot it. And since the landing must take place within fighter range of England there is no way to disguise the fact our attack is going to take place somewhere between the Cherbourg Peninsula and Dunkirk. Because moon and tide data dictate when we will be able to land our amphibious troops ashore, it is no great feat for the other side to estimate the narrow time window each month when that is possible.

"So, the fact is the Nazis know we are coming, they have a general idea where we intend to land – only two geographic locations are suitable – and they can reasonably estimate when. Oh, and the German defenders will significantly outnumber our forces when we go ashore. In addition, they possess the ability to counterattack the beachhead with heavy concentrations of infantry and armor.

"What we have is OPERATION FORTITUDE – an elaborate ruse designed to bottle up the Germans where we want them and keep them away from where we do not want them.

"I have been asked to keep my remarks brief today in order for you gentlemen to move on to the more pressing business of cocktail hour. So in conclusion . . . as the Chinese military genius Sun Tzu laid down in his book *The Art of War*, 'Deception is the basis for all warfare.' To cover your D-Day operations, MI-5, ably assisted by Section V of MI-6 and X2 of OSS, is in the process of carrying out the largest, most aggressive offensive military deception campaign in the history of organized conflict.

"From time to time you may be asked to participate in certain activities that may not seem to make a great deal of sense and may be an inconvenience. All part of FORTITUDE – thank you in advance for your cooperation. Rest assured, gentlemen, we have a few tricks up our sleeve to help level the playing field.

"Wish I could elaborate, but alas . . ."

It did not escape the senior officers present that while they might compose the top tier of Supreme Headquarters Allied Expeditionary Force they were not cleared to know all the details of OPERATION FORTITUDE. Even though they would be BIGOTS...the codeword meaning on the short list cleared to have the Need to Know when and where the D-Day landing would take place.

Strangely enough that was reassuring.

THE LOBBY OF THE BRADFORD WAS ALWAYS A BUSY PLACE. Senior Allied military officers, visiting politicians in from the States, Peers of the House of Lords, Members of Parliament (MP) from the House of Commons, high government ministers, exiled heads of European states, movie stars, etc. used the hotel as a meeting place. Quite a lot of high-level government and military business was being conducted on premises at any given time. Normally the ambience was one of understated elegance . . . and power. Not so today.

When Colonel John Randal walked in he heard the sounds of laughter and hands clapping in rhythm. Lieutenant General "Geronimo" Joe McKoy was putting on an impromptu show twirling his pistols and juggling knives. Probably a first for the buttoned-down Bradford. How it got started was a mystery, but a crowd had gathered.

Major the Lady Jane Seaborn was sitting with Major General Sam Houston Blackwell and Brandy Seaborn. Col. Randal joined them as Lady Jane was saying, "Brandy, is there any chance you happen to know an MI-5 officer named Tar Robertson?"

Brandy said, "I do – why would you ask?"

"Colonel Robertson wants to recruit Mandy for certain duties – what's your opinion of him?"

Brandy said, "Immensely personable. Monstrously good-looking with charm that could melt an iceberg. It masks a ruthless streak. Married and by all accounts madly in love with his wife. Mandy has no worries about his being a skirt chaser now though that was not always the case. Before the war Tar had an almost suicidal appetite for beautiful women, partying and fast sports cars. Nowadays it's said he is a recovering womanizer.

"Might suffer a relapse – that is possible in marriages."

Lady Jane laughed. "So I am told."

Brandy said, "Tar's the best MI-5 officer no one has ever heard of, which makes him very good."

Lady Jane said, "Excellent."

Col. Randal said, "General, I understand you might be able to assist with shuffling my personnel from Seaborn House to RFHQ and vice versa?"

Maj. Gen. Blackwell said, "Beverly's already talked to me about it. As has General Donovan. I'll have Troop Transport Command's G-3 set up a schedule. My boys can use the long-distance navigation practice. Always more realistic training when we have an actual mission transporting people.

"Due to our other commitments we'll probably have to do it on a shuttle basis – two plane flights in most cases."

Col. Randal said, "That works, sir."

"When do you want to get started?"

"As soon as possible, sir."

Maj. Gen Blackwell said, "What's your thinking, Colonel?"

"General Donovan wants Raiding Forces' pre-D-Day operations to be primarily U.S. personnel," Col. Randal said. "In order to conform to his wishes I need to swap out Seaborn House men who are predominantly British for SOG and the Maritime Unit. Then rotate in the rest of the 575th Ranger Task Force."

Maj. Gen. Blackwell said, "Bill's going to like that. Putting his OSS Frogmen front and center right off the bat – good plan. I'll go make a call."

As the general walked away, Col. Randal said, "Jane can I ask you to send a telex to RFHQ?"

"Love to."

"Advise Lieutenant Starrett to Standby Ready for a permanent change of duty station to Seaborn House with SOG and the Maritime Unit Special Warfare Operators. Put the remainder of Major Hoolihan's Red Frogs on alert for movement to the UK at the next possible date."

When Lady Jane left to send the TWX, Brandy said, "Well-played, John. Now that we are alone, tell me about Bronc. I want to know everything."

Col. Randal said, "Maybe you should talk to Beverly."

BRIGADIER GENERAL WILLIAM "WILD BILL" DONOVAN walked in the front door of the Bradford Hotel accompanied by a tall Commando captain wearing the red and black Commando shoulder title over the Combined Operations formation "badge" that depicted an eagle, a Thompson submachine gun and an anchor stitched on his shoulder. The eagle represented the RAF, the submachine gun represented the Army and Royal Marines and the anchor represented the Royal Navy. Thus the name Combined Operations – the first unit of its kind in military history. The two proceeded straight to the VIP area.

Brig. Gen. Donovan said, "Colonel, we need a word."

The three moved to unoccupied chairs, pulled them in close and took seats.

Brig. Gen. Donovan said, "This is Captain Edmond Harlequins of No. 12 Commando – a semi-independent outfit specializing in small-scale raids that's primarily been operating against enemy-occupied Norway. Recently elements of No. 12 transferred down here to Combined Operations Headquarters.

"COHQ planned a series of raids for them on the French coast but only one, a reconnaissance of a German strongpoint, was approved for sea transport by Admiral Pridham-Whippel. And now that too has been canceled. Captain Harlequins has a mission but no way to cross the Channel. As a result, COHQ is breaking up No. 12 to use as fillers to infuse into the Commando brigades it's in the process of forming."

Capt. Harlequins said, "The big lie being told is pinprick raids have been put on hold because of a fear they will simply cause the Nazis to reinforce the Atlantic Wall. Not true. The Germans are reinforcing it anyway.

"The truth is the bloody Navy hates supporting small-scale raiding because they would rather be hunting U-boats. The staff at COHQ believes bigger is better – brigade-sized units translate into more and higher promotions all around."

Brig. Gen. Donovan knew what Capt. Harlequins said was accurate. The rationale COHQ was alleging was the basis for allowing the Royal Navy to cancel the small-scale raiding program without a fight was simply not true. LCS and MI-5 were working round the clock to come up with ingenious ways to *entice* the Germans to reinforce certain sections of the Atlantic Wall. This was an example of compartmentalization and obsessive Need to Know preventing one organization from being aware of what the other was doing. Or it was an outright lie for some reason unknown.

The small-scale raids No. 12 Commando had planned were not slated to take place anywhere near where the invasion was going to land. In fact, had they been allowed to go forward they would have dovetailed nicely with the FORTITUDE SOUTH deception campaign.

Colonel John Randal said, "Maybe I can help, Captain."

He made eye contact with Mandy Paige who was sitting with Lady Jane, Waldo Treywick and Rikke Runborg. She immediately excused herself and came over.

"Do you know where Jack is?"

"In the pantry room shooting dice with the porters."

Mandy had recruited Captain Billy Jack Jaxx to penetrate the Bradford Hotel's backstairs intelligence network. Col. Randal had given her the assignment. His thinking was it might not be a bad idea to know what was going on in the rest of the hotel. Lady Jane signed off on the idea provided she had access to the reports. She loved gossip.

"Tell the captain I said Standby Ready."

"On the way, John."

Brandy Seaborn was sitting with Major General Sam Houston Blackwell, Captain Pamala Plum-Martin and King. She glanced across at Col. Randal, spoke to the Merc – they both stood up and came over. By that time Mandy was returning with Captain Jaxx.

Brig. Gen. Donovan made the introductions.

Col. Randal said, "OK, Captain Harlequins, take it from the top – tell us your story."

COLONEL JOHN RANDAL PULLED MAJOR THE LADY JANE Seaborn aside. "Do you happen to know Lord Tredegar?"

Lady Jane laughed, "Why would you ask?"

Col. Randal said, "When Capt. Harlequins was describing a mission No. 12 Commando has planned he mentioned the team would be taking carrier pigeons along to signal the MGB standing offshore when to come in and pick them up. He said Lord Tredegar had formed a carrier pigeon unit. Something I've never heard of."

Lady Jane said, "If you are seriously interested in the idea talk to someone else. The man is a candidate for the glass house."

"Crazy?"

"Strange . . . an occultist even so he has been the chamberlain to two popes, openly gay but married twice, mixes royalty with rabble and it is no secret prior to the war he was connected to well-placed Nazis who dabbled in the dark arts. Lord Tredegar's favorite parlor trick is to have a pet parrot crawl up his trousers leg and poke its head out the fly."

Col. Randal said, "Really?"

Lady Jane laughed. "He was doing something for MI-5 involving pigeons – oddly enough called the Falcon Unit. Unfortunately for Evan he told two Girl Guides the details of the project. The girls, aware of the 'Loose Lips Sink Ships' campaign, reported his indiscretion to the authorities."

"That probably wasn't good."

"Lord Tredegar was arrested, court-martialed and thrown in the Tower of London for a brief time for violating the Official Secrets Act," Lady Jane said. "It was quite the scandal. Brandy can provide more details if you like."

Col. Randal said, "You do know some colorful people."

"I know you, John Randal," Lady Jane laughed. "Even before the trouble with the Girl Guides my godfather recommended I never be in the same room with Lord Tredegar."

"Said that about me too."

"Yes he did."

COLONEL JOHN RANDAL BRIEFED CAPTAIN BILLY JACK JAXX and King on the mission to be led by Captain Edmond Harlequins of No. 12 Commando. Brandy Seaborn and Captain Penelope "Legs" Honeycutt-Parker, who had recently arrived at the Bradford with her husband Lieutenant Colonel Lionel Honeycutt-Parker, sat in.

"Tonight is a reconnaissance of a small isolated fishing village on the French coast five miles east of Calais. A party of Germans of undetermined strength is billeted there. According to Captain Harlequins this will be his fourth attempt to carry out this particular mission. Twice they were forced to turn back – once for rough weather and another because of dense fog. On the third attempt the team made it ashore but were unable to find a way up the cliff off the beach.

"I want you two men to accompany his team and report back to me why they're having so much trouble. You're along as observers. This is Captain Harlequins' operation. Don't interfere except in exigent circumstances – at which time, should they arise, you are authorized to take command, Jack."

"Yes, sir."

Col. Randal said, "I want to know what's going on with cross-channel small-scale raiding. Three failed attempts seem excessive. I've heard a report of another COHQ mission that took ten. Something's not right. We need to find out what that is and fix it."

Capt. Jaxx said, "Roger that."

Brandy said, "I can manage this one alone, Penelope. A quick over and back. You stay here with Lionel."

Capt. Honeycutt-Parker said, "No, I want to do the navigating."

That was how Capt. Jaxx and King found themselves in France standing on a small shingle beach below a sheer cliff at 2315 hrs with Capt. Harlequins and seven men, one of which was a French corporal from No. 10 Inner-Allied Commando along as interpreter. Whoever had selected this location to land a team had clearly never done much climbing. And did not know the first thing about small-scale raiding from an operational standpoint. The landing site would have made a great location for an Achnacarry-style training exercise. It was a bad place to launch a quick in-and-out recon patrol. Especially since time ashore was a pressing issue.

Capt. Harlequins led the way and they started their assault on the face of the cliff. It was a challenging climb for men encumbered with .45 M1928 Thompson submachine guns, grenades and other items of equipment of which four were pigeons in their little containers that looked like they were designed to hold tennis balls. Capt. Jaxx wondered if birds got claustrophobia. Two hours later as the team was nearing the top, the climbers found the way barred by a large overhang.

King, being Swiss with high mountain experience, could have completed the climb. Capt. Jaxx, having grown up in a flat West Texas county could not. Neither could the rest of the Commandos. Capt. Harlequins reluctantly decided to return to the beach.

Refusing to give up, he had his pigeon handler dispatch two birds with instructions to Brandy to return for their exfiltration in forty-eight hours. The use of two birds was SOP to increase the odds of the message getting through.

As they watched the pigeons wing their way into the dark, Capt. Jaxx said, "How do they know to return to the *Silver Arrow*?"

Capt. Harlequins said, "Trained to fly to a boat – bloody birds cannot distinguish the difference between the battleship *King George* and a German E-boat."

While the rest of the men stashed their kit at the base of the cliff, Capt. Jaxx and the French Commando, Corporal Laurent Casalonga decided to patrol up the shingle toward the village, the route the team should have taken to make its approach in the first place.

They moved along the edge of the cliff face staying in the rocks next to the wall where it would have been difficult to bury mines. While the Germans had placed millions of antipersonnel mines along the Atlantic Wall they were careful about how they went about it. Too many people, to include their own troops, moved around the coastline for them not to mark the mines' locations.

So they did with signs facing *in* away from the water – a black skull and crossbones stenciled on a board with *ACHTUNG MINEN* in capital letters. Anyone landing from the sea would not be able to read them night or day unless they went around and were standing in the mine field.

Capt. Jaxx and Cpl. Casalonga returned before sunrise having spotted a small guard post which may or may not have been manned. This would have been the perfect opportunity to effect a prisoner snatch if it were. However, Jack Cool restrained himself. He had his orders to be an observer. Still ...

Once back in the IRP/ERP the patrol spent the first part of the morning getting caught up on sleep. Capt. Harlequins used most of the rest of the day searching for an alternative route up from the beach. No joy. Why he was so determined to scale the cliff was a mystery.

Every gully up the height had concertina wire entanglements blocking it and most likely were seeded with antipersonnel mines. King could have made the climb up the face of the precipice alone and conducted the reconnaissance – he liked to work by himself. But that never came up. As they kept reminding themselves, Capt. Jaxx and the Merc were along only to observe so they did not offer the suggestion.

More or less out of desperation, Capt. Harlequins decided to risk making contact with a fisherman who came down the beach to check on his nets. King, who spoke fluent French, and Cpl. Casalonga were dispatched to bring him in.

Capt. Jaxx – having had a recent bad experience with fishermen – was not entirely comfortable with the plan. However, once the Frenchman got over his initial concern they might be Nazi counterintelligence agents masquerading as British Commandos to find out whether the locals were aiding the enemy, he went out of his way to be helpful.

The fisherman told them about a path leading into town that was not guarded at night. He advised there was a forty-man German platoon stationed in the village made up of disillusioned veterans rotated in from hard service on the Russian Front. They were willing to live and let live – up to a point.

He claimed when there were no officers around the troops said, "Hitler kaput."

As it was getting late the fisherman agreed to come back and meet them the next morning.

At 2230 hrs Capt. Harlequins, Capt. Jaxx and Cpl. Casalonga patrolled back up the shingle. They came to the gap in the wire exactly where the fisherman said it would be. A path led to the village. When they approached the center of the town moving as stealthily as possible, they heard footsteps up ahead. In enemy-occupied France, a curfew went into effect at sundown. Anyone moving around in the dark was fired on by the Germans, most often without the customary challenge, so the three believed the steps belonged to a sentry walking his post since the locals did not go out at night.

They went to ground and listened. After an agonizing hour, they could still hear the sentry up ahead. He seemed very vigilant.

It was not possible to approach any closer. The white shingle offered no cover at all. Plus the moon was out now which did nothing to help concealment. And while Capt. Jaxx was wearing rubber-soled raiding boots, Capt. Harlequins and Cpl. Casalonga were in hobnailed ammunition boots. The shale crunched every time they took a step.

Capt. Harlequins decided it best to return to the IRP/ERP. He did an about-face and began to move away. At that moment a challenge rang out in German. The three froze briefly then tried moving again.

Immediately came a second challenge followed by a rifle shot. Then a 7.92mm MG 42 light machine gun commenced fire from the top of the cliff. These veteran German troops might not be aggressive but they were experienced and dedicated to their personal safety. Initially the firing was off-target, but after a couple of bursts the Germans were beginning to get the range.

The patrol was caught in the crossfire. Now was no time for indecision. Being an observer could only go so far. This definitely qualified as exigent circumstances.

Capt. Jaxx ordered, "Break contact!"

Then, leading the way he jumped to his feet and made a mad dash to the sea and dived in. This distracted the Nazis long enough for Capt.

Harlequins and Cpl. Casalonga to make it out of the killing zone. They ran to take shelter at the bottom of the cliff where the Germans were not able to depress their LMG enough to fire down on them.

No such luck for Capt. Jaxx. The machine gunner had him in his sights. He tried to stay submerged as much as possible. But he was swimming through a beaten zone of machine gun bullets. Jack Cool was treated to an underwater fireworks display as tracers laced the water and glowed for a second or two before flickering out – a light show he could have well done without.

It was high tide. He swam down the coast for some distance before cautiously making his way back to shore. There he ran into Capt. Harlequins and Cpl. Casalonga edging along the base of the cliff.

Upon linking up with the rest of the team at the IRP/ERP Capt. Harlequins informed the men he had decided to try to infiltrate the village again the next night. Capt. Jaxx had no idea why he would believe that plan would work, but he had to admire the captain's stick-to-itiveness.

Wet, cold and having just survived being machine gunned, Capt. Jaxx was not having a good night. There was no way to get dry or warm until the sun came up. And now Capt. Harlequins wanted to do it all over again tomorrow night.

Carrying out the new plan required notifying the *Silver Arrow* to reschedule their rendezvous again. There were still two carrier pigeons to carry the message. Capt. Harlequins wrote identical notes on tiny slips of pink rice paper, rolled them up to about the size of a postage stamp, and put them in the little canisters fitted to the birds' legs. He requested Brandy extend their extraction by one night.

The instant the two pigeons started on their journey, five peregrine falcons swooped down from the cliffs after them. The Germans had falcon handlers in falcon destruction units – *"Falkenabschussstaffel,"* stationed all along the Atlantic Wall to intercept pigeons winging their way across the Channel. Unknown to most, a brutal bird war was in progress. Both British and Germans were thought to be using carrier pigeons to carry messages. Both sides also employed falconers to hunt down each other's birds. Whether the five raptors attacking Capt. Harlequins' pigeons were Nazi falcons or local birds of prey there was no way to know.

The two pigeons sought refuge on a ledge. When one tried to continue its mission it was pounced on by the waiting falcons. The other bird took the opportunity to disappear out of sight but there were no illusions about what was going to happen to it.

The fisherman who had agreed to meet them that morning was a no-show. Had he turned them in? No one knew for sure. Team morale that had been taking a steady drumbeat of hits from the moment they first landed ashore sank to a new low. Now there was something else to worry about. They were trapped on a tiny beach with no way home until Brandy came back. Capt. Jaxx was having a flashback to the fisherman he encountered when he washed up on Hydra – which did nothing to improve his spirits.

The Frenchman finally did arrive. He was upset to learn there had been a German sentry on the path where he told them there would not be one. Trying to make up for it, he asked, "Would picture postcards of the village be of any interest?"

Responding through the No. 10 Inner-Allied Commando interpreter, Capt. Harlequins said, "Bring all you can obtain."

The British War Office had put out a request for people to send in their family photos taken of vacations on the coast of France. It was a stark testament to how unprepared England had been when the war started. Now the country was having to play catch-up. The intelligence services were wading through thousands of photos of people frolicking in the sand in order to put together a mosaic of potential D-Day landing sites. It was the only thing that could be done at this point.

The fisherman disappeared in the direction of the village. Two hours later he was back with a sack of postcards. The Frenchman pointed out where the Germans had guns, mines, barracks, and their headquarters. Reasonably good field intelligence.

That night at 2330 hrs Capt. Harlequins led a five-man patrol back up the shingle with Capt. Jaxx and King both along this time. However, a cloud passed over the moon limiting visibility and somehow they got tangled up in the concertina wire outside the small guard shack. An explosive charge was detonated under the coils to cut through it, to no avail. It was an act of frustration and not a very wise one in Capt. Jaxx's opinion.

Finally Capt. Harlequins resorted to firing at the sentry post with a bolt-action, bull-barreled, magazine-fed, 8-round, suppressed .45ACP De Lisle Carbine. He had hopes of driving the guard out of the shack. This was the first time Capt. Jaxx had ever observed a De Lisle in action – he had never seen one before.

It was very quiet. And since .45 rounds are subsonic there would not be the distinctive "crack" in the event of a miss when the bullet went past like would happen with a 9mm. However, follow-up shots were slow and racking the bolt to chamber a round created a distinctive metallic signature. Capt. Jaxx made a note to see about obtaining one of the carbines to evaluate – .45 rounds were big and fat with substantial knockdown power at close range.

Why Capt. Harlequins thought plinking at the sentry box would force the German out in the open was not clear. In any event the guard chose not to come outside. With time running short the patrol gave up on trying to capture a prisoner, called it a night and moved back to the IRP/ERP.

The Life Boat Service Men were waiting when they arrived having already ferried the rest of the No. 12 Commandos out to the *Silver Arrow.*

Capt. Jaxx and King were having breakfast with Col. Randal at the Bradford by morning. They ran through the events of the mission from start to finish. He was pleased with the photo postcards of the objective.

Col. Randal was not as impressed with the after-action report.

6

NOTHING IS FOREVER

A KING'S MESSENGER DELIVERED A DISPATCH TO COLONEL John Randal in the dining room where he was having breakfast with Captain Billy Jack Jaxx and King. Inside was "Reconnaissance of Widerstandsnest," a set of grid coordinates and the message "Forthwith."

Col. Randal had no idea what a Widerstandsnest was. He had no problem with the assignments arriving fast and furious unannounced at all hours. But he was starting to resent the peremptory "*Forthwith.*"

Hasty missions had become the norm in the Aegean. Raiding Forces did a lot of them. That did not mean Col. Randal liked it. "Poor Prior Planning Produces Poor Results" was one of Raiding Forces' maxims that did not originate with the unit but was said a lot.

Col. Randal preferred raids against point-type targets be planned in detail so the Actions on the Objective could be rehearsed and rehearsed and rehearsed prior to. Which gave the best chance for success on the night of. That required target data. The three ops since arriving in England did not have any discernible prior planning and no Plan B – they had limited to zero intelligence to act on. If that continued to be the way Raiding Forces was expected to conduct cross-channel operations there would eventually be a price to pay.

That was a given.

King looked at the order Col. Randal handed him, "Widerstandsnest means 'resistance nest,' Chief. Sometimes the Germans call them Tobruks. They can be as small as a single fighting position. No two are exactly alike. The Germans incorporate them into the local terrain to be more formidable."

Capt. Jaxx said, "Sir, if we're going to keep getting alerts like this while we're here at the hotel, we need to set up a map room somewhere."

Col. Randal said, "Get with Lady Jane and see if you can make that happen."

"Wilco."

On the way out of the dining room Col. Randal stopped by the table where Major General Sam Houston Blackwell was dining with Brandy Seaborn.

Col. Randal held up the envelope. "Standby Ready."

Brandy said, "We have a problem, John."

"What might that be?"

"The engines on the Silver Arrow are acting up. I would be reluctant to take her out until we can perform a complete maintenance overhaul," Brandy said. "Sitting in dry dock all these many months has been less than ideal."

Col. Randal said, "How long?"

Brandy said, "Weeks, possibly months. With the war on, civilian pleasure craft have zero priority. Raiding Forces has no pull with the local Royal Navy yard."

"Enjoy your breakfast. I'll get back to you," Col. Randal said.

When he walked away Maj. Gen. Blackwell said, "You two are close?"

Brandy said, "Very."

In the lobby, Col. Randal ran into Major the Lady Jane Seaborn and Capt. Jaxx. They were headed toward the elevator. Give Jack Cool marching orders – he stepped off.

Lady Jane said, "Do not go anywhere, John. We shall be setting up your London headquarters here in the Bradford. I have options to show you momentarily."

Col. Randal said, "We were only thinking about someplace to hang a few maps."

Lady Jane laughed. "General Donovan said you require a London office, as you recall. Did you actually believe I would allow it to be anywhere else?"

Col. Randal said, "What could I have been thinking?"

He walked over to the concierge's desk. "Is General Donovan still in the hotel?"

"May be in his room, sir. He has not left the premises. Would you like me to ring him, Colonel?"

"Ask the general to meet me in the lobby at his earliest convenience."

"Straightaway, sir."

By the time Brigadier General William "Wild Bill" Donovan arrived, Col. Randal was seated in one of the high-backed chairs in the VIP section. Rita Hayworth and Lana Turner were sitting on the floor leaning against his legs like a pair of faithful gun dogs. The exotic Kit-Kat Club dancers were attracting a lot of attention around the hotel. He had the impression the girls were bored.

The former slaves had taken all of the etiquette classes Lady Jane put on for the Officer Candidates. Nevertheless, given the opportunity the two still plopped down on the floor like they were living in a tent. Which for most of their lives they had. Lady Jane liked to do that too – just not in the lobby of her hotel.

Brig. Gen. Donovan said, "You needed to see me?"

"We have a situation, sir. Brandy provided her boat for our last mission," Col. Randal said. "It's developed engine trouble and needs maintenance – we've been alerted for another operation . . ."

Brig. Gen. Donovan said, "That's not a problem, it's a crisis."

Just when he was finally beginning to get OSS – meaning Raiding Forces – involved in the deception campaign's OPERATION FORTITUDE SOUTH, this almost insurmountable obstacle cropped up.

Col. Randal said, "We're caught in the middle of an interservice catfight, General – there's not an easy fix."

"I spend more time doing battle with our Army, Navy, Marines, FBI, MI-5, MI-6 and SOE than the Germans – I'll see what I can do," Brig. Gen. Donovan said.

"By the way, those M3 Grease Guns you requested arrived today and are being trucked to Seaborn House as we speak."

Col. Randal said, "Captain Jaxx tells me SOE has a suppressed .45 caliber weapon called the De Lisle Carbine. No. 12 Commando took one along on the raid last night. Jack says it's quiet, sir."

Brig. Gen. Donovan said, “I’ll instruct Colonel Bruce to locate one and have it delivered to you to field test.”

The Director of the Office of Strategic Services was a combat veteran in his third war and a lifelong hunter. Wild Bill was fascinated with special weapons. He fired one of Raiding Forces’ suppressed .22 High Standard Military Model D pistols into a pillow in the Oval Office when the President was looking the other way to demonstrate how silent it was.

One of the reasons he liked to visit Raiding Forces was because they were always experimenting with something new of interest. As Lieutenant General “Geronimo” Joe McKoy said, “Toys for big boys.”

Col. Randal said, “Thanks, General.”

“Those two Zār priestesses still not talking to you?”

“Negative.”

“Strike me as good company.”

MAJOR BUTCH “HEADHUNTER” HOOLIHAN, DSO, MC, MM, RM, walked in the door of the Bradford having hitched a ride on one of Major General Sam Houston Blackwell’s Troop Transport Command’s planes flying in from Cairo. He had Happy on a leash. Major the Lady Jane Seaborn and Captain Billy Jack Jaxx were stepping out of the elevator across the lobby when the dog spotted her. He broke free, raced the length of the room, and leapt up with his paws on her shoulders. Living up to his name – he was happy.

Lady Jane was so overjoyed to see the dog that there were tears in her eyes.

Lieutenant General “Geronimo” Joe McKoy was having a conversation with Colonel John Randal and Beverly Blackwell, said, “That animal purely loves Lady Jane. But you’re his huntin’ buddy, John. There’s a difference.”

Beverly said, “Do you think the Bradford Hotel will ever be the same after our little visit?”

Col. Randal said, “Who said anything about after? Lady Jane’s designated the Bradford as our London HQ. In a few minutes she’s taking us around to check out space available.”

Beverly said, “There goes the neighborhood.”

Lady Jane escorted Maj. Hoolihan upstairs to get settled in his room before taking Col. Randal to view his options. While waiting for her to return he took the opportunity to have a word with Lieutenant Colonel Lionel Honeycutt-Parker. They moved off to a pair of chairs in the VIP area for privacy.

Col. Randal said, “We’re getting ready to initiate a major reorganization. Seaborn House personnel, for the most part, will be relocating to Castelrozzo while the 575th Ranger Task Force and other elements in the Aegean will effect a change of station to England.

“So, here’s the deal, Colonel. You can take my place at Advanced Base Castelrozzo or you can assume command of that armored cavalry regiment I understand you’ve been offered. Take your choice.”

Lt. Col. Honeycutt-Parker said, “How did you find out about the regiment, sir?”

“I get paid to know things like that.”

“Are you suggesting I leave Raiding Forces, sir?”

“Negative, not a chance. I’d like you to take over operations at ABC,” Col. Randal said. “That said, the opportunity to command a newly formed regiment is too great an opportunity for a career cavalryman like you to turn down. Promotion goes with it.”

Lt. Col. Honeycutt-Parker said, “If I take the regiment, sir, would it be possible for Penelope to be assigned to Seaborn House so we could spend time together before the invasion?”

“Roger that . . . absolutely.”

“In that case, it has been an honor and a privilege, John.”

Col. Randal said, “Those young troopers are going to need an officer of your caliber to see ’em through the rest of the war, Lionel. Lucky men. So are their wives and mothers.”

And that was that. Nothing is forever. Not in the Army.

Lady Jane returned with Capt. Jaxx and Beverly. “Time for your showing.”

Rita and Lana tagged along, as did Happy, who was not about to leave Lady Jane’s side. Three spaces readily available in the hotel could be quickly converted into a Raiding Forces’ Rear HQ (RFR), which is different from a Tactical Operations Center (TOC). The space was mostly expected to be used to coordinate logistics and as a point of contact for the various agencies Raiding Forces would be working with in the London area. While its presence would not be a secret, the RFR needed to be discreet. In fact, the idea was for hotel guests not to realize it was there.

The last stop on their tour was the basement. Most of it had been converted to serve as the hotel's air raid shelter during the Blitz. Col. Randal had ended up there late one night during the first Luftwaffe bombing raid on London wearing one of the Bradford's silk robes with a monogrammed "B" on it – after carrying Brandy down six flights of stairs because she sprained her ankle.

A large area that was not part of the bomb shelter served as storage for odds and ends like old buckets and mops for housekeeping. No windows. It was a dark, damp underground bunker.

Col. Randal said, "What do you think, Jack?"

Capt. Jaxx said, "This is perfect, sir."

"Roger that."

Lady Jane said, "I shall have engineering install better lighting. A phone bank. We shall move desks down here. The hotel has oriental rugs we shall use to cover the concrete floor. A giant wall map of the French Coast . . ."

Col. Randal said, "No sign on the door."

Lady Jane said, "Fun."

Happy was poking around in the back.

Beverly said, "Hope he doesn't find a rat."

BRIGADIER GENERAL WILLIAM "WILD BILL" DONOVAN walked into the Bradford Hotel. He spied Colonel John Randal in deep conversation with Major the Lady Jane Seaborn and Beverly Blackwell.

Brig. Gen. Donovan approached the VIP section and was immediately ushered inside the velvet rope by the Vulnerable Points Wing security operator.

Col. Randal was saying, "So how long is all this going to take?"

Lady Jane said, "My construction manager assures me he intends to work around the clock – two days."

Brig. Gen. Donovan said, "What are you three conspirators plotting?"

"Lady Jane's building out a space in the basement for the Raiding Forces' Rear per your suggestion, sir," Col. Randal said. "She's on mission."

Lady Jane laughed. "We are also installing a privacy entry that blocks off the wing of the penthouse floor where our suites are located. You may be temporarily inconvenienced, General.

"The hotel will be placing an additional security desk outside to restrict access. The other guests on the floor shall no longer be able to stroll down the hall and knock on our doors anytime they choose."

"I like that," Brig. Gen. Donovan said. "I want to see the space you're building out for the RFR."

Lady Jane said, "Beverly and I shall give you the grand tour."

Brig. Gen. Donovan said, "On another subject – about which time is of the essence, Colonel. It may be of interest for you to learn a flotilla of six 80 ft. Elco model PT boats arrived from the States as part of Lend Lease a week ago. They were offloaded from a Merchant Marine Liberty ship at Portland Naval Base. Scheduled to be trans-shipped to Russia in a convoy that's being formed as we speak.

"Currently the boats are berthed at one of the docks prior to being loaded on their transport. Portland's a very busy Naval base . . ."

Col. Randal said, "We can take it from here, sir."

With a perfectly straight face, Brig. Gen. Donovan said, "Take?"

Lady Jane laughed. "Midnight requisition – a time-honored Raiding Forces' tradition."

Beverly said, "Exactly."

Changing the subject, Lady Jane said, "Do not forget we have a dinner tonight for you and Colonel Bruce, General."

Brig. Gen. Donovan said, "Looking forward to it."

The idea was for Col. Randal and Lieutenant Colonel David Bruce, the head of the OSS London Station, to have an opportunity to get to know each other in a small intimate setting. Lady Jane was at her best arranging social events like that.

Col. Randal said, "Beverly, see if you can pry Brandy away from your father for a few minutes – we need to talk."

COLONEL JOHN RANDAL AND MAJOR BUTCH "HEADHUNTER" Hoolihan were sitting in the VIP section when Captain Billy Jack Jaxx walked past. Col. Randal made eye contact and he came straight over. These were his two most trusted small-unit commanders.

"Change of plans. A major reorganization of Raiding Forces is in our immediate future. I was just explaining to Butch the Maritime Unit and SOG are being flown in to Seaborn House. I want the two of you to coordinate with Commander Fleming. He has plans for us to move forward with a Raiding Forces' troop for his NID 30 Assault Unit.

"I want you to organize separate independent elements for Raiding Forces – A-team and B-team. Jack, you command the American A-team composed of OSS MU personnel and your SOG operators. Butch, you take the British B-Team composed of Royal Marines – yours and the few of Fleming's original Red Indians who made the cut. I don't like breaking Raiding Forces down into national units. However, there are reasons I'm not cleared for to reorganize this way.

"You're both going to be running 30 Assault Unit-type missions across the Channel into France commencing on and following D-Day – possibly through the end of the war. You'll be going against high value priority targets on the Continent. Commander Fleming has lined up specialist training that sounds interesting. Keep me in the loop. I want to be actively involved.

"Questions?"

Maj. Hoolihan said, "What about the remainder of my Royal Marine troop, sir?"

"We'll get your Marines here but understand they're dead last on travel priority," Col. Randal said. "They'll be the most experienced operators remaining on Castelrozzo. I need to keep 'em in place conducting missions for the time being while we complete shifting the 575th Ranger Task Force to Seaborn House."

He did not elaborate on his plan to use the 575th RTF, reflagged as the 575th Ranger Regiment, as cover for Raiding Forces – it having been designated the new OSS Operational Group Branch Europe (OGBE). They could have that conversation at a later date. There were still issues that needed to be resolved. Right now things were in flux moving too fast to be distracted by name change for deception purposes details.

While Col. Randal's response was not what he wanted to hear, Maj. Hoolihan said, "Wilco, sir."

Col. Randal said, "I know you're a Royal Marine at heart, Butch. Give me ninety days. If you're not completely satisfied with the NID's 30 Assault Unit program and the work you're doing out of Seaborn House, then at that time I'll have Commander Fleming find a Royal Marine Commando company in one of the Special Service Brigades for you to command on D-Day."

In the British Army, majors commanded companies.

Maj. Hoolihan said, "I am not transferring out of Raiding Forces, Colonel."

Col. Randal said, "Round pegs need to go in round holes, Butch. I'm good with it if that's the way you decide to go. Wouldn't blame you if you did."

Capt. Jaxx said, "I'm to put SOG through Commander Fleming's training program too, sir?"

"Affirmative."

Capt. Jaxx said, "Over half of my people are Brits, Colonel."

Col. Randal said, "Yeah, well, I'm only going to follow the directive to make Castelrozzo a UK operation and Seaborn House U.S. just so far, Jack."

Capt. Jaxx said, "Roger."

Both young officers had legitimate concerns. They had worked hard to hone their commands to a level of professionalism seldom achieved in any army – ever. Now that was subject to change. No commander appreciates a major unit shakeup at the start of a new campaign.

Col. Randal said, "Let's see how this plays out ... could have possibilities."

LIEUTENANT GENERAL "GERONIMO" JOE MCKOY, CAPTAIN Billy Jack Jaxx and Captain Sinclair Lovelace were preparing to conduct the first interviews of the volunteers from the soon-to-be stood-down super-secret GHQ Auxiliary Units. They had no idea what to expect. The men coming in today were members of the clandestine, stay-behind underground guerrilla army in the counties immediately surrounding London. The initial evaluations would be conducted in one of the small conference rooms in the hotel.

The candidates were to appear in their Home Guard uniform to not cause undue notice. Soldiers in wartime England were thick on the ground. Troops were required to carry their primary weapon and their flat-rimmed WWI Brodie Mark 2 steel helmet everywhere they went. No one paid them any attention. They were invisible. Men and women in uniform were part of the landscape.

Since the Auxiliaries from different counties did not know each other they would be arriving at different times and kept separated. Their anonymity needed to be protected. Secrecy at all costs even when it did not accomplish anything. The AUs were slated to be broken up. Being able to know who was a member of a nonexistent clandestine unit no longer posed any security problem.

While waiting for the first applicant to show up, Capt. Lovelace, who had an admitted eye for the ladies, asked Capt. Jaxx, "How would you describe the experience of having Lady Seaborn as your patroness?"

Capt. Jaxx said, "Like having a former Miss America as your favorite aunt."

Lt. Gen. McKoy said, "You got that right, Jack."

Capt. Jaxx said, "Notice the scar on the colonel's face?"

"I did."

"Lady Jane cheekboned him making out. Dangerous woman. If the heart attack smile doesn't get you one of her European cheek-to-cheek kisses will. Keep a tourniquet handy – I do."

Jack Cool.

A BRADFORD HOTEL LIMOUSINE DEPOSITED MANDY PAIGE at MI-5 Security Services Headquarters. While the door still did not have a knob, today she came armed with the knowledge there was a concealed button under a certain piece of decorative wrought iron. She slid it aside and rang the doorbell.

One of the Security men opened the door. Having been briefed she was now in training to be MI-5, he was all smiles today. The Security Service was a cloistered organization. Its charter was to suspect everyone in England of being an enemy spy until proven otherwise – which had a chilling effect on the agents' social lives – otherwise, once admitted to MI-5's ranks it was an exceptionally nice place to serve.

Mandy was escorted to Lieutenant Colonel Thomas Argyll Robertson's office.

Lt. Col. Robertson said, "I will be personally handling your orientation. The first few days are going to be spent going over case studies of the double agents we work with here at MI-5. I trust you shall find the details interesting."

"I am looking forward to it, Tar."

Lt. Col. Robertson said, "As we are doing that, our technical boffins will be setting up the transmitter at the Bradford as Lady Jane and I discussed. While being read in on XX/B1-A history and your new responsibilities, in your capacity as her case officer you can supervise Rocky when she sends her first transmission. I shall be there to assist."

Mandy said, "Perfect – as Colonel Randal says, 'Hit the ground running.'"

"It is time to inform Rommel Miss Runborg has relocated to London," Lt. Col. Robertson said. "I have an idea for her cover story to pass by you, Mandy. What if we say she is living at the Bradford under the protection of General McKoy – your thoughts?"

Mandy said, "The Desert Fox knows the general works with Colonel Randal. Raiding Forces made his life miserable for nearly two years. He has a dossier on us."

"I am aware of that."

"Only makes sense John would be brought in to handle SHAEF's Special Operations. He is the best there is. General McKoy would come with him."

Lt. Col. Robertson said, "Quite right."

Mandy said, "The general's arrival in London is easy enough for the Abwehr to verify. Especially if we plant a few squibs in the newspapers. I believe it is a splendid idea, Tar."

"Brilliant minds think alike."

"I shall take that as a compliment," Mandy said.

Lt. Col. Robertson said, "Let us dive right in and go it from the start. I am the chief of Section

B1-A. We handle MI-5's double agents and play them back against the Abwehr. The first German agents we turned were duds. My initial attempt at being a case officer resulted in dismal failure. Except that in the end by pure dumb luck my man led us to a clue that allowed our technical boffins to crack a certain MSS, MOST SECRET Source, code. The result turned out to be so highly classified that even I am not cleared to know what it does – some sort of Signals Intelligence.

"My takeaway from that experience – and this is key – was no matter how satisfying it might be to imprison German spies, stand them up in front of a firing squad or send them to the gallows, it does not offer our side any long-term benefit. If the Abwehr believes their operatives are in place, alive and functioning, the Germans may not feel the necessity to send over additional agents. Which makes MI-5's job that much easier.

"Now this next item is crucial to understanding the why/what we do. The questions the Abwehr spymasters ask their agents under our control reveal what the Germans do *not* know. And they tell us what it is they *are* interested in finding out. Once we figured out how that worked it became the original mission statement for Section B1-A.

"Only later did a lightbulb go off and I realized the *answers* we crafted for our double agents to send back to their Abwehr case officers were the perfect vehicle for B1-A to perpetrate a deception on the Germans. It was an epiphany. Now counterintelligence – which is by definition defensive in nature – could be used in the *offense*. Changed the game."

Mandy said, "Very impressive. Sounds so simple it is almost as if you have the Abwehr working for you."

"Very good, Mandy, you grasped the concept of the operation on the first pass," Lt. Col. Robertson said. "Bottom line – a live spy is more useful than a dead one. Though quite a lot more trouble as I shall explain.

"A pair of Scandinavians were recruited by the Abwehr to spy on Great Britain, whom we shall call Mr. Brown and Mr. Miller. Brown had lost a fortune in a silver fox farm. Miller was a Danish Fascist – a true believer. The men may or may not have been given parachute training . . . for all the good it did them. They were dropped into England separately.

"Mr. Miller was inserted by parachute on 9 October 40, made a bad job of his landing fall, staggered into a ditch to try to sleep off a concussion and was spotted by a farmer who noticed his feet sticking out of a hedge.

The local authorities were summoned. At the time of his arrest the Dane was found to be carrying a transmitter that could only send, not receive – a most ineffective communications system for an enemy agent if there ever was one – two hundred pounds sterling, and a loaded 9mm Luger.

"Mr. Brown dropped in two weeks later, sprained his ankle badly, limped into a village wearing a blue suit and speaking in a heavy foreign accent. Might as well have had a sign around his neck that said 'GERMAN SPY.'

"'Tin Eye' Stephens, nicknamed for his monocle – you met him at the prison – gently persuaded both of them the wisdom of becoming double agents. However, Brown developed second thoughts. One night in their safe house when his minder was playing solitaire he snuck up from behind and tried to strangle him with a telephone cord. When that failed, he apologized, tied the case officer to a chair and escaped with a can of sardines, a pineapple and a large canvas canoe. He then stole a motorcycle and rode toward the coast with the canoe balanced on his head. His plan – paddle to Holland.

"A report came in to the local police station stating a man carrying a canoe had fallen off his motorcycle. Mr. Brown was arrested, deemed to no longer be of any value to the XX program and thrown in the Tower of London for the duration.

"Mr. Miller, the Fascist, is still on duty to this very day. The one-time political fanatic is now the longest-serving double agent MI-5 has on its books – funny, that."

Mandy said, "You could not make that story up, Tar."

Lt. Col. Robertson said, "One would not have reason to believe Rocky might attempt to throttle you, would they?"

"Hope not . . . she is awfully physically fit.

COLONEL JOHN RANDAL AND MAJOR THE LADY JANE Seaborn were in one of the Bradford Hotel limousines en route to 1 Richmond Terrace, the home of Combined Operations Headquarters. Lady Jane had an appointment to see WREN Third Officer Christen Mary Lamb to make arrangements to install a map of the French coastline in what was now being called the "Bunker." 3/O Lamb was responsible for updating

COHQ's chart of the French coast – a work in progress. Col. Randal was along because he was hoping to obtain aerial photos or at least a topographical map of the section of the French coast where the Raiding Forces' next objective was located.

Upon arriving they were first ushered into Major General Robert Laycock's office. This was not expected. He was a Royal Horse Guards officer who, as a colonel, had commanded Layforce, an assortment of elements from several Commando units – when it went out to Middle East Command. The general had experienced a colorful if unfortunate war so far. It was almost as if the stars were aligned against his command. Laycock lost over 600 men captured on Crete. He escaped taking one of the last boats off the island leaving the bulk of his troops behind to their fate – a decision he was never apologetic about.

Later Col. Laycock went along with a party from No.11(Scottish) Commando to observe their raid on Rommel's HQ . . . or supposed HQ. There was no record of the Desert Fox ever having been at the location even on a visit. The operation was a disaster resulting in all but two of the raiding party being killed or captured. Col. Laycock was one of the two people who got away. After an epic escape across the desert he was ordered back to England. Instead of court-martialed he found himself promoted to major general. He replaced Vice Admiral Louis Mountbatten at COHQ.

Some workings in the military are difficult to explain.

When Maj. Gen. Laycock was informed that Lady Jane would be visiting his headquarters he had leapt at the opportunity to personally offer his assistance. While the two had never met she was well-known. He knew Col. Randal by reputation – everyone at COHQ did.

After a brief conversation Maj. Gen. Laycock escorted them to the map room. There 3/O Lamb spent her days putting together a giant patchwork puzzle. It looked like a mosaic. Consisting of aerial photos, vacation snapshots and picture postcards that took up one big wall, the pieces created a partially completed map of the French coast.

"Make sure Lady Seaborn leaves here with everything she requires."

"Aye, aye, sir."

Lady Jane pointed at the collage. "I want one of those."

3/O Lamb said, "As you wish, Lady Seaborn. We have copies of everything. I can dispatch a team of WRENs to the Bradford to assemble it for you at your convenience. As you can observe there are still quite a few gaps we hope to fill in eventually."

Lady Jane laughed, "I see that. Thought you were going to tell me what I was asking for was out of the question. You have a big project on your hands, Third Officer."

3/O Lamb said, "COHQ has set up several of these for other headquarters and agencies. We have everything annotated on the back. It was only difficult the first time we tried to fit the pieces together. For fillers we put topographical maps in the gaps as placeholders until photos or post cards become available. We shall keep you updated as they do."

Lady Jane said, "John?"

Col. Randal said, "That works."

He handed 3/O Lamb a slip of paper with the grid coordinates of the next Raiding Forces' objective. "What might you have on this location?"

3/O Lamb went to the wall map and found the coordinates requested. Col. Randal came over to inspect it. No photos or postcards – just a folded contour map pinned up as a temporary placeholder.

What the topographical map indicated was not good. In fact, it could hardly have been worse. The contour lines were so close together starting from the beach for several inches they formed an almost solid brown band. The compacted lines indicated a vertical slope from the water's edge up to the objective – running along the waterfront for several thousand yards in each direction.

As depicted on the map there were ten yards between lines – the trick was to picture that in your mind's eye.

Col. Randal said, "How high would you say that cliff is?"

3/O Lamb said, "As you can see, sir, this is a 1:25000 topographical map. The incline would be approximately 250 feet – almost vertical. But then I suspect you knew that sir."

Col. Randal said, "Lovely."

BRIGADIER GENERAL WILLIAM "WILD BILL" DONOVAN WAS in the bunker checking on the state of its remodeling. He was killing time before the private dinner Major the Lady Jane Seaborn had planned with

Lieutenant Colonel David Bruce, the chief of the OSS London Station. A team of WRENs from COHQ was hard at work installing the map of the French coastline on one freshly painted wall. The room had undergone quite a transition in the short time since it had been selected to be Raiding Forces' Rear (RFR).

Brig. Gen. Donovan said, "You really whipped this place into shape fast, Lady Jane."

"Not my first rodeo, General."

Colonel John Randal said, "Have you ever been to a rodeo?"

"Well no, but Beverly has been teaching me how to be a barrel racer."

Brig. Gen. Donovan was studying the 1:25000 topographical map placeholder that filled in the location of Raiding Forces' next mission. Reading a contour map is different than reading a road map. You have to be able to look at the wiggly green and brown lines and visualize the terrain features they depict. It's an art as much as a skill set. Not everyone is able to do it and of those who can, few are good at it. Wild Bill could read a topo map as well as anyone.

Scaling the cliff was not impossible. But it was a dangerous climb due to the terrain along the coast in the Pas-de-Calais region consisting of chalk, marl and clay. And with the short time window given to land, make the climb, conduct the raid on the Widerstandsnest, snatch a prisoner, then climb back down, reboard the transport and arrive back at Seaborn House before getting caught at sea with the sun coming up – wishful thinking.

Brig. Gen. Donovan was fully aware of Col. Randal's often stated, "Hope is not a course of action." So, wishful thinking was not on. What to do?

After evaluating the after action report on No. 12 Commando's mission Captain Billy Jack Jaxx and King had observed, Col. Randal ordered a ban on raiding parties staying ashore overnight. It was a dangerous practice bordering on foolhardy. For future special operations teams would have to land, carry out their assignment and return same night. Brig. Gen. Donovan concurred with the order. Why take a chance? Another phrase he had picked up from time spent around Raiding Forces.

When Col. Randal joined him at the map, Brig. Gen. Donovan said, "That cliff is not scalable with a team in the amount of time you have ashore to execute your mission, Colonel – what's your plan?"

Col. Randal said, "I'm working on it, sir."

Which was not exactly true. Col. Randal knew exactly how he was going to carry out the operation. And he had from the moment he saw the 1:25,000 terrain map at COHQ. He could play the Need to Know game as well as anyone – even when there was no point to it.

LATER THAT EVENING MAJOR GENERAL SAM HOUSTON Blackwell, friends called him "Bronc," Brandy Seaborn and Colonel John Randal were looking at the mosaic map of France. Maj. Gen. Blackwell did not like what he saw. He could read a contour map and what this one told him was the mission was not doable as he understood small-scale Commando raids. That means hit and run at a predetermined time and place, utilizing surprise, speed and violence of action, then away and gone.

Because of the close connection he had developed with Raiding Forces and because of his lifelong interest in military subjects the general had been studying small-scale Commando/Ranger-type special operations. Particularly those delivered by parachute, Troop Transport Command's specialty.

Maj. Gen. Blackwell said, "What fool dreamed this one up?"

Col. Randal said, "Sir, that's not exactly clear."

"Beverly tells me a King's Messenger arrives with your next assignment – you don't have any idea who the sanctioning authority is?"

"Negative."

Brandy said, "If it takes too long for you to scale the cliff we shall be caught at sea when the sun comes up on the return."

Maj. Gen. Blackwell said, "That's not good. What's your plan, Colonel? I know you have one."

"Yes sir, here's what we're going to do . . ."

COLONEL JOHN RANDAL PLACED A CALL TO THE NAVAL Intelligence Division and spoke with Commander Ian Fleming. The Commander said, "I need to wrap up a few things here, Colonel. Then I shall be on my way to the hotel straightaway."

"Thanks, Commander."

Brandy Seaborn and Captain Penelope “Legs” Honeycutt-Parker were waiting in the VIP section with Col. John Randal, Major the Lady Jane Seaborn and Beverly Blackwell when the naval intelligence officer arrived.

Col. Randal said, “The Admiral in charge of the Dover Straits AO is refusing to support Raiding Forces’ missions. Brandy has her personal yacht at Seaborn House and has used it for operations in the past. Problem is it needs a complete maintenance overhaul. The Admiral’s not going to authorize work on a civilian craft.

“We have a mission and no way to carry it out.”

Cdr. Fleming said, “I can arrange for support from the Navy. Unfortunately that may require a few days. You say you may have another solution?”

Col. Randal said, “We do. There’s a flotilla of PT boats bound for Russia docked at Portland Naval Base. I’d like two.”

Cdr. Fleming said, “I take it you do not wish to bother with paperwork?”

“Negative.”

“Excellent, I can supply sailors for a boarding party but it would be better if you are able to handle that part yourselves,” Cdr. Fleming said. “The less people outside your command in the know the better. We do not want any unnecessary blowback.”

Brandy said, “Raiding Forces has a small naval contingent that shall be adequate for the task.”

Cdr. Fleming said, “I always wanted to be a pirate.”

At 0100 hrs a small convoy consisting of a jeep with two Royal Navy Patrol Service (RNPS) personnel as an escort, a command car containing Cdr. Fleming, Lady Jane, Brandy, Capt. Honeycutt-Parker and Beverly, followed by a Bedford truck carrying the *Silver Arrow* crew arrived at the security gate outside Portland Naval Base. Cdr. Fleming stepped out and approached the two-man guard post. He produced his credentials.

“I was never here. You never saw me. If you are ever asked, these vehicles did not pass through this gate. Should either of you make any statement to the contrary you both will be permanently assigned to the Murmansk convoys for the duration of the war. As you know, the run is under constant attack the entire way to Russia and quite often on the return leg of the voyage as well.

"Do we understand each other?"

It was widely known around Portland Naval Base that out of a convoy of thirty-six ships – PQ17, outbound for Murmansk – only eleven arrived. The rest were lost to U-boats and air attack. Survivability for a sailor abandoning ship in Arctic waters was measured in minutes – possibly less than fifteen. The security guards were petrified by the threat.

"Sir!"

Cdr. Fleming loved his job.

The two RNPS sailors in the lead jeep had been chosen for the detail because they were familiar with the massive Portland Naval Base. They drove straight to the dock where the six PT boats were tied off in a neat row. Upon arrival, Lady Jane, Brandy, Capt. Honeycutt-Parker and Beverly stepped out of the staff car. The young *Silver Arrow* sailors climbed out of the back of the truck.

Cdr. Fleming said, "Take the two with ribbons tied off on their masts. I shall remain here until I hear your boats depart – have a nice night, ladies."

Brandy led the way down the pier to where the six sleek PT boats were bobbing. She and half of the sailors boarded one sporting a long white ribbon attached to the antenna mast. Capt. Honeycutt-Parker and the rest of the sailors boarded the other boat with a matching ribbon. Lady Jane went with Brandy, Beverly with Legs Parker.

Pre-start checks began immediately. When the PT boats had been unloaded from their transports after arriving from the States they would have had their gas tanks partially filled, their engines would have been checked and the motors run briefly – SOP. Cdr. Fleming had called ahead to the MI-6/SOE detachment housed in a restricted area at Portland and ordered the gas tanks on two boats topped off. The ribbons were tied off to identify them.

Brandy's engineer and his assistant who was on Capt. Honeycutt-Parker's boat went through the pre-startup sequence. Wise sailors always subscribe to one of Raiding Forces' unofficial mottos, "Why take a chance?"

The engineers checked to see that there was sufficient fuel – 100 octane aviation gas – and that all oil lines were properly lubricated. Then they checked the cooling systems to ensure they were functioning properly. Each of the three engines on the boats was inspected individually to make sure they were primed with fuel and oil. The electrical system's generator was started and checked for proper voltage and current output.

Engines were then cranked up sequentially, beginning with the center engine and then moving to the outside engines, left to right. Once the engines were running they were allowed to warm up properly before being put under load. It seemed to take forever considering they were pirating the boats.

Still, some things it is best not to rush. Brandy and Capt. Honeycutt-Parker were experienced boat captains with extensive time running special operations to dark shores. They were not going to cut corners. While the inspections were modified tonight, they were not dangerously so. The good news was if anything went wrong with a boat on the voyage to Seaborn House the other could effect a tow.

The powerful four-stroke, liquid-cooled V-12 marine engines equipped with centrifugal superchargers rumbled as the PTs slowly made their way out into the Channel. On shore Cdr. Fleming flashed his staff car's lights three times, "Godspeed."

Now Raiding Forces had an off-the-books navy. When it was eventually discovered there were only four PT boats instead of six it would most likely be attributed to an administrative error. It was a big war. Things went missing. No one would have an explanation. Besides, chances were less than half the ships in the convoy would reach their destination anyway.

From the day the unit was formed, Raiding Forces had been forced to resort to "midnight requisitions," improvising equipment from castoff gear or captured from the enemy – they were good at it.

CAPTAIN RICHARD "DYNAMITE DICK" COOGAN, LIEUTENANT Ricky Mascuch, Lieutenant Chase Starrett, Captain Jake Novak aka "Jake the Snake" and the two Lovat Scouts rolled into the lobby of the Bradford Hotel looking exactly like what they were – a rough and ready crew of paratroopers armed to the teeth. The men had just flown in from Castelrozzo. The Raiding Forces' eagles were gathering. Colonel John Randal and Captain Billy Jack Jaxx were in the VIP section talking to Lieutenant General "Geronimo" Joe McKoy when they came in. The arrival of his officers and the Scouts changed Col. Randal's plans for that night. He was getting his people around him – that was good.

Major the Lady Jane Seaborn walked over to greet them. Happy was dancing around glad to see old friends. There were not enough rooms available to accommodate every Raiding Forces' arrival, but this group would not be checking in.

Col. Randal said, "Show these studs to the Bunker, we'll join you there."

Lady Jane said, "Follow me, lads." Then she led the way downstairs.

Lt. Gen. McKoy said, "What're you thinkin,' John?"

"I wasn't expecting these people to get here this fast but since they did why not put 'em on the manifest tonight?"

Lt. Gen. McKoy said, "Yeah, good idea."

Capt. Jaxx said, "Roger that, sir."

Col. Randal made eye contact with King. The Merc was sitting in another part of the VIP area talking to Captain Pamala Plum-Martin. He immediately came over.

Col. Randal said, "Warning Order – you ready?"

King said, "Affirmative."

The Bunker smelled of fresh paint. Lady Jane had the walls painted snow white to help offset the total lack of windows. More lighting was up. Large-paddled ceiling fans had been installed to help circulation. Oriental carpets covered the floor. There was nothing oppressive about this room, but it was a bunker. And a war room. Except for the colorful rugs, the atmosphere was strictly military – crisp and professional.

Royal Marines and FANYS were starting to show up from Seaborn House, MI-6, MI-5, and SOE to handle clerical duties and to effect coordination with their respective agencies. The Bunker was going to be a busy place when fully staffed.

Mandy Paige and Beverly Blackwell were at a small table in the back talking to Lieutenant Colonel Thomas Argyll Robertson aka Tar. Beverly had officially been named as Brigadier General William "Wild Bill" Donovan's liaison to B1-A and XX. What that entailed initially was attending the weekly meetings and reporting back. She most likely would have additional responsibilities later.

It was a good plan. If either she or Mandy were unavailable for any reason they could fill in for each other. Lady Jane would be able to sit in on Rikke Runborg's transmissions with Beverly when Mandy was not available because the UT beauty queen did not speak German. A must, because it was necessary to be *absolutely* certain that Rocky was transmitting the approved message word for word. B1-A had learned that lesson the hard way. MI-5 never trusted their double agents. No matter how much they liked them.

The details of what Lt. Col. Robertson originally had in mind for Rikke Runborg were not working out exactly as he intended. The current set-up was better.

When Brandy Seaborn and Major Butch "Headhunter" Hoolihan arrived in the Bunker, Col. Randal assembled his officers around the wall map mosaic. "Are you prepared to accept a Warning Order?" – the traditional statement made prior to the beginning of every alert order.

It was not a question.

Lt. Col. Robertson, Mandy and Beverly stopped their conversation and came over to observe the briefing. Not a problem. Anyone allowed in the Bunker was cleared to know the details of Raiding Forces' missions. Compartmentalization and Need to Know – at least for the most part, stopped at the door. Besides, like Lady Jane said, Tar was one of them now.

Col. Randal said, "Situation: This is WWII, the Germans are in France and we're in England."

Tension ratcheted down.

"Mission: Raid on a point-type target off the Vieux Lighthouse, which translates to 'Old Mole Lighthouse.' It is classified as being located 'at sea.' Meaning it can only be reached by boat or by walking on a long breakwater that leads to it. Footing on the stone is reported to be treacherous when the waves are high which is pretty much always.

"Raiding Forces will land on the mole, assault the lighthouse, attempt to snatch a prisoner, capture signals codebooks and/or anything else of intelligence value. While the search is in progress, demolitions will be emplaced. Then we withdraw.

"This is a hasty mission. There is not much intelligence on our target. We are trying to develop additional intel at this time – don't count on much. The lighthouse was raided about four years ago by the Small-Scale Raiding Force – an early SOE outfit. Unfortunately, subsequent to that time all the principal players on the mission have been killed, captured or transferred elsewhere and the unit disbanded. Obtaining after-action reports from actual participants is unlikely.

"Execution: An eleven-man Raiding Forces' team will depart Seaborn House at 2400 hrs by PT boat under the command of Mrs. Seaborn. Time to target is approximately ninety minutes. The PT will stand a mile offshore while the raiding party goes in by dory and/or rubber assault raft.

"Lieutenant Mascuch, you will land and establish the Initial Rally Point/Extraction Point with the Life Boat Service Men from the two dories transporting the main party.

"Lt. Starrett, there is a light anti-aircraft gun position known to be located on the mole between the lighthouse and the shore. You will land by rubber raft with a party of three men armed with suppressed 9mm M3 Grease Guns to take down that gun position.

"Once you've neutralized the site, set up a blocking force to prevent German reinforcements from shore being able to reach the lighthouse via the mole.

"Captain Jaxx, you will land and assault the lighthouse with a party of four men armed with suppressed 9mm M3 Grease Guns. I'll follow you in with General McKoy, Captain Novak and King. Once the objective has been secured, turn over any prisoners to Captain Novak who will be standing by outside the objective on the mole – King will assist as needed.

"At that point a search of the premises will be initiated. Priority to signals codebooks and/or anything else of intelligence value. I say again, prisoners – don't shoot 'em all, Jack.

"Captain Coogan, while the search is underway you will emplace demolitions. Set your charges to detonate following our withdrawal. Make sure to get a report on the last lighthouse we blew – consult with Major Hoolihan. It needs to go up *after* we're well away.

"I'll be in overall command. Chain of command is me, General McKoy, Captain Jaxx. Initially I will be traveling with Captain Jaxx's Assault Team. Go in hard, fast and quiet. Everyone carries a suppressed 9mm M3 Grease Gun. Speed, violence of action and maximum stealth at all times. We do not want to alert the Germans ashore we're there. Time on the objective is to be no more than thirty minutes – a quick in and out. Again, no one on shore is to know we've been there until the lighthouse goes up.

"Administration and Logistics: We'll revisit that once we reach Seaborn House.

"Command and Signal: "Tonight we'll be using a handheld SCR-536 walkie-talkie to communicate between the shore party and the PT boat. Range is said to be three miles over open water so we're good on signals. Lieutenant Mascuch, in addition to securing the IRP/ERP you will be Signals Officer responsible for maintaining contact with our ride home.

"What are your questions?"

Capt. Jaxx had been waiting patiently, it being SOP in Raiding Forces for all questions to be held until the end so as not to interrupt the briefers' train of thought. "Sir, what's a mole, exactly?"

Col. Randal said, "A stone structure like a pier or a jetty, the difference being water can't flow under it. Think of it as a breakwater with a walkway on top."

No one laughed. Jack Cool was not the only person present not to know the answer.

"We don't have any of those in West Texas."

Col. Randal said, "Any more questions?"

Lt. Starrett said, "Sir, our objective is a lighthouse. Won't they be able to spot the PT boat? And the dories when we go in?"

Col. Randal said, "Mrs. Seaborn, you want to take this one?"

Brandy said, "Lighthouses are designed to be a navigational aid. The light is aimed high on a fixed automatic rotating pedestal to be seen from a great distance. No search function."

As soon as the Warning Order was concluded Maj. Hoolihan approached Col. Randal. "Sir, are you leaving me out on purpose?"

Col. Randal said, "I have another assignment for you, Major. No. 12 Commando is being disbanded. I need you to recruit as many of their personnel as you can before the SAS beats us to them."

Clearly not pleased to be ordered to stay behind, Maj. Hoolihan said, "Sir!"

Col. Randal said, "Butch, you've been on three times as many amphibious raids as any man in this room including me. You can afford to skip this one. I need you to enlist those No. 12 operators."

"Understood, sir."

Lady Jane came over and handed Col. Randal a manila envelope. Inside was a grainy 8x10 black and white low oblique aerial photo of the objective taken by a Supermarine Spitfire Mark XI photoreconnaissance aircraft. The picture was not much to look at but it showed the lighthouse, the mole and the anti-aircraft position. Good enough for military work.

"Three-O Lamb sent it over from COHQ while you were issuing your Warning Order."

"We need to make friends with her."

"My thoughts exactly."

GENERAL DWIGHT D. EISENHOWER WAS IN THE BRADFORD Hotel's dining room with his core group of senior staff officers, both British and American – becoming known as the SHAEF inner-circle. Also there was his attractive Mechanized Transportation Corps Driver Kay Summersby. She was currently a private but Ike was in the process of having her transferred to the U.S. Women's Army Corps (WAC) in the rank of second lieutenant. Drv. – soon to be Lieutenant Summersby had become an integral part of the Supreme Headquarters Allied Forces Europe commander's entourage.

The SHAEF staff was developing an affinity for the Bradford. It catered to upper echelon military and government clientele. A good place to be seen – making the statement, "There is a new sheriff in town."

Major General Sam Houston Blackwell was at the table. In addition to his other duties he was now the designated SHAEF Air Transportation Officer – with expanded duties. All air transport was now under his command with some elements of the US Eighth Air Force attached for operations. Maj. Gen Blackwell had the ability to move in any military circle. He provided the planes for the great ones to travel.

An eclectic stream of people consisting of the most influential Allied intelligence officers in England were making their way into one of the side rooms off the main dining area. Major General Sir Stewart Menzies, Chief of MI-6, Commander Ian Fleming and his new boss Rear Admiral Edmond Rushbrooke, Director of Naval Intelligence (DNI), Lieutenant Commander Thomas Argyll Robertson and his boss Major General Sir David Petrie,

Director General of MI-5, Lieutenant Colonel John Henry Bevan, Controlling Officer of LCS, Major General Francis Henry Davidson, Director of British Military Intelligence (DMI), Lieutenant General "Geronimo" Joe McKoy . . .

Gen. Eisenhower said, "Good heavens, Bronc, who is that general with all the hair? I have seen him here before."

It was not true, as was widely believed, that general officers in the United States Army are authorized to design their own uniforms. Or, as in this case, ignore military grooming regulations. There were simply not many people high enough in rank to order one of them not to. Certainly not lieutenant generals.

Maj. Gen. Blackwell said, "That's Geronimo Joe McKoy. Medal of Honor recipient – Blackjack Pershing's aide during the Punitive Expedition. He was standing next to Patton when they shot those Mexican bandits off their horses. Photos of the dead Villastias strapped on the fenders of Georgie's Model A Ford were in all the papers.

"Made Old Blood and Guts famous."

Gen. Eisenhower said, "He needs to get a haircut."

Maj. Gen. Blackwell said, "I'd tread lightly, General – word is Joe's the President's Special Envoy for Irregular Warfare."

Gen. Eisenhower said, "Any idea what is taking place over there?"

"Lady Jane's planned a surprise promotion party for General Donovan," Maj. Gen. Blackwell said. "I'm going to need to excuse myself and head on over – my smoking hot date just walked in."

"Do you believe it would be all right if I came with you? Like to see Bill get his second star. He's a good man."

Maj. Gen. Blackwell said, "Sure, maybe we can twist Lady Jane's arm a little. Get her to find you a suite here at the hotel. She's the hostess . . . owns the place."

Gen. Eisenhower laughed. "So I understand. Appears to be a couple of junior captains staying here and the Supreme Allied Commander can't get a room. What is wrong with that picture?"

"Pays to be one of Lady Jane's 'lads.'"

BRANDY SEABORN SLIPPED THE DOCK AND SET TO SEA AT 0130hrs en route to the Vieux Mole lighthouse. It was a dark and stormy night without there actually being a storm. Typical English Channel weather. On occasion the water was so choppy even veteran Royal Navy sailors suffered from seasickness. Not the case tonight, but the crossing was no pleasure cruise.

Colonel John Randal's SOG team – actually it was Jack Cool's team with him in command – was going against a point-type target. Their specialty. Because of the configuration of the mole and the small amount of square footage in old 19th-century searchlight towers – typically two stories with storage on the ground level and sleeping quarters on the second floor, there were not many enemy personnel expected to be on the objective. But that was not known for sure.

The beautiful thing about this raid was if the Germans on shore realized it was taking place the only way to reach the breakwater was by boat or to counterattack straight down the mole. It would take time to organize boats. Lieutenant Chase Starrett's blocking force would make attacking down the mole suicidal – the Nazis would be channelized with no way to deploy. Exposed in the open with no cover caught in his killing zone – the dream scenario for an ambush team.

There was another thing that made the lighthouse an attractive target. It was going to be easy for Captain Penelope "Legs" Honeycutt-Parker to pinpoint. The light was operational. She could see it from the PT boat shortly after heading out into the Channel. In good conditions the beam was visible up to thirty miles away.

Lieutenant General "Geronimo" Joe McKoy, Captain Billy Jack Jaxx, Captain Richard "Dynamite Dick" Coogan, Lieutenant Ricky Mascuch and Captain Jake "The Snake" Novak huddled around Col. Randal on the deck. They were watching the searchlight in the far distance on the enemy shore.

Col. Randal said, "Capt. Coogan, did you to talk to the Headhunter about OPERATION TOMCAT?"

Capt. Coogan said, "Roger, sir, he said when the lighthouse blew, it was pretty spectacular. Claimed no one knew it would go up like that. Told me you took out another one off Crete that ran it a close second."

Col. Randal said, "You make sure we're away and gone before this one goes up."

Capt. Coogan, a cigar-chomping explosives expert, always had the stub of a blunt in his jaw. His father owned a demolitions company in Atlanta, Georgia. He had grown up taking down buildings. Thus the nickname "Dynamite Dick."

"No problem, Colonel," Capt. Coogan said. "I checked into French-built lighthouses. Acetylene is the preferred fuel source. It's believed to produce a superior beam for penetrating fog for some reason. Most have six pressurized tanks containing 850 cubic feet each. Acetylene is highly explosive and flammable when contained.

"Not only that, sir, it's an unstable gas. Decomposes rapidly if subjected to an explosive initiator. Acetylene is characteristic for producing a big flash-bang detonation. I understand the magnitude of the fireball during TOMCAT caught you off guard."

Col. Randal said, "That would be an understatement."

Capt. Coogan said, "Tonight I'll use a pair of explosives starting with a thirty-minute delay, sir. The first charge will blow the seals on the containers. The acetylene will escape, fill up the lighthouse, and the second charge will ignite the gas. No shrapnel effect but it'll be like the tower is Mount Vesuvius erupting. If the idea's to make a statement the Germans will definitely know we came calling."

Col. Randal said, "Works for me."

As the PT boat closed in on the target, the sweeping beam of the Vieux Mole lighthouse grew from a speck into a full-blown shaft of white light rotating back and forth hypnotically. If the Ranger SOG team, as the men were calling themselves now, were not standing by to land and blow the place up it would have been a beautiful sight. Going in on a sleek PT boat, watching your objective grow larger and larger as you approached was not, in Raiding Forces'-speak, "For the weak or faint of heart."

Col. Randal could not help reflecting on the experience of that long-ago OPERATION TOMCAT mission. The Ranger SOG team tonight consisted of the most professional small-scale raiders Allied Forces had to offer. By comparison, the Commandos on that early raid were rank amateurs. His war had come full circle.

As the PT boat made its approach, studying the target up ahead it almost felt like he was waking up from a dream – Rip Van Winkle. Only in this case, nothing had changed except now his team consisted of experienced combat veterans and he had a hard edge.

There was one other difference. He now found himself a recognized special operations expert – how did that happen? It was a surreal feeling. Col. Randal did not plan on telling anyone about the feeling. He glanced at his Rolex and, as usual, wondered what Lady Jane was doing right this minute. Chances were he would tell her – maybe.

The PT boat came to a full stop. They were a mile offshore with the beam of the lighthouse slowly sweeping back and forth over their head. It did not illuminate the boat. That did not seem right. You would think they would be exposed.

Two Goatley dories were put over the side. Each was capable of transporting ten men. The second boat was for redundancy – a very important aspect of mission planning for a raid. A rubber raft for Lt. Starrett's team was also prepared. As soon as it was in the water he and his men climbed aboard and on the command "Give Way Together" they started rowing in sync with the two LBSM. They would go in first and take out the Flak 30 anti-aircraft gun mounted on the mole about twenty-five yards from the lighthouse. Flak stood for Fliegerabwehrakanone – "Aeroplane Defense Cannon."

It was critical for the 20mm fast-firing gun and its four-man crew to be eliminated quickly. If the automatic cannon was turned on the main party, the raid would be over before it was started. Lt. Starrett was an aggressive small-unit leader who was working his way into Col. Randal's circle of trust. He had not been chosen at random for the assignment – "Right Man, Right Job."

Giving the rubber assault raft a five-minute head start, the LBSM in the Goatley dories started for shore. The Goatley was an interesting design, perfect for Commando work. It was double-ended, meaning it could be paddled in either direction. To go the other way all the LBSM had to do was turn around and paddle. A useful feature when extracting from a raid. There was no need to take the time to bring the dory about. A much appreciated time saver by all parties on board when executing the all-important "Getting the hell out of Dodge" phase of an operation.

A mile seems like a long way over water. The LBSM covered the distance in short order. During the approach the Rangers studied the target like a pack of starving hyenas. They were predators. Switched on. "Ready to rock."

The water was choppy. A great deal of seamanship was required to bring the dories alongside the stone mole without being overturned or smashed into matchsticks. The LBSM were more than equal to the task.

Lt. Mascuch was out first with the security people. He and his team set up a small perimeter. Initially a threat could come from either direction.

Capt. Jaxx went next, hoisting himself onto the concrete walkway. He was followed by Col. Randal and King, then Lt. Gen. McKoy, the Lovat Scouts and two SOG Rangers. When Capt. Jaxx moved off toward the lighthouse they shook out into a tight column formation as briefed. The men had their suppressed 9mm M3 Grease Guns at their shoulders, ready to engage. The only problem was that during the movement to contact the narrowness of the mole only allowed for the two Lovat Scouts, who made up the point element, to bring fire in the event the team was spotted by the Germans.

As advertised, the footing on the mole was slippery. Waves were breaking over it, and this was when there was no storm. In rough weather conditions it would have been impassable. The men's rubber-soled raiding boots gave good purchase on the wet stone but they moved warily in a modified semi-airborne shuffle.

Lt. Starrett and his team had only just arrived even though they had a head start. He rolled up on the mole about ten yards from the Flak 30. His three Rangers were right behind him. The original plan was to low crawl up to the 20mm gun for maximum stealth and surprise. Raids rarely go according to plan.

The lieutenant was faced with a command decision. Stick to low crawling, which would require more time, or move in and assault with M3s blazing? It was imperative the 20mm automatic cannon not be allowed to fire on Col. Randal's party. He was behind schedule. Time was of the essence.

Lt. Starrett whispered, "Let's go, boys – fire 'em up."

Unruffled, the Rangers shifted into the change of plan and within a second they were on their feet moving toward the target. The footing was treacherous. They moved methodically, suppressed 9mm M3s to their shoulders looking out over the sights, both eyes open. Slow is smooth. Smooth is fast.

The Germans manning the Flak 30 were not all asleep. The gun crew was on a 25 percent alert. There were four men. One was supposed to be awake at all times while the other three slept. They rotated the duty after an hour.

Being awake does not mean being vigilant. There are few things more boring for a soldier than to be a long way from home on guard duty, standing a post where nothing ever happens. Until last week there had not been a Commando raid in this part of France for nearly two years. And reports of those recent attacks had been nowhere near the Vieux Mole.

A guard was on duty. He was lying flat on his back staring up into the sky daydreaming about his girlfriend. Lt. Starrett's Rangers were on him before he could give warning to his sleeping crewmates. By the time he noticed them, the suppressed 9mm M3s were already hissing.

SSSSS,SSSSS,SSSSS . . .

There was a mad scramble by the now-alerted remaining three Germans to grab their individual weapons. No chance. The Nazis were down – shot dead before fully awake.

Lt. Starrett had the 20mm Flak 30 wheeled around and pointed down the mole in the direction of the shore. One Ranger manned it. The rest stood by to repel boarders. Mission accomplished – so far.

The Lovat Scouts on point, closely followed by Capt. Jaxx, were moving toward the lighthouse. Behind Jack Cool the order of march was Private First Class Norvel "Horn Dog" Hansen, then King, Col. Randal and Lt. Gen. McKoy, with Capt. Coogan and Capt. Novak bringing up the rear. Small waves were splashing over their raiding boots making a rhythmic soothing sound.

When the Lovat Scouts, followed by Capt. Jaxx and PFC Hansen made entry they would break right and start to clear the ground floor. King would break left and proceed up the stairs to the second floor followed by Col. Randal and Lt. Gen. McKoy. The other men in the team would flow in – initially to back up Capt. Jaxx and then to be on call to move to the second floor in the event the situation required their support.

Once the tower was secured a search of the premises would commence.

Capt. Coogan would start placing his charges as soon as he got the all-clear. Capt. Novak would stand by the door to the lighthouse to either reinforce the two assaulting parties as needed or take charge of prisoners should any be captured. Considering the close quarters, action on that last was unlikely.

Upon reaching the lighthouse tower Capt. Jaxx resumed the lead. When he turned the doorknob it was unlocked. He opened it, stepped inside with PFC Hansen so close behind he was pressing up against him and nearly bumped into a wide-awake German soldier.

SSSSS

Stacked behind him, PFC Hansen shoved his way past ready to do battle. King brushed by and moved up the spiral staircase that ran up against the inside wall of the tower with Col. Randal and Lt. Gen. McKoy right behind. There were no lights on. However, the 18-foot, eight-sided glass lantern on the roof that housed the light traversing slowly back and forth caused a bluish glow to filter into the windows as it slowly swept the horizon.

It is often said in military circles, "No plan survives the first contact with the enemy." That is not always true. Sometimes they do. However, the ability to improvise and adapt on the fly with no let-up in intensity or purpose of mission is what sets special forces operators apart from run-of-the-mill line infantry combat soldiers.

It was anticipated – "hope" being a banned word in Raiding Forces – that the Germans manning the lighthouse would be asleep. They may have been. But by the time King and Col. Randal arrived in the sleeping quarters on the second floor the Nazis were awake, armed and ready to fight.

A blazing close-quarters gun battle immediately broke out at virtual contact range. The Germans were armed with Karabiner 98 bolt-action 7.92 rifles. King, Col. Randal and Lt. Gen. ' were armed with suppressed 9mm M3 submachine guns. A wild shootout ensued with the heavy caliber 7.92 K98s booming like thunder in the enclosed space and the 9mm M3s hissing like angry snakes. In the constricted space the 9mm M3 Grease Guns spit out tracers that barely had time to flash before being swallowed up.

It being dark, the initial impression was there must have been a full enemy platoon barracked in the room. In fact, there were only six Germans. They never had a chance. Raiding Forces trained for situations like this. And Col. Randal, Lt. Gen. McKoy and King were among the best snap shooters in the unit.

The trick was to stand to your weapon, fire short, crisp bursts and call your shots – which sounds easier than it is when a dangerous encounter breaks out in your face. All the team could see in the dark to fire at were muzzle flashes.

As for the Germans, firing their weapons was a death sentence. Close-quarters engagements – when one side is the quality of Raiding Forces' operators and the other side consists of rear-echelon occupation troops caught off guard – are over fast . . . usually in seconds.

As soon as the K98s ceased thundering, Col. Randal, Lt. Gen. McKoy and King retreated a short distance down the staircase. The Merc then tossed a No. 69 concussion grenade into the second-story room.

WHUUUUUPH! The explosion in the small contained space rocked the upper floor.

As soon as the grenade detonated they rushed back upstairs, slinging the M3s, drawing their sidearms and producing red-filtered hook-nosed flashlights as they went. All six of the Germans were down – most shot in the face by a tight pattern. The Nazis must have had their rifles to their shoulders when a swarm of 9mm rounds came back aimed at the muzzle flash.

There were not going to be any prisoners taken at the lighthouse tonight. Resistance put a stop to that. While Lt. Gen. McKoy, King and the Rangers conducted a search Col. Randal went back downstairs to talk to Capt. Novak. He was standing by the door outside on the mole.

Col. Randal was concerned about the noise made while securing the second floor.

"Think we alerted the Germans on shore?"

"Negative, sir. Pretty muffled out here. Not much louder than some of the wind gusts blowing in off the Channel."

"Go help General McKoy search the upper floor."

"Roger that, sir – prisoners?"

"Negative."

Col. Randal walked down the mole to check on Lt. Starrett. When he came past the IRP/ERP Lt. Mascuch said, "How did it go in there, sir?"

"We're good. Contact Brandy, inform her we'll be pulling out in zero five."

When he reached the Flak 30 position, Lt. Starrett was waiting. "No sign of any enemy activity on shore as far as I can tell, sir."

"Good."

"Afraid my people were a little hyped up, Colonel. Four bad guys .. KIA."

"Nice job, Lieutenant. Give my compliments to your Rangers. We'll be pulling out as soon as I walk back to the lighthouse. Stand ready for the signal to withdraw."

"Can do, sir."

"Don't forget to leave that canteen cover behind when you pull out."

"Yes, sir."

When he arrived back at the lighthouse, Capt. Coogan was standing outside chomping on the stub of his unlit cigar. "Demo is up. Good to go. On your command, sir."

Col. Randal ordered, "Stand by."

He went inside. Capt. Jaxx was still searching, "We didn't find much, Colonel. There's an SOI – signals operating instructions."

Col. Randal said, "Good enough – time to go."

Capt. Jaxx shouted, "Rally – break contact!"

He stood by the door and counted everyone out. Never hurt to be completely sure. "Good count, sir."

Col. Randal said, "Shove off, Captain. As soon as you reach the ERP signal Lieutenant Starrett to pull out. Have your people board the Goatleys – we'll be right behind you."

"Roger that, sir."

Col. Randal ordered, "Make it happen, Captain Coogan."

"Fire in the hole." Normally the warning is shouted three times, each one in a different direction to make sure everyone understands explosives are about to be set off. Not on Commando raids when the idea is to get away without alerting nearby enemy troops they were there. The practice, being an ingrained habit from childhood working with his father, Dynamite Dick said it under his breath.

When Capt. Jaxx reached the ERP he flashed his red-lensed light three times in the direction of the Flak 30 position. Two red flashes came back – Lt. Starrett confirming he was withdrawing. Last thing before departing he pulled the ring lighter on the fuse initiator attached to a block of Composition C-3 on the anti-aircraft gun.

Then the Rangers climbed off the mole into their waiting raft. The LBSM held it steady as the men clambered aboard. Then set out to break the world speed record for a one-mile row back to the PT boat – they were trying to make it in under twenty minutes. That was the kind of small boat handlers the LBSM were. Always competing against themselves. One of the many things that made them such valuable assets for Raiding Forces.

Col. Randal and Capt. Coogan arrived at the ERP. All was quiet on shore. There was no reaction from the German occupiers.

Col. Randal took one last look around before boarding – all was quiet.

The two dories raced each other to the PT boat. A *BOOOOOM* came rolling across the water from the mole as the charge on the flak gun detonated. No more stealth. The troops were on board and the Goatleys recovered when the lighthouse went up.

The explosion was spectacular.

First there was a brilliant flash – blinding. Then a monster-sized orange fireball leapt three hundred feet in the air – maybe more, forming a towering mushroom-shaped cloud. The lighthouse's two-story tower, illuminated by the fireball, seemed to come apart brick by brick all at once like in a cartoon, vaporized as if the Great Teddy had waved his magic wand, "Hey, Presto!" That was followed by a massive *BOOOOOM!* rolling across the water that made the charge on the 20mm automatic cannon sound like a firecracker.

The Vieux Mole Lighthouse was no longer there.

The Rangers and the sailors on the PT boat started cheering. It was fantastic. Not quite the life-altering experience as when the lighthouse Captain "Pyro" Percy Stirling blew during TOMCAT went up. That explosion, because of their close proximity to it, had seemed like the end of the world. As if the fabric of the universe had been ripped in half. Still, this was impressive.

Brandy said, "How close were you to the lighthouse Percy blew?"

Col. Randal said, "A hundred yards, maybe a little more."

Brandy laughed. "Must have been quite the experience – Randy says it was."

Col. Randal said, "You have no idea."

Then the shockwave rolled across the PT boat. Rocking it. No one was cheering now, awestruck.

Had they done that?

Col. Randal said, "Let's get the hell out of Dodge."

7

SNAKES

COLONEL JOHN RANDAL AND BEVERLY BLACKWELL WERE sitting in the VIP section in the lobby of the Bradford Hotel. Beverly had been traveling to 58 St. James Street to begin her indoctrination into the mysteries of counterintelligence. Because she would be a part-time case officer handling Rikke Runborg, the OSS S2 Counterespionage Officer assigned to Raiding Forces and now the designated OSS liaison to the Double Cross Committee, a certain amount of training was necessary to bring her up to speed on how the British conducted counterintelligence. Every morning at 0800 hrs one of the hotel limousines would drop Beverly off at MI-5 and then return to pick her up at 1200 hrs unless she and Lieutenant Colonel Thomas Argyll Robertson – who she called Tommy, decided to have lunch.

Beverly was enjoying her training, which unknown to her, was heavily redacted compared to Mandy's. Lt. Col. Robertson was personally handling her introduction into the Top SECRET/MOST SECRET art of spy catching and incidental dissemination of false and misleading information to the Germans through the use of notional and turned German agents. Certain material was being left out of her training syllabus because she was undergoing a sort of internship. Her suitability for the assignment was yet to be determined. And there was the fact Beverly was an American. MI-5 was a clannish organization. It had staked out a claim to all things counterintelligence – specifically deception-related – for the entirety of Allied Forces. The Security Service did not want the US OSS Counterespionage Branch encroaching on its private preserve. Not that there was any chance of that. OSS had never staffed X-2.

Nevertheless, Lt. Col. Robertson had every intention of using Beverly for as much B1-A business as possible. He took great pains with her lessons. While he planned to have minimal contact with OSS London Station the idea of a direct line to Major General William "Wild Bill" Donovan offered possibilities he had never imagined.

Unknown to him, Beverly went straight back to the Bradford and told Col. Randal everything she had learned that day. In violation of every principle of security. But it was what she did.

Need to Know or not.

Lady Jane, a highly trained intelligence officer in her own right, thought Beverly briefing Col. Randal on her MI-5 activity was priceless. However, she felt it advisable to have a quiet word with her. "If you are going to brief John on your activities, you cannot tell anyone – ever – not a soul. Keep it a secret strictly between the two of you."

Lady Jane smiled every time she thought about it – one had to love Beverly.

Beverly said, "Do you know the difference between counterintelligence and counterespionage?"

Col. Randal said, "Negative – I don't."

"Counterintelligence, called CI, is like playing defense," Beverly said. "Counterespionage, CE, is offense."

"Really – how's that work?"

"Counterintelligence focuses on preventing enemy intelligence gathering, sabotage and assassinations inside the country. Basically it's spy catching in your home base. Reacting to a threat.

"Counterespionage detects, neutralizes and exploits enemy espionage activities through penetration, manipulation and deception by the use of double agents," Beverly said. "The way it works is captured enemy spies are turned and used to send back false reports our side writes to their handlers in Germany."

Col. Randal said, “You picked up all that today?”

“I did.”

“You’re a quick study, Beverly. Must have come in handy at UT. All those classes you squeezed in between your Tri-Delta sorority social life and beauty queen pageants.”

Beverly laughed. “I was an art and drama major. Slept with my professors. Made straight As.”

Col. Randal said, “Don’t tell anybody that – they might believe you’re serious.”

Beverly said, “Do you know what chickenfeed. . . .”

WHILE MANDY DATED AROUND, BEVERLY NEVER WENT OUT. Except with Captain Billy Jack Jaxx and they were just friends. She had known him in college.

There were drawbacks to being one of the University of Texas’ Ten Most. Going out with cowboys in South Texas or football players and fraternity men at UT nearly always turned into “hand-to-hand combat.” Soldiers were worse. Beverly was on a self-imposed stand-down from dating. Which did not mean automatic rejection if the right person presented himself – Lieutenant Chase Starrett for example, maybe.

That was classified.

COLONEL JOHN RANDAL ARRIVED AT SEABORN HOUSE WITH Major the Lady Jane Seaborn, Captain Billy Jack Jaxx and King. Lieutenant General “Geronimo” Joe McKoy was already there having traveled earlier to set up the suppressed United States Submachine gun, caliber 9mm M3s that would be issued to all hands on the night’s operation. Typically as issued the M3, aka “Grease Gun,” was .45 caliber. SOE had ordered 9mm conversion kits from the Guide Lamp Division of General Motors – the submachine gun’s manufacturer. The High Standard Manufacturing Company – the same organization that made the .22 Military Model D pistol Col. Randal favored – built the M3’s suppressors.

Col. Randal elected to go with the OSS issue 9mm configuration for Raiding Forces. The lighter caliber made the already extremely controllable M3 Grease Gun even more controllable. An operator could carry a third more 9mm ammunition than .45 – an important feature for small-scale raiding. And when operating behind enemy lines, ammunition was readily accessible – you only had to kill or capture a German soldier to obtain a resupply. The 9mm variant with the suppressor was quiet – not unlike a snake hissing.

There were some who would argue .45 caliber would have been the better choice. It fired a heavier bullet. And in their minds, more importantly, it was subsonic. Meaning it did not break the sound barrier. Unlike with a 9mm round which does – there is no signature "*Craaack.*"

Col. Randal was not swayed by that argument. The crack is only audible when a round travels past. The sound is heard *behind* the intended target making a sharp ringing snap not unlike what you would hear if a firecracker went off an inch or so behind your ear. It is a telltale sign to those who have been shot at and missed – those who have not been do not even know it exists. Over the distances Raiding Forces operated – typically night at virtual contact range, there should not be very many rounds going past whoever it was they were firing at. As far as knockdown power is concerned, a burst of fully automatic 9mm center of mass works perfectly fine. And since 9mm rounds provide superior penetration they might even possibly be better.

The target for tonight's raid was a 60-centimeter German searchlight position in the vicinity of Saint-Valery-en-Caux. The mission was about as complicated as a small-scale operation could be – cross the Channel, scale a 150-foot chalk cliff, attack a target at the top, capture a prisoner, collect anything of intelligence value, exfil down the cliff and return home. Col. Randal had the distinct impression the assignment was designed to fail. Not as in getting men killed or captured. Most likely the idea was the mission was impossible within the time parameters Raiding Forces operated. Therefore, it would not be attempted.

That translated into failure – why?

For starters the German searchlight was located at the top of a chalk cliff. Given the unstable nature of chalk experienced climbers are reluctant to go near the stuff because it can collapse without warning. There was no way to go around the precipice because the escarpment ran the entire length of the only beach within range of the objective. A ten-man raiding party complete with arms and equipment would have to land ashore, scale the vertical incline, attack the target, search it, return to the beach, row back to the PT boat and make it home before sunrise. Not a realistic concept of the operation in the time allotted, even if the team managed not to get caught in a landslide.

Brandy Seaborn and Captain Penelope Honeycutt-Parker were at Seaborn House, preparing one of the PT boats for the night's mission. Since there were no organic weapons on board – the Russians had been expected to supply their own deck guns – it was believed the boat would be a few knots faster than the normal PT, in the range of forty-two knots, or slightly over fifty miles per hour. The intention was to operate under cover of darkness so there was no need for an anti-aircraft capability. Still, it was not likely Brandy would leave the PTs unable to defend themselves from enemy aircraft for long. She was a great believer in shooting back.

Col. Randal huddled with Capt. Jaxx and Lieutenant Chase Starrett. He had decided to employ SOG for the assignment. It was his most qualified unit for difficult missions like this one. They had just flown in from the Aegean along with the highly trained OSS Special Warfare Operators. The Frogs would not participate in this operation.

Col. Randal showed his two officers a topographical map of the objective. There was dead silence as they studied it. Both young officers had a history of being given tough assignments. This one was more than simply hard – it was complex. A lot of things could go wrong. If any did the team would be stranded in enemy-occupied France.

Col. Randal said, "I'll go over the Concept of the Operation in detail when I give the Operations Order in about thirty minutes. Here's what you need to be thinking about. Actions on the Objective – Captain Jaxx, you will select and lead a team of three men and attack the searchlight located on the objective. Lieutenant Starrett, you will lead a team of three men to clear and secure the area immediately around the target. I will initially travel with you, Jack. Horn Dog's my Number Two. King and one man will be carrying ropes to rig a rappelling line down the cliff to speed up our exfil.

"What are your questions?"

Capt. Jaxx said, "Does whoever dreamed this one up realize what he's asking us to do, sir?"

Col. Randal said, "Wasn't me."

Major General Sam Houston Blackwell and James "Baldie" Taylor flew to Seaborn House in a Piper L-4. Bronc landed on the long drive outside the country house. He dropped off Jim and his Troop Transport Command G-2 Intelligence Officer then immediately took off again.

Jim had learned about the mission in his role as LCS liaison officer to Raiding Forces or maybe in his role as MI-5's liaison officer to LCS – how that was supposed to work was still not exactly clear. Without being asked or informing anyone he immediately sprang into action attempting to locate information on the Raiding Forces' objective. No joy. No aerial photos were to be had. Not a shred of intelligence about the enemy forces in the area was available. All he had to offer Col. Randal was general background material describing the quality of the German Army guarding the Atlantic Wall. Most of which he already knew.

Maj. Gen. Blackwell's G-2, Lieutenant Colonel Mark Westinghouse, was on orders from Bronc to brief German searchlight tactics. All he could provide was a general description of how the German Army deployed searchlights as part of their coastal air defense system. Lt. Col. Westinghouse had contacted his counterpart, the United States Strategic Air Forces Europe (USAFE) G-2, but he had no specific details relating to the Wehrmacht or Luftwaffe air defense units in Raiding Forces' target area.

Col. Randal was in conversation with King when the two walked in the TOC.

The Merc said, "Affirmative – can do, Chief."

When King walked away, Jim said, "Colonel Randal, this is Colonel Westinghouse – General Blackwell's G-2. We are here to provide what limited intelligence there is on your objective."

Col. Randal said, "Let's do it then, gentlemen. I'm pressed for time. About to issue my Operations Order."

Jim said, "There are currently two German Armies in France – the 7th in Normandy and the 15th in the Pas-de-Calais region where your target is located. Fighting the US/UK on one front, meaning Africa and Italy, and the Russians on another has all but exhausted German manpower reservoirs.

"The Wehrmacht has been forced to raise units from the countries it has overrun – Dutch, Belgians, Norwegians, Frenchmen, Czechs, Danes, Hungarians, Austrians . . . whatever. There's even a small number of English turncoats in what is styled as the British Free Corps – Waffen SS. German Divisions in France guarding the Atlantic Wall have had their rosters combed and combed again for replacements to send to the Russian front.

"Those troops sent East have been replaced with men rated as less fit for combat – one entire division is made up of men with stomach problems because it is easier to treat them all in one unit. Divisions from France transferred to the Russian Front were replaced with new formations that are often a polyglot mixture of fit, unfit, experienced and green troops.

"The Nazis have even been reduced to recruiting Russians from POW camps who 'volunteer' to serve. These are formed into 'Ost' battalions, originally intended to fight exclusively in the East but some are now in France as well. The Russian battalions are the lowest grade units in the Wehrmacht – considered essentially armed but worthless."

Col. Randal was growing impatient, but he knew Jim was trying to make a point.

"The racial purity of the German Army the Nazis like to brag about so much has been badly diluted. As has the fighting quality of many of its front-line divisions. Morale is a problem, command and control is challenging, officers and NCOs have a difficult time communicating with their troops due to language barriers. What this means is you are not going up against the Afrika Korps at its best, Colonel."

Col. Randal said, "Good to know."

Jim said, "That said, even the Russians in the 7th and 15th Armies can be dangerous when put in a position where they have to defend themselves. Then they will fight to the death. For the record the Geneva Convention does not apply to traitors like them."

Col. Randal said, "Roger."

"Air Intelligence indicates a substantial number of Russian volunteers are being used to man searchlights," Lt. Col. Westinghouse said. "We do not know if that will be the case on your objective – be advised.

"German tactical deployment of searchlight batteries calls for clusters of three lights spread out in a checkerboard pattern a mile and a half apart.

Batteries are layered in-depth dropping back from the coastline toward the interior."

Col. Randal said, "What's the spacing of the individual searchlights?"

Lt. Col. Westinghouse said, "Fairly close, a hundred yards or so . . . there doesn't seem to be an exact standard. The Nazis don't have the manpower to defend every square inch of the coastline from Norway to the Mediterranean. They don't even have the people to provide individual security for each searchlight's position. There's tens of thousands of them on the Continent. Seems like hundreds of thousands or maybe millions when you're overhead in an aircraft at night.

"We believe you will be going up against the smaller 60-centimeter model – eight-hundred million to a billion candle power with a range of three to four miles, depending on weather conditions. The generators are powered by six-cylinder BMW automobile engines. Each light has a crew of three . . . light operator, generator operator and team leader/spotter – like I said, no organic security detail.

"Air Intelligence rates German searchlight performance as poor. Due in no small part to nonuniform equipment much of it captured from countries the Nazis overran, a mixture of troop nationalities, personnel shortages, inadequate training, low morale, etc.

"Hope some of this is useful – it's all I have for you, Colonel."

Col. Randal said, "Appreciate your input."

And it was helpful. Based on Lt. Col. Westinghouse's intelligence, he was going to have to rethink his planned Actions on the Objective. Maj. Gen. Blackwell making the effort to fly his G-2 to Seaborn House was a last-minute game changer.

Jim said, "What I want to know, Colonel, is how you intend to scale a dangerous cliff face in the dark without waking the nesting seagulls? The sound of all those birds screaming will surely alert the Germans, Russians or whoever they are at the top."

Col. Randal said, "Not a problem."

MAJOR THE LADY JANE SEABORN SAID, "YOU WISHED TO SEE me, John?"

Colonel John Randal said, "I need to take the SOG Ranger team personnel on a walkthrough of one of our anti-aircraft searchlight positions. Not the big ones. The 60-centimeter ones – is that possible?"

Lady Jane said, "Searchlight teams are scattered all along the coast. A number are located here on the estate. When would you like to do it?"

Col. Randal said, "Right now would be good."

Lady Jane placed a phone call to the local detachment of the Auxiliary Territorial Service (ATS) 93rd Searchlight Regiment. The first all-female searchlight regiment in the British Army – 1,500 women strong. In a few moments she reported back to Col. Randal.

"A Bedford is being brought around to truck the lads to one of the small searchlight positions here on the estate. Only a ten-minute drive. We shall lead the way in the hotel limousine."

Col. Randal said, "Outstanding!"

Lieutenant General "Geronimo" Joe McKoy had Captain Billy Jack Jaxx, Lieutenant Chase Starrett, King and the seven SOG Rangers out on the front lawn demonstrating the suppressed 9mm M3 Grease Gun. Not all of the operators had carried one on an operation. Each of the men fired a magazine of 9mm rounds into one of Lady Jane's flower beds to test-fire their weapon. The SMG was compact with a sliding wire stock, fully automatic only, with a low cyclic rate. Almost like squirting a water hose giving the shooter the impression he could write his name in bullet holes with it.

The SOG Rangers liked the suppressed 9mm M3 a lot.

When the Bedford pulled up they climbed aboard for their inspection tour. Capt. Jaxx's people were used to being called out on late-breaking, fast-developing operations. But this one was taking the term "hasty mission" to another level considering the operators had just arrived in a new AO, different than most of the unit's current members had ever served in before. No matter how you looked at it, the ten-man SOG Ranger team would be carrying out their own invasion of France – something to think about.

The spotlight team leader, ATS Corporal Bernice Woodbine showed them around her position. The light was mounted on a wheeled carriage. It did not escape notice there were no slit trenches dug. The women were expected to fight their light and not take cover. Aiming a spotlight at a

German intruder bristling with 7.92mm MG81, 13mm MG131 machine guns and or 20mm MG15 automatic cannons was best left to those with nerves of steel.

The ATS was living rough – in tents. They manned their lights at night and slept by day. And doing it for two-thirds the pay of their male counterparts.

Col. Randal made sure everyone in the assault team had the opportunity to learn how to traverse the light – a fairly simple process. Then, time being short, the SOG Rangers mounted back up in the Bedford and returned to Seaborn House. The brief walkthrough had been instructive. Now when they arrived on their objective everyone would know what to expect.

Little details count.

In the limousine on the ride back Lady Jane said, "I intend to make other billeting arrangements for the girls – at least those stationed on the estate. We have the space."

Col. Randal said, "I think that's a good idea."

Immediately upon arriving back at Seaborn House Col. Randal issued the Operations Order in a clipped staccato military manner. He broke down the key tasks step-by-step in simple, easy-to-understand bullet points. Short and simple, per Raiding Forces' Rules. The delivery was an impressive tour de force that left no questions in anyone's mind about what was going to take place and what was expected of each individual involved. All those present – SOG Rangers, TOC staff, support personnel, PT boat crew – were left feeling assured by the presentation. The Colonel knew what he was doing. That was clear.

Col. Randal said, "Concept of the Operation: German searchlight tactics call for the lights to be deployed in a cluster of three with approximately one hundred yards spacing between lights – a distance of a mile and a half between clusters. Which means we have to take down all three lights in the cluster where our target is located in order to ensure against a counterattack.

"The order of march to the objective will be King with the SCR-536 walkie-talkie and one Ranger, Captain Jaxx with two Rangers, I will be third with one, followed by Lieutenant Starrett with two Rangers.

"Actions on the Objective: Upon reaching the first searchlight position the lead team will immediately attack and eliminate the crew, keeping in mind a prisoner is part of our mission brief. Suppressed M3s or coshes only. Surprise, speed and violence of action.

"King's team will then peel off, move to the cliff to rig a line to the beach. He will send the radioman with the SCR 536 Walkie Talkie down to signal the PT boat to have the Life Boat Service Men come in for our extraction. And to coordinate with them when they arrive.

"My team will flow through Captain Jaxx's followed by Lieutenant Starrett with his team to advance on and take down the second spotlight.

"At that point our presence will likely have been compromised. With that in mind we will manually traverse the light on my objective and place its eight-hundred-million-to-one-billion candlepower beam directly on the third position. The result should blind, dazzle, and/or otherwise disorient the crew. Lieutenant Starrett's team will leapfrog my people, advance down the beam and attack out of the light.

"As soon as Lieutenant Starrett eliminates resistance on his objective, conducts a search and places demolitions on the light he will fall back to my location. We'll have conducted our search and placed our explosives. Both teams will then withdraw and consolidate with Captain Jaxx's team. From there we move to the extraction point where King will have rigged a rope, rappel down to the beach, board the dories and get the hell out of Dodge..."

Following the conclusion of the Operations Order, Col. Randal led the team outside and conducted rehearsals.

THE SPECIAL OPERATIONS GROUP RANGER TEAM WAS trucked to their departure airfield. Brandy Seaborn was already at sea in her PT boat. Major General Sam Houston Blackwell briefed the mission.

"As soon as Mrs. Seaborn signals she is three miles off the French Coast, two C-47 Dakota aircraft from the Troop Transport Command will take off from here. Their mission is to fly over the target area at an altitude of two-thousand feet then circle to draw the attention of the German searchlight batteries. The purpose of the exercise is to create a diversion.

"Fifteen minutes after the C-47s depart I'll take off in a third Dakota with you Rangers on board. We'll be flying in at wave top level to the Initial Point to avoid being picked up by radar. Upon reaching the enemy coastline I'll swoop up to five-hundred feet. The green light will come on and you men go. This is a flight of short duration. Things are going to happen fast. Be ready.

"Once we pass overhead the PT boat will close to within one mile of the beach from which you will be extracted following the successful conclusion of your mission.

"What are your questions?"

The SOG Ranger team consisted of all highly experienced Special Operations veterans. There were no questions. Gen. Blackwell had covered the relevant points. Most of what the troops might like the answer to was unknown – they knew that. Professionals do not ask questions it is clear the briefer has no answer for.

One of Maj. Gen. Blackwell's aides stuck his head in the door at the back of the room. "PT boat reports it's on station at this time, sir."

Maj. Gen. Blackwell said, "OK, boys, saddle up."

The SOG Rangers moved directly to their jump aircraft. While the troops chuted up in the dark beside the plane, Colonel John Randal huddled with Captain Billy Jack Jaxx and Lieutenant Chase Starrett. Lt. Gen. McKoy listened in.

Col. Randal said, "This mission sounds basic enough. It's not. I want the jumpers stacking the door – tight exit. If we land dispersed we won't be going home. If we give our presence away before the second searchlight is taken down the Germans will counterattack. Should the Nazis retake the top of the cliff as we're making our extraction they can place plunging fire on the team and the dories."

One of the props on the C-47 wheezed, turned over, then began running rough, sounding like a giant Harley Davidson motorcycle.

Col. Randal said, "Go in hard and fast. You two conduct the jumpmaster inspection of your individual teams. I need a word with Bronc."

The two Dakotas that would be carrying out the diversion roared down the airstrip and took off into the midnight sky. Col. Randal threw his X-type parachute over one shoulder, boarded the airplane and made his way to the cockpit. Maj. Gen. Blackwell was in the left seat running up the motors.

Col. Randal said, "Dispersion on the drop is my primary concern. We have to reassemble fast. It's OK with me if you put us out lower than 500 ft, sir."

Maj. Gen. Blackwell said, "Due to pilot error the 82nd made a training drop in North Africa at 250 ft. No one was killed. Lot of jump injuries."

Col. Randal said, "Yeah, well that might be a little low, General."

"How does 350 ft sound?"

"Works for me."

"You still want to drop as close to the searchlight as we can?"

Col. Randal said, "Affirmative – right on top of it."

The C-47 was taxiing before he got back to the rear of the plane. Lt. Gen. McKoy was sitting there chuted up with a suppressed M3 Grease Gun strapped to his chest where the reserve normally rode. He was not slated to be on the mission.

Once the plane was airborne, the general helped Col. Randal into his parachute while he conducted one last officer's call with Capt. Jaxx and Lt. Starrett. "Talk to your men. Everyone has to be on their A game. Each action has to be sharp and crisp. We'll be exiting the door at 350 ft – tell your teams it's out and down."

The SOG Rangers would not be jumping reserve parachutes tonight.

When they were sitting alone with the C-47 droning toward the drop zone, Lt. Gen. McKoy said, "It ain't a big show. And it sounds simple enough. But this might just be the most technically complex operation we've ever took on, John – we're playin' for all the marbles tonight."

Col. Randal said, "That is a fact."

"On the bright side at least we won't be havin' to count on pigeons for our ship-to-shore commo. One of the dumbest ideas I've heard of lately."

"Roger that."

Capt. Jaxx stood up and sang out, "C-47 rolling down the strip. Eleven Rangers on a one-way trip."

The men laughed, stamped their boots and Private First Class Norvel "Horn Dog" Hansen shouted "Hell yeah, AIRBORNE!"

The red light, indicating ten minutes out, came on almost immediately. Col. Randal struggled to his feet and shuffled over to the exit door. It was open. He looked out and saw the C-47 was skimming the waves per Maj. Gen. Blackwell's last minute briefing.

There was no time to waste.

"Stand up and hook up!"

Tonight the jump commands would be condensed. Everyone was going to exit the aircraft. There was not going to be time to correct any last-minute equipment deficiencies.

"Check static line!"

The rasping metal-on-metal sound of SOG running their snap links back and forth on the metal cable was strangely reassuring in the darkened troop compartment. In addition to the small jump light there was only a dim red light glowing in the troop compartment to protect their night vision. Night jumps were always an eerie experience no matter how many a paratrooper has made. Especially when factoring in the additional stress of getting ready for a low-level drop on the continent of enemy-occupied Europe. The idea seemed insane.

"Sound off for equipment check!"

Col. Randal realized he could have probably left that one off – if any jumper found anything there was no time to do anything about it.

Like a string of dominoes, "OK, OK, OK . . ." rippled from the last jumper to King, who would be following Col. Randal out.

"Close on the door."

Having been instructed to make this a tight exit and understanding the consequences of being dispersed on the DZ, the SOG Rangers surged forward. King had to brace himself to keep from being shoved into Col. Randal who was spread-eagled hanging outside the door making a totally useless safety check. It was muscle memory.

What was he thinking?

Tonight Col. Randal had elected for a DZ as close to the target as possible. Assembly was the big threat. If it took long the mission was doomed to failure.

The plane flashed over the PT boat. Maj. Gen. Blackwell was doing his own navigating tonight. Bronc nailed it. The boat was a reference point. He might have been showing off for his new girlfriend.

Col. Randal swung back inside and shouted, "Brace yourself."

The C-47 swooped straight up. The stick of paratroopers was fighting hard not to get thrown off their feet. Simultaneously with the plane starting to level off, the green light came on.

"Go!"

Then Col. Randal was out the door, feeling King's knees on his parachute pack. As far as he could see in all directions pencil-thin beams from what appeared to be hundreds of searchlights were pointing up into the night sky, teetering back and forth like they were on stilts – probing for targets. A number in the distance had formed a light pyramid locked on one of the diversionary aircraft. Fortunately, there was not as much anti-aircraft fire as might have been expected – it was sporadic.

WHAAAAAM! Col. Randal was down. Expecting a hard landing, it was a surprise to find himself having made one of his better PLFs. Automatically going with the momentum of the roll, he ended back up in a standing position hammering the quick release to drop his parachute. It would be reasonable to say adrenaline helped make that possible.

King was right there, as was PFC Hansen, Col. Randal's No. 2 tonight. Capt. Jaxx arrived with Horn Dog's running buddy and partner in crime, PFC James "Wildman" Terrell.

Col. Randal ordered, "Move out, King – let's go."

The Merc and his radioman dashed off toward the objective, which was only a short distance away on a small point on the edge of the cliff jutting out into the English Channel. Capt. Jaxx and PFC Terrell rushed past Col. Randal to take the lead as the rest of the team shook itself out into the correct order of march on the run. A few of the operators were banged up from the low-level drop but everyone was functioning at a high level of performance.

Maj. Gen. Blackwell's diversion plan was working to perfection. His C-47 Dakota had come and gone so fast the searchlight crew had no time to react when it roared up and over the escarpment at such low altitude. The Germans were fixated on one of the other planes caught in their beam. They never noticed the paratroopers exiting.

The low-level drop paid off. The team was down and assembled. On the move.

As Maj. Gen. Blackwell brought his plane around headed toward the Channel a burst of heavy caliber anti-aircraft machine gun fire tore through the right engine. Rounds penetrated the cockpit, killing the co-pilot instantly and blowing out part of the windscreen.

Then the wing caught on fire. C-47s are designed to fly with one motor. They cannot fly with one wing.

Bronc was going down.

Capt. Jaxx, King and PFC Terrell arrived at the target coming in from the rear at a dead run. The searchlight crew were all looking up for aerial intruders.

There was a stuttering sound not unlike a snake hissing, *SSSSSSSS, SSSSSSSS, SSSSSSSS* – the bolts of the suppressed M3s making a louder noise than the discharge of the 9mm rounds. All three enemy soldiers manning the searchlight were swept off their feet.

Col. Randal said, “Sorry Horn Dog. I couldn’t keep up the pace. Leg’s not a hundred percent.”

PFC Hansen said, “That’s OK, Colonel. We’ll get ours on the next one.”

The rest of the stick pounded up.

Col. Randal said, “Move out, Hansen, let’s roll.”

His team charged directly at the nearest spotlight along the cliff. It was searching the sky, the beam seeming to lean back and forth in slow motion as if it would topple over. The crew was not going to spot anything. The two diversionary aircraft were already winging their way home – mission accomplished.

Maj. Gen. Blackwell’s C-47 was headed back across the Channel on fire, losing altitude – then it splashed down.

Lt. Gen. McKoy, Col. Randal and PFC Hansen arrived at the second searchlight with their 9mm M3 Grease Guns to their shoulders. They went straight in. As before, the Germans were all looking up, focused on an empty sky searching for a target.

A short three-second burst of suppressed SMG fire, *SSSSS, SSSSS, SSSSS,* and the light’s generator operator, light operator and spotter were neutralized. It was fast. When they dropped, it was almost as if their heads hit the ground before their feet left it – one of those things that cannot be replicated in true action war movies.

Lt. Gen. McKoy jumped in the aimer’s chair. He manually cranked the light around and brought it down pointed toward the third target. It was positioned substantially less than the prescribed 100 yards away – more like fifty yards. The brilliant beam – pushing a million candle power, blasted into the position like a gigantic science fiction ray gun out of a comic book.

Lt. Starrett said, “I’ve got this, sir.”

His team flowed through going over to the attack, charging straight down the beam with the wire stocks of their suppressed 9mm M3 Grease Guns to their shoulders. At that point-blank range the scorching white light turned night into brighter than day on the third target. The three-man crew was caught like deer in the headlights.

Not only were the Germans blinded, they were disoriented. Only at the last second did they observe three vague silhouettes of the SOG Rangers arriving out of the beam. By then it was too late – the snakes were hissing, *SSSSS, SSSSS, SSSSS.*

While his men searched the position for anything of intelligence value Lt. Starrett slapped a prepared charge on the spotlight. With nothing of intelligence value recovered, he ordered, “Fall back” – then pulled the ring on the fuse lighter and set in motion a fifteen-minute delay.

As that was taking place, Lt. Gen. McKoy and Col. Randal searched their position. They did not find anything meaningful. PFC Hansen placed a charge on the spotlight. He stood by waiting for orders to initiate the standard issue U.S. Army pull-type M-1 fuse igniter.

Lt. Starrett and his men returned on the double. Col. Randal ordered, “Light it off, Hansen.”

Then the two teams commenced running back in the direction of Capt. Jaxx’s position. Upon arriving, Col. Randal was shown a strange-looking oversized pair of binoculars – possibly night glasses? They were of a type he had never seen before.

“Good job, Jack. Bring those when we pull out. You didn’t manage to take a prisoner?”

“No-go on prisoners – how about you, sir?”

“Negative.”

Col. Randal pitched a canvas first-aid pouch with “U.S.” stenciled on it on the ground per his standing orders to leave something behind that identified the raiding party. “Light it off, Captain.”

Capt. Jaxx pulled the ring on the fuse lighter. “Fire in the hole, Rally, move out boys – Go, Go, Go.”

The SOG operators raced toward the Rally Point. King was standing by on the edge of the cliff. He had driven a piton into the ground to secure the line down to the beach. Col. Randal sent Lt. Gen. McKoy over first to organize boarding the dories. A record may have been set for the time it took the team to rappel down to the beach. He and Capt. Jaxx were last.

Loading the dories went like clockwork.

As the LBSM were pulling for all they were worth rowing back to the PT boat, up on top of the escarpment, the demolitions on the three searchlights started cooking off like a string of dominoes. In the distance out in the Channel Bronc's C-47 was on fire. The flames could be seen reflecting off the water. The sight curbed the euphoria normally associated with the final stage of a successful mission – the heading for home part.

On the PT boat Brandy had spotted a burning C-47 flying toward her at extremely low altitude. The plane came directly overhead with the flames trailing from the right engine engulfing the wing. Then the Dakota went into the water.

Maj. Gen. Blackwell realized his aircraft was not going to make the short hop across the Channel. If the fire ate through the wing the plane would roll over and crash. So, getting down fast and ditching as close to the PT boat as possible was his best option for rescue.

Seeing the C-47 go in, Brandy ordered, "Carley float over the side! Double the boat team."

Normally two LBSM would man the Carley float – a raft. However, they were all committed to the extraction of Col. Randal's SOG Rangers. Four teenage sailors, ex-Sea Rover Scouts recruited back in the desperate dark days, leapt into the raft and started paddling like madmen. All hands were by now long-service veterans well-trained in small boat drill – just not as skilled as the LBSM.

By the time the Carley float arrived at the C-47, Maj. Gen. Blackwell and his crew chief were standing on the left, not burning, wing. The plane was taking its time about sinking, attesting to Bronc's ability as a pilot. With a less skillful landing it could have broken up on impact. Water landings are not something that can be practiced. Making one with the handicap of an engine out is no small accomplishment.

The two stepped off the wing into the raft, never getting their feet wet. They were back to the PT boat before the Goatley dories arrived. Brandy was waiting when Bronc came aboard.

"Are you all right, Sam?"

Maj. Gen. Blackwell said, "Yeah, we had an unfortunate operational conclusion."

Brandy laughed. "Looked like a crash to me?"

Maj. Gen. Blackwell said, "Got to be an easier way for us to have a late date."

In the distance, back onshore over the top of the escarpment searchlights were still tilting back and forth, sweeping the sky. German air defense efforts had picked up substantially. Light and medium caliber anti-aircraft machine guns blazed away, the tracers seeming to chase each other before curving off into the dark and then flickering out. Heavier caliber guns were booming.

The Germans were doing battle with phantom intruders. There were no Allied aircraft presently over this part of France. They had returned to base.

The Goatley dories pulled alongside the PT boat. The SOG Rangers scrambled aboard. When the operators could see Bronc and his crew chief had survived the water landing, the repressed post-mission euphoria kicked in hard. End of mission is a rare fine feeling.

When Col. Randal came on deck, Maj. Gen. Blackwell said, "How'd it go, Colonel?"

"We didn't accomplish one thing tonight, sir . . . let's get the hell out of Dodge."

Maj. Gen. Blackwell said, "I've always wanted to hear you say that – just never pictured it'd be this way."

8

CONFUSION TO THE ENEMY

MAJOR THE LADY JANE SEABORN ARRIVED AT WHITE'S WITH Happy on a short leash. Groom came to the door. Women were not allowed inside the premises. Not even the lobby. The sole exception being Major General Sir Stewart Menzies' granddaughter, Lady Mary Stewart. She delivered documents from his official MI-6 office at 54 Broadway to him at his club on a daily basis and was allowed to step inside during inclement weather. When she arrived "C" would come to the front since Lady Mary was required to physically place the highly classified material in his hands.

Groom said, "May I help you, Lady Seaborn?"

"I need to see my godfather, Colonel Bevan."

"He is in conference at the moment. Do you have a message? I shall deliver it the moment the colonel has concluded his business."

Groom did not mention Lieutenant Colonel John Henry Bevan was in with Maj. Gen. Menzies. When either officer was meeting with someone at the Club, he had strict orders they were never to be disturbed. And under no circumstances was he allowed to reveal to anyone who they were in conference with.

Lady Jane said, "Tell my godfather he needs to come to the door right now or I shall come inside and sic my dog on him."

Reacting to the change in her tone of voice, Happy went on alert.

Groom had a wealth of experience dealing with wealthy, famous, powerful, pampered men of high rank possessed of runaway egos and inflated senses of self-importance. Women not so much – Lady Seaborn was not to be denied, that much was obvious. He realized to his dismay one Club rule or another would have to be broken or at the very least bent.

"Allow me to inquire if the colonel can be disturbed."

"Inform him of what I said."

In minutes Lt. Col. Bevan arrived at the door having never known his goddaughter to behave like this. It was not done. And totally out of character for her. Eyeing Happy he chose not to step outside but spoke to her through a crack in the door. The hackles on the dog's neck were standing up.

Lady Jane was livid. "What could you have been thinking, Uncle? Were you trying to get John killed on a suicide mission? One of absolutely no importance whatsoever?"

The Chief of LCS wondered how his goddaughter was aware he was behind designing the raids. That was Need to Know. Lady Jane was not on the list.

Lt. Col. Bevan said, "Never anyone's intention for the colonel to *actually* carry out the operation, Jane. It was a test. LCS was simply trying to establish the parameters of what we can reasonably expect of Raiding Forces in the future.

"The unit is slated to be employed on highly sensitive classified assignments. It is vital to understand how to best utilize them. We need to know what Raiding Forces is capable of and more importantly what they are not."

Lady Jane said, "You clearly do not understand John Randal."

"No one anticipated him parachuting into France. Never crossed my mind. We intentionally gave him a mission he would have to decline," Lt. Col. Bevan said.

"I was mortified when notified of the development late last night."

Lady Jane said, "You are supposed to have my best interest at heart, Uncle. I expect you to be more responsible. And you need to be nicer to John."

"I shall, on my word. Does that dog bite?"

"He can – test those parameters."

Lt. Col. Bevan said, "Rather not."

MAJOR THE LADY JANE SEABORN WAS HAVING FUN. HER godfather, Lieutenant Colonel John Henry Bevan, had called to invite her to lunch. The stated purpose of the exercise was to solicit her help with a deception project, but he was also mending bridges. The United States Army was developing what the LCS called "notional" – and what OSS called "ghost" – units. The idea was to cause the Germans to believe the U.S. had far more troops in the pipeline en route to the UK to stage for the invasion than it could possibly raise. Lt. Col. Bevan provided her with a chart depicting fake unit patches developed by the U.S. Army's Heraldry Division for the imaginary outfits. Some were of a particularly blood-curdling design.

Lt. Col. Bevan said, "What I should like you to do, Jane, is create a unit insignia for the 575th Ranger Regiment for Colonel Randal to wear. And one for a Cavalry Corps for General McKoy. General Donovan tells me Geronimo Joe prefers a cavalry command.

"Then you need to have other individuals outfitted with notional unit insignia selected from the chart – and send them out into the city to be seen."

Lady Jane knew this was her godfather's way of trying to make amends. "Love to."

Lt. Col. Bevan said, "Accepting the assignment means you shall need to quit spending all your evenings here at the Bradford. You and the colonel must hit the town. Be seen in all the right places – for King and Country."

Lady Jane laughed. "Tough duty, Uncle. I shall do my best to rise to the occasion."

That evening she had a word with Major General Sam Houston Blackwell. "Beverly and I are about to be involved with a highly classified deception operation – a small project but vital. We could use your assistance, General."

Maj. Gen. Blackwell said, "Just ask. If it's in my power, consider it done."

Lady Jane said, "I need leather A-2 bomber jackets."

"What for?"

Lady Jane said, "USAAF bomber jackets have been authorized as optional wear in place of the Class A uniform blouse. Beverly and I shall be painting unit patches on them. I did something like that a few years ago for Raiding Forces."

Maj. Gen. Blackwell said, "Not a problem. I'll have my Four get in touch. How many jackets are we talking about?"

"Less than a dozen initially, more later – what exactly is a 'four?'"

Maj. Gen. Blackwell said, "G-4, my TTC supply officer. All USAAF aircrew wear Jackets, Flying, Type A-2 with their name tag, squadron insignia, pinup girls and other stuff painted on 'em – they call 'em 'Painted Ladies.' Where's the deception part come in?"

Lady Jane laughed. "The patches we shall paint are not for real military organizations. Incognito Raiding Forces' officers are soon to be spotted around London wearing A-2 bomber jackets with make-believe insignia on their chest."

Maj. Gen. Blackwell said, "And that makes sense – why?"

"Beverly and I shall be helping to deceive Hitler by creating an imaginary order-of-battle."

"I'm for that. Count me in, Lady Jane," Maj. Gen. Blackwell said. "You can put some of my USAAF people in uniforms wearing infantry branch insignia and your phony Painted Ladies – have 'em go bar hopping. If that helps."

Lady Jane said, "Perfect."

After serious deliberation, Lady Jane and Beverly set up easels in the lobby of the hotel. They chose a highly trafficked location instead of an out-of-the-way corner. The idea was to initiate the deception immediately. People passing through and stopping to watch them paint were informed the jackets were for officers belonging to the advance parties of units soon to be arriving from the States.

First they draped one of the A-2 bomber jackets over an easel to use as a reference. And so passersby could easily understand what they were doing – or said they were doing. Then the unit insignia was painted on a separate piece of leather cut in the shape of the patch. Once completed it was cut out and stitched on the jacket.

Colonel John Randal's seal brown leather Jacket, Flying, Type A-2 sported an oversized RANGER scroll consisting of "RANGER" in bold white letters on a black background outlined in red. It was modeled on the 1st Ranger Battalion's shoulder patch. Only the forked end of the banner on the left side said "575th" and on the right, "RGT." A pair of silver U.S. Army Parachute Wings was pinned under it.

Lady Jane had to admit it looked "pretty macho."

There was no such unit as the 575th Ranger Regiment, but the Germans would have no way to know that. They were about to be informed by a reliable source there *was* a Ranger Regiment and that elements of it had already arrived in England.

Rikke Runborg would be sending a message composed by LCS for MI-5's B1-A to transmit to Field Marshal Erwin Rommel to that effect. She would explain Raiding Forces was attached to the 575th Ranger Regiment. And that the combined unit was to fall under the personal command of Col. Randal. The Rangers' mission was to perform strategic reconnaissance for SHAEF prior to the upcoming invasion.

As Beverly explained to Col. Randal, "We make the Germans work for it but we don't want them to have to think too hard…so we eventually disclose what conclusion to draw."

In Normandy the Desert Fox would not have to guess at what the sudden increase in raids on the Pas-de-Calais portion of the French Coast meant – Rikke Runborg was going to tell him. He could pass it on to his counterpart in Calais.

Carefully placed leaks in the press and indiscreet conversations about the 575th Ranger Regiment's arrival in the UK at cocktail parties and other social events would be taking place in embassies around neutral countries in Europe. Lady Jane was about to drag Col. Randal to high society parties all over London wearing his Ranger bomber jacket.

Troop movements being classified the indiscretions would be attributed to "unfortunate" lapses of security. Other messages from XX agents under B1-A's control would mention SHAEF was furious about the order-of-battle gossip going round.

Lieutenant General "Geronimo" Joe McKoy's notional Cavalry Corps patch was a tongue-in-cheek masterpiece. Lady Jane named it "XXX Corps" as a salute to one of his Hungarian dancer "friends" at the Kit-Kat

Club in Cairo who was known for her X-rated performances. The insignia was based on the real 1st Cavalry Division shoulder patch. The First CAV would be serving somewhere in the Pacific so there were no concerns about it arriving in the ETO and blowing XXX Corps cover.

The distinctive horse's head silhouette remained in the upper right-hand corner of the patch. However, below the black diagonal bar dividing it in half was a five-pointed star encased in a circle – the badge of the U.S. Marshals Service. To make it easy to figure out what unit was being denoted XXX was stenciled on the jacket over the top of the patch. When completed, Lt. Gen. McKoy's bomber jacket was a showstopper.

Lady Jane provided Captain Billy Jack Jaxx a chart of the Heraldry Divisions notional units. It took him about three seconds to make his decision – the 135th Airborne Division. Its notional patch consisted of a gold circle under a black and gold AIRBORNE flash. In the center of the patch was a giant black widow spider poised to bite. The cover story was Capt. Jaxx had recently been placed on TDY to command the Division's Pathfinder Company for the D-Day invasion.

When Col. Randal saw the 135th Airborne's patch he said, "Jack's name is written all over it."

Lieutenant Chase Starrett was provided with an A-2 jacket with a patch for an actual stateside unit – the 13th Airborne Division. The division had been cannibalized of officers and men to fill out the 101st and the 17th Airborne Divisions that were in the act of deploying or marshaling to deploy to England. The Golden Unicorns – the unit's nickname, derived from the image on its shoulder patch depicting the head of a unicorn – were not going to be able to replace their administrative losses fast enough to arrive overseas in time to take part in the invasion.

Again, the Germans had no way of knowing that. The Nazis would have every reason to believe the 13th Airborne Division would be dropping on France leading the charge on D-Day. Articles would appear in Stateside newspapers informing the public the division was on orders to be deployed to England in the immediate future. The XX Committee's double agents in England would be reporting paratroopers being seen wearing the Golden Unicorn.

The more the Nazis were tricked into spreading out their troops to guard against ghost airborne divisions, the less available to defend the actual drop zones of the 82nd and 101st Airborne Divisions when the D-Day invasion commenced. The choice of the Golden Unicorns for the LCS operation was a nice touch – from a deception standpoint. A make-believe creature was the perfect mascot for the imaginary pre-invasion deployment of a very real parachute division that was stuck in the States.

Lt. Col. Bevan's favorite toast was, "Confusion to the enemy" – he loved Lady Jane choosing to have the U.S. 13th Airborne Division be a part of the deception.

A pair of horsehair brushes, a little paint and no small amount of talent were helping make the confusion happen. People stopping by to watch Lady Jane and Beverly practice their art had no idea they were witnessing a military deception in progress. One that would contribute to influencing how the German 7th and 15th Armies deployed its defensive forces behind the Atlantic Wall in anticipation of an airborne assault.

And it was being conducted in full view.

THE KING'S MESSENGER DELIVERED A NEW DISPATCH TO Colonel John Randal. Compared to the other cryptic orders, this one was like the *Encyclopedia Britannica*. It said, "Prisoner snatch from a searchlight/gun position on the pier located at 41855674." Unlike the other orders, this one did not say "Forthwith." Perhaps that was because this mission would require special equipment and/or personnel be organized?

Col. Randal went downstairs to the Bunker. It was becoming a busier place. FANYs from MI-6, MI-5, SOE and some of Major the Lady Jane Seaborn's Royal Marines from Seaborn House were moving in to set up shop. He found the location of the target on the wall map mosaic. The pier was located in the town of Calais proper. He knew it fairly well. It was the same one he had landed at and later escaped from with the surviving members of Swamp Fox Force four years previously. Was it possible whoever was orchestrating this raid was aware of that fact? He was beginning to question almost everything.

None of those Swamp Fox Force men who had volunteered for Raiding Forces later were left in England at Seaborn House. The handful still serving, after all these years of intensive virtual nonstop operations, were now all NCOs or had taken direct commissions, operating out of ABC. That was unfortunate, as they might have had a personal interest in this mission.

Col. Randal knew the objective was a long wooden wharf jutting far out into the Channel. An aerial photo taken on a high-speed, low-level run over the pier by an RAF photoreconnaissance aircraft ingressing from over the water was tacked to the mosaic. It was of a type called a "low oblique." The black and white 8x10 photo showed a small searchlight and a twin-mounted 7.92mm MG 42 anti-aircraft machine guns.

Lady Jane came over to see what he was studying. "Do we have a new assignment?"

Col. Randal said, "Prisoner snatch off this pier."

"Calais... in the vicinity of where you brought your men out before we met?"

"Roger that – this very dock."

Lady Jane said, "The target must be the gun position located on the tip end of the wharf. Near the edge of the town. How do you plan to pull that off?"

"Time to unleash our Special Warfare Operators."

"Let me find out what recent intelligence is available."

Col. Randal said, "Can you get Lieutenant Slade back here from Achnacarry?"

Lady Jane said, "Eight hours or so by train. I can have Westly here by tonight. If you need faster, possibly we can arrange to have him flown down."

"Faster is better. I need his input," Col. Randal said. "This is not your typical Raiding Forces' mission."

Lady Jane said, "I shall have to check with meteorological. As you would know the weather in Scotland is mercurial. Flying is not always possible due to chronically heavy ground fog in the Highlands."

"See what you can do – contact Seaborn House and have the Special Warfare Operators placed on Standby Ready alert."

Two hours later Lady Jane returned to the Bradford from her trip to COHQ to gather intelligence. She found Lieutenant General "Geronimo" Joe McKoy and Col. Randal sitting in the VIP section. They were wearing their one each, Flying, Type A-2 bomber jackets.

Col. Randal was feeling self-conscious. Lt. Gen. McKoy was not.

Lady Jane laughed. "You two certainly look handsome in those jackets."

Lt. Gen. McKoy said, "I like mine so much, Lady Jane, I just might sleep in it."

They went down to the Bunker to take a look at the wall map.

Col. Randal said, "What's your report?"

Lady Jane said, "The prisoner snatch off the Calais dock is not a new idea. It has been attempted twice before. The first time, inclement weather made a No. 12 Commando team turn back. Reports state the Channel was so rough the Royal Navy sailors from 15th Motor Gun Boat Flotilla became violently seasick.

"On the second try, when the raiding party paddled to the pier the spotlight caught them. When they attempted to escape the beam seemed to follow their dory. Believing the mission to be compromised the Commandos withdrew to their MGB and returned to base.

"Now in retrospect, cooler heads believe the light was on a fixed automatic timed sweep like a lighthouse and merely appeared to follow the dory."

"Hate it when that happens," Lt. Gen. McKoy said.

Col. Randal said, "When was that last attempt?"

Lady Jane said, "Back before COHQ ordered a stand-down on small-scale raiding."

"So, we're good on time then?"

"Yeah, those Nazis won't be expectin' us to come callin' after all that time," Lt. Gen. McKoy said. "That's gonna be some bored men sittin' out on those planks in the dark a' night damp n' cold wonderin' if their girlfriends or wives are thinkin' about 'em.

"Maybe got their selves a Dear John in the mail and ain't feelin' real good about the fairness of it all and in no mood to… 'understand'."

Lady Jane said, "The nearby town of Calais is not heavily defended. While it is believed the Germans are of the opinion the invasion shall take place in the Pas-de-Calais region the town itself is no longer considered a desirable site for a large-scale amphibious assault. So many ships have been sunk in the harbor over the last four years it is no longer navigable."

Col. Randal said, "Any idea about enemy forces in the area?"

"Exact details on enemy troop strength in Calais proper are not known. Elements of the 708 Static Division and the 1st Panzer Division are stationed nearby," Lady Jane said. "In addition you can expect the normal coastal artillery defense personnel, anti-aircraft batteries, searchlight crew, etc. Intelligence indicates the Germans are focused on defending other potential landing sites in the Pas-de-Calais district that have more to offer an invader."

Lt. Gen. McKoy said, "Here we go. Tough mission. Zero intel."

Col. Randal said, "I see possibilities."

Lady Jane said, "You always do."

Beverly Blackwell walked into the Bunker. "Well, Daddy's jealous."

Col. Randal said, "What of?"

Beverly laughed. "He wants an A-2 bomber jacket like Billy Jack's – with a big spider."

"The Abwehr have a dossier on the general. They shall know he commands Troop Carrier Command," Lady Jane said. "That would prohibit him from taking part in our deception."

Col. Randal said, "Maybe not. German airborne divisions are commanded by Luftwaffe generals. The Abwehr might not see anything unusual about Bronc getting a new assignment for the invasion – let him have one, Jane."

Lady Jane said, "What the general would really like is an A-2 you paint for him, Beverly. Why not the two of us design a more appropriate unit insignia for Troop Carrier Command. The one they have now is not bold enough for a man like Bronc."

Lt. Gen. McKoy said, "Give him a tarantula."

Beverly said, "Or a rattlesnake."

Lady Jane laughed. "Oh, we shall come up with something special – like a man-eating tiger dangling from a parachute."

Col. Randal wondered if the stress incidental to the change of duty station to England, the dramatic adjustments to their individual job descriptions and/or the intensity of the raids coming hard and fast with no advance warning and little time to prepare was making everyone a little crazy.

"I like it."

MAJOR THE LADY JANE SEABORN CONTACTED HER godfather, Lieutenant Colonel John Henry Bevan. The Chief of Deception then placed a phone call to the Air Ministry. The Air Marshal he spoke to called the Royal Air Force base closest to Achnacarry, Scotland. The base commander phoned the Basic Commando Training Center. Lieutenant Westly Slade, USMCR, was pulled from training and driven to an airfield where he boarded a De Havilland Mosquito – a twin-engine light bomber that was faster than a Spitfire fighter – and flown to London. One of the Bradford's limousines was waiting at the airport when he landed.

Lady Jane escorted him to the hotel's restaurant where a meal was waiting. She knew Commando students were sometimes only provided one meal per day during training. Food-and sleep-deprivation being important elements in evaluating performance under stress.

Colonel John Randal and Captain Billy Jack Jaxx were waiting when Lt. Slade finished. They escorted him to the Bunker where he was briefed on the proposed prisoner snatch from the Calais pier. For a minute the lieutenant wondered if this was some kind of test – part of Commando training?

Col. Randal said, "This is a mission tailor-made for your Special Warfare Operators. I want you to proceed to Seaborn House with Captain Jaxx and plan the raid. I'll be down later today to go over the details. Coordinate with Mrs. Seaborn – she'll provide transport to the target area."

Lt. Slade said, "Wilco, sir."

This was no drill.

Col. Randal said, "Captain Jaxx will be along as an observer. However it's your mission, Lieutenant. You're in command."

Lt. Slade glanced at Capt. Jaxx. It was clear he was going along on this first OSS Maritime Unit cross-channel operation to be available to step in if things went sideways. That was perfectly fine with him. There was no one he respected more than Jack Cool. And he was aware of Col. Randal's crawl, walk, run approach to officers leading raids – a practice he thoroughly approved of.

Col. Randal said, "So, Lieutenant, do you have any idea how you're going to make it happen?"

"Yes sir, I do."

U.S. Marine Corps officers are known for decisiveness.

COLONEL JOHN RANDAL, MAJOR THE LADY JANE SEABORN and Happy took her private rail car to Seaborn House. The coach was going to be busy shuttling people back and forth from the hotel to the estate. Lady Jane had been planning to use it to take Mandy, Beverly and Major General Sir Stewart Menzies, an avid fox hunter, on a day trip to ride with the exclusive Beaufort Hunt – she and "C" were both members. The fast pace of events since they had arrived in London had not allowed the time so far.

Col. Randal said, "I wasn't anticipating a permanent change of duty station when we flew in. This was supposed to be a two-week leave. Now we have to come up with an entirely new plan for how to restructure Raiding Forces."

Lady Jane said, "Agreed."

"Before we departed I had Percy replace Terry. But that was based on me being there in command. That's not going to happen now."

"What would you have done differently had you known?"

Col. Randal said, "Baltimore Farquhar may be the better choice to take my place permanently. Mongo has a broader level of command experience. And he's better connected. I've always had you for that – Percy doesn't."

Lady Jane said, "Hard decision."

"Major Dance had the opportunity to command an airborne battalion in either the 82nd or 101st but he chose to stay on in Raiding Forces. He would be the logical choice as my replacement. But my orders are to make our Aegean operations a British affair as much as possible."

Lady Jane said, "Do you believe the major was motivated by a desire to stay close to Stephanie?"

"Could be."

Lady Jane said, "I am going to need her here, John. Operating the Bunker and the TOC at Seaborn House simultaneously shall undoubtably become more and more challenging the closer we get to D-Day. With our deception and counterintelligence commitment, the MI-6 and SOE agent insertions/extractions, and all the raids we are being tasked with, our support staff are starting to be overloaded as it is now."

Col. Randal said, "So, what do you want to do?"

"I have no idea who to select to replace Stephanie at ABC."

"What about Veronica? Bring her on board as one of your Royal Marines," Col. Randal said. "She's capable of wearing two hats – Escape and ABC Operations."

Lady Jane laughed, "Reading my mind again . . . one has to be careful with you, John Randal."

"Roger that."

Captain Billy Jack Jaxx met them at the train station. On the drive to Seaborn House he gave Col. Randal a report on the state of planning for the Pas-de-Calais mission. He was clearly impressed with Lieutenant Westly Slade's mission prep.

"This may be the first assignment we've given the Frogs they've actually trained for, sir."

Col. Randal said, "In what way?"

"When the MUs arrived on Castelrozzo we immediately sent them on raids. But we did it the way we operate. You know, Commandos arriving out of the dark of night with knives in our teeth," Capt. Jaxx said. "The idea was to get the OSS people up to speed on how Raiding Forces does things as fast as possible."

Col. Randal said, "That was the plan."

Capt. Jaxx said, "The difference between OSS MUs and Navy Underwater Demolitions Teams is the UDT's responsibility stops at the water's edge. OSS has always intended for the MUs to be able to land ashore clandestinely, go inland and gather intelligence. We've never asked 'em to do anything like that, sir," Capt. Jaxx said.

Col. Randal said, "How's this prisoner snatch any different, Jack?"

"The idea is to slip in, nab a prisoner and slip out without anyone the wiser, sir. Right under the noses of the Germans. It requires a stealthy approach, stealthy violence of action on the objective and a stealthy extraction. Finesse all the way.

"Raiding Forces' direct action missions typically end up not being very stealthy, sir."

Col. Randal said, "There is that."

When they arrived at Seaborn House, Lieutenant General "Geronimo" Joe McKoy was out on the lawn with Lt. Westly Slade. He had six Special Warfare Operators with him. They were assembling three canvas kayaks.

Lt. Slade gave Col. Randal a briefing on the flimsy-looking "gliders." "These are British-designed Cockle Mark I kayaks adopted for use by OSS, sir. The two-man version is a collapsible portable boat on a plywood frame covered by a rubberized canvas outer sheath. All up, the boat is two feet, nine inches wide, thirteen inches deep, sixteen and a half feet long and weighs one hundred four pounds. It can be assembled by two men in less than five minutes.

"The eight-man canoe is built on the same principle as the two-man boats. It's twenty-four feet long, nineteen inches deep – weighs two-hundred-forty-five pounds. There are detachable outriggers capable of mounting a pair of eight-horsepower, silent-running electric outboard motors. We will not be using the outriggers or motors tonight sir. There's not been time to test them after shipment. And in training they have not proven to always be reliable.

"The shaped plywood frames for both type boats are fitted together by lengths of metal pipe which also serve to stabilize the craft. Disassembled, the kayak can fit in one haversack, sir.

"The double paddle blades are collapsible to facilitate packing and transport. May not look like much, Colonel, but this is one versatile warfighting craft."

Lady Jane was not so sure. "Does not do much to inspire one's confidence, Westly – not for weak swimmers."

Lt. Slade said, "There are no weak swimmer Frogmen, Lady Seaborn. Eskimos have been using kayaks like these Cockles covered in seal skin from the beginning of time – rubberized canvas is lighter and tougher. I'll take you out in one after we return. You'll see, they're very stable."

Lady Jane laughed. "Deal."

Lt. Gen. McKoy said, "You ain't gettin' me in one a' those contraptions – Eskimo or no Eskimo."

Major General William "Wild Bill" Donovan arrived in time for the Operations Order. Not only was he demonstrating loyalty down the chain of command – a lot rarer in the military than might be believed, he was there for a reason. While OSS had a worldwide commitment, Raiding Forces was one of his only two operations of any meaningful size.

The other was Detachment 101 in the China-Burma-India (CBI) Theatre of Operations. It was the first guerrilla warfare, espionage and sabotage unit in U.S. history. Even so, Det. 101 numbered less than two hundred OSS operators. The Office of Strategic Services was finding it difficult to get into the war in any meaningful way.

Raiding Forces was very important to OSS.

Maj. Gen. Donovan was at Seaborn House to be on hand to see his troops off on their mission. OSS had a lot riding on their performance. And Wild Bill wanted to ensure for himself the Maritime Unit was receiving the support needed. Not that he had a concern about how Raiding Forces was treating them – Col. had a reputation for taking care of his troops. It was the other services that were a problem.

The white haired, fatherly-looking director of OSS was wildly popular with his Special Warfare Operators. The Frogs were pleased he was taking such an active interest. It was a major morale boost.

Lt. Slade briefed the mission. He did it strictly by the book for an Operations Order. Nothing else the Frogs were going to do tonight was in any book.

While bold in the extreme, the mission was not reckless or suicidal. The Special Warfare Operators would be going into the heart of the most heavily guarded district in France – Pas-de-Calais. However, they would not enter the built-up area. The plan was to slip in, conduct a prisoner snatch off of one of the piers on the edge of the town and slip out. The Frogs had trained for nearly two years to do something like this.

There was no actionable intelligence available on the target other than what could be gleaned from a single aerial photo. It showed a small-caliber anti-aircraft gun – dual-mounted 7.92mm MG 42s and a searchlight. It was not one of the sixty-centimeter anti-aircraft searchlights. What the picture showed was a much smaller spotlight mounted on a pedestal. It was anticipated a German crew of three to seven soldiers would be on the objective. That was an estimate. Two Nazis were visible in the low oblique photo.

Lt. Gen. McKoy was known to say, "There's WAGs and SWAGs – your WAG is a wild-assed guess. A SWAG is a scientific wild-assed guess."

Enemy troop strength was a SWAG. There would be at minimum a single operator on the light, a gunner for the twin-mounted MG 42's and two loaders. There could be an NCO and one or two other men. However, it was not believed there would be a large party on the tip end of the pier who would remain overnight (RON).

The possibility the Wehrmacht had the dock wired for demolition had to be considered. In the event of an attempt to land in strength it could be blown up to deny its use to the Allies. In that eventuality the German crew would be expendable.

Not a problem for the Special Warfare Operators tonight. While they were highly trained naval demolitions experts and knew how to dismantle explosives, that skill would not be necessary. Blowing the pier would be done remotely from shore if it were about to be captured. And then only provided the 15th Army commander authorized the destruction – as a last resort. Lt. Slade's plan was to sneak in, carry out the mission and extract without alerting the Germans of their presence and leaving no trace behind they had ever been there.

And *if* they were found out – to be gone before permission could work its way down the chain of command.

Col. Randal had suggested it would be better if the Frogs did not leave any bodies behind. Best-case scenario was for the sun to come up and the Germans on the pier to have vanished. Lady Jane's godfather, the Chief of Deception, would be proud of Raiding Forces getting into the spirit of mystifying and misleading or at least considering the idea: "Confusion to the enemy."

And it was true Col. Randal's tactical thinking, which he was passing down to his subordinate commanders, was beginning to shift. In addition to the importance of how to improvise and adapt, he was now also contemplating how to mislead and bewilder.

Lt. Slade's Concept of the Operation sounded simple. It was not, unless you had trained extensively for a mission like this one. You could not simply put a few Commandos in kayaks and send them out on an operation and expect success. Small-boat raiding was a highly specialized skill set.

Brandy advised the PT boat would not approach closer than three miles to the objective. The Special Warfare Operators would have to offload the two Cockle Mark Is and the eight-man canvas canoe and paddle to the pier. The distance was well within their capability.

Initially the three boats would travel together. A half mile from the target they would split up. The two kayaks would approach the pier fifty yards past the gun position behind it on the port side. The canoe would mirror that approach on the starboard side.

On arriving at the wharf, the bow paddlers from the kayaks would each throw up a grappling hook onto the pier. Then they would climb hand-over-hand up the rope. The stern paddler would remain with the boat. On the starboard side. Capt. Jaxx and Lieutenant Chase Starrett, who also requested to come along to observe the Special Warfare Operators in action, would be scaling a grappling line along with the canoe's bowman.

Capt. Jaxx took advantage of every opportunity to mentor his junior officers. His were always so capable they were constantly being promoted then transferred out of SOG and given their own troop commands within Raiding Forces. At this time he was down to one, Lt. Starrett. Arguably his best since taking command of the Special Operations Group.

When the assault team went in there would be five Raiding Forces' personnel force-on-force for the attack on MG 42/spotlight position. Each was armed with a suppressed 9mm M3 Grease Gun and an OSS Cosh.

The assaulters would kill or subdue the Germans on the objective and immediately withdraw. The attack would be very fast maximizing surprise, speed and violence of action. From the time of landing on top of the wharf the team would not be on it for longer than five minutes. Tonight, using one of Maj. Gen. Donovan's legal terms, on this raid "time was of the essence." Every effort was to be made to bring out the bodies of any enemy KIA. The kayaks and canoe would return to the PT boat at all due speed.

It sounded like a good plan if possibly optimistic about the allowed time to remain on target.

Following the Op Order, Lt. Slade issued Capt. Jaxx and Lt. Starrett a small metal pipe a little over half a foot long. Then he gave them a brusque military style briefing on what they were.

"This is an OSS Telescopic Steel Spring Extendable Baton – commonly called a 'cosh.' It consists of two heavy concentric springs enclosed in a tubular, diamond-patterned steel grip, with a hole at the skull crusher end to insert a leather thong, and a lead ball mounted on the tip end forming the main striking element. The cosh is carried closed. To activate it grasp the handle in the small of your palm fingers extended and joined then cupped around the diamond-patterned handle, arm held at a forty-five-degree angle, press the button with your thumb and give the handle a vigorous shake toward the ground. The spring-loaded mechanism will automatically extend the weapon to its full length. Closed, the baton is seven inches in length.

Extended it's seventeen and a half inches. Normally carried concealed up a sleeve for our purposes tonight it will be tucked through your pistol belt for easy access."

Capt. Jaxx said, "Hey, Presto!"

Then he pressed the button and whipped the end of the cosh toward the ground with a snap of his wrist. As if by magic the spring-loaded baton sprang out to its full length. Hard and deadly. Ready for action – a true "toy for big boys."

Lt. Gen. McKoy said, "I'm gonna want one a' those, Westly. Need to ship it to the U.S. Marshals Service to take a look at. They'll want all they can get."

Capt. Jaxx said, "Yeah, I need one to send to my grandfather – the sheriff."

Maj. Gen. Donovan, having walked over to observe the briefing and demonstration, said, "I will contact my office to arrange it."

Lt. Gen. McKoy said, "Lot a' law enforcement applications for that little beauty."

"I know I'd sure like one," Beverly said.

Lady Jane said, "My Royal Marines shall want a cosh to carry in their purses. The perfect Christmas present for the girls. Put us on the list too, General."

Maj. Gen. Donovan said, "My pleasure."

Lt. Gen. McKoy said, "You already got yourself a killer dog, Lady Jane. A stiletto concealed in John's . . . I mean *your* ivory walkin'-out stick. A Browning 9mm P-35 on your pistol belt. A 7.65mm Walter PPK in your purse. And now you want an extendable steel baton. . . ."

Lady Jane said, "One can never be too sure."

For once she was not laughing.

Then it was time for rehearsals. There was no dock in the immediate vicinity to train on so they simulated climbing up the grappling lines to the pier. The movement to contact was simple. All five operators lined up shoulder-to-shoulder with Capt. Jaxx in the middle and advanced on where the gun position would be. On coming into sight of the target the two operators to his left and the two to his right lowered their suppressed 9mm M3 Grease Guns on their carrying straps around their necks and deployed their steel batons.

Capt. Jaxx kept his weapon to his shoulder as they advanced. In the event a German spotted the assaulters prior to their reaching the objective it would be his responsibility to engage. Lt. Slade had completely bought into the Raiding Forces' ethos – "Right Man, Right Job." Jack Cool was a gunfighter.

Then it was time to test-fire their weapons. Lt. Starrett performed a commo check with the SCR 536 hand-held transceiver, aka walkie-talkie, he would be using to coordinate the return trip to the PT boat with Brandy. Lt. Slade went to check in with the TOC to see if there was any late-breaking information – there was not.

After that, the team loaded on a Bedford truck and departed the staging area for the drive to the loading point. Lt. Gen. McKoy, Maj. Gen. Donovan, Col. Randal, Lady Jane and Beverly followed in the hotel's limousine. By now night had fallen. There was no moon. It was pitch dark. Perfect conditions for a raid on a pinpoint type target on an easy to locate objective.

There were Commando and Royal Navy officers who would not have felt that way. It was fairly common practice to wait for a full moon cycle to launch a raid. They wanted the light to see by. Not Raiding Forces. They went when ready, and there were times pitch-black was best because it provided a slight increase in cover and concealment during the movement to contact phase. They trained to operate in the dark.

Dark nights also offered a slight additional element of surprise. The Germans knew Commandos liked to raid during periods of full moons. They did not expect them on moonless nights.

Col. Randal stepped out of the limousine. He had stayed out of the briefing, rehearsal and other preparations – which was difficult for him. The idea was for Lt. Slade to go through the troop-leading tasks without interference. The Lieutenant had a lot of high-ranking observers watching his every move. That may have been more stressful for him than the upcoming mission.

Unable to restrain himself, Col. Randal pulled Capt. Jaxx aside, "The purpose of the exercise is to bring back a prisoner. Try not to shoot everybody, Jack – clear?"

"Crystal, sir."

"Unless you have to."

Time to board. Brandy was impatient to depart. She revved the engines. Lt. Slade came over and reported to Col. Randal. "Sir, we are preparing to move out at this time. Any last instructions?"

Col. Randal said, "You know your job. I'll be here when you return. Good luck, Lieutenant."

Lady Jane was saying something to Capt. Jaxx. Then the OSS Maritime Unit (MU) Special Warfare Operators began filing onto the PT boat. The three powerful Packard 4-M-2500 engines – producing a total of 4,500 horsepower – were warbling.

Tension mounted among the observers on the dock who would not be going on the raid. It is never easy to see off a team going into harm's way. Each of the recent Raiding Forces' missions out of Seaborn House had an element of desperation to them. Any small mistake and the team might not make it home. It was a heavy responsibility to put on young junior officers and the equally young operators they commanded.

The PT was an 80-foot "Elco" boat. Brandy had wanted it camouflaged. Not having access to any of the nine different colors of authorized U.S. Navy paint, she had her boat painted flat black – no gloss. That may or may not have been the best naval camouflage for nocturnal operations, but since it was all that was available it was going to have to do.

There was no hull number because Brandy had it painted over. PT boat numbers were assigned at the factory and referred to the contract number for the boat when it was ordered. Not theatre of operations, specific squadron or any other official U.S. Navy numbering system. Brandy's PT boat was part of a Lend Lease package to Russia and came with a number indicating such. She wanted it gone in the event anyone ever came looking for a missing boat.

The PT boat was stripped down. There were no anti-aircraft machine guns, torpedo tubes or depth charges. It had a range of 500 miles with a top speed on paper of forty knots (47mph.). Without the weapons it might be capable of slightly more.

Brandy liked PT boats. While it was a step or two slower than her MAS boat and slightly more conspicuous in silhouette, the Elco was more seaworthy. That was important when operating in the English Channel where the water was choppy more often than not.

And – of extreme importance to small-scale raiding or agent insertion/extraction – when closing on an enemy shore, the PT boat could run almost silently at fifteen knots.

The Frogs went below to rack out during the trip across the Channel. Capt. Jaxx remained on deck to talk to Brandy. They were friends and colleagues and shared a mutual respect. She had transported him to – and brought him home from – more bad places than he could remember. And she had posed for a swimsuit photo to put in his pistol grip.

Captain Penelope "Legs" Honeycutt-Parker was on board as navigator. There would be no problem finding their objective tonight. The firm of Seaborn & Honeycutt-Parker were arguably the most experienced duo in the Royal Navy when it came to delivering small units of Commandos to and from their targets.

Brandy timed her speed so the PT boat arrived three miles off the coast at 2400 hrs. It would take approximately two hours minimum likely a little more for the kayaks and Mark I Cockle to row to the target and back. She wanted to be home before sunrise. That was doable with room to spare unless the weather deteriorated

Lt. Slade had the Frogs up on deck as soon as the boat hove to. The men moved with an ease that came from long practice of small boat operations in low-light conditions. No wasted movement. No stumbling around. The prospect of a three-mile open water row was business as usual – they trained for much longer distances.

Col. Randal had thrown so many raids at the Special Warfare Operators when they first reported to ABC the prospect of another, while not without a certain amount of pre-mission jitters – tonight was no big drama. The Frogs had arrived at Raiding Forces as professionals. Now they were veterans. The combination of the two made them dangerous small unit operators.

The two kayaks and the canvas canoe were put over the side.

Lt. Slade ordered, "Lock and load."

There was the rattle of weaponry as rounds were racked into the chambers of the 9mm M3 Grease Guns and the SMGs clicked on safe. Everyone touch-checked their equipment in the dark one more time. It would not be for the last time this night.

Lt. Slade said, "Let's go, boys – stay frosty."

He still did not know what that meant. Jack Cool liked to say it. Good enough for him.

Then the Frogs were over the side into the boats. In the choppy water of the Channel no small feat. Capt. Jaxx and Lt. Starrett were last to go down. Two Special Warfare Operators held the canoe close alongside the PT boat as they clamored in trying not to put a boot through the bottom.

Lt. Slade ordered, "Away all boats."

Once they cast off from the PT boat all three bowmen took out their M1938-lensatic compass and shot an azimuth to the dock. Although the PT was made from mahogany fir and oak there was enough metal in it to affect the compass reading. Once the needle was lined up the compass men dialed the azimuth in on the bezel ring. Now they could take out their compass from time to time and check the luminous dial to make sure they were on course. But they were not going to have to. The team could see the searchlight rotating hypnotically back and forth straight ahead.

A ground infantry patrol can keep a pace count to see how far it has traveled. That was not possible over water. So the navigator on each boat would check his watch to see how much time had elapsed from launch. That would give a rough idea of distance traveled. Basic navigation is azimuth and distance/or time. Like land navigation it's an art as much as a science with a lot of extra guesswork on distance traveled.

It's not as easy as it sounds.

Capt. Jaxx was an ace land navigator. This was his first experience over open water. He wore his compass on a cord around his neck tucked into his left breast pocket. From time to time he took it out, locked his thumb in the brass thumb ring, rested the compass on his trigger finger, jiggled it to make sure the dial was floating free, and verified if they were staying on course.

Double- and triple-checking never hurts a navigator. Neither does having someone else verify your work. It is a lot easier if you can see your objective in the distance – like the light on the pier. The navigation was not necessary tonight. But the Frogs did it anyway. It never hurt to be on the top of your game during an operation.

Time stood still. The three miles to the target seemed to take forever. However, finding it was made even easier when a number of searchlight batteries on the shore inland behind the pier suddenly switched on and starting to sweep the sky. They must not have spotted anything because no anti-aircraft guns began firing.

Capt. Jaxx spent his time studying the layout of the lights. A light fog gave the beams penetrating it a ghostly appearance. The batteries were grouped in threes with seventy-five to a hundred-plus yards between individual lights in places. In spots two were closer together. Information to be filed away that might be useful to know for later raids. The lights were pretty much set up like the battery his SOG Rangers had jumped on. What he was observing squared with the intel Raiding Forces had on German searchlight batteries prior to that parachute raid.

The spotlight on the end of the pier was a much smaller light. It was sweeping back and forth in a slow, lazy arc. The light appeared to be on timed rotation as reported. It was not searching.

The lead kayak with Lt. Slade in the bow hove to. The other kayak and the canoe pulled alongside. The target was a half mile straight ahead as per the plan.

Sound carries a long way over water so Lt. Slade whispered, "Everybody ready?"

The coxswains in the second kayak and the canoe whispered back, "Affirmative."

Lt. Slade said, "Time to go to work, boys."

His kayak made way with the canoe following. The other kayak slid out of sight to come in on the pier from a slightly different angle on the opposite side. The last half mile to the target had a dream-like quality to it. The spotlight created a strangely hypnotic effect, slowly swaying back and forth in a 180-degree arc. That was deceptive. There was danger ahead.

Aboard the canoe the Frogs did the paddling. Capt. Jaxx and Lt. Starrett were passengers. That gave them time to continue studying the target as the boat silently made their way toward it. The light grew bigger and bigger. The approach seemed to be taking place in slow motion.

The low-profile small craft were like sharks moving in silently for the kill. Smooth, silent and deadly, knifing through the choppy water. The choppiness was good. It made the boats difficult to see. At least Capt. Jaxx hoped it did. The beam swept past, illuminating the canoe briefly as it moved on.

Now they were under it, making their final approach. No matter how many times he had done something like this, when committed to going in on the final movement to contact, Capt. Jaxx always experienced a full on adrenaline rush. Tonight was no exception – he was locked in, tightly focused.

The bowman feathered his paddle and then used it to fend off the wooden pylon. The stern man expertly brought the canoe alongside. They had arrived. Fifteen feet away Lt. Slade's kayak was already there. The Marine had thrown up a grappling hook and was beginning to climb up hand over hand.

The bowman in his canoe tossed up a grappling hook, tested it, then went up. Capt. Jaxx followed. Lt. Starrett came right behind him. As soon as they rolled over the top they took up a prone position facing the end of the pier where the spot light was sweeping back and forth. They could see the dim outline of the twin MG 42 position. No sentries were visible.

The bowman from the kayak on the other side came up on the pier. He low-crawled over and took up a position with the other operators. Lt. Slade studied the target for a few seconds to determine if they had been discovered.

Apparently not. The light continued playing back and forth. Other than that there was no movement on the objective.

Under his breath Lt. Slade ordered, "On line."

The team stood up silently shoulder-to-shoulder. Everyone had their 9mm M3 Grease Gun pointed in the direction of march. Ready to advance on command.

"Move out."

The team stepped off on their left foot as if on parade. Moving carefully to maintain cadence they advanced in the school solution, "Slow is Smooth. Smooth is Fast," patrolling technique espoused by Raiding Forces for movement to contact on the final objective. There was a powerful group dynamic from being shoulder-to-shoulder with men who were committed to take it to the enemy.

Capt. Jaxx noted, not for the first time, the Special Warfare Operators were very silent – tightly focused as they moved closer, padding, knees slightly bent, in their rubber-soled raiding boots. The target was backlit by the bluish beam of light sweeping the Channel.

Lt. Slade whispered, "Coshes."

Everyone but Capt. Jaxx lowered their 9mm M3 Grease Guns on the slings around their necks, broke out their spring-loaded coshes and continued to march without slowing the assault. There was the business-like sound of metallic clicks as the Frogs deployed their batons to their full length.

Now the team was closing on the end of the pier. They still did not see any Germans. It was dark – suddenly four enemy soldiers rose up from where they had been sleeping. Apparently no one was standing watch. Maybe one of them had been but dozed off.

SSSS, SSSS, SSSS – Capt. Jaxx shot three of them fast before the Frogs had a chance to react. Then they were on the fourth Nazi. He went down under a storm of whipping blows.

Lt. Slade said, "Nice shooting, Captain."

All four Germans were dragged to the canoe. The Special Warfare Operators lowered them into the boat. Then everyone went down the ropes and the race was on to see who could make it back to the PT first.

Halfway home in the middle of the Channel the three dead Nazis were thrown overboard.

Col. Randal was waiting on the dock when Brandy pulled in. While Lady Jane talked to Lt. Slade, and *her* Special Warfare Operators – Raiding Forces was known as "Lady Jane's Own" behind her back – he pulled Capt. Jaxx aside.

"How'd it go Jack?"

Capt. Jaxx said, "A thing of beauty, sir."

THE TWENTY COMMITTEE WAS REFERRED TO BY ITS members as "the Club." It met every Thursday in MI-5's office building at 58 St. James Street. The Committee was unofficially approved by Prime Minister Winston Churchill but not subject to ministerial responsibility. That way the Club could not claim it had been authorized to do what it was doing – much of which was illegal. This gave XX – always pronounced "Double Cross," unusual freedom of action.

There was another reason. It was hoped that not being officially sanctioned might help keep the Prime Minister at arm's length. He was so fascinated by deception the Club was concerned he would attempt to become actively involved on a case-by-case basis. The thought terrified MI-5 and all the rest of the agencies represented on the XX Committee.

So the Club introduced the PM into their program slowly a little at a time in the form of monthly reports. The first stated: "In all, 126 spies have fallen into our hands. Of these, twenty-four have been amenable and are now being used as Double Cross agents. In addition twelve real – and seven imaginary – persons have been foisted upon the enemy as Double Cross spies. Thirteen have been executed . . ."

As feared, Prime Minister Churchill was hooked from the first instant – scribbling across the bottom of the report in blue-black ink using his favorite Conway Stewart fountain pen, "Deeply interesting."

After reading a report concerning a certain party who was spying in the service of the Germans and the Italians he wrote, "Why don't you shoot him?"

That was the kind of Prime Ministerial response MI-5 worried about. To their relief it was merely an observation. The PM made comments. He did not issue orders to the Club. And he was very supportive of XX.

The Club had twenty members consisting of a representative from every one of the nine British intelligence agencies. No Allied intelligence organizations to include the United States Office of Strategic Services were represented on the XX Committee. Major General William "Wild Bill" Donovan could not get OSS appointed to a seat.

As a concession, OSS was offered the opportunity to have a liaison to the Club who would be able to attend meetings – provided MI-5 could nominate that person. Acting on a recommendation from Lieutenant Colonel Thomas Argyll Robertson aka Tar, John Cecil Masterman, the chairman of XX Committee, requested Beverly Blackwell.

It was an astonishing choice.

Two things happened almost simultaneously. First Maj. Gen. Donovan rushed to the Bradford Hotel to see Colonel John Randal. The two retreated to a secluded spot in the lobby behind the velvet rope for a private conversation.

Maj. Gen. Donovan said, "Everything I am about to tell you is classified TOP SECRET codeword. You have the clearance but are not authorized to know the codeword. That means I'm not telling you what I'm about to tell you. Am I perfectly clear?"

Col. Randal clicked on. "Affirmative."

Maj. Gen. Donovan said, “There exists an organization so highly classified I am not able to appoint a member to it.” Wild Bill was unaware Beverly was briefing Col. Randal about XX and B1-A on a daily basis. “Generally speaking it has some connection to counterintelligence though catching spies is not what it is primarily concerned with.”

Col. Randal gave no indication he had any idea what the general was talking about – but he did.

Maj. Gen. Donovan said, “Knowing I can fight being stonewalled all the way to the White House and eventually prevail, resulting in hard feelings on both sides of the ocean, an offer has been proffered to allow OSS to send a liaison officer to the committee’s weekly meetings. With one caveat. MI-5 gets to pick that individual.

“Security wants Beverly.”

Col. Randal said, “Really?”

Maj. Gen. Donovan said, “I rushed straight here as soon as the Security Service’s nominee became known to me. I wanted you to be aware it was not my doing. Knowing how close you and Beverly are it is important to me for OSS not to do anything that might undercut our relationship. I have no intention of taking her away from Raiding Forces.

“What is your thought on the idea, Colonel?”

“Great.”

“You understand if Beverly accepts the assignment her flying days are over until after the invasion? She will be in possession of some of the Allies’ closest-held secrets. She will be a ‘BIGOT’ – which means cleared to be in the loop for all matters concerning the invasion. Beverly will know when and where D-Day takes place.

“That means no exposure to risk of capture.”

Col. Randal said, “Works for me, sir.”

“Hardly the response I was anticipating,” Maj. Gen. Donovan said.

Col. Randal said, “I don’t want Beverly flying missions to France, General. When it comes to air operations the ETO is more dangerous than the Aegean. Radar-controlled anti-aircraft artillery, night fighter capability...”

Maj. Gen. Donovan said, “Bronc will be pleased. Though we can’t tell him the actual reason his daughter is being taken off flying duties. We need to come up with a cover story.”

Col. Randal said, “The general knows she’s working with MI-5 in a limited capacity, sir. Blame them for being obsessed with security. Don’t go into details – say that’s classified.”

Maj. Gen. Donovan said, “We’re good then – the two of us?”

“Absolutely, sir.”

Beverly was waiting to see Col. Randal as Maj. Gen. Donovan was leaving. She took his chair. For once it was not all sunshine and happiness.

“We need to talk, Johnny.”

“OK.”

“Tar just informed me I had been nominated to be the OSS liaison to the XX Committee. He had mentioned it before. But I didn’t understand the details.”

“Really?” Which was what Col. Randal said when he was surprised, did not want to expose his true thoughts or reveal how much he knew about a subject.

Beverly knew that. “How does it strike you, Johnny?”

Col. Randal said, “I’d say you’ve come a long way from the pretty college girl I first met in Washington doing a summer internship at OSS. Make it happen, Beverly. I’ve got faith in you.”

Beverly said, “No, you don’t. Well, maybe you do – a little. Tar is only recommending me for the job because he thinks I’m a dizzy blonde. Probably believes I’ll forget what’s said in the meetings before I can report back – I won’t be allowed to take notes. He has an ulterior motive, I know it.”

“Well, you are a dizzy blonde.”

Beverly laughed. “Too true.”

“You’ve been offered a ticket for a front row seat to the biggest show in history – make the most of it. Just so you know, General Donovan and I agreed days ago you’d be a valuable asset as the OSS/MI-5 liaison officer,” Col. Randal said. “Being tapped for the XX Committee job is a big step up from there.”

Beverly said, “Could be fun – too bad Daddy can’t know.”

Col. Randal said, “Lady Jane will be proud.”

“Those sneaky British double crossers.”

LIEUTENANT GENERAL GEORGE S. PATTON JR., AKA OLD Blood and Guts, arrived at the Bradford Hotel. His aide was trailing behind carrying a brand new U.S. Army Air Force Jacket, Flying, Type 2 on a hanger. General Patton was at his most magnificent best. He was wearing a brightly polished helmet liner sporting three gleaming stars denoting his rank and the decal of his new command, First United States Army Group (FUSAG). Since his ivory gripped .45 Colt Single Action Army revolver was around his waist he was "under arms." Which meant he could keep his hat, or in this case helmet liner, on indoors if he so chose. In addition to the three stars on the liner there were three stars on each of the epaulets on his blouse. And three on each collar of his shirt. A total of fifteen gleaming silver stars.

There was no First United States Army Group. It was as phony as the XXX Cavalry Corps or the 575th Ranger Regiment. Lt. Gen. Patton was commanding a phantom army – the centerpiece of OPERATION FORTITUDE SOUTH. He was not happy about it.

Old Blood and Guts was in the doghouse.

When ordered to London from exile, after having been relieved of his command of 7th Army for slapping two U.S. soldiers, Lt. Gen. Patton arrived from doing nothing in North Africa for four months believing he would be appointed to lead the U.S. contingent ashore on D-Day. It was a shock to find out his former deputy, Lieutenant General Omar Bradley, was now to have that honor as a result of his indiscretion.

Lt. Gen. Patton was a decoy, or as he described it, "A damned wooden duck." His assignment in the greatest military endeavor in world history was to be a bright shiny object. The idea was to misdirect the attention of the Germans standing to on the Atlantic Wall to one location while his former deputy, Lt. Gen. Bradley, commanded the U.S. troops coming ashore somewhere else. It was a stroke of genius from a deception point of view. The FUSAG command played to the Nazis' preconceptions that the Allies most flamboyant commander who had a string of amphibious masterpieces under his belt would certainly command the invasion.

He should have never slapped those malingering GIs. For his actions Old Blood and Guts had been held out of combat for four long months with no end in sight. He was not going to be allowed to command in the most important operation in the history of organized warfare. Newspapers in the States were still howling for him to be fired, court-martialed and sent home.

Now Lt. Gen. Patton was left with no option but to throw himself into playing the role of FUSAG commander. He had been informed it was the only way he "was ever going to get back in Eisenhower's good graces."

He lived in fear of missing the entire rest of the war – it was a possibility.

After stopping by the concierge station, Lt. Gen. Patton and his aide approached the VIP section. Spotting Lieutenant General "Geronimo" Joe McKoy sitting with Colonel John Randal he shouted, "Hey, Joe, your XXX Cavalry Corps is being assigned to me for the invasion. Imagine that. The two of us old horse soldiers back in the thick of it again.

"Just like down in Mexico."

Col. Randal signaled the Vulnerable Points Security operator to allow Lt. Gen. Patton in.

Lt. Gen. Patton continued to shout. "Randal, you're in charge of strategic reconnaissance for SHAEF. I need you to work out a plan to provide me regular briefings on the state of German defenses in and around Calais. I want FUSAG to hear it first, not filtered down through layers of rear-echelon, pencil-pushing staff SOBs before it reaches my warfighters."

Lt. Gen. Patton's voice boomed loud enough to be heard all over the lobby. People turned to glare. The general was committing criminally bad security. Or so it seemed.

Col. Randal said, "My pleasure, General."

Lt. Gen. McKoy said, "What can we do for you, Georgie?"

"Word is there's a couple of artists here in the hotel who paint bomber jacket patches. I need one with my First United States Army Group insignia on it," Lt. Gen. Patton said. "I want it big and bold."

Lt. Gen. McKoy said, "That would be Lady Jane. She and Bronc Blackwell's daughter Beverly do the paintin.' You may have to get in line, they're in high demand."

Col. Randal made eye contact with Major the Lady Jane Seaborn. She was sitting with Lieutenant Colonel Thomas Argyll Robertson, Mandy Paige and Beverly Blackwell. What they were discussing *was* classified.

Lady Jane walked over. Unlike most generals, who tended to look like college professors, Lt. Gen. Patton looked as if he had stepped off the Silver Screen. He exuded command presence. Old Blood and Guts was a fighting soldier and he wanted everyone to know it. She liked the general from the first time they met – loved his ivory-handled revolvers.

"How nice to see you again, General."

Lt. Gen. Patton said, "Word is you are a world class painter of A-2 bomber jackets, Lady Jane. I need one for my new First United States Army Group Command – FUSAG. We're getting ready to go kick that paper-hanging Hitler's . . ."

Lady Jane flashed one of her best-grade heart attack smiles. "Love to, General."

The aide handed over the bomber jacket with a copy of the FUSAG device – pentagon-shaped with a red border around a faded gray background. In the center was a bold black Roman Numeral I denoting the First United States Army Group.

Lt. Gen. Patton said, "Make it big and bold, Lady Jane – I want people all the way to Berlin to know who we are and that we're coming."

"Where are you staying in London, General?"

Lt. Gen. Patton said, "Tried to get a suite here but this place's booked up solid. So Ike's boys stuck me in Claridge's. It's like a French bordello – has a mirror on the ceiling over my bed. Hate to open my eyes in the morning."

Lady Jane laughed. "I shall have your jacket delivered to your hotel in the next few days."

She did not mention owning the Bradford.

9

DOUBLE CROSS XX

COLONEL JOHN RANDAL WAS IN THE VIP SECTION SITTING with Lieutenant General "Geronimo" Joe McKoy and Waldo Treywick. They had unlit cigars in their teeth and were discussing OPERATION LONG NECK/CARD GAME. With the shuffling of most of the CARD GAME personnel to Seaborn House on a semi-permanent basis, the diamond interdiction program needed to be rethought.

Lt. Gen. McKoy said, "Me n' Waldo been plannin' to head on down to the Congo to touch base with Frank right after Christmas. And Waldo, bein' Mr. Big, needs to check in with the Three to keep 'em in line. So, we've got us some LONG NECK biness needin' to be taken care of, John."

Col. Randal said, "Coordinate your travel with Bronc. He's letting Raiding Forces use his personal C-47 now that he has a new plane. General, I want you to take charge of LONG NECK at least until after the invasion. Almost all the voting members of CARD GAME will be here in England through D-Day. You'll have to work out how to handle command and control of the operation."

Lt. Gen. McKoy said, "No problem, John. Can do. You got a lot on your plate. The Commander General needs to know we'll be checkin' up on him from time to time. We don't want any a' those sparklers Frank's been collectin' to slip into his pocket.

"As for the Three, Waldo needs to shake 'em up pretty regular. Maybe shoot one of 'em – let those crooks understand he's still top dog."

Waldo said, "Yeah, we don't want 'em thinkin' we run off and forgot about 'em."

Lieutenant Colonel John Henry Bevan appeared at the velvet rope. Col. Randal nodded to the Vulnerable Points Wing operator to allow him in. The arrival of Lady Jane's godfather was not expected.

Major the Lady Jane Seaborn and Mandy were away meeting with Lieutenant Colonel Thomas Argyll Robertson at MI-5. But then the Controller, London Controlling Section knew that. He had called ahead to the hotel and spoken to James "Baldie" Taylor prior to driving over.

Lt. Col. Bevan said, "I was hoping to have a word with you in private, Colonel."

Lt. Gen. McKoy and Waldo decided their presence was required elsewhere. They knew who Lt. Col. Bevan was. And were aware Lady Jane's godfather and Col. Randal did not enjoy the warmest of relationships. Which made Bevan *persona non grata* in their eyes.

Col. Randal and Lt. Col. Bevan moved to a more secluded spot in the VIP section.

Lt. Col. Bevan said, "I received a telex from Vice Admiral Ransom this morning. There were two items both concerning you. First, the Admiral is most unhappy to learn you shall be having a semi-permanent change of duty station. Blames me for the development. Second, I am to ask you about a sensitive matter involving Jane's husband, Mallory."

"I see."

Lt. Col. Bevan said, "You and the Razor enjoy a warm relationship?"

"We do."

"Interesting, almost no one else can say that."

"Admiral Ransom is the best senior commander I have ever reported to," Col. Randal said.

Lt. Col. Bevan said, "And the matter of Jane's husband?"

Col. Randal made eye contact with Beverly Blackwell. She was talking to Captain Billy Jack Jaxx and Lieutenant Chase Starrett. The two young officers were sporting their new A-2 bomber jackets hoping a German spy might be passing through the hotel and see the unit patches. Excusing herself, she came over.

"Colonel this is Beverly Blackwell. Lady Jane's personal assistant. Recently she's been named the OSS liaison to a committee so highly classified I am not cleared to know its name."

Lt. Col. Bevan wondered how Col. Randal had *any* information about the XX Committee even if only enough to claim he did not know what it was called. The Club was classified above TOP SECRET. Col. Randal would never be cleared to learn anything about its activities.

He already knew about Beverly's appointment. James "Baldie" Taylor had briefed LCS on the development. He was not expecting someone so young and attractive. It was a serious assignment, not one passed out on a whim to beauty queens – he knew about that too, or the daughter of a general.

Lt. Col. Bevan said, "A pleasure, Miss Blackwell."

Beverly knew who he was. "Likewise."

Lt. Col. Bevan had the impression he had been snubbed.

Col. Randal said, "Beverly I'd like you to sit where you can keep the door in line of sight. If Lady Jane walks in, go intercept her. Colonel Bevan and I are about to discuss a matter she's not cleared for."

"Does that mean we're not having this conversation, Johnny?"

"That's what it means."

Beverly said, "Done."

Lt. Col. Bevan noted the chemistry between the two – what was that about?

As soon as Beverly walked away Col. Randal ran it down for Lt. Col. Bevan in clipped bullet points. "Mallory Seaborn was captured by the Japanese. He was interned in a slave labor camp tasked with constructing a railroad through triple canopy jungle in mountainous terrain. It was a death camp. The POWs were worked eighteen hours a day and starved.

"Mallory was caught stealing food. He was tried by a kangaroo court made up of prisoners he stole from. Found guilty his sentence – carried out same night, was to be boreholed."

"Boreholed?" Lt. Col. Bevan sounded like he had no idea what that was. He was being disingenuous. Jim had briefed him about Commander Seaborn's gory demise.

Col. Randal said, "Held up by his heels. Lowered headfirst down a latrine. Held there until he drowned."

Lt. Col. Bevan said, "That has to be the most appalling punishment I have ever heard of. Mallory and Jane were thought to be the perfect match. It was an arranged marriage as occasionally occurs in the Six Hundred. Only thing I ever fundamentally disagreed with her father about.

"Does Jane know?"

Col. Randal said, "Jim brought me the intel in confidence. I informed Admiral Ransom. We agreed nothing was to be gained by telling Lady Jane at this time."

Lt. Col. Bevan tended to think of Col. Randal as a blunt instrument. Useful but possessing no great intellect and definitely not a gentleman. Even though well-aware of the colonel's military record, he had never been much impressed by the man until he parachuted into France to go after those searchlights – that was extraordinary. Above and beyond.

If Col. Randal was pursuing his goddaughter for her money, as Lt. Col. Bevan suspected, all he needed to do was to provide Jane the information her husband was deceased. They could be married almost immediately. By holding his silence, if Mallory was classified as MIA – the POW's were never going to confirm what happened to him, it might take years after the war to have him legally declared dead. Not telling Jane out of a desire to spare her feelings was one of the more selfless decisions Lt. Col. Bevan had ever personally encountered. Not one he could relate to.

In civilian life he was the financial advisor to heads of state, the rich and famous, titans of industry. In his world the accumulation of wealth trumped everything. Try to do right when enormous amounts of money were at stake . . . never in a million years. Reluctantly he was coming to the conclusion he might be forced to reassess his assessment of the colonel.

"Why share this story – you could have told me anything or nothing at all?" Lt. Col. Bevan *was* curious about that.

Col. Randal said, "When Lady Jane finds out we withheld Mallory's death from her, if she's not happy with the decision I'm going to blame you for keeping it secret."

Lt. Col. Bevan had no idea Col. Randal could be so mendacious – a compliment coming from Great Britain's Chief of Deception. "You would too, you right bastard."

Col. Randal said, "Roger that – what's family for?"

MAJOR GENERAL SAM HOUSTON BLACKWELL ARRIVED AT the Bradford. Major the Lady Jane Seaborn and Beverly Blackwell were expecting him. Brandy Seaborn was on hand as well. They had his new A-2 bomber jacket ready.

It was magnificent. Troop Transport Command was getting a new unit emblem. It was a disc-shaped patch that showcased a parachute with a glider in the background. Three gold lightning bolts were stacked on top of each other, angled down left to right, across the lines and risers. Dangling in the parachute's harness was a giant tiger – based on the one in the insignia designed by the Walt Disney Studios for the 1st American Volunteer Group aka Flying Tigers. The big cat was coming down roaring, its huge fangs bared, claws showing, paws outstretched like an Olympic diver. The man-eater appeared to be raring to get at whoever it was down below. Over top of the emblem was a large black and gold "AIRBORNE" flash – while not an airborne unit, TTC dropped the U.S. Army's paratroopers and towed their gliders.

Silver Command Pilot Wings, Jump Wings and Glider Pilot Wings were pinned one on top of each other over the leather MAJ. GEN. SAM H. BLACKWELL name tag stitched above the TTC patch.

Bronc said, "It doesn't get any better than this!"

Beverly said, "Lady Jane and I put our initials on it."

"I can see that. I'm having this emblem painted on every single one of TTC's aircraft – initials and all. It's going on the wall of every building in my command. I'll probably have it painted on our runways."

Lady Jane said, "Try it on, Bronc – we are dying to see how it looks on you."

Maj. Gen. Blackwell ripped off the jacket he was wearing. Beverly held the new A-2 for him. "I need to go find a mirror, baby."

Brandy said, "Check inside the jacket on the left side first, Bronc."

Maj. Gen. Blackwell pulled it open, “This what I think it is?”

An enlarged copy of the pinup swimsuit photo of Brandy that Captain Billy Jack Jaxx had carried in his plexiglass pistol grip was stitched in the liner under a clear plastic overlay signed, “Love Brandy.”

Maj. Gen. Blackwell said, “I’m having a really good day.”

LIEUTENANT TED HAMILTON, OBE, MC, “THE GREAT TEDDY” arrived at the hotel.

Colonel John Randal said, “Where have you been, Lieutenant? I haven’t seen you since we got here.”

Lt. Hamilton said, “Being indoctrinated into my new assignment, sir.”

“What new assignment?”

“Can we speak in private, Colonel?”

They moved off to a secure spot in the VIP section.

Lt. Hamilton said, “An organization called the London Controlling Section has created OPERATION FORTITUDE, the overall D-Day deception campaign designed to cover the D-Day invasion. FORTITUDE SOUTH – a subset of FORTITUDE – is aimed at presenting Pas-de-Calais as the target for the invasion. Which means it’s not, sir.

“FORTITUDE SOUTH has been assigned to the new Supreme Headquarters Allied Expeditionary Force to execute certain aspects of the operation in conjunction with other agencies. A SHAEF section called Ops(B) is being organized to coordinate the deception programs for D-Day with MI-5 and the LCS, sir. Brigadier Dudley Clarke’s deputy, Colonel Noel Wild, is en route as we speak from Cairo to run it.

“Ops(B) will be broken down into Operations and Intelligence. I am assigned to Operations. We will be responsible for handling physical deception – specifically sir, in my case, inflatables. My understanding is Colonel David Strangeways will also be brought in from A-Force to oversee the implementation of the physical deceptions so I will be working for him.”

Col. Randal said, “What is it you’re supposed to do, exactly?”

Lt. Hamilton said, “Because of my background as a military conjuror I have been assigned to create an illusion, sir – my personal biggest ever.”

“What does that mean?”

Lt. Hamilton said, “My specific duties initially involve repairing to Seaborn House and setting up a couple of dummy airfields and activating an armored division, sir.”

Col. Randal said, “And how do you intend to do that?”

“Inflatables . . . big balloon-like tanks and airplanes, sir. You blow them up like you would a child’s rubber swimming pool. Hey, Presto – a division of tanks and a wing of airplanes magically appears overnight.

“The idea is for the RAF to allow an occasional German photo reconnaissance aircraft to overfly the estate at Seaborn House to observe my handiwork. With any luck, sir, I can convince the Germans to bomb us.”

Col. Randal said, “Try to get ’em to miss the house.”

He was reasonably confident the part of Lt. Hamilton’s report about the Pas-de-Calais not being where the Allies would land on D-Day was *supposed* to be one of the most tightly guarded secrets of the war. It was definitely not information to be shared with the commander of the Special Operations unit tasked with conducting boots on the ground missions in the district where the invasion would *not* be taking place.

From what Lt. Hamilton said it sounded like Brig. Clarke was strategically placing A-Force’s key officers in the top echelon of SHAEF to oversee the deception phase for D-Day. As a result he would be like a puppet master pulling the strings of FORTITUDE SOUTH long-distance from Cairo. The Brigadier was tricky like that. Was his long-time relationship with Raiding Forces the reason he recommended them to the London Controlling Section?

Col. Randal said, “If anyone even suspects you suggested to me Calais is not the actual site of the invasion I’ll be sidelined until after D-Day. You could end up behind bars in the Tower of London. Is that clear?”

Lt. Hamilton said, “Absolutely, sir.”

Col. Randal said, “Good – keep me in the loop, stud.”

“Always, sir.”

“What else have you been up to?”

“Working with Political Warfare Executive, sir.”

“Oh yeah, doing what?”

“Engaging in the ongoing battle for the hearts and minds of the German fighting men stationed in France, sir. Bringing enlightenment. Provoking despair.”

"How does that work?"

"Pornography, Colonel."

"Really?"

"PWE conducts photo shoots depicting beautiful blond women having sex with sinister-looking individuals who do not take their hats off so you know they are civilians. Then we write some catchy phrase like, 'When you are stationed far from home she is *not* alone.' The RAF scatters the photographs over France, sir."

"You think that works?"

"No way of knowing. Could stimulate second thoughts. Lots of fun, sir."

"Keep up the good work, Lieutenant. Just don't let Lady Jane know about the porn."

"Can I tell Captain Jaxx . . . ?"

MAJOR GENERAL WILLIAM "WILD BILL" DONOVAN SAID, "I have a Canadian officer I'd like you to talk to."

Colonel John Randal said, "Yes, sir."

Maj. Gen. Donovan signaled a Royal Canadian Navy Volunteer Reserve, RCNVR lieutenant over to the VIP area. He made introductions. Then the three moved to a quiet place behind the velvet rope where they could have a conversation.

Maj. Gen. Donovan said, "Tell the colonel your story, Lieutenant."

Lieutenant Bruce Wright said, "Two years ago, sir, I was in St. Johns, Newfoundland, awaiting an assignment to a Canadian corvette on Atlantic escort duties. One day the boom patrol skipper of one of the patrol boats guarding the harbor reported in sick. I filled in for him. My orders were to patrol up and down the net protecting the harbor and to keep an eye out for any U-boat that might come nosing around.

"Pleasant if somewhat boring duty, sir. I passed the time pondering how one would go about defeating the antisubmarine net that was closed across the mouth of the harbor and only opened to allow ships to enter or depart. I concluded that this could best be accomplished by underwater swimmers. I recalled having read a magazine article about abalone divers in California utilizing paddle boards, dive masks and swim fins.

"It occurred to me if such a diver could be put overboard from a submarine outside the boom defense he could cut a hole in the net then tow a limpet mine through and place it against the hull of a warship or merchantman. Soon after that I boarded my ship and went to sea, sir. To amuse myself when not on watch I wrote a dissertation titled *The Use of Natatorial Assault and Reconnaissance Units in Combined Operations.*

"My skipper on the corvette liked it and forwarded the paper up the chain of command. It reached the desk of the Flag Officer, Halifax, who dispatched it to the Director of Naval Intelligence in Ottawa. From there it was sent to the Director of Naval Intelligence at the Admiralty in the UK, sir.

"A rocket arrived ordering me to report to Combined Operations Headquarters in London forthwith to 'develop' my proposal. I was instructed to bring a surfboard, dive mask, swim fins and an 'underwater spring gun' complete with arrows.' That was the problem, Colonel.

"Not only did I not have the gear requested, I had never laid eyes on any of it. I only read the one magazine story, sir. Incredibly, I now found myself attached to the Naval Intelligence Department for 'TOP SECRET Special Duty' – an expert in a field I knew nothing about.

"I won't bore you with the details, sir, but I traveled to Los Angeles to find out what kind of skin-diving equipment was to be had. I located a small firm that manufactured most of what was needed. Except for the speargun. I had to settle for pictures of one of those, sir. The diving gear company had an employee who was an abalone diver. He demonstrated how to use the gear.

"Then I sat down and wrote another paper titled, *The Organization and Equipment of a Natatorial Unit,* sir."

Maj. Gen. Donovan said, "At that point Lieutenant Wright was brought to my attention. OSS had come into possession of his paper, reviewed his work, and adopted it as our training syllabus for the Maritime Unit. We were particularly impressed with his mission statement, 'To conduct special reconnaissance of landing beaches, to attack shipping and shore objectives in defended harbors, and to act as scouts and raiders in inland waters . . .'

"When he arrived in London COHQ authorized Lieutenant Wright to raise a team of one hundred men for a unit called the 'Amphibious Reconnaissance Party' – later changed to 'Sea Reconnaissance Unit' . . . SRU. They were to be trained in the use of fins, masks and paddle boards to include body surfing, riding in on and returning through heavy breakers, night paddle boarding, long distance swimming, etc.

"Lieutenant Wright is a visionary when it comes to developing new naval warfare techniques and planning training programs. And he turned out to be something of an overachiever as a troop leader. The SRU trained and trained and trained. In the States. In the Bahamas. With the U.S. Navy UDTs, the Army's Scouts and Raiders, my MUs. And spent time with the Marine Corps at Camp Pendleton to develop tactics for dealing with sentry dogs patrolling landing beaches.

"When the SRU returned to England it was shipped to Achnacarry for Commando training in scouting, patrolling, stalking, cliff climbing – you know the drill. Then Ringway for jump school."

Lt. Wright said, "All that took time. The war moved on. The senior officers who knew about the unit had been reassigned elsewhere and we did not have a mission. The SRU had fallen through the cracks. Morale plummeted, the men started volunteering out. At this point we are down to thirty-two swimmers."

Col. Randal said, "Have you or any of your SRU operators ever been on an operation?"

"Negative, sir."

"Here's what's going to happen," Col. Randal said. "SRU will be flown out to Egypt tonight. Immediately upon arrival at Advance Base Castelrozzo – meaning same day, you will commence an intensive amphibious raiding campaign against island targets in the Aegean Sea."

Lt. Wright said, "Actual targets?"

Col. Randal said, "That's what you're here for isn't it, Lieutenant?"

"Yes sir, absolutely!"

Col. Randal said, "I wouldn't write any more papers for the time being if I were you."

Lt. Wright departed to put his SRU people on alert for immediate departure to Egypt. Col. Randal sent for Major Butch "Headhunter" Hoolihan and Captain Billy Jack Jaxx. They were both in the hotel. Maj. Gen. Donovan sat in on the conversation.

Col. Randal said, "How's your recruiting of No. 12 Commando personnel progressing, Major?"

Maj. Hoolihan said, “Afraid we got there late, sir. SAS beat us to them. I was only able to enroll eleven Commandos who were away at the time the recruiters showed up.”

“Not a problem. We’ll take what we can get. I have a change of mission for you and Captain Jaxx.”

Both officers perked up. Having recently been handed new assignments this announcement was not expected. New developments were coming hot and heavy.

Col. Randal said, “I have a new TO&E for Major Hoolihan’s 40 Assault Unit troop. General Donovan brought us an unassigned outfit called Sea Reconnaissance Unit. It’s led by a Royal Canadian Navy Volunteer Reserve lieutenant and consists of personnel from the British Army, Navy and RAF. They’re the British equivalent of the OSS Maritime Unit. Overtrained, under-experienced.

“Major, you’re to take command of the SRU – thirty-two men, one officer. You will fly out with them for ABC as soon as you can effect coordination with TTC. Possibly as soon as tonight. Combine the SRU with the 40 AU Red Indians and the remainder of your Marine troop. Feel free to reorganize what will continue to be called 40 Assault Unit as you see fit.

“I want you to conduct a series of raids utilizing the SRU to give the swimmers combat experience. At some point prior to D-Day your 40 AU will be transferred back here to Seaborn House to go through specialized training Commander Fleming has lined up.

“Questions?”

“No sir, thank you!” Maj. Hoolihan was thrilled with the new assignment. Now he had his old Royal Marine troop. They had a long history of raiding the Via Balbia from the sea side. He had not been pleased to have lost part of his Marines due to the transfer to Seaborn House.

Col. Randal said, “Captain Jaxx, you will continue your amalgamation of the OSS Maritime Unit into your Special Operations Group. The combined unit will become an OSS Operational Group – OG Ranger.”

“Wilco.”

“Later when Major Hoolihan brings his people back to Seaborn House we’ll go back to the Team A and Team B concept we previously discussed without calling them that,” Col. Randal said.

"I want both of you capable of operating independently. Butch, you remain 40 AU. Jack, you will be OG Ranger. You two studs will be conducting Special Operations for NID and OSS for some time to come. Maybe through the end of the war.

"Is that clear?"

Capt. Jaxx said, "Yes sir, sounds good."

Maj. Hoolihan said, "Roger."

Col. Randal said, "General, anything you would care to elaborate on?"

"Not at this time," Maj. Gen. Donovan said. "Understand you two officers are being groomed for a very important mission. One with long-range national defense implications for both our countries."

Capt. Jaxx said, "I have a question, sir. What kind of specialized training? You've mentioned it before."

Maj. Gen. Donovan said, "Lock picking, key making, safe cracking..."

That gave Jack Cool and the Headhunter something to think about.

Maj. Gen. Donovan had chosen not to inject himself into the conversation but he was well-pleased with Col. Randal's plan. OSS was going to get involved in the war in Europe one way or another. Now he would have stories to tell the President that took place somewhere other than remote places no one had ever heard of before. Raiding Forces was about to be front and center in the secret war on the Continent of Europe.

Col. Randal went to place a phone call to the Naval Intelligence Division. He spoke to Commander Ian Fleming. "There's been a new development involving 40 Assault Unit. You need to come by the hotel as soon as possible. You're going to want to meet your new contingent of Red Indians. They'll be flying out to ABC later today or tonight."

Cdr. Fleming said, "I am on my way."

LIEUTENANT GENERAL "GERONIMO" JOE MCKOY, MAJOR General Sam Houston Blackwell and Waldo Treywick were sitting in the VIP section chewing on Waldo's long, thin cigars. They were watching Major General William "Wild Bill" Donovan talking to Colonel John Randal and a Canadian naval officer none of the three had ever seen before.

After the Canadian left, Major Butch Hoolihan and Captain Billy Jack Jaxx arrived for what was clearly a serious discussion.

Maj. Gen. Blackwell said, "Beverly said this was billed as a two-week leave. Look at the colonel. He hasn't quit wheeling and dealing since he got here – nonstop."

Lt. Gen. McKoy said, "John suspected we might be walkin' into a hornet's nest. That's why me 'n Waldo are here . . . in case he needed us for somethin.' We were headed to the Congo until this UK trip came up."

He did not mention why. Maj. Gen. Blackwell was not cleared for LONG NECK. Even though his daughter was a plank-holding member of CARD GAME.

Maj. Gen. Blackwell said, "You spent some time in the Philippines. The other night Ike called John 'The Butterfly.'

"What does that mean?"

Lt. Gen. McKoy said, "Filipino women – meanin' mostly hookers – refer to American servicemen who, not havin' a steady girlfriend and 'flit from flower to flower' as 'Butterfly Boys.'"

Maj. Gen. Blackwell said, "No kidding?"

"Since that definition pretty much fit ever soldier, sailor and marine in country, a man would a' had to run up a pretty big score to earn the permanent monicker 'Butterfly'," Lt. Gen. McKoy said.

Waldo said, "Must a' taken a lot a' flittin'."

Lt. Gen. McKoy said, "John ain't volunteerin' n' I ain't askin.'"

"I may have underestimated Johnny," Maj. Gen. Blackwell said.

Lt. Gen. McKoy said, "How'd it come up, Bronc?"

"Something about a bandit named Smiling Jack."

Waldo said, "Colonel shot him."

Lt. Gen. McKoy said, "That's all we know."

Waldo said, "Which don't mean we ain't interested, in case you ever find out, General."

IT WAS TIME FOR BEVERLY BLACKWELL TO ATTEND HER first XX Committee meeting. She was more than a little anxious. The men – there were no other women except for an MI-5 stenographer – on the committee were some of the most brilliant minds in Great Britain. All highly experienced senior intelligence officers. Beverly was not.

To the uninitiated it might have seemed as if the Club spent its time planning schoolboy pranks to play on the Nazis, but there was more to it than that. The fate of the D-Day invasion might be decided by a single misstep. Every piece of information had to be vetted before the B1-A's double agents passed it on to his or her case officer in the Abwehr. A single scrap of information could reveal the entire German spy network in England was under MI-5's control. The weekly XX Committee meeting were serious affairs.

XX sessions were characterized by another element. Everyone in the room was keeping a secret. Beverly's was she did not have a clue what she was doing there.

Lieutenant Colonel Thomas Argyll Robertson had explained to her what XX did in simple terms he thought she would understand. "The Club plays for all the marbles – tens of thousands of lives are at stake when D-Day finally arrives." Beverly was not comforted by Tar's explanation.

It was imperative she make a good first impression, so she called in Major the Lady Jane Seaborn for consultation. This was classic "Right Man, Right Job" only "woman" was more appropriate in this case. What to wear was extremely important especially to men who judged others by the stitching on their button holes or the number of pleats on the back of their gloves. There would not be any blue jeans and pee-wee cowgirl boots.

Lady Jane said, "We shall put your hair up in a severe French Twist. Full warpaint – there's a make-up artist here in the hotel."

Beverly had two options in her quest to "dress for success."

Option 1: Beverly was OSS. She was not a WAC. Nor did she hold a military rank. Therefore she could go dressed as a civilian. Wear one of Lady Jane's outfits that cost a year's salary of anyone on the Double Cross Committee. That would make an impression.

Option 2: Beverly was OSS. She was not a WAC. Nor did she hold a military rank. However, Maj. Gen. Donovan, whom she was representing, could change that with the stroke of a pen by giving her a direct commission. Or she could attend the meeting in uniform displaying U.S. lapel insignia and no rank – as U.S. Army CIC agents and some OSS personnel commonly did. This would allow her to display her valor awards and qualification badges while concealing her military status.

Colonel John Randal said, "Option two."

Lady Jane said, "Agreed."

Beverly's decorations consisted of the Silver Star, the Distinguished Flying Cross with two oakleaf clusters and the Soldier's Medal plus service and campaign medals. Her qualification badges, worn over her heart above the decorations were Pilot Wings, Jump Wings, Glider Pilot Wings and a pair of British Special Forces parachute wings over the right breast pocket.

Col. Randal said, "You may fool XX into believing you're Superwoman, but you're still a dizzy blonde to me."

Beverly laughed, "Roger that."

She was scared to death.

Lady Jane said, "Think of the meeting as play acting. You were a drama major at UT. Walk in, shake hands with everyone you are introduced to – Tar shall be there to handle that part. Firm grip. Look them in the eye. Be poised. Be attentive. No big beauty queen smiles.

"The less you say the better. Absolutely nothing would be perfect."

Beverly said, "I can do that – maybe."

Lady Jane said, "Be the first to leave once the meeting is over. No small talk with the Committee members afterwards. Remember they are all intelligence officers. Do not provide them with any personal information about yourself to evaluate you on other than you are beautiful, highly decorated and deadly focused.

"One of the hotel's limousines will be waiting to whisk you back here."

"Play it strictly professional," Col. Randal said. "Walk in with a Commando knife in your teeth and blood in your eye."

Beverly laughed – Johnny always had a way of making her feel better. "I don't want to let you down."

Col. Randal said, "You won't."

Lady Jane said, "One last thing. You do *not* work for XX. You work for General Donovan – a fine distinction to keep in mind at all times."

Col. Randal and Lady Jane rode in the limousine with Beverly to drop her off at the meeting. She was getting into character on the way to mask her anxiety – it helped. A little.

When the car arrived, before Beverly stepped out Col. Randal said, "Beautiful women are often discriminated against because of their looks. Go in there and use yours as a weapon. You've got this."

On the ride back to the hotel Lady Jane said, "That was nice of you to say to Beverly. Most insightful on your part. I had no idea you understood how often beautiful women are prejudged for their looks."

Col. Randal said, "I just said that, Jane – everybody knows good-looking women aren't very smart."

Lady Jane laughed. "Oh, you are going to pay, John Randal."

10

WHY TAKE A CHANCE

JAMES "BALDIE" TAYLOR ARRIVED AT THE BRADFORD HOTEL in the early afternoon on Christmas Eve. There was a buzz of excitement in the air, tinged with a certain amount of well-concealed homesickness, as the staff and guests went about their business in anticipation of celebrating the holiday away from home and family. The war did not slow down for Santa Claus.

Jim had not been there much lately. His liaison duties between LCS, XX Committee, MI-5 and SOE kept him on the move. And he was still a career MI-6 officer – he reported in to Broadway almost daily. A fact he did not advertise, but it was true that once in the Secret Intelligence Service always in – or on at the very least on call.

It was fine with him if that reality was overlooked by all the other agencies.

The multi-tiered assignment was taking some adjusting to. The liaison job was a tightrope balancing act. Mixed loyalties had to be navigated. Personalities and egos had to be managed. Survival, meaning job performance, meant not allowing the players to know if he had an agenda, which he did, or showing sides to one faction or the other, which he also did. It would be easy to get caught in the crossfire between agencies and highly placed intelligence officers with competing mission statements – the experience was not unlike tiptoeing through a minefield.

Jim found himself one of the unseen players at the very heart of the D-Day deception program. While not in a position to be able to directly influence the outcome except in an advisory capacity – he was of vital importance to ensuring the assorted personalities understood each other and worked together as smoothly as possible. The role called for him to be an intelligence officer, soldier, diplomat, confidant – a chameleon.

Today he was here to coordinate a late-breaking mission on behalf of Special Operations Executive. While his primary responsibility as it pertained to the "Baker Street Irregulars" was to keep them at arm's length from LCS, MI-6, MI-5 and specifically Colonel John Randal – even though Raiding Forces had an ongoing commitment to insert/extract SOE agents into/out of enemy-occupied France.

Major General Sam Houston Blackwell's Troop Transport Command's two Special Operations Squadrons were in the process of establishing an efficient system for dropping SOE agents and supplies. However, doing so was complicated and was never going to be any easier.

In a perfect world air supply missions for MI-6 and SOE would have been an RAF responsibility. Unfortunately the British did not have enough aircraft or aircrew available at any given time to interrupt their normal operations to fly a time sensitive clandestine mission on call. That was a problem. Intelligence jobs were more often than not time-critical. TTC had stepped in to take up the slack – likely in no small part influenced by Maj. Gen. William "Wild Bill" Donovan's relationship with Maj. Gen. Blackwell. Having his longtime friend handle supply drops for SOE gave OSS some small control over their guerrilla operations on the continent.

Air drops were the lifeblood of the French Resistance. However, all air operations were wholly dependent on weather conditions. And it did not always cooperate.

There were three basic types of SOE missions that required air support. 1) To drop agents by parachute; 2) To drop arms, demolitions and other stores to the Resistance; 3)To land on improvised landing strips to insert or extract agents.

Dropping agents or cargo into enemy-occupied France required extensive advance planning and coordination. While not always the case with agents who could be dropped in blind without a reception committee or even informing the Resistance they were arriving – dropping arms, stores and equipment was a lot more complicated than simply sending an aircraft to some preselected location and having door kickers put the bundles out as they flew over.

First a DZ had to be selected by the on-scene Resistance group that would be receiving the supply drop. They then had to inform SOE where the DZ was be located. Next TTC had to notify the Underground fighters when the mission would be flown. Communications were often a crude affair. Carrier pigeons and/or secret messages at the end of certain British Broadcasting Radio shows often were the only means of communicating between SOE Baker Street and the French Resistance cell requesting the air drop.

The DZ had to be marked in a specific way so the pilot could confirm the drop was being made to the Resistance and *not* the Germans, who were known to set up false drop zones to trick the aircrew. The signals information had to be transmitted to SOE Baker Street who supplied it to TTC prior to their flying the mission. The communications back and forth could be a lengthy and somewhat unreliable process as not all French Underground guerrilla units were in direct wireless contact with SOE.

On the night of a reception committee had to be organized to recover the parachutes, collect the weapons and materiel, and transport arranged to spirit the stores to a safe location. This operation was entirely contingent on wind conditions that had to be conducive to an air drop. Excessive winds would result in the supply chutes becoming scattered. It was not desirable for parachutes to drift and become stuck in trees and still be hanging there when the sun came up. That would be disastrous for the local Underground. If every single item dropped to include the parachutes was not recovered it would be a dead giveaway to the Germans that an air supply mission had taken place. They would come calling in force with a vengeance.

And last but not least, the TTC navigators had to be able to fly to and locate the DZ – not all that simple.

Lieutenant General "Geronimo" Joe McKoy's frequent observation, "There's been many a slip betwixt the cup and the lip" was in full force and effect on aerial drops.

Landing a plane behind the lines in France on an improvised airstrip to deliver agents was a high-risk proposition. Extractions posed their own problem. It was not always possible to bring out some people by air in an emergency because more PAX showed up than the number originally anticipated. If a plane made a bad landing, became stuck in the mud, broke its landing gear or had any one of a hundred other equipment failures incidental to landing on a rough strip, the mission would end in disaster. The aircraft would be sitting there the next day – an open invitation to the Gestapo to descend on the area and sweep up anyone they suspected to be in the Resistance.

Small boats, MTBs, MGBs and PTs were the preferred method of choice for supplying the French Resistance in the coastal region. Much more in the way of passengers, stores and equipment could be transported by sea. The problem was the Royal Navy had other commitments. The Vice Admiral-in-Charge of Channel Operations, Dover, did not appreciate having his limited resources diverted by the intelligence agencies for missions he believed were of dubious value. He was not cooperative.

That left Raiding Forces. They seemed to have recently found their own way of delivering small-scale raiding parties to the coast of France. How Col. Randal managed the trick was not clear to all interested agencies. But they sought to take advantage of it.

Maj. Gen. Donovan wanted Raiding Forces to provide the service to MI-6 and SOE as long as it did not interfere with the missions delivered by King's Messenger. Those had top priority. Under the new mandate for SFHQ Col. Randal had to sign off on every SOE operation up to five miles inland and that included agent insertions/extractions and resupply missions. Wild Bill wanted the 5-mile mandate enforced. He had ulterior motives. But then that was usually the case.

Jim came straight to the VIP section. Col. Randal was sitting off to one side with Beverly. She was telling him about her recent meeting with the XX Committee – information he was not cleared to hear. It was an interesting story.

Beverly was saying, "There's lots of secrets being kept from each other behind those closed doors. Jim was there. He's the liaison from MI-5 to LCS and XX. And there was a major from Political Warfare Executive, Hawthorne Merryweather. I met him at Oasis X.

"He and Jim acted like they didn't know each other. Major Merryweather pulled me aside to whisper he was Raiding Forces by way of Force N in Abyssinia. Doesn't want anyone in the Club to know for some reason. He asked me to tell you he would be dropping by the hotel..."

Col. Randal said, "Hold that thought."

The Vulnerable Points security operator let Jim in. While he was clearly there on business, Col. Randal did not ask Beverly to leave. He wanted her to hear what Baldie might have to say.

And he wanted it clear that doing so was his intent.

Jim said, "I am wearing my SOE hat today, Colonel. The Baker Street Irregulars at the Ministry of Ungentlemanly Conduct, as they like to call themselves – working in conjunction with MI-9 Escape – has a mission request."

Col. Randal said, "Let's go down to the Bunker where we can look at the map while you lay it out."

"Good idea."

Col. Randal said, "Beverly do you know where Jack is?"

"I think he's shooting dice with the porters again."

"Round him up and bring him downstairs."

When Jim arrived, Brandy Seaborn looked their way. Col. Randal nodded. She joined them after excusing herself from a conversation with Captain Penelope "Legs" Honeycutt-Parker and her husband.

Col. Randal said, "Jim has an SOE/MI-9 mission he's getting ready to brief. We're heading down to the Bunker. You might want to bring Parker along."

Downstairs there was now a Vulnerable Points Wing operator at a security desk in front of the door. The Bunker was getting organized. Drop-in visitors were not encouraged.

Col. Randal, Jim, Major the Lady Jane Seaborn, Lieutenant General "Geronimo" Joe McKoy, Captain Billy Jack Jaxx, Brandy, Capt. Honeycutt-Parker, Beverly and Brandy gathered around the large wall mosaic of the coast of France. While a few more photos and picture postcards had been added to fill in blank spaces, it was not a lot.

Col. Randal felt the urge to laugh every time he looked at it. The montage of aerial photographs, vacation photos, picture postcards and topographical maps was one of those stories you could not make up. No one would believe it.

Lt. Gen. McKoy said, "It's a good thing folks back home can't see what it is we're fightin' the war with over here. Wouldn't be real reassurin' to learn it's a lot like a sandlot football game."

"Exactly," Beverly said.

Jim said, "SOE has a two-pronged mission needing to be executed same night. Immediately upon conclusion of this briefing you will depart this location by a method of your own choosing for Seaborn House. Upon arriving you will rendezvous with a two-party team of Joes under the supervision of an SOE conducting officer. From there you will travel by boat to France to insert the agents at grid coordinates 41345646.

"As soon as the Joes are ashore you are to proceed to 42735682 where you will bring off a party of thirty to forty SOE 'parcels' for transport back to England.

"What are your questions?"

Col. Randal said, "Signals?"

"An SOE officer will be linking up with you at Seaborn House to brief the signals," Jim said. "Then he will accompany the mission in order to handle your ship-to-shore communications. His only responsibility is signaling."

Beverly said, "What's a parcel?"

Jim said, "A quote taken directly from my marching orders. Spy talk. Meaning PAX or personnel."

Beverly said. "Who does SOE think they're fooling?"

"Your guess is as good as mine," Jim said. "You are a high-level liaison officer now, Beverly. As you know our job is to observe and report – no opinions unless specifically asked. Then very little of that unless it's an operational detail I refrain from idle questions."

Beverly laughed, "I don't ever say anything,"

Capt. Jaxx said, "Looks like a desolate stretch of coastline – no villages. The beach is small. The Germans probably don't have a lot of troops in the area."

Jim said, "That is the idea."

Lady Jane said, "I shall call upstairs to arrange hotel transportation to Seaborn House."

"Good," Col. Randal said. "Will you get a message to Lionel to come down here?"

When Lady Jane walked away, Capt. Jaxx said, "Sir, are you planning to lead this one?"

Col. Randal said, "We're going to continue having these types of missions for MI-6 and SOE. I want Colonel Honeycutt-Parker to use his best team for this op. I thought you and I might go along to see how they work."

Capt. Jaxx said, "Yes, sir."

Col. Randal said, "Jim, what I need you to do for me is let it be known to everyone you're working with that Beverly attended your briefing today because she's wired in on all of Raiding Forces' operations."

"I can do that."

"Make it clear Beverly's been Lady Jane's personal assistant from the time she was recruited for Raiding Forces. Effective immediately she's mine too – has been for a long time," Col. Randal said. "And as you are aware in addition to her liaison duty she also works with Colonel Robertson at MI-5 as a case officer."

Jim said, "I can make Beverly's duties general knowledge within the intelligence community."

He understood what Col. Randal was doing. Fortifying her bona fides – taking care of one of his troops.

Beverly laughed. "Can I indent for overtime?"

Lt. Col. Lionel Honeycutt-Parker walked in. "You wanted to see me, sir?"

"Raiding Forces has been tapped for an SOE mission," Col. Randal said. "An agent insertion in one location and an extraction of a fairly large party from another. I need you to advise me on the composition of the Raiding Forces' support team."

Lt. Col. Honeycutt-Parker said, "Captain Dick Courtney has recently returned from a classified operation he's been involved with on a recurring basis. When he is back at Seaborn House I have used him for these types of assignments on numerous occasions. Typically a shore party consists of five or six men."

Col. Randal had not seen the former Gold Coast Border Patrol policeman since their gun jeep patrolling days out of Oasis X. "Does he still have his two strikers, X-Ray and Vanish, with him?"

"He does. The three have been seconded to the Naval Intelligence Division on a TDY basis on-call for an ongoing operation Raiding Forces has supplied personnel on a rotating basis for the last two years,"

Lt. Col. Honeycutt-Parker said. "While I am not cleared for the details of their assignment what I do know is he and his strikers have spent a year pulling multiweek deployments for NID behind the lines somewhere in France. They go in, stay ten days to two weeks, come out for a week or two and then go back in."Capt. Courtney is my best pure reconnaissance operator. Highly decorated for who knows what? The NID assignment is classified."

While they were talking, his wife, Capt. Honeycutt-Parker, was studying the map mosaic working with her protractor plotting the route. It was straightforward navigation. Provided, that is, the receiving party on the second landing was alert and signaled when they arrived. There would not be any going in to the extraction point blind.

No signal, no landing. Wrong signal, no landing. Raiding Forces' unwritten rule: "Why take a chance?" would be front and center on everyone's minds for the duration of these kinds of cross-channel missions. A lot of things could happen on an enemy shore in the dark of night – most all of them not the desired outcome.

Col. Randal, Lady Jane, Capt. Jaxx and Beverly arrived at Seaborn House as twilight was falling. Brandy and Capt. Honeycutt-Parker had come down earlier. They linked up with the SOE signals officer and the SOE conducting officer who was escorting the Joe's, a man and a woman. An MI-9 Escape officer would also be along to facilitate the linkup with the party to be extracted.

As was protocol, security was so tight neither the "Seeing Off Officer" nor the two Joes introduced themselves. The less anyone knew about their business the better. They had a bicycle with them. It was a standard single-seat model. While everyone on the Raiding Forces' side of the operation wondered how that was going to work, no one asked.

At 1830 hrs a call came through from 64 Baker Street, London, to confirm the operation was indeed "on."

"Brandy and "Legs" Parker went to inspect the PT boat. The ex-Sea Rover Scouts now Royal Navy Volunteer Reserve crew were hard at work. The sailors had been spending all their time since the two craft arrived at Seaborn house familiarizing themselves with the boats. They had been living on them. A mission to France was not the stage to learn your way around your ship. Brandy's young crew was well-prepared. They were experienced small unit cross-channel veterans. Arguably the best in the business.

The Warning Order had been sent ahead by courier. It was given to Capt. Courtney who issued it to X-Ray, Vanish and three Seaborn House operators – all veterans of this type of mission, who had been selected for the night's work. Col. Randal did not know the men.

Brandy went first. Tonight would not follow the standard five-paragraph order format. Being a hasty mission, it would pretty much consist of, "Get your gear, let's go."

Then Capt. Courtney briefed. It was a straightforward mission. Drop off the two agents. They would go ashore without a beach party. When the LBSM returned, Brandy would set sail for the second objective. Upon arrival he would lead Vanish and X-Ray plus the three operators ashore, link up with the SOE conducting officer, escort the party to be extracted to the beach, where they would be rowed to the PT boat and return to Seaborn House.

When the briefing was concluded, Beverly said, "Johnny, what do you want me to do?"

Col. Randal said, "You monitor the mission from the TOC with Lady Jane."

Beverly said, "But you and Jack are . . ."

Col. Randal said, "You're prohibited from going into harm's way until after D-Day – no flying, no PT boat jaunts. Besides, we're only along as observers."

"I may not like XX liaison duty," Beverly said. "Is it too late to back out?"

"Sorry, you've already been initiated into the mysteries of MI-5," Col. Randal said. "Why do you think Tar issued you that L-pill?"

Lady Jane said, "Make sure not to let anyone know you feel that way, Beverly. The intelligence services have a secret prison they call the 'Forgetting School.' People who go through training and fail to meet minimum standards, have a change of heart for any reason or turn down an assignment once they have been briefed are sent there for the duration. Put in isolation to forget what they know because they learned too much to risk letting them talk."

Beverly said, "Wow, are you making that up to scare me?"

"Not in the least. There is one in the UK and one in Egypt," Lady Jane said. "Commander Seligman of the Levant Schooner Flotilla was recruited by SOE in Cairo. After hearing what they had in mind for him he turned down their job offer on the grounds it violated the Geneva Convention.

"SOE threatened him with Forgetting School. When he still refused they attempted to arrest him."

"What'd he do?"

Lady Jane said, "Jumped off a two-story flight of stairs, ran out in the street and escaped. Agents chased him but he managed to get away. If SOE believed Adrian knew too much after one recruiting pitch, how do you think MI-5 is going to feel about you?"

Beverly said, "I wouldn't want Tin Eye after me."

Following the Operations Order there was no time for rehearsals. Other than Col. Randal and Capt. Jaxx, everyone on the Raiding Forces' side had carried out operations like this before. At least from the standpoint of inserting or extracting agents.

This would be the largest extraction Seaborn House had ever attempted – an unspoken concern. The MI-9 Escape officer and the SOE Signals Officer were of unknown ability. They would bear watching.

Col. Randal had time for a brief reunion with Capt. Courtney, X-Ray and Vanish. The young White Hunter, Gold Coast Border Patrol Policeman – now Raiding Forces' special reconnaissance operator – had not changed much from the last time they had worked together. The captain was in charge, confident, self-reliant – one of the better junior officers he had ever served with.

X-Ray and Vanish were all smiles when they saw Col. Randal. If spending as much time behind the lines had been hard duty, none of the three showed it. The same could not be said for Col. Randal.

Noticing the scar on the left side of his face, Capt. Courtney said, "Cut yourself shaving, sir?"

Col. Randal said, "Something like that." Capt. Courtney had already heard Jack Cool's version of the story. Lady Jane was a hot topic of conversation among the bachelor set of Raiding Forces' officers at Seaborn House. As were Mandy and Beverly.

When the two Joes boarded the PT boat their conducting officer did not come with them. He remained on the dock with Lady Jane and Beverly.

The role of a Seeing Off Officer was to ensure last-minute mission preparations were completed. Then check to guarantee the agents they were escorting had the correct false ID card, ration card, work permit, transit papers, weapons, explosives, communications devices, etc. And conduct a thorough body search looking for anything such as a letter, photograph, a personal engraving on a ring, or anything else they might have on their person that could blow their cover. Any British-made item such as a wristwatch could lead to interrogation, imprisonment or execution.

The Seeing Off Officer's last act was to watch the Joes depart, which some thought was the most difficult aspect of the assignment.

In the run-up to departure, an SOE conducting officer spent a lot of time with his charges. He/she was responsible for providing emotional support for the Joes during the highly stressful waiting-to-go period. This process was described in the pocket-sized SOE field manual, *How To Become A Seeing Off Officer*, as "…catering to the agent's emotional needs." Generally that consisted of taking them out to dinner or a show. Some went so far as to stretch their interpretation of the guidebook's instructions to include such things as supplying them with a hooker.

Lady Jane had served as a Seeing Off Officer for a brief time. While not supplying any ladies of the evening for her Joes, she did occasionally have to provide emotional support to some anxious spy experiencing a last-minute case of nerves. She confided to Col. Randal knowing the survival rate of an SOE operative in the field was less than 50 percent, made her feel like a "Judas Goat" when seeing them off.

Col. Randal had said, "I can see how it would."

On board the PT no one went near the female spy. Women SOE agents were primarily tasked with being wireless operators. The Germans, while having a comically inept offensive spy operation in England, were the war's absolute masters of technology. The Abwehr had a highly aggressive Direction Finding (DF) program in France. Transmitting messages was suicidal if an SOE telegrapher stayed on the air for long. It was claimed once in the field a wireless operator's life expectancy was only six weeks – possibly less.

If captured a female agent could expect to be subjected to enhanced interrogation, torture, rape, being turned under duress and eventual execution. The job of wireless operator for SOE in enemy-occupied territory was as dangerous as any assignment in the military and more than most – to include combat infantrymen. Still, there was never a shortage of women volunteers.

Lady Jane was standing on the dock with Col. Randal and Capt. Jaxx who arrived carrying a duffel bag slung over his shoulder. They were watching Capt. Courtney's team file on board. "You and Jack are not getting off the boat tonight." It sounded more like a direct order than a question.

"Don't worry," Col. Randal said.

"Captain?"

"I hear you loud and clear, Lady Jane."

"If the colonel attempts to go ashore shoot him with your .22 pistol some place he shall have to be restricted to light duty for a long time – that is an order, Jack."

Brandy revved the Packard engines. Final boarding call. Col. Randal and Capt. Jaxx stepped off the pier onto the flush deck and the boat slipped the dock. Arrangements had been made with the black site SIS/SOE naval base in Dover to utilize their twenty-five-foot SN6 surfboat for extracting the "parcels." Since the PT was not fitted with a derrick capable of hoisting the boat aboard Brandy decided she would tow it across. Three of the no-nomenclature canvas canoes – the Special Warfare Operators nicknamed them "Mark I Frog Boats" – would be carried on deck for redundancy. Tonight there was an eight-man LBSM boat team to operate the SN6 and six Maritime Unit Frogmen to handle the canoes.

Knowing the SN6 was in their future, the Life Boat Service Men had been familiarizing themselves with the craft and knew its capabilities. It could carry more passengers, row faster, and handle more easily in surf when loaded than the Mark I Frog Boats or the Goatley dories they primarily used. Provided the weather remained cooperative, it should be easy to tow.

In a rough sea all bets were off.

As the Rules for Raiding stipulated, "It's Good to Have a Plan B." That was why the three canoes and boat teams were aboard – backup.

SOE had a party standing by with the SN6. The hawser was quickly rigged. Sub Lieutenant Jeffery Macomber of the Inshore Patrol Flotilla came on board to supervise the towing.

And so at 2200 hrs on Christmas Eve, Brandy slipped the dock at Admiralty Pier and on the last of the ebb tide nosed slowly downstream toward the open waters of the Channel. The radio was blaring full blast – Bing Crosby singing *White Christmas*. As the last notes were fading away the PT boat pulled out into the open water. The civilian radio channel was switched off and a commo check on the tactical frequency transmitting to the TOC at Seaborn House conducted.

This mission was a go.

The weather had taken a turn for the better. The sea was calm with a long swell from the southwest. At 2225 hrs with a northwesterly wind behind them they took their departure from the D7 buoy on the inner side of the swept Channel. Speed was increased to fifteen knots – coincidentally silent running started at that speed for a PT. Tonight it was also All Ahead Full because of towing the SN6.

Brandy set a course straight for the drop-off point on the French Coast to put the two Joes ashore. Since the plan called for the agents to make their way inland to a road that ran parallel to the coast it was not particularly challenging navigation for a pilot of Capt. Honeycutt-Parker's class. The beach was a linear area type target and she did not have to hit it on any particular point.

Col. Randal was standing next to Brandy on the bridge, impressed by what he was observing. This was a true small-scale multi-agency combined operation. Everyone on board was conducting themselves in a highly professional manner. Thinking back to the early days when his men were not capable of paddling their dories through the surf without capsizing – the difference between now and then was stark. That crisis was only solved after Lady Jane brought in Life Boat Service Men to handle the boat work.

That was a long time ago. Lieutenant General "Geronimo" Joe McKoy claimed a year in wartime was measured in dog years. One equaled seven. Col. Randal thought the general was right. What he was witnessing now was like the difference between daylight and dark. Everyone knew their job. And they were carrying it out as if setting sail for enemy-occupied France to land ashore twice was routine.

The ex-Sea Rover Scouts had grown up at Seaborn House serving on Raiding Forces' boats. The OSS Maritime Unit Special Warfare Operators were at home on the sea. Capt. Courtney's team had spent two years on runs to France. They moved around the boat going about their tasks with no wasted effort – even X-Ray and Vanish were good sailors.

The young former Gold Coast Border Patrol officer had developed into a mature small-unit commander. By sheer force of character he instilled confidence in the troops under his command – that much was easy to see. Col. Randal had no intention of sending Capt. Courtney to ABC to gain amphibious raiding experience.

Because speed was reduced due to towing the SN6, the trip across the Channel took longer than normal. At 2345 hrs Brandy cut back to dead slow ahead. The coxswain started taking soundings off the bow as the PT edged in toward the shore.

Brandy made a command decision to dispense with the traditional standing one to three miles off shore and sending in the boats. It was her belief in certain circumstances the better idea was to go in as close to shore as possible like they did in the Aegean. Doing so reduced the amount of time the boat had to remain in close proximity to the beach. That outweighed the risk of being picked up by radar or sound detection. Even if that happened, the Germans would likely not have any way to react to their presence in such a remote location as this in the short amount of time they had before the PT would be gone.

One of the canvas canoes was put over the side. Two OSS Special Warfare Operators climbed in. The bicycle was gingerly lowered down and placed in the bottom of the canoe. Both agents followed behind it.

It was a short pull for the Frogs. Because time was short and they were landing in an isolated location on a beach that was too small to be an invasion site and therefore would not likely be guarded, Capt. Courtney did not feel the necessity to take a party ashore to secure it. There was a road paralleling the coast a short distance inland. Once the Joes landed they were on mission. The agents hit the beach, pushed the bicycle through the sand dunes in the direction of the road, then disappeared. Swallowed up by the night.

It was hard not to feel sorry for them.

Brandy was away in less than fifteen minutes. She ran down the coastline approximately a quarter mile off the shore. This might have been thought of as suicidal by some but then they did not have her experience at inshore operations. Her audacity contributed to the element of surprise.

The plan was to land opposite of what was believed to be an abandoned stone house a hundred yards off the beach. There were two groups of escapers to be picked up. They were under the supervision of an MI-9 Escape officer and a small team. Fourteen Royal Navy sailors, survivors from boats sunk during Channel operations who had managed to swim to shore and fifteen RAF pilots and aircrew who had been shot down were anxious to return to base. Six other SOE agents, two women and two members of a French family also needed passage to England – for a total of 32 PAX.

SOE's primary interest in the night's mission, other than to recover its personnel, was because the extraction presented an opportunity to bring out the Secret Mail Bag, which was of high intelligence value.

This second phase of the nights operation stood to be more challenging. There were Germans known to be in the area of the extraction point. However, the EP was fairly remote. And the beach was not large enough to be an invasion site – which meant it would not likely be heavily guarded.

There was one other factor. It was zero dark thirty on Christmas morning – the time was now 0225 hrs. In all probability the Nazis had been drinking like fish since sundown.

The plan was for Capt. Courtney, X-Ray, Vanish, the three Raiding Forces' operators, the MI-9 agent and the SOE Signals Officer to land with two of the Mark I Frog boats. The Special Warfare Operators would remain behind and secure the beach while the rest of the team went inland to link up with the MI-9 Escape officer shepherding the evaders. Once physical contact was established with the escapers, the SOE Signals Officer would radio Brandy to send in the SN6.

As they cruised down the coast, the MI-9 party on shore flashed a blue filtered light out to sea. One Raiding Forces' Rule that did not get quoted as often as some of the others was "It Never Hurts To Cheat." They didn't need to because the concept was completely ingrained in all of their tactical thinking.

The blue light made locating the EP easy. The SOE Signals Officer equipped with an S-Phone reported he was in contact with the MI-9 officer on the beach.

The S-Phone was a 15 lb UHF man-portable, duplex radiotelephone system developed by the Royal Signals Corps. The radio was worn on a harness with a headset. It was primarily designed for SOE agents operating behind enemy lines to communicate with friendly aircraft to coordinate dropping of supplies and operatives or for landing of aircraft to insert or retrieve operatives from the field. But it had other uses for clandestine messaging.

The S-Phone had one drawback. It was directional – the operator had to face the direction of whoever it was he was communicating with. It could be used for ship-to-shore or vice versa. The phone had a range of thirty miles and had the useful trait of not being able to be picked up by German ground monitoring stations more than a mile away – which more than checkmated the directionality limitation.

The thirty-mile range meant in this, the narrowest part of the English Channel, the S-Phone could provide a secure voice link to the secret SIS/SOE base in Dover for coded conversations. That capability was priceless.

The OSS Signals Officer relayed the message the mission was a go.

Two of the canvas canoes were put over the side. The Special Warfare Operators, the MI-9 officer on board and the SOE Signals Officer boarded. Capt. Jaxx opened his duffel bag, extracted two 9mm M3 Grease Guns with suppressors and a pair of canvas bandoleers containing 30-round magazines.

He passed one of the M3s and a magazine pouch with three thirty-round magazines to Col. Randal. Then the two went over the side into a canoe.

Capt. Jaxx said, “It’s probably better if I wait to shoot you until we’re back on the PT, sir.”

Col. Randal said, “No problem Lady Jane will take care of that when we return to base.”

The canoe knifed through the water. They were on the beach in minutes. The MI-9 escort officer was waiting when they came ashore.

The SOE Signals Officer radioed Brandy the beach was clear and to send in the SN6. The two

MI-9 officers led the way to where the evaders were waiting among the sand dunes. It was going to take the SN6 two trips to bring everyone out.

Capt. Courtney established a loose perimeter defense. The first lift started moving toward the beach. Then they heard voices.

Capt. Jaxx whispered, “What’s that?”

The MI-9 escort officer who had brought the evaders to the beach said, “Germans – in a shed behind the dunes.”

Col. Randal said, “Don’t you think you should have mentioned that?”

"They are all drunk, sir. When the wind blows you can hear. Singing Christmas carols."

Col. Randal looked at Capt. Jaxx. They had done a lot of strange things. Standing on a beach in enemy-occupied France on Christmas morning listening to drunk Nazis singing carols had to be at the top of the list.

Col. Randal said, "Captain Courtney, we'll be right back."

"Sir . . ."

Col. Randal and Capt. Jaxx were gone. One second they were there and the next they had disappeared. It was spooky.

Moving through the sand dunes was easy going and quiet. The farther they went inland the louder the singing became. Soon a light could be seen coming from the shed where the Germans were celebrating.

The Nazis were bored, a long way from Germany, and homesick. They did not pose an immediate threat. Nevertheless, they were still the enemy.

Col. Randal had a long-standing personal policy of killing every enemy combatant he encountered with no exceptions unless the mission was to take prisoners. Not everyone felt that way. But it was his belief if he did not take them out then at some later time and place those very same Nazis he chose not to engage might kill one of his men.

He was not about to let that happen if he could help it.

Upon reaching the edge of the dunes they could see the shed. It was an ancient structure for some undetermined farming use sometime in the distant past. The building offered a measure of comfort out of the elements that was superior to the improvised lean-to position the Germans normally manned. From the singing it sounded as if there were four or five people inside.

As they were crouched down studying the shed a Nazi staggered out the door. The instant he stepped away, Col. Randal shot him with a crisp burst. *SSSSS, SSSSS, SSSSS.* The German went down without a sound.

He and Capt. Jaxx advanced on the door of the shed. In fact, there was no door, just the opening where there had been a door in days past. Making eye contact with Jack Cool the two of them stepped inside, M3 Grease Guns to their shoulders.

The Germans were startled. It was a fairly constricted space with a dirt floor. The only light was provided by candle lamps which gave off a mellow glow. It seemed like there were fifty of them packed in the room but in fact it was only five.

The two M3s were hissing like a pair of evil snakes. The singing was quickly replaced by panicked shouting. The Germans were scrambling to get to their rifles, which were leaning against one wall. Nazis were dropping – shot at point-blank range.

Then Col. Randal and Capt. Jaxx changed magazines. Everyone was down. Jack Cool went around and put a short burst in each man. "Why take a chance?"

By the time they returned to the beach the second lift of evaders was loaded on the SN6 and away. Capt. Courtney pulled in his security. Everyone boarded the canoes. It did not take the Special Warfare Operators long to paddle the short distance to the PT boat.

By 1000 hrs Col. Randal, Lady Jane, Capt. Jaxx and Beverly were having Christmas brunch at the Bradford Hotel.

Lady Jane said, "You and Jack remained on board the PT boat?"

Col. Randal said, "Those were our marching orders."

"So how exactly did you two get all that mud on your boots?"

MAJOR THE LADY JANE SEABORN HELD A FORMAL DINING IN for the "Raiding Forces' family." Prior to the event the Bradford catered a Christmas dinner for the troops at Seaborn House. Colonel John Randal, Lady Jane, Captain Billy Jack Jaxx, Mandy Paige and Beverly Blackwell stood in as servers. Then it was back to London for Lady Jane's party. When they arrived the Bradford was a beehive of activity. The guests were a long way from home and family. Some had loved ones in the service stationed all over the world. Virtually everyone in the hotel was in the restaurant hoping to make the best of a holiday they both looked forward to and dreaded. Extra tables had to be set up to accommodate them.

The Raiding Forces' event that evening was held in one of the private rooms. A star-studded group started to arrive. Lady Jane had decreed the men were to wear full awards and decorations. The ladies were in evening gowns. She, Mandy and Beverly had been planning this party almost from the time they arrived in London. Christmas was a time that made hard men and strong women sentimental. Their idea was to arrange for the day to end on as an enjoyable note as possible by spending it in the company of people they served with and respected – a group you could not be born or buy your way into.

Col. Randal and Lady Jane – in a black mermaid dress that fit her like a snakeskin – greeted the guests at the door.

Lieutenant General "Geronimo" Joe McKoy arrived with a statuesque beauty who was said to be one of the "nude actresses" from the notorious Windmill Theatre. The manager had somehow managed to convince Lord Chamberlain, the Official Censor of the British Theatre, that if the models stood perfectly still they were no different than Roman statues – equivalent to works of art. The rule was "to move was lewd." Lieutenant Colonel Sir Terry "Zorro" Stone's father, the Duke, had introduced the two – he maintained a box at the club.

Sir Terry arrived with Red, the Clipper Girl.

Major General Sam Houston Blackwell was with Brandy Seaborn.

Major General William "Wild Bill" Donovan had Mrs. Veronica Paige as a dinner companion. She was in from ABC to discuss taking over Captain Stephanie Fawcett-Tatum's duties on ABC. The two women had flown in to work out the details of their new assignments.

Capt. Fawcett-Tatum was with Major Jack Dance. He had traveled with Veronica and Stephanie to assess the possibility of his taking over from Lieutenant Colonel Lionel Seaborn after his departure from Raiding Forces.

Waldo Treywick brought Rikke Runborg,

Lieutenant Colonel Thomas Argyll Robertson, known as "Passion Pants" among the staff at MI-5, brought his lovely wife, Joan.

Lieutenant Colonel John Henry Bevan was with his wife, Lady Barbara.

Jim "Baldie" Taylor was stag – so Lady Jane arranged for one of the FANYs to be his dinner companion.

Mandy was with Captain Sinclair Lovelace – she was known to date around.

King was with Captain Pamala Plum-Martin.

Captain Dick Courtney brought a beautiful WRNS.

Captain Dan Bonham, Captain Jake Novak aka Jake the Snake, Captain Clint Hays, Captain Richard "Dynamite Dick" Coogan, Lieutenant Ricky Mascuch and Lieutenant Westly Slade escorted Lady Jane's Royal Marines.

Lieutenant Ted "The Great Teddy" Hamilton arrived with a stunning WAAF – Col. Randal wondered if she knew how old he was.

Beverly Blackwell, surprise of surprises since the UT beauty queen was not known to date, was with Lieutenant Chase Starrett – she asked him.

And Captain Billy Jack Jaxx brought the Gypsy Dancer from Bob Hope's USO Show who had told him she was a lesbian – and maybe she was.

It was a magical Christmas night. A good time was in full swing.

Then a King's Messenger arrived.

THE MISSION CONTINUES IN

–Stand To! –

BOOK XIX IN THE RAIDING FORCES SERIES

COMING SOON

The Raiding Forces series continues all the way to VE Day.

Be the first to get updates and know about upcoming releases. To be on our notification list, scan the QR below and sign up!

ABBREVIATIONS
ORDERS & AWARDS

Bt	Baronet
CB	Companion of the Bath
CMG	Companion of the Order of St. Michael & St. George
DCM	Distinguished Conduct Medal
DFC	Distinguished Flying Cross
DSC	Distinguished Service Cross
DSM	Distinguished Service Medal
DSO	Distinguished Service Order
GC	George Cross
GCB	Grand Cross in the Order of the Bath
GM	George Medal
KBE	Knight Commandeer of the Most Excellent Order of the British Empire
KCVO	Knight Commander of the Royal Victorian Order
LG	Lady Companion of the Order of the Garter
MC	Military Cross
MM	Military Medal
MVO	Member of the Royal Victorian Order
OBE	Order of the British Empire
SS	Silver Star Medal
VC	Victoria Cross

ACRONYMS

AB – Able Body
ABC – (RFHQ) Advanced Base Castelrozzo
AO – Area of Operation
ATS – Auxiliary Territorial Service
AU – Auxiliary Unit

B1-A – A section of MI-5 that handles Double Cross agents
CBI – China Burma India
CIB – Combat Infantry Badge
CIC – Counter Intelligence Corps
COHQ – Combined Operations Headquarters

DF – Direction Finding
DZ – Drop Zone

ERP – Extraction Rally Point
ETO – European Theatre of Operations
ETOUSA – European Theater of Operations United States

FANY – Field Auxiliary Nursing Yeomanry
FEBA – Forward Edge of the Battle Area
Flak – Fliegerabwehrakanone – “Aeroplane Defense Cannon”
FUSAG – First United States Army Group

G-2 – USAFE Intelligence Staff
G-4 – Troup Transport Command supply officer
GHQ – General Headquarters

HMPS – His Majesty’s Prison Service

IRP – Initial Rally Point

KM – King’s Messenger

LBSM – Life Boat Service Men
LCS – London Controlling Section
LD – Line of Departure
LMG – Light Machine Gun

Cont…..

MGB – Motor Gunboat
MG – machine gun
MI – Military Intelligence

MI-5 – Counterintelligence (SS)

- B1-A – A section of MI-5 that handles Double Cross agents

MI-6 – Secret Intelligence Service (SIS)
X-2 – Counter Espionage Branch

MOS – Military Occupational Specialty
MP – Members of Parliament
MP-40 – German 9mm Maschinenpistole 40
MSS – Most Secret Source
MTB – Motor Torpedo Boat
MTC – Mechanized Transport Corps
MU – Maritime Unit (OSS)

NCO – Non-Commissioned Officer
NID – Naval Intelligence Division
NLSI – National Lifeboat Service Institution

OCTS – Officer Cadet Training School
OG – Operational Group
OGBE – Operational Group Branch Europe
OPCON – operational control
ORP – Objective Rally Point
OSS – Office of Strategic Services (The Outfit)
Special Warfare Operators (the Frogs)

PAX – passengers
PIB – Parachute Infantry Battalion
PM – Prime Minister
PT – Patrol Torpedo (boat)
PWE – Political Warfare Executive

RCNVR – Royal Canadian Navy Volunteer Reserve
RF/DF – Range Finding/Direction Finding
RFR – Raiding Forces Rear HQ
RNPS – Royal Navy Patrol Service
RNVR – Royal Navy Volunteer Reserve
RON – Remain Overnight Position 8
RP – Rendezvous point
RTF – Ranger Task Force

Cont….

SAS – Special Air Service
SFHQ – Special Forces Headquarters
SHAEF – Supreme Headquarters Allied Expeditionary Forces
SI – Secret Intelligence
SIME – Security Intelligence Middle East
SIS – Secret Intelligence Service (British) 2 Commonly known as MI-6
SMG – submachine gun
SO – Special Operations
SOE – Special Operations Executive
SOG – Small Operations Group
SOI – Signals Operating Instructions
SOP – Standard Operating Procedure
SRU – Sea Reconnaissance Unit
SS – Security Service

TDY – Temporary Duty
TOC – Tactical Operations Center
TO&E – table of organization and equipment
TTC– Troop Transport Command
TWX – Teletypewriter Exchange Service

UDT – Underwater Demolition Team
USAFE – United States Strategic Air Forces Europe

WAC – Women's Army Corps

CHARACTERS

Bevan, MC, John Henry, Lt. Col.
Bevan, Lady Barbara
Blackwell, SS, DFC, Beverly
Blackwell, Sam Houston "Bronc", Maj. Gen.
Bonham, Dan, Capt.
Bruce, David, Lt. Col.
Casalonga, Laurent, Cpl.
Chauncy, Maurice, Sgt. Maj.
Coogan, Richard "Dynamite Dick", Capt.
Courtney, Dick, Capt.
Dance, Jack, Maj.
Davidson, Francis Henry, Maj. Gen.
Davis, Thomas Jefferson, "TJ", Col.
Donovan, William "Wild Bill", Maj. Gen.
Eaker, Ira C., Maj. Gen.
Eisenhower, Dwight D., Gen.
Fawcett-Tatum, RM, Stephanie, Capt.
Fenwick, Lionel, Scout
Ferguson, Munro, Scout
Fleming, RNVR, Ian, Cdr.
Godfrey, John Henry, RAdm.
Grand, Lawrence, Maj. Gen.
Groom
Hamilton, OBE, Ted "The Great Teddy", Lt.
Hansen, Norvel "Horn Dog", PFC
Happy
Harlequins, Edmond, Capt.
Hays, Clint, Capt.
Hayworth, Rita
Honeycutt-Parker, Lionel, Lt. Col.
Honeycutt-Parker, OBE, GM, RM, Penelope "Legs", Capt.
Hoolihan, DSO, MC, MM, RM, Butch "Headhunter", Maj.
Jaxx, MC, SSM, SC, DSC, Billy Jack, Capt.
King
Kirk, Adam G., RAdm
Lamb, WREN, Christen Mary, 3/O
Laycock, Robert, Maj. Gen.

Cont....

Leigh-Mallory, Sir Trafford, ACM
Lovelace, MC, Sinclair, Capt.
Macomber, Jeffery, Sub Lt.
Mascuch, Ricky, Lt.
Masterman, John Cecil (J.C.), Lt. Col.
McKoy, OBE, "Geronimo" Joe, Lt. Gen.
Menzies, DSO, MC, Stewart, Maj. Gen.
Montgomery, Bernard, Gen.
Novak *aka* Jake the Snake, Jake, Capt.
Paige, OBE, RM, Alexandra (Mandy)
Paige, OBE, Veronica
Patton Jr., George S., Lt. Gen.
Petrie, Sir David, Maj. Gen.
Plum-Martin, DSO, OBE, DFC, RM, Pamala, Capt.
Prescott-Davies, DSC, RNVR, Cavin, Lt.
Ramsay, Sir Bertram, Adm.
Randal, DSO, OBE, DSC, MC, John, Col.
Red (Clipper Girl)
Robertson, Thomas Argyll "Tar", Lt. Col.
Rollins
Runborg, Rikke (Rocky)
Rushbrooke, Edmond, RAdm.
Seaborn, GC, Brandy
Seaborn, LG, OBE, RM, Lady Jane, Maj.
Slade, Westly, Lt.
Smith, Walter Bedell, Maj. Gen.
Starrett, Chase, Lt.
Stephens, Robin "Tin Eye", Col.
Stone, KBE, DSO, MC, Sir Terry "Zorro", Lt. Col.
Summersby, Kay, Pvt.
Taylor, James "Baldie"
Tedder, DSO, OBE, DFC, Sir Arthur, ACM
Terrell, James "Wildman", PFC
Treywick, OBE, Waldo
Vanish
Westinghouse, Mark, Lt. Col.
Woodbine, Bernice, Corp.
Wright, RCNVR, Bruce, Lt.
X-Ray

ABOUT THE AUTHOR

Phil Ward is a highly decorated combat veteran commissioned when he was nineteen. He served as an instructor at the Army Ranger School. Now days he lives in Texas on a mountain overlooking Lake Austin.

~ ~

OTHER BOOKS IN THE RAIDING FORCES SERIES:

Those Who Dare
Dead Eagles
Blood Wings
Roman Candle
Guerrilla Command
Necessary Force
Desert Patrol
Private Army
Africa 1941
The Sharp End
Raiding Rommel
Strategic Services
The TIP of the Sword
Always So Few
The War That Never Was
Economy of Force
The Magnificent Mission
Military Deception
Stand To!

www.ingramcontent.com/pod-product-compliance
Lightning Source LLC
Chambersburg PA
CBHW020303030826
48979CB00027B/2039/J
9798992064520